GLORY: HUMANITY FIGHTS BACK

GLORY SERIES
BOOK 2

IRA HEINICHEN

CRAIG MARTELLE

Connect with the Authors

Craig Martelle Social

Website & Newsletter:
https://craigmartelle.com

Facebook:
https://www.facebook.com/AuthorCraigMartelle/

Ira Heinichen Social

Website & Newsletter:
https://iraheinichen.com

Facebook:
https://www.facebook.com/iraheinichen/

Twitter:
https://twitter.com/iraheinichen

Instagram:
https://www.instagram.com/iraheinichen/

Copyright © 2022 Ira Heinichen and Craig Martelle

Published by Craig Martelle, Inc

PO Box 10235, Fairbanks, AK 99710

First US edition, November 2022

ACKNOWLEDGMENTS

Glory: Humanity Fights Back
    Thanks to our Beta Readers

Micky Cocker (in memoriam), James Caplan, Kelly O'Donnell, and John Ashmore

If I've missed anyone, please let me know!

Editor Lynne Stiegler
    Cover designed by Chris Kallias

We can't write without those who support us
    On the home front, we thank you for being there for us

We wouldn't be able to do this for a living if it weren't for our readers
    We thank you for reading our books

For Micky

EARTH

Terran Federation Space

CHAPTER ONE

"I swear upon my dear grandfather's grave, Cap, if I have to fill out another requisition form, I'm going to join him in the afterlife."

Doctor Broussard's complaining was sotto and heavy with breathing as he huffed to keep up with his captain. "What do you want?" Drake asked him, not breaking stride or taking his eyes off his data pad, which was filled with dozens of flashing action items, all with self-proclaimed urgency. "And speak up."

The Brit harrumphed, straightened, and put his diaphragm into it. "Antiseptics. Bastards cleared me out when they took inventory. How am I supposed to run a sick-bay, Captain, if I can't *clean* anyone?"

"I'd suggest you speak with our quartermaster."

"I have."

"And?"

"He handed me a requisition form."

"Did you file it?"

"Two weeks ago."

"Then you have nothing to worry about."

"Captain, that was *two weeks ago*."

Drake took a hard right, which sent the good Doctor straight down the corridor by himself for several steps before he realized. Ahead of Drake, just in the peripheral of his view, he caught sight of a small group of officers and crew. Among them was Fredrickson, his chief engineer. "Lieutenant," he bellowed, fishing out a second data pad tucked under his armpit. He handed it to the younger man in stride. "Your updated power curves, as requested."

"And the inspections, sir?" he called as Drake swept past.

"0800 tomorrow. And a structural team at 1430."

Fredrickson groaned, which Drake took as receipt of the information. Doc, meanwhile, huffed his way back up alongside Drake. "You know, you shouldn't be walking this much," he said. "Not so soon after your injury."

The doctor was referring to Drake's hip, which had taken damage on their last mission; in particular during hand-to-hand combat with his second officer, Commander Carrol. She'd been under the influence of a Paragon parasite, not in her right mind of course, and had nearly stopped them all from destroying the planet-killer that was about to blow Earth to bits—yes, the entire planet—with one shot. But Drake, *Glory,* and her crew had prevailed. The planet-killer was destroyed. Humanity had survived to fight another day. Now everyone was trying to pick up the pieces, repair what could be repaired. For Drake, that meant his ship, injury be damned.

"Hip feels fine, Doc," he said.

"I believe my orders were two weeks of limited use—"

"I am limited. To these corridors."

"Captain?" came a new voice, deep and gruff. Drake gave a brief sidelong glance. Smith. Their enhanced-marine.

At his side was a giant dog, matching him stride for stride. Cheddar. Also enhanced.

"Walk with me," Drake said to the Marine, intuiting that he wanted something. He'd have to ask it on the move, as Drake was slowing for no one.

He didn't get the chance to ask, however, as Doc interjected. "With a *cane,*" he hissed to Drake, still on about the hip. "Limited use with the cane for support, Cap. Those were the orders."

Finally, blessedly, Drake reached the destination to which he'd been hustling so intently: *Glory's* main hangar bay. It was a cacophony of sound, with the whirring of power tools building and un-building crates, the beep-beep of wheeled anti-grav lifts moving palettes, shouting crew members, and the rumble of shuttle- and cargo-craft landing and taking off. All of it was music to Drake's ears. The sound of progress, and repair. Though, from the flashing items on his data pad, which had grown by several lines in just the time it had taken to walk to the hangar bay . . . said progress was moving at a snail's pace, with no fault lying in his crew or their efforts.

Drake stopped to survey the scene. Doc nearly ran into him; it was so sudden.

"I say, Cap," the doctor blustered, accent particularly thick in his surprise. "Give a warning. I could have bowled you over."

What Drake was waiting for—a very specific shuttle carrying a very specific person—hadn't yet arrived, so Drake took a moment to finally regard Broussard straight-on. "What do you want, Doctor?" he asked, straightening, and making his tone of voice formal.

Broussard did the same. "Antiseptics. Captain."

"But you've already requisitioned them."

"I know you were listening when I said that, yes."

"So, what you *really* want is for me to speak with quartermaster."

Broussard flushed ever so slightly. "He hasn't returned my inquiries, Cap. I think he'll have to return yours."

Drake shook his head, looking back out over the hangar bay. The shuttle he'd come down to greet was arriving. Before moving off toward it, he tapped a new entry line into his data pad, and waved it at the doc. "I'll see what I can do," he said to him. Another item added to his long and growing list he intended to share with the person arriving on that shuttle.

"And if you're not going to use the cane," Doc called to Drake as he let the captain stride away, "then *slow down.*"

"I'll see what I can do," Drake repeated over his shoulder with no small hint of sarcasm. Truth be told, the hip was sore, but Broussard had done a bang-up job stitching it all back together, as he always did. He felt fine. And Doc was a worrywart anyway. The entire conversation left Drake's mind in the same instant it was over.

As Drake sidled up to the empty mooring that the newly arrived shuttle was about to inhabit, he caught sight of a group of crew and officers huddled around a craft in the adjoining space. They were loading bags and gear into what Drake recognized as a planet-bound transport. Among the group were several faces he knew from the command deck: Li, an enlisted tactical sensor operator, Ensign Foley, a communications engineer.

"Camping?" he asked them, eyeing the gear. Tents, sleeping sacks, folding chairs. A cooler . . . full, from the way it was sweating.

He'd authorized XO to allow *Glory's* crew shore leave in staggered waves. Repairs were pressing, but they would take weeks—if not months at their current glacial pace—and after the hell they'd all been through saving Earth, R&R was well-earned. Requisite, Drake would argue. He was glad to see them excited about it.

"Yes, sir," Shannahan answered, another member of the command deck squad Drake recognized; their A shift helmsman. Another thing that warmed Drake's heart and helped to lift his anxious, all-business mood: this group was getting tight. Spending their free time together. It would only help them on duty, where cohesive teamwork could literally save your life. "Foley grew up in the pacific northwest, sir. Says she has a nice spot."

Drake nodded, wishing he could join them.

On cue, the shuttle transport's tug clunked the craft into its berth, and there was a crack-hiss of the sealed door opening. On the side of the shuttle was the insignia of Fleet Admiralty. Drake straightened. This was indeed the craft he'd been waiting for.

The person who emerged from the shuttle, however, was not.

"Captain Drake," a squeaky, wide-eyed junior officer said as he strode up to greet him. He, too, wore the insignia of the Admiralty. An aide, and a new one at that. The young man gave a crisp salute.

Drake returned it, scowling. "I was under the impression the Admiral was coming here, personally." Drake referred to Admiral Jack Sturgess, longtime head of Fleet Intelligence and Special Operations, an oft-involved commander of *Glory's* missions, and the man who'd drug Drake out of retirement to save the world.

See, it wasn't just Doc who was having a hard time getting necessary supplies or equipment. It was *everyone.* From his frequent discussions with the dry dock quartermaster that were happening almost daily at this point, Drake knew it wasn't even just *Glory* who was having issues. It was the entire system. The damage the Paragon had done with their attack went far beyond the ships they'd destroyed, or even the entire planet of Mars that they'd vaporized on their way toward Earth. The impact of those losses, surely, were seismic. But it had affected the very foundation of the Fleet in the solar system: its infrastructure. Supply lines. Manufacturing facilities. Transport. Logistics. Personnel. Technology. It was all in shambles. And *Glory* was suffering because of it. The entire Fleet around Earth was. They weren't getting repaired and refitted fast enough with the Paragon still out there. Fought back for now, sure, but still out there. Still a threat to attack at any time.

So, Drake had run it up the command chain. He'd reached out directly to Jack. *We need to be operational.* His response was that he would come to *Glory* and assess the situation. But now, at the specified time and place, Drake was looking at a teenager.

The aide gulped under Drake's scrutiny. "He sends his regrets," he said, voice breaking. He held out a data pad. "And your new orders."

Drake knitted his eyebrows and took the pad. He scowled further as he began to read what it contained. It wasn't what he expected.

"If you can just thumbprint here for me," the aide asked, shakily holding out another data pad. This one was a receipt document to show that Drake had been given his orders. Drake pressed a thumb in the appropriate spot on its bottom right corner, and with that, the aide scampered back into his shuttle. The tug was pushing it back from its mooring and out toward the takeoff queue before Drake even looked back down at the pad.

Another figure sidled up next to him. "Idri," he said, surprised.

Idri was the ship's Navid navigator, an alien species that could fold space-time and jump ships with their minds. It was she who'd dealt the planet killer its death blow by jumping *Glory* inside it, and then back out again. The sudden collision of so much mass taking up the same space for an instant had proven to be . . . explosive. And a stroke of genius. No navigator had ever attempted such a jump, but Idri had, and executed it so that the jumping ship came out intact on the other side. It was good to see her on her feet again, though Drake was having a hard time fathoming exactly what she was doing there.

"Captain," she responded, brightly. "Are you going camping with them?"

Drake blinked. Camping? He looked back over at the command deck crew and their nearly full, earth-bound shuttle. "Ah," he said. "No." The pad of orders he held in his hand didn't have good news for them.

"Stuck aboard *Glory* with me, then?" she asked.

He watched as the young navigator looked wistfully over at the camping group. Drake recalled receiving a leave request from her to accompany them, one which he'd denied. Idri was still recovering, not to mention it was dangerous for her to be off ship in any capacity. Idri was the only navigator left in the known galaxy. It made her quite the asset to protect. All the same, Drake hadn't relished denying that request. She looked away from the group and back at him, covering her own disappointment with a good-natured smile. "We certainly have enough to keep us busy," she said.

"Indeed, we do."

"Well," Idri said after a beat, looking over at Smith, who Drake had completely missed was standing close by. Had . . . he been there this whole time, following from all the way back in the corridor with Doc? Drake had lost track of him entirely. Idri rocked on her heels, looking excitedly at the Marine. "Did you show him?"

"I've been waiting for the captain to have a moment," Smith answered her without the slightest hint of impatience or annoyance.

"I'm sorry, crewman," Drake said, rubbing the bridge of his nose. "I'd completely forgot you wished to speak with me. My apologies."

"Unnecessary, sir," the Marine said in deference. "You are very busy."

That was an understatement. "How can I help you?"

"He just wanted to show you something," Idri said, smiling at Smith as if prompting him.

Drake inclined his head. "You have my undivided attention, Mister Smith."

The Marine cleared his throat. "As you know, sir, like me, Cheddar has many engineered abilities." Drake nodded. He was talking about the dog. Where . . . was the dog? Hadn't he seen the two of them together back in the corridor? "Well, I'm not sure if you're aware, sir, but many of those abilities were suppressed when she was neglected for so long. Malnutrition, anxiety, loneliness, and plainly and simply not practicing certain skills, sir, will cause an enhanced canine to lose the ability to do many of the things they were engineered for."

"I'm following," Drake said, although he wasn't really.

"But," Smith continued, "with proper nutrition, attention, and practice, many of those abilities can be recovered. Restored."

"Okay."

"You just need to show him," Idri prompted. She then turned to Drake. "He wants to show you."

"By all means."

Smith nodded. He looked down at his side, which was empty, just air, and he gave a soft command.

And suddenly Cheddar, the dog, was sitting there looking up at the Marine, tongue out to the side, panting softly. Drake felt like rubbing his eyes to confirm what he'd just seen wasn't a trick. She'd . . . literally appeared out of nowhere.

"How . . .?"

"She can conceal herself," Smith explained as he reached into his uniform pocket. "Either by command, or on her own as an instinctual defense mechanism." From his pocket, Smith produced a morsel of cheese, which he tossed, and she caught in midair. She munched it, contentedly. Her name, 'Cheddar,' had been chosen for obvious reasons.

Drake was impressed.

"Isn't that amazing?" Idri said, beaming.

"She can't even be tracked," Smith said, obviously proud. He retrieved a small screen from his uniform pocket, dusted cheese crumbs from it, and showed it to Drake. "See," he said, pointing to a dot on the screen, "she's visible here on my tracker now." He gave the dog another quiet command, and in the same blink with which she'd appeared from thin air, she disappeared right back into it. Gone without a trace. Smith gestured to the tracker. Even the dot was gone. "And this is quantumly entangled, so it's not a matter of distance. If she's off my screen, it means she's concealed herself. Visually, infrared, all scopes, Paragon, Fleet or otherwise."

"Impressive," Drake said, and he meant it. That was quite the ability. How she'd been engineered with it, he didn't want to know; the history of such augmented and enhanced soldiers was a grisly one, which is why there were almost none of them left, but they certainly could do some things nobody else could.

"It means she's healing," Idri said, smiling to Drake, and he understood why she'd wanted him to see it. Smith, too.

There was healing happening. It was slow, frustratingly so, but the signs of it were all around him if he took the opportunity to slow down, poke his head up, and look. Things were becoming whole again. "Thank you for sharing," Drake said to the two of them, and he meant it.

Cheddar was back, now, after another command, taking a fresh cheese treat. Smith looked at her with utter devotion. "We're going to go hunting with Ensign Foley's group," he said. "Practice concealment in the field."

Drake made a pained expression. He looked back down at his data pad, the one from Admiral Jack, and the orders that it contained. "I'm afraid there's been a change in plans," he said. Smith and Idri looked at him, expectantly. "We're not going to complete our repairs to the ship here, at Earth."

"Oh?" Smith asked, frowning. "Where else would we dry dock?"

"The Freepoint shipyards," Drake said, reading the pad. He wasn't familiar with the facility personally, but he was aware of it. A massive installation that had begun construction while Drake had still been in service the first time, then finished while he was in forced retirement, and had since taken over as the Fleet's main ship-building facility. This was Jack's solution to their lack of resources: send them to Freepoint. Where Earth was suffering dramatic shortages of materials, equipment, and personnel, Freepoint was overflowing. "Apparently, they have capacity to refit much of the damaged fleet here, including us."

"But, sir," Smith said, eyebrow raised, "Freepoint is weeks away."

"Two," Drake said, reading the orders, then looking up. "By tug."

Smith's expression soured further. "Tug?" he repeated.

Drake sympathized. *Glory* couldn't maintain her own power yet, something Fredrickson was working on furiously despite their predicament, and Idri wasn't yet cleared by the Doc to resume jumping the ship. A tug would be their only way out there.

"I take it that shore leave is canceled," Smith said, more stating the obvious than asking a question.

"For the moment," Drake affirmed with a grimace. He'd make damn sure they'd find some once they reached Freepoint; whatever amenities and destinations they could offer. "We're underway in twelve hours."

"Understood," Smith said, with a crisp nod. He'd taken the news in stride. A good soldier. The best.

Even Idri didn't seem put out by it. "Would you like us to bring those orders to XO?" she asked with a glance at the data pad.

"That would be very helpful," he said, and he handed it to her. "I'm sorry," he said to both.

"Whatever it takes to get the ship whole again," Idri replied in earnest. She wasn't upset, disappointed, or even deflated; just purposeful and focused.

Drake thanked them, wishing he could adequately

express how much their unblinking support meant, and then they left.

Whatever it takes to get the ship whole again.

Apparently, that meant Freepoint, and her ample facilities. A little grin-and-bear-it in the meantime would be worth it if it meant that *Glory* was back in action. Drake felt that way, and he knew his crew did, too. They'd take the news in stride just as Idri and Smith had. In that way, Idri was right, and Cheddar was *Glory's* shining example. The healing had started. Drake needed to make sure they finished it.

The Paragon were still out there, waiting. The attack on Earth was just the beginning, and the Fleet needed every single ship it could muster for the fight to come. *Glory* would be among them.

Drake resolved to make up the sacrifice he was about to ask of his crew. Shore leave would have to wait.

But just for now.

BEACON PRIMA

Paragon Imperial Space

CHAPTER TWO

THE PALACE of the Supreme had changed much since Hadras last set foot on its polished stones. Gone were the ornately carved statues of Severus and the ceiling-to-floor tapestries of Anchilo or Cate depicting the Illumination of the Primo Supreme ten thousand years ago. Such ornateness was frowned upon in the New Fundamentalism, and the Supreme—the current one, descendent of the ancients depicted in those magnificent, missing paintings—had deferred to the political whims of the Diocese.

Hadras had heard as much, but it was another thing to see the palace halls so barren. The bastards had stripped the place. His footsteps, and those of his Second and the guards that accompanied them, echoed like a drill team marching in unison. It earned them spiteful looks from the others who had assembled about the hall.

Hadras would have earned those looks regardless. His reputation preceded him like it always did. And always would. Hadras' appearance flew in the face of the loathing; he marched in head-to-toe armor of stark white inlaid with gold, and a blood-red headdress that plumed from a wrap-around helmet that broke only to form an open slit across the eyes. Blood-red was the signature color of an archgeneral, very nearly the highest rank to which one could rise in the Paragon Imperium.

Hadras' very existence was profane. His blood was not pure, tainted as it was with the genetic strains of off-worlders. He was a sin against the Divine, impure in an order obsessed with purity.

Hadras was an impossibility. How he could have risen through the ranks of the Paragon clergy was an outrage to many, particularly in the Fundamentalist sects. Yet here he was, archgeneral's plume bouncing gloriously with each clacking step of his boots on the palace stones, on his way to meet with the Supreme. It had been twenty years, two decades and a lifetime of fighting, scratching, and clawing, but Hadras was back. Back where he needed to be.

Members of the Diocese, he realized, had assembled to watch his return. His reappearance in the Holy Palace had certainly not been at their behest. No, this was the Supreme's doing and the Supreme's alone. If it were up to the Diocese, Hadras would have been executed, not banished, when the New Fundamentalists had seized power.

They all had the stench of bitter defeat on them now. The Diocese had failed. Spectacularly. And opened the door for this very moment.

Hadras relished the scorn. He drank it in like wine, let it intoxicate him, fill him up, and propel him toward his destination. They would remember who he was. He would succeed where they had failed, and he would make every last one of them pay for their lack of faith in the Divine's plan.

A solitary knock shook Hadras from his thoughts. He

hadn't noticed they'd reached the stone doors that led to the Supreme's inner sanctum, and he chided himself for letting his rage get the better of him, no matter how righteous it might be. He unsheathed his ceremonial dagger and knelt at the doors, genuflecting even before they were opened by the attending guards.

He could feel his second do the same and led him by prostrating himself, placing his arms and head on the floor as well. The doors yawned silently, belying their mass and size. Hadras could smell the Supreme's sanctum through the slit in his armored helmet, sweet but not cloyingly so and tinged with earthy spices and stone. What a contrast to the stench in the hallways. It smelled like nothing else in the galaxy, and it brought tears to the archgeneral's eyes. It had been so long. Divine, how had it been so long?

"Too long," said a voice that matched the heavenly smell, and Hadras felt a firm hand caress the back of his neck. It was a reassuring touch. Familiar, even after all the time and distance.

Hadras did not rise for the Supreme until he was instructed to do so. The Supreme indicated he could with a tap on the back of his neck, and took his hand as he stood. The person Hadras saw before him had changed, just like his palace. The lines on his face were deeper, the arch in his back more curved, and the flesh between the bones of his arms and hands had sunken deeper.

Even his robes were more muted, and his celestial head-dress smaller. However, the grip on Hadras' wrist was strong, and his eyes, pure white against his alabaster skin, were as fierce and sharp as Hadras remembered. Even if they were blind.

"Leave us," the Supreme commanded everyone else, and he led Hadras farther inside his chambers, rubbing his sight stones in his free hand as he went. Hadras sensed his second tarry and looked him away as well to wait outside.

The blinding had been by ritual, the optic nerves deadened on purpose. The Supreme did not need his terrestrial sight. No clergy of a certain status did, and no one had higher status than the Supreme. He had the sight of the Divine now, and the sight stones made up for any shortfall. Almost any shortfall.

"Remove your headdress," the Supreme commanded softly once they were alone and the doors were closed behind them. "I wish to touch your face, Archgeneral."

Hadras obliged, moving slowly and deliberately. He removed his helmet, knelt again, and lifted his face to the old cleric. He closed his eyes in shame, even if the Supreme could not see. He never removed his helmet for anyone else. Why remind them of the difference? That his genetics made his skin the wrong hue, or his features askew and more pronounced.

Why let them see the scars there, mostly self-inflicted by the demands of his faith and piousness? But for the Supreme, anything. Anything at all. The bony fingers swept over his blasphemous features gently, caressed each of his many scars, and lingered by the corners of his eyes to wipe away the residue of his earlier emotion. He smiled. "You have grown older, too."

"Cursed is the flesh," Hadras responded, his cheeks flushed.

The Supreme nodded. Hadras had given the appropriate response. "It is auspicious, I think, you coming here. A sign."

"May it be the will of the Divine."

"The Diocese is displeased." The Supreme cast a sightless look toward the closed door and the multitude of seething clergy beyond it. He didn't dwell there too long, however, before turning back to Hadras with another and slyer smile. "I do not care. You've never lost my favor, Hadras. Only theirs."

Hadras nearly teared up again, his heart swelled so, but he fought it back this time. It was a confirmation of what he'd hoped was true. He'd been banished to the darkness for all those years by those faithless bastards, so far away from where he was at this moment.

But no longer. "I only seek the favor of the Divine, Supreme."

The elder finally let go of his face. "A true believer." He stepped away from Hadras and strode toward a nearby seat, stumbling slightly when he reached it. Hadras instantly rose to aid him but was waved off as the elder sat. The Supreme was reaching the end of his span; the signs were clear.

Of all the changes in this place Hadras had missed in the past two decades, this was the most alarming. He cursed the Diocese in his mind. Oh, he hated them through and through. Surely, they'd had some part in this decline, greedy thoughts about replacing him before his time. But the Supreme sensed and waved that off, too. With vigor. He was nearing the end, perhaps, but the end was not yet.

Hadras compulsively took the old cleric's hand and kissed it, relishing the sweet smell of his skin and letting his gratitude pour from his touch. An entirely silent exchange from beginning to end, but with zero meaning lost between the two.

"I've considered your plan," the Supreme said, getting Hadras to release his hand with a pat from the other.

"Yes, Supreme."

"It is tricky. Audacious. Many on the other side of that door would say blasphemous, and they have."

Hadras chose his words carefully. "Our enemy is tricky, audacious, and blasphemous, Supreme."

"Indeed they are. The humans have dealt the Diocese a particularly stinging blow."

The Supreme referred to the Paragon's recent failed direct assault on Earth, the homeworld of their most persistent enemy for the past several hundred years. Virtually all of the Paragon's military efforts had been poured into the ill-fated venture, one that Hadras had vehemently and vocally opposed from the start.

No one had listened to the opinions of the banished, however. Not until they'd been proved to be right. "My plan is what the humans require to be beaten, Supreme. Cunning, ruthlessness, and respect."

It was the last word so many in the clergy couldn't wrap their heads around. They never had, but Hadras did. He'd met humans in battle for decades. He'd studied them with an interest and fervor matched by no one else in the Paragon's hierarchy, and his success in battle against them was unmatched because of it.

He knew what made them tick, what made *their* cheeks flush and *their* eyes weep. He knew they were not to be taken lightly. That was what made them so blasphemous, an unmatched, unrivaled test sent to the righteous by the Divine. They were technologically inferior, but they persisted, and of late, they had defeated the Paragon's best.

The Diocese was failing that test, but Hadras would not. Not this time. Not with this plan.

The Supreme was right; what he was proposing was audacious. Reckless, even. But the extremity of the times, the corner the Diocese and their stupidity had put them all in—humans included—with their failed attempt to destroy Earth, demanded nothing less than every ounce of audacity the Paragon could muster. Hadras was convinced. Was the Supreme?

"You have always had to try harder, Hadras, haven't you?" The Supreme looked at him with a mixture of sorrow and hesitancy. It was Hadras' first whiff that it was possible he could walk out of this meeting with an answer other than the one he was seeking. "To do more than your peers." The Supreme rolled his sight stones in his hands, and he could feel their tingle prick his face, lingering on the scars like the Supreme's fingers had earlier.

"I have no peers." Hadras bowed his head. The response was rote, meant in humility, but thinking of the Diocese, he couldn't help but intend the phrase to mean the opposite. He could see that the Supreme took it that way—a way that, in the wrong company, could end him. He held his breath.

The Supreme's sorrow remained, but his hesitancy evaporated as he regarded his bowed archgeneral. He had decided. "We are all nothing in the glory of the Divine," he said. "Your audacity might be distasteful, but it may also be exactly what we need."

"Yes, Supreme." Hadras' blood rushed to his head.

"You are an impossible contradiction, Hadras. Your very flesh is an affront to the Divine, but your works speak for themselves. You are among the fiercest warriors ever to spread the Light."

"Yes, Supreme." He could hardly respond, his breath had become so shallow, and his heart was beating so fast.

"But consider this," the Supreme continued gravely. "If you fail in this, it will be the end for you. Even I cannot shield you from what the Diocese will do."

"My plan will work." He spoke without hesitation, for he knew it to be true.

"And it will cost you," the Supreme said, moving closer to him and speaking softer. "Personally."

"That's why it will work, Supreme."

The elder considered that, then leaned back with a small, sad smile. "Then go forth," he commanded. "And spread the Light."

Moments later, after Hadras had been allowed to recover his shameful face and withdraw into the comfort of his armor, the doors swung open. He thanked the Supreme for his infinite wisdom. He had the sense he could never thank him enough and that the Supreme knew that. He considered that the old man's warning, *Fail, and this will be the end of you,* applied to his leader as well. They were both taking a risk, both being audacious.

"We have approval," Hadras said to his second as they re-secured their daggers outside. He considered his long-time friend and the key part he would play in the events to come and channeled the gravity of the Supreme. "We must not fail."

VORKUT V PENAL COLONY

Paragon Imperial Space

CHAPTER THREE

LIEUTENANT HENRY WARREN felt the stab in his back from the guard's rifle butt for the thousandth time and nearly whirled to punch the bastard.

Unlike the majority of the other prisoners on this nasty-ass transport, Warren was taller than their armored Paragon captors. He was certain he'd have the time, surprise, and strength to get his hands on either side of the guard's helmet, give the necessary yank, and snap the life out of the fuck. Maybe he'd even tear the helmet off so he could see who it was he was snuffing out and look into his Paragon eyes as they died.

It would cost him his life. The other guards and their plasma rifles would see to that in an instant. But goddammit, enough was enough.

"Move," the guard said as if the rifle butt or the open door hadn't communicated that. Warren refrained from making the comment aloud.

Ahead of them, beyond the newly opened gangplank hatch, a bitter cold bit at his nose, and for a moment, all he could see was white snow. Somewhere in the distance was Warren's new home, a Paragon labor camp.

That was a phrase Warren was not familiar with: Paragon labor camp. He'd expected to be summarily executed when they picked him up several weeks prior in his fighter over Corvus. "Several" was as close a time estimate as Warren could come up with; he had no idea how long it had been.

Warren, on what was supposed to be his *very last mission* before retirement, had been escorting a Navid named Idri to Earth when disaster had struck. The Paragon, apparently, hadn't wanted her to reach Earth. It was just a guess, since Warren was never told the true nature of his missions, but he figured it was because the Navid was a navigator—the first in a hundred years—and the Paragon didn't want her running around the galaxy jumping Fleet ships. Well, he'd seen to it they didn't get their hands on her. But they got their hands on him in the process, and he'd expected to die as soon as they did.

Execution was standard operating procedure for the Paragon as far as he'd seen. Their goal was the extermination of all the unclean, unholy filth in the galaxy, everyone and anything not Paragon. So it was much to his surprise when he'd been thrown into a guarded cell with dozens of other humans and humanoids, eventually loaded into this transport, and finally dropped on this iceberg.

Not the way he'd envisioned spending his post-service days.

The transport had a single consolidated space, cockpit included, so he'd seen their approach into the system. An odd one, this "Vorkut," as he'd heard them call it. Hard to tell if it was proto or collapsing, but it was dominated by a thick, soupy cloud full of gases and asteroids, none of which appeared to be valuable.

Inner-system had a small star. Not much heat to be found here. It was the gas giant that gave the system its name, the lone planet around which everything swirled, and Vorkut V was its fifth moon. Nearly Earth-sized, but frozen white from pole to pole. Not a deep freeze, Warren thought as he stared out the door at the swirling snow flurries, but enough to make one reconsider one's life choices.

Warren didn't wait for the Paragon guard to poke him twice since he may not have been able to contain himself and was the first of the prisoners to step onto the lowered gangplank. Peering through the falling snow, Warren could see that he was stepping out onto a mountain plateau. There were jagged peaks above them, tall enough to reach past the tree line.

And there were trees. Evergreens, mostly, with their branches bending under the thick snowfall. They surrounded the compound into which he was being taken, which was on the plateau.

To the left, nestled into the mountains, was what Warren recognized as a mining pit. From the color of the slurry pools and tailings piles, it was a magnesite-07 mine— the stuff starships used to scrub CO_2 from recirculated air. It was labor-intensive to mine and not very valuable when extracted by hand. Inefficient was the nice way to put it. Surely the Paragon had at least the Terran Federation's level of automated mining capabilities. Nobody mined magnesite by hand. Cruel would be an accurate way to describe it, especially with forced labor.

Even cruelty didn't explain this camp, Warren realized, not given the level of security forces he saw as he trudged into the snow and more of his surroundings took shape.

There were guards *everywhere,* five to one for each prisoner, if not more, all decked out in the signature faceless, completely covered, head-to-toe white Paragon suits of armor. They'd have blended right into their snowy surroundings if it weren't for the bright blue dots spaced out over their bodies; their eyes, it was assumed. Nobody really knew what was under those suits. They self-immolated instantly when killed.

Simple cruelty also failed to explain the facility to the right side of the plateau, away from the mine pit, perched on a cliff ledge that fell hundreds if not thousands of feet to some unseeable valley floor below. Most of the guards were stationed on that side. There, shrouded in the falling snow, lay a sprawling facility. One would expect it to be a magnesite-07 refinery, but there were no material handling systems or furnace stacks. There were no outward features of any kind to the facility, not even windows; it was nearly a perfect black cube.

Between the pit and the facility was the camp, a sprawling mess of wooden huts, fencing, burn barrels, and many guards. A fenced, heavily guarded corridor led out of the camp on either side, one to the pit on the left and the other to the facility on the right. Warren saw more prisoners shuffling through the facility side than the mine pit side by a factor of three or four to one. Odd, indeed.

The windowless facility, the plethora of guards, and the mine pit were far from the most interesting thing about this godforsaken camp. That honor belonged to the ship that hung over the top of the facility. Likewise windowless, it was pure black, angled oddly, and relatively small, which was odd for a Paragon vessel. Warren had never seen anything like it. It floated two or three hundred meters above the facility, thrusters silently keeping station, with a tether cable attached to its underbelly that descended into the mysterious building below.

Like the facility, one might think the vessel was involved with the magnesite, perhaps as a cargo carrier, but Warren was a warrior. He knew a warship when he saw one, even if it looked like no ship he'd ever seen. It sent a chill down his spine. Dark, unnaturally shaped, and hungry-looking, it wasn't good.

Behind it, a meteor streaked across the sky, catching flame in the atmosphere. Must have come from the thick, soupy asteroid field they'd flown through. With a ground-shaking *boom*, a plasma turret fired from somewhere up along the mountain range. The flaming rock exploded an instant later, becoming smoke and dust. A meteor defense system. That was going be fun to hear at night.

Warren must have been rubber-necking too long because he got a verbal "move" from one of the multitude of new guards that lined the path to the prisoner camp. No rifle this time, thank the stars.

"In here," called a raspy squeak of a voice.

The fence from the landing pad angled in on both sides until it terminated at a gate staffed by more guards. It was open for them to pass through, "them" being Warren and his fellow prisoners. Beyond that was a wooden hut with a ramp leading up to an open door like one might see on a chicken coop. Inside sat a man who matched the rasping, squeaking voice. He was hunched over a stack of papers and gesturing impatiently at Warren and the others. "Quickly, quickly," he said.

Not a man. As Warren lumbered up the ramp, in no particular hurry, he recognized the white hair, wrinkled persimmon skin, and hunched back of a Trew, a humanoid species on the far side of the Paragon Imperium. Not much was known about them since the Terran Federation had little to no direct contact, but what Warren saw, he didn't like. The alien was wearing the same type of jumpsuit the others inside the fence line had been. A fellow prisoner.

"Name and race?" the Trew squeaked.

Warren was first in line, and the others from the transport shuffled into place behind him. "You work for these guys?" he asked the Trew in response, finding it impossible to hide his disgust.

The Trew didn't look up. "In the camp, everyone works. Name and race?"

"Name and race," the Paragon guard closest to him repeated with a smack from his rifle barrel. What was it with these guys?

"Warren, human," he answered through barely controlled rage. "Terran Defense Force Serial Number 4478—"

"Not necessary," and the Trew cut him off with an impatient wave, then held up a paper. "I have you right here." He finally looked at Warren, squinting between him and the paper he held.

The guard gave him a mirthless glare. "Hands out," he commanded when the Trew appeared satisfied that Warren was who he said he was. "Feet spread apart."

Warren rolled his tongue inside his mouth but obliged. The guards on either side of him advanced, which made Warren involuntarily brace to defend himself, but it wasn't an attack. Not yet. One unlocked his hand restraints and the other his feet, setting them free.

Warren rubbed his wrists and thought about how quickly he could take out the guards on either side of him. Did he have enough time to make it to the transport? Blast off before they could call in the bigger guns to shoot him down? No. Not even close. It was a way to go out, sure, but Warren had resigned himself to staying alive a little longer. Dammit.

"Strip."

Warren blinked. "What?"

"*Strip,*" the Trew said. He gestured at the Fleet armor Warren still had on. Its power core had been removed the second the Paragon had subdued him at Corvus, and was currently in the possession of one of the guards behind him, but Warren had . . . convinced them to let him leave the suit on. It was a wonder he was still alive. This bastard apparently needed some convincing as well. "All prisoners wear the same clothing," the Trew stated before Warren could speak in protest. "You will remove your armor."

This motherfu—

The plasma rifle barrel from the rear left guard was back in his rib cage, poked between articulating plates on his torso. It was primed to fire. He could feel the heat wisping up and through the underlayers.

Warren obliged. For the first time in months—the first time ever in the field—Warren was out of his boots, shin and thigh guards, backplate, breastplate and torso covers, shoulder assembly, neck guard, and the underlayers, too. They already had his damn helmet, which the guard to the right rear of him tossed onto the pile on the floor; the suit power core rattled inside it, and Warren looked at both forlornly. The cold was bitingly harsh, but Warren refused to shiver. He took his sweet time when they asked him to fold the whole contraption into an orange storage box, making sure each piece was neatly packed so as not to bend out of shape.

Behind him, several of the other prisoners in line grumbled and groaned for him to hurry up. They were stuck out in the snow and wind until he finished his intake. Warren didn't care. That shit was fitted down to the millimeter of his body shape. He'd be damned if this prison camp would ruin *his* armor.

"Holy fuck!" The shock came out of nowhere and surprised Warren. He whirled to see one of the guards holding a sanitizer gun, still glowing from being discharged on him. The smell of his burned hair filled the small wooden cabin, a rancid scent. His muscles involuntarily twitched, but he was free of topical parasites. Not sure it was better than getting naked and sprayed with a hose like in the pictures from history, though. He couldn't shake off the twitching sensation.

"You have a choice," the Trew said after he handed Warren his jumpsuit. He laid out two small strips of fabric on the table between them. One was a faded red, the other a faded green. They looked like scarves.

Warren was putting his last arm through and zipping up the thin and inadequate garment. "A choice?" he repeated and frowned at the scarves.

The Trew pointed to Warren's left in the direction of the magnesite mine and indicated the red one. "You can go there and break your back like every prisoner who works in the pit for long enough does, with the minimum amount of privileges allowed by the Interstellar Treaty on the Treatment of War Prisoners or . . ."

He pointed in the other direction toward the windowless facility with the ship hanging above it and indicated the green scarf. "You may choose to work in the research facility and assist the Paragon in their holy war to cleanse the cosmos of the blasphemers and the unfit and receive the extra privileges afforded to friends of the Paragon." He leaned forward, a sneer on his wrinkled orange face. "As a

Terran Fleet officer, I'm sure they would find your insight on weapons and knowledge of human warships to be quite valuable indeed."

Warren sneered back and reached down to pick up the red scarf. The Trew smiled as if he had hoped Warren would make that choice. "The Paragon can *rigarrut*," Warren said to his face. He was digging into his interstellar social studies, but it was Trew for "Go fuck yourself." Or he thought it was.

"There is no cursing at this camp, human," the Trew said, smile growing larger and more punch-worthy by the millimeter. "In any language. Offenders will be shot." He gestured at the red scarf in Warren's hand. "You will have that tied around your right arm at all times. Offenders will, of course, be shot. On sight. Is that clear?"

"Crystal." Warren barely suppressed the urge to strangle him then and there.

"Excellent. Welcome to Vorkut V." The small alien leaned sideways, looked past Warren's hulking frame, and shouted out into the snow. "Next!"

CHAPTER FOUR

GREEN WOULD HAVE BEEN the better choice. Conditions in the mine were much worse than Warren had imagined they could be. The mountain range in which they were situated was volcanic, that much was abundantly clear, and the rock the prisoners were tasked with mining the magnesite from was like glass. It shattered into pieces so sharp they'd have cut through gloves, which nobody had.

That ignored the pace they were forced to maintain, the loads they were compelled to carry, and the hours they were required to work. After the first few days, Warren and every other new prisoner who'd chosen the red scarf was covered in blood, every inch of their body ached, and was considering that they'd made a grave mistake.

Every evening, the largest groups of Greens, which was what Warren had learned the other prisoners called the collaborators, shuffled in from the research facility and lined up for their extra chow and blankets, and the Reds would holler at them viciously. It was jealousy, but it was also contempt for their weakness. A hard pill to swallow when you were dying as they survived, but Warren held onto it like honey.

The Greens were kept in a separate section of the camp with extra guards. Necessary, or Warren was sure they'd all have slit throats by dawn the next morning. There were still raids in the night. Groups of Reds would slip into their huts for food, clothing, or simply to satisfy bloodlust. It wasn't an activity exclusive to the Reds. The Greens ran counterraids. The penalty for being out of bunk past sundown was the same as it was for everything else in the camp: being shot on sight.

Warren was approached by one such raiding faction early on, Red, of course, probably because of his size. It was a group of Serm, a non-humanoid species of mineral-based life forms that fed off sunlight. They didn't need their allotted food or blankets, so they hoarded them to trade with other prisoners. A distasteful, brutal group of murderers and thieves who were nonetheless suffering along with everyone else since there was little sun on Vorkut V. However, the Serm were blood enemies of the Paragon, and these Serm lived up to that reputation and poured that hatred into the collaborators who wore the wrong color. Warren wanted nothing to do with them, but he did come to share their hatred of the Greens.

There were small perks, however, to the existence of the collaborators. The camp barter network was flush with goods. Warren used it to trade some extra hand-damaging assignments in the mines for a few choice goods; among them a small imager he could hide in his rags. He took holographic images wherever he went, including that of the mine, the outside of the facility, and the camp in between them; entrances, exits, guards, huts, the ship, its tether, the meteor defense system in action, blowing rocks to bits.

Why, he wasn't really sure. But it hadn't cost him much, the imager, and though he wasn't sure what the facility or the ship above it were all about, they just *looked* important. So, special ops soldier that he was, he took images.

Just before dawn on the seventeenth day in hell— Warren knew the number since he'd been counting days meticulously because he actually could—minutes from the morning siren, a commotion roused him to raise his head from his bunk and peer out the single-paned, hand-hewn window of his cabin. He shared it with a couple other cast-aways, humanoids from a race he didn't recognize, who all huddled together on the floor for warmth.

Warren slept alone with a Green blanket he'd procured from a raiding band other than the Serm. On that particular night, the meteors had been falling in numbers, each marked with the same *boom* of the defense system that rattled the camp and kept everyone awake. In the gray pre-dawn, through exhausted, half-lidded eyes, Warren watched as a man was led out of the research facility by two Paragon guards. He was human, tall, desperately thin, and old. His skin was stretched over every inch of his visible body like parchment, and his eyes had sunk deep into his skull.

"Here!" one of the guards who was handling him commanded, and they tossed him into the snow near Warren's window. The man fell hard, but he didn't let out a sound. He just picked himself up out of the cold slush and turned to stare at the pair of guards. They took exception to the eye contact, and one of them raised his rifle over his head and butt-stroked him in the face. The old man toppled back into the snow. Again, he didn't cry out, but he didn't get up, either.

The second guard activated his plasma rifle and pointed

it at the man, who was nothing more than a crumpled mass of skin and bones. Paragon soldiers wore head-to-toe armor, so you could never see their facial expressions, but Warren could read body language. These two were *furious*. The one holding the rifle quaked with anger, finger twitching on the trigger. But he didn't pull it, and eventually, his fellow guard put a hand out to have him lower the weapon.

"Leave him," he said.

The other guard nodded and stalked toward the facility gate.

"This goes for all of you!" the guard shouted into the morning air, his words amplified through his suit's external speakers to make his voice boom. Nobody was outside their cabins yet, but the entire camp was watching and listening. The guard knew it, too. He pointed at the old man. "Impertinence will be dealt with harshly. Help this one, and you will be shot." He left for the facility as well, following the other guard.

It was silent after that. Warren lay in his bunk with the man a meter or two from his window, close enough to hear that he was still breathing. Raggedly, a worrisome wheeze and gurgle with each breath, but he was alive.

The morning siren went off not long after that. Warren rose, exited with his bunkmates, and saw that the man was still face-down and bleeding into the snow from a cut on his temple.

He would be surprised if the man made it through the day.

He was still alive after morning chow, though not in much better shape. He'd managed to pick himself up off the snowbank and was kneeling upright and muttering to himself. The wound on his head was still bleeding, and he was barely conscious. He swayed on his knees, and his eyes were half-lidded; he was clearly concussed. The mutter, Warren realized, was prayer. The man was praying. For all the good it would do him. There was chatter in the chow line, at the tables, and everywhere. His green armband was unmistakable, and not an ounce of that chatter was devoid of bloodlust. Warren stuck with his initial estimate that this man would not last through the day.

He found himself thinking of the other prisoner as he worked, and when the end-day siren went off close to sundown, he made sure he was at the head of the line returning back to camp to see what state the old man was in. Much to his surprise, the man was still there, still alive. He was shivering violently, but he was on his knees, praying, his eyes were clearer, and it looked like his head wound had scabbed or crusted over in the extreme cold. His eyes . . . they were something else, too. It was hard to tell from far away, but they almost seemed to glow in the dimming light. Crazy colors, depending on which way he looked.

As Warren watched him from evening chow, the chatter growing ever louder and the glances ever sharper, particularly from the Serm, he revised his estimate to a worse fate. The man would make it to nighttime, and that would be the end of him. A shame. It would have been better for him to die before sundown to spare him a more gruesome fate. An odd thought to have about a Green, Warren realized, but he had it, nonetheless.

After chow, as Warren was trudging back to his cabin, he paused to get a good look at the man. It was starting to rain, which might sound like a reprieve from the snow, but Warren knew better. Rain meant the water soaked into your clothing and got you wet so that when it froze later, you were far colder than if it just kept snowing. At least in the snow, it was possible to stay dry. Warren couldn't see the old prisoner well through the precipitation, so he stepped off the path and waded a few steps into the slush.

The old man snapped into a crouched defensive stance. It took Warren aback. The movement had been lightning-quick, and the pose he'd struck was defensible. Trained. Military. Warren wasn't sure how it was possible, but the man before him was Fleet. He recognized the defensive stance drilled into himself during basic training. The soldier's sunken eyes shone at him through the rain, steelier and more resolved than Warren would think possible. This man would stand his ground.

Admirable.

A plasma bolt ripped through the air between them. A Paragon guard stood twenty meters away, and the multitude of light dots that covered his uniform shimmered in the rain. The barrel of his plasma rifle glowed from the shot. Warren put his hands in the air and reversed his few steps back onto the path to the cabin. The old man watched him back away, eyes still steely. Warren felt them follow him into his cabin.

THAT NIGHT, the Serm came for the old man. Warren was asleep but awoke to grunts. He rolled over in his sack and wiped at the single-pane window, which had frosted over. That let him see the dim shadows of three of the rocklike aliens circling the old man. Another Serm was writhing in the snow, a spear of some sort sticking out of it.

A stick, Warren realized. The old man had found some discarded wood and sharpened it. Siding from the cabin, maybe? He held another piece of wood in his hands, a heavier piece meant to crunch rather than stab. An unfortunate weapon against the Serm. They didn't crunch. Their mineral skin was too tough. Poking was better, but that was probably why the old man had used the other weapon first.

None of them made a sound, not even the Serm on the ground when it managed to extract the stick from its side. The circling aliens closed on the man in unison. He swung his club wildly, trying to connect, and he did, with one of their heads, but the Serm didn't go down.

Instead, it grabbed the club from him and yanked right as the other two tackled the man. None of them made a sound beyond the grunting and hissing and clawing of a brawl. Warren saw the Serm with the club raise it just as the tussle rolled into the wall of his cabin, and his view was blocked.

There was a thud and a gasp and then one more of each, followed by more grunting and tussling, but Warren's view remained blocked. Then, there was a sharp crack, the sound of someone's bones breaking, and a sickening moan. Silence for a moment after that. The tussle was over. The Serm had won. They clicked among themselves, and then there were more thuds.

It was much worse listening to it than watching it. Warren's stomach churned as he heard another thud and another. The first couple were punctuated with moans, but the blows coming now were met with silence. The man was being beaten to death, and the sound of it was driving Warren mad. All he could think about were his eyes, unafraid, determined, and asking for nothing.

If the man had begged for his life, it would have been easy to hold onto his disgust. Lump him in with the other cowards and collaborators. But that dying man out there was no coward. That was the goddamn surprise of it all.

Even more surprising was when the sound of the blows drove him from his bed onto his feet. Surprise turned to astonishment when he tossed his sack aside and ripped two of the bed slats off his bunk. Astonishment gave way to something unnameable when he snapped those slats into sharp points and busted out through the cabin door into the freezing night.

The Serm had no idea he was coming. They were huddled around the limp form of the old man, throwing their version of fists and stomping on him with their boulderlike feet, beating him to a pulp. There was blood everywhere. Warren slipped in it as he drove one of the bed slats deep and hard into the neck of the closest Serm.

Serm didn't bleed. Fluids ran through their bodies, but they were more like pitch-black wet sand than blood. A lot of it ran between their lumpy heads and ample shoulders and the neck, which was where the majority of their seven "eyes" were located. Those eyes were a softer tissue than the rest of them, and Warren struck in the middle of one. Lucky. He got the wet black sand all over him, but he drove the stake in deeper, undeterred.

The other two Serm noticed him when their comrade crumpled on the snow, twitching in its death throes. Warren, dripping black sand, attacked the next closest Serm. He stabbed for the neck again but missed this time and hit the alien in its torso.

Unlucky. The alien howled, the first widely audible sound of the entire affair. Warren ducked around the creature to get behind it and use its body for leverage, then pushed the wooden stake as hard as he could. The alien howled again, and the stake went deeper.

It snapped when Warren couldn't push it any farther in, and he tumbled off the alien into the snow. He leapt to his feet, sure one of the other Serm would be upon him in an instant. The bastards could move shockingly fast for organisms with no muscles. Instead, their many legs scrambled them away from him, and they disappeared into the night.

Their howls had echoed across the camp. Warren could hear people moving about in their cabins, trying to get a look at what was happening. Guards would be outside in seconds, too, sweeping the area and shooting anyone they saw. He had to move and fast.

He looked at the old man. He was lying on his face, crumpled. Warren crab-walked back to him and reached out to touch the man's neck. It was feeble, but there was the thump-thump of a heartbeat. The same fingers held under the other prisoner's nose confirmed that breaths were still being taken. Incredible. The man was alive. A problem for Warren but incredible all the same.

A shout rang out from one of the guards' barracks, and Warren saw the blue lights of Paragon armor flashing between buildings as they moved. They would be upon him in seconds. He sucked in a deep breath, then exhaled it as he slung the old man's dead weight over his shoulder in a fireman's carry. Starry fuck, he was heavier than he looked. Grunting and wondering how much strength this place had sapped from him in just seventeen days, Warren hauled the man away from his cabin and deeper into the camp and the night.

CHAPTER FIVE

"STILL. STAY STILL."

Warren had to restrain the old man's thrashing with all his body weight, and he hissed his words through clenched teeth. A day and a night had passed since the old man had been attacked. Warren had managed to set the two of them up nicely in one of the older abandoned huts at the far end of the camp.

It hadn't been easy. The old man had been out cold when he'd finally found a hut no one would see them enter, and it had been a risk to leave him there. So easy for him to either freeze to death before Warren could return with supplies or wake like he was now and make enough noise to call attention to his whereabouts.

It was an even greater risk, however, for Warren to return to his previous cabin. Guards had been everywhere after the fight, and so were the watching eyes of the camp, many of whom would be happy to finger him to the Serm as their surprise attacker. If he could get back into his cabin before the dawn siren, not only could he get his hands on his supplies, but he could also plead ignorance of the whole affair.

His black ops experience got him through the camp undetected by the guards, and hopefully, cross his fingers, his eyes, and whatever else he could cross, without having been seen by his fellow prisoners. He was back inside his cabin just minutes before dawn. His cabin mates were asleep. A good sign, he thought. They were a bunch of loners like he was. He doubted they'd snitch on him if no one suspected the assailant had come from their midst.

At morning chow, Warren slipped his gruel into an insulated container he bartered from another human. A civilian woman, and the same he'd bartered for his imager before. She was in one of the rival factions of the Serm and wanted to talk about the attack. The whole camp was abuzz. But Warren had feigned disinterest.

Hard to tell if that tactic made him more or less suspicious, but it was consistent with the persona he'd adopted from the start. He got some med pills and a thermal warming pad from her, too. The latter was the most expensive item he'd ever bartered for. Six extra shifts, three of his meals when she asked for them, *and* he owed her whatever favor she wanted whenever she wanted it. From the way she said it, he doubted it would be the sexual kind. More likely the stabbing kind.

It was worth it, though. When he was finally able to sneak back to the abandoned hut after chow and off the work line with his goods in tow, the old man's lips were blue, as was the gash where the Serm had broken his jaw. Nasty fracture, but it looked like it might heal on its own if the man stayed alive long enough. Warren stuffed him into his sack, the thermal pad along with him, and stayed with him until the color started to come back into his cheeks.

When Warren was back on the work line, hauling magnesite ore, he wondered what in the stars he was doing. Why should he stick his neck out like this for someone he knew nothing about and a Green at that? He didn't have an answer, not even later that evening when he again didn't eat his meal at chow and brought it back for the old man instead.

The Green soldier was still unconscious but was sleeping now, and there was sweat beading on his brow. That had seemed like an improvement. It wasn't. It was a fever setting in, and the man woke in a half-dream, screaming and fighting off Warren's attempts to quiet or contain him. He flailed with a zeal that got Warren smacked in the face several times. The fever dreams tore at the man's psyche.

"Hush," Warren growled, trying to sound reassuring. It was a vain attempt with one hand clamped over the old man's mouth and his body weight on top of the dreamer to stop the thrashing. "Hold . . . the fuck . . . *STILL.*"

The thrashing stopped, and Warren tentatively lifted off enough to look at the man's face. His eyes were open and still wild but conscious. Warren locked eyes with him, then risked using his free hand to put a finger to his own mouth. The man nodded, and Warren removed the hand over his mouth. His lips were still crusted with blood.

"I . . . alive," the Green said, barely managing words through his broken jaw and swollen mouth.

"For now," Warren said bluntly. "You have a fever."

The man nodded, and Warren seized the opportunity to take his patient in for the first time. His face was more than parchment skin pulled over old bones. There were spiderwebs of scars, some of them ancient-looking and faded, others fresh. They formed intricate patterns Warren didn't understand, and he wondered if they were from self-inflicted wounds. They were certainly deliberate.

The blood that had crusted on the man's face from his many wounds glittered in a way that normal blood didn't. Warren hadn't noticed it in his rush to hide the other man, but there were flecks of something metallic in it, even the fresh blood. He'd seen such blood before, oozing in a glittering white from a Paragon's body armor. The old man's eyes were the most distinctive, for sure, particularly this up close. His irises had shattered into a multitude of blues, greens, and browns. There were other colors in there too, inhuman yellows and reds and purples. They were kaleidoscopes that also seemed like they might glow on their own.

What had the Paragon done to him?

The old man felt the scrutiny. He turned away from it, shivering as his fever became chills. He groaned. His face wasn't the only thing the Serm had broken.

"Take these," Warren said, fishing the med pills out of his jumpsuit and shoving them toward the man. They were catch-alls, the pills: pain reliever, antibiotic, antiviral, and tissue growth accelerator. Some came with a stimulant, others which components that helped you sleep. Warren had the latter, or that was what the woman he had gotten them from had said. "You have to beat this fever," he pressed when the man ignored him, "or you *will* die."

Grudgingly, the old man turned back to him. He hated being taken care of, being sick, weak, and dependent on someone else. Warren could tell. He'd have felt the same way. But he took the pills being offered, popped them into his mouth, and swallowed. He couldn't contain the gasp of pain that followed, that broken jaw barking at him, but Warren wasn't done with him yet. "Swallow it down with this," he said and unscrewed the top of the insulated container he'd put his last two meals inside.

The contents were still warm. The man balked, but Warren insisted. He kept insisting until the container was three-quarters empty and the man could not physically swallow any more of the hot, pasty-white porridge the Paragon called food.

"Good," Warren said, satisfied he'd done everything he could to get his patient through another day or even just the night. The old man grunted something that sounded like an aggrieved "Thank you." "I'm Warren," he said as the man started to drift back to sleep, the pills taking hold.

"Mm . . . arkus," the old man said with great difficulty.

"Markus," Warren repeated. "You'd better not fucking die tonight after what I went through to get you this far."

The old man winced. Warren assumed it was from the pain. It wasn't. "Don't," he rasped, eyelids closing. "Curse."

Warren almost laughed. The wince was from the *cursing*? "How did you ever survive out here without cursing?" he asked him.

But, the Green soldier was already asleep.

MARKUS DIDN'T DIE that night. Warren slept next to him, huddled back to back, wrapped in his blanket, trying to ignore the freezing wind whistling through the missing slats on the cabin's roof, and the periodic thunderclap and shake of a meteor being blown to bits. He didn't die the next day or night that followed either, or the next, or the next. On the fourth day, when Warren returned from the work line, the bastard was sitting up in the cabin, clear-eyed and face washed. He'd done it out in the snow, he said. He'd walked!

"Anyone see you?" Warren asked, none too impressed.

Markus shrugged.

Warren flared. "Goddammit, man. The entire camp knows what you look like. The only reason anything has quieted down is they think you're dead. Give them a reason to think otherwise, and there will be a shitstorm. I killed a Serm for you."

Markus flared in return but stewed rather than say anything. It took him several minutes to finally say he would be careful. "It's not a very tenable long-term plan," he stated. Tenable. Jaw must be feeling better, using fancy words like that. "And I'd appreciate it if you watched your language in my presence."

"There is no long-term plan right now." That was the truth. "And what is it with this cursing thing? Is that some kind of Paragon shit?"

"It offends the Divine."

Of course it did. "I make you no promises, old man," Warren told him.

The questions of how long they could keep this up and how ill-advised it had been to get involved in this mess were eating at Warren, but he'd done what he'd done, and there was no going back now. If the camp discovered Markus, they'd discover his part in keeping the old man alive at the same time, which meant the Serm would tear him apart. Tear them both apart. Their fates were tied, whether they liked it or not.

The two men left it at that, and they ate their slop in silence.

On the fifth day, Markus was praying when Warren came into the cabin. They were Paragon rites; Warren recognized them. He was flat on his back, palms pressed together and resting on his nose and forehead.

He waited for the man to finish, posting up against the wall nearest the only unbroken window in the dilapidated cabin. He spoke when the old man was sitting up again, eyes open. "So, that's who you pray to? The Paragon?"

Markus blinked at him. "Yes."

Warren flexed his jaw. "But you're Fleet."

"I was."

"Who?"

Markus looked down at his green arm scarf and slid it off, considering it. "I was an officer. Computer tech, then a lead in the AI division before I was picked up by the Paragon."

Warren frowned. "AI?" Fleet hadn't messed with artificial intelligence in decades.

"I served in the Third Paragon Wars."

There was a stunned silence. "That was over a hundred years ago."

Markus' eyebrows rose. "Has it been that long?" he asked, sharing Warren's surprise.

That surprised Warren. People these days lived well into their nineties on average, some even hitting their hundred and twenties, but the man before him looked like he was in his seventies at most. Malnourished, with some weird shit going on, sure, but it was not possible this man was a hundred and forty or fifty. "So, what are you now?"

He pointed at his eyes and the myriad colors they contained and to wounds healing on his face where the blood still shimmered. "I'm a Blaspheme," he explained.

Warren had to drag out the history book in his head to make sense of the term, but he recognized it. In those earlier conflicts, the Paragon had often taken prisoners. Some of them to run their labor camps, like this one. He had no doubt that the cabin they were huddling in had been built around that time when this mine was running at five or ten times its current capacity. Many prisoners were released, eventually, when hostilities died down.

The Paragon had been less hell-bent on extermination in those days, apparently. Less high on their own superiority. However, some prisoners were never returned. Some went missing. And the rumors about where they disappeared to were horrifying. Experiments. The Paragon poked and prodded them to find out what kept them alive and what killed them. Others were subject to genetic manipulation, surfacing after years with deformities or diseases. The Blasphemes were rumored to have been infused with Paragon DNA to see if the Paragon superiority could be achieved through means other than war. If *everyone* could become Paragon.

They couldn't.

"I thought the Blasphemes were failures," Warren said slowly. "And all of them died."

"Most of us did. I didn't."

"It made you live longer?"

"Among other things."

"You started praying to their god because your blood turned into glitter?"

"Among other things." There was another defiant pause. "I don't expect you to understand."

Warren put his head down and rubbed the bridge of his nose. He *didn't* understand. For right then, Warren decided he didn't need to. He would at some point. They were in this together, now. He pushed himself off the wall and grabbed their pot to go and get some snow they could melt for drinking water. "Just keep it down, I guess," he said before he left. "And don't go outside again."

CHAPTER SIX

"Markus. Wake up."

Six Serm were stalking outside their cabin. How they'd found them, Warren didn't know. One of the sandy bastards must have followed him the last time he got off shift, or maybe from chow. He'd been careful never to come here directly, always watching out for a tail. Dammit. Or maybe one of his previous bunkmates had finally talked.

Markus was up in an instant. Light sleeper, Warren had noticed. Hell when he was trying to get some shut-eye, but helpful here.

"Can you travel?" Warren hissed at him. Markus nodded. He hoped the old man knew what he was talking about. It had been a little over a week, and while he'd been improving each day, those Paragon supergenes no doubt helping, he'd yet to see him walk more than a few slow steps at a time. He still had several broken ribs and a fractured jaw.

He either could or couldn't walk. They'd find out in seconds.

Warren Army-crawled to the back corner of the dilapidated cabin and carefully lifted several of the floorboards, then slid them aside in silence. Bitterly cold air wafted up from the opening, bringing frosty white flakes with it. It was snowing outside. Aside from the temperatures, that was a plus. It lowered visibility.

Warren gestured for Markus to go through the opening, which led into the crawlspace between the floor joists and the ground upon which the raised foundation had been built. More slowly than Warren would have liked, he grunted his way through the small opening. After he was through, Warren tossed his sleeping sack and the heating pad after him. When he went to grab his own pack and blanket, he froze.

A Serm was standing in the doorway.

Warren almost made the mistake of attacking him, but the momentary shock of seeing the lumpy figure froze him. Warren stayed frozen as he realized the Serm wasn't attacking him. It stayed in the doorway, slowly turning its torso—its eyes—to sweep back and forth over the cabin, looking. It couldn't see him.

The Serm stood in the doorway, slowly sweeping the interior, long enough for Warren's muscles to start aching. Behind him, through the hole in the floorboards, he could hear Markus breathing. Surely they were going to be discovered. It wasn't they who were seen in the end, however. It was Warren's stuff, still by the window. The alien tensed when it caught sight of the telltale signs of habitation.

It was game over, but the Serm handed Warren one small piece of good luck. Rather than approach the items, it took a half-step outside and called for its friends. Warren seized the moment and dove for his blanket and the pack. He grabbed something and yanked it, then dove into the hole.

From the sounds above, he knew the Serm had seen him that time. He heard pounding footsteps as he scrambled away from the opening, then a giant rocklike fist rocketed through it, causing a puff of dust and ice as it hit the ground.

"Go, go, go," Warren hissed to Markus, who was crawling ahead of him, not trying to hide his painful grunting any longer. "Dead ahead." There was a grate in the foundation. Access to the crawlspace. Warren doubted the Serm knew where it was, but they'd find it soon enough. He and Warren had to beat them to it.

They did. It was pure luck, but they did. The Serm were nowhere to be seen. They were either still looking for them inside or had run to the other side of the cabin. Warren would take it. He threw Markus' arm over his shoulders to give the man extra support, and they ran into the snowy night.

Behind them were shouts, the ruckus of breaking glass and shattering timber. Something whistled past Warren's ear and exploded with a smack on the rail of another abandoned cabin. He didn't dare pause or even slow down to see what it was. Their only chance was to outrun the bastards.

They did that, too. Credit to the old man. He needed the help Warren provided, but once those legs got moving, he kept them moving. The shouts receded quickly. When he was satisfied that the Serm were far behind them, Warren altered their course to take them zigzagging through the compound. Then they'd crouch in the snow or behind machinery to wait and listen.

It was goddamn freezing. Warren could hardly hear through the chattering of his teeth, but each time they stopped, there was no sound of pursuit. When he believed they had lost the Serm, he hauled Markus and their provisions toward his fallback position. His final secret place. There were no more after this one.

It was a lean-to underneath an outcropping of rock. An old earth-mover had been parked there decades ago and never moved again. Bridging the gap between the rusting hulk and the outcrop was a strip of canvas suspended by rope. It was unclear if that was because someone else had used this as a hideout or if it was to protect the mat, but it didn't matter. Warren hadn't put it up.

It had been there for longer than he had, so it wouldn't be noticed. It was drafty, worse than the cabin for sure, and the ground was rock-solid, but it was hidden, the wind couldn't rip through at full force, and it offered a spectacular view of the research facility. Above it, stars were peeking out, and the snowstorm was moving south off the ridge.

"Thank you," Markus wheezed as Warren got him set up to go back to sleep. He hadn't lost the sleep sack or the warming pad. The latter would keep them alive through the night, but beyond that . . . "You couldn't grab your pack," Markus observed.

Warren shook his head. He'd only managed to grab the blanket. Beyond that and whatever was in his pockets—a few pills, and his imager—all their food, the meds, the extras Warren had traded and bartered for in his time at the prison were in the hands of the Serm, and they knew it was him. Now, neither could show their face in the camp again and not get jumped.

Markus looked like he wanted to tell his savior he was sorry, but wisely, he didn't. He just pointed at the sky.

The clouds had cleared. The meteors were quiet. The Vorkut gas giant was a brilliant ice-blue high above them, and reflecting some of its light as it hung above the research facility was the black prototype ship. Its tether was gone. It floated free from the facility, and there was activity in the air around it, with drones and work pods flying this way and that. Same for the ground below. It seemed like every light the facility had was turned on, and the shadows of people moved everywhere.

Then, the activity quieted. The drones left, as did the work pods. It was like an inhalation. Warren watched intently. The damn thing would move, wouldn't it? It was preparing for a trial run. He pulled out his imager, propped it in the snow, and set it to record.

"Don't watch where it is," Markus said, and he pointed far into the distance in front of the shining gas giant. "Look there."

Warren didn't know what he meant until it was almost too late.

Silently, without spinning up energy or movement or preamble of any kind, the ship shimmered with blinding multicolored light and disappeared. Except it wasn't gone. Warren had shifted his eyes just in time for the nearby flash to happen in his peripheral vision, and he caught a second, seemingly instantaneous smaller flash in front of the gas giant. If he hadn't seen it, he'd have missed the tiny black dot that was left behind. As it was, he could only track it for a second before it was lost in the vast distance between them.

It was the prototype ship. From Warren's experience in the Fleet, he knew he was looking at a distance of several hundred thousand kilometers crossed in an instant. A jump. Something nobody other than Idri, who was hopefully a thousand lightyears away at that moment, safe on Earth. So, how had the Paragon just jumped a ship? The question sent shivers down his neck and spine.

"Okay, Markus," Warren breathed. "Who the fuck are you? And what do you know about that ship?"

Markus didn't even acknowledge the 'fuck,' he just nodded as if this was a question he'd been expecting. It made Warren want to punch him in the goddamn face; why not just spill the beans earlier, then? "I've been an AI specialist with the Paragon for . . . a long time," the Green soldier started. "Decades. Top-level clearance. General research and development across every conceivable deployment, including much of the security systems used at this camp, for example. But, for the past several years, I've been working one single project. Here. With the archgeneral."

"Archgeneral?" Warren had heard the term in the camp. He didn't know what it meant.

"Hadras. This is his facility."

The name meant nothing to Warren, but it seemed to mean a lot to the old man. "Okay. So, what I just saw is . . . AI?"

"Yes. Sort of."

"Sort of?"

"Allow me to speak, and I will explain."

"Fine."

"I've been working on a computer with sufficient intelligence to operate a displacement drive on that vessel. We've recently had a breakthrough. A large one."

Markus was about to continue, but Warren held up a hand, blinking. He was stuck on "displacement drive." "Y-you mean," he stammered, "you mean a computer just jumped that ship? Like a Navid can?"

"Yes."

"An AI?"

"Yes."

Holy shit. Warren suddenly felt as though he needed to

sit down, but his legs started pacing instead. It was . . . It was inconceivable. Even at the height of the humans' AI exploration, such a thought was laughable. Whatever the Navid did, it was unique in the known universe and several million orders of magnitude beyond the computational power of any known artificial intelligence. And Markus had been at the heart of it.

"So, what landed you out here, then?" Warren asked him. "With me?"

Markus shifted uncomfortably. "I did not expect to make the leap to a working, artificial interstellar displacement drive. Not in my lifetime, Warren, so this breakthrough was a surprise. Things happened very quickly after that. Hadras plans to use this ship to turn the tide in this new war. That much was clear from the directives I was getting, the updated timelines and who he started to share the work with. Those ramifications on that scale were . . . not something I ever expected to consider."

Warren scoffed. "A bit late, don't you think?"

"I hope not."

Warren picked up on the subtext of what the man was saying and where this story was going. He stopped pacing. "You sabotaged it."

Markus looked satisfied that Warren had figured that out. "Only temporarily, but as much damage as I could do. At first, I tried to diminish the AI in ways they would write off as malfunctions and not detect, but the leap the AI had taken made that impossible.

"The only way to slow the project down was to do obvious damage. So, at my first opportunity, I deleted large chunks of the AI's code. It was detected instantly, of course, and I was thrown out." He blinked, that moment of him in the snow, bare and exposed, replaying in his kaleidoscope eyes. "I thought they would kill me right then and there." He considered. "If Hadras had been here, I'm sure they would have, but the guards didn't want to risk upsetting him, I think. I don't really know."

"Why did you suddenly have this change of heart?" Warren asked.

Markus opened his mouth, about to answer, then closed it uncertainly. Warren saw the defiance, haughtiness, and piss and vinegar melt out of him. When he finally answered, he looked very old and very small. "I do not know," he said. He shook his head, lost and angry with himself. "I don't know why. I think I regret it."

Not the answer Warren was hoping for, but he believed him. If the old man had answered in any other way, actually, Warren probably *wouldn't* have believed him. This angry, confused, disoriented uncertainty had the ring of truth. Especially the regret. "How close is the ship to being operational?"

"Hard to say. Before I did what I did, days. Now, weeks?"

Warren's body felt several kilos heavier with the knowledge. He looked back up at the night sky. The oddly-angled black ship was there, as it always was, stark against the dark.

If that thing did what Markus said it could, it could be curtains for the Fleet, especially since AI was re-producible on a mass scale. Even when the Fleet had been chock full of Navigators at the height of that time, they had been a limited resource and had to be deployed strategically. This? This would be a massive change. A game-changer. It was hard to believe. He said as much to Markus.

"I can offer you one sliver of recompense," Markus said. "For saving my life and perhaps for all of my crimes against my own kind."

Warren shook his head. He wanted to tell the man it was over. There was nothing left for them in this camp but death. As for humanity, based on what he had just witnessed, it was probably curtains for them, too. However, what the old man said next changed his mind on both accounts.

"I know how to get us out of here."

Warren turned, trying to assess if Markus had gone crazy. It was hard to tell. "I'm listening," he said very slowly.

CHAPTER SEVEN

THE CAMP's Trew intake officer, the one who Warren had the displeasure of meeting when he'd first arrived, was named Skrill. Unfortunately for him, there were fewer guards around his hut when no new prisoners were arriving, particularly before dawn. The Trew collaborator liked to go to his office in those gray hours before the other prisoners woke. It was less conspicuous, and nobody liked him, the Reds included.

Warren and Markus used this to their advantage. While the fence lines, the main corridor between the rows of inmate huts, and the other main buildings like the kitchen and bathrooms were constantly patrolled by the plethora of guards, the rest of the grounds were not. That meant Skrill was alone and out of the sight of any patrol for about twenty meters of his morning walk to his office.

They jumped him in those twenty meters. Markus clamped the small alien's mouth shut, and Warren pressed him in the back with a shard of magnesite ore, right where he knew the Trew's heart was.

"Remember me?" he asked, relishing the moment.

They used the cover of the morning siren and its coinciding shift change to slip into Skrill's office unseen. The alien didn't resist, even when they tied his hands and feet to his desk chair with twine. It didn't surprise Warren, but it did make him dislike the spineless little shit even more.

"Where are the access cards?" Warren asked him when the small alien was satisfactorily secured. He passed his magnesite shard to Markus, who posted up by the door.

Warren pounded on the desk and repeated his demand. "The cards!"

It made Skrill jump. "In the top drawer," he said and pointed a quivering finger at the desk cabinet to his left. Warren tore the drawer open, and inside, he found a stack of palm-sized plastic rectangles. They otherwise had no markings. "Won't do you any good," Skrill squeaked. "They're blank. They don't even let me program them."

Warren had seen the cards on the Greens. He knew they opened doors once they were allowed to pass through the gates into the facility. Green armband got you past the gate, access card got you to where you were allowed to work. "Don't worry about that."

He took two of them and tossed them to Markus, who caught them with ease. Nothing wrong with the old man's sight or dexterity. He watched as Markus expertly snapped a previously-invisible tab out of the edge of one of the cards and began to tap in a complicated code. Skrill's eyes widened.

"You think you can do that and handle this guy?" Warren asked, pointing at Skrill.

"Sure."

"Good." Warren straightened and turned to the open door behind the intake desk. Beyond it was the storage room. "I have to check on something."

The storage room was dark at this time of the morning. Warren didn't want to turn on the lights and attract undue attention to the intake cabin, so it took him longer than he wanted to find what he was looking for since every second or so, he checked the outer office.

Credit to Skrill, his storage containers were clearly marked and meticulously sorted. Warren found the day of his intake, hauled it onto the floor, and cracked it open. Inside, with a paper tag that had his name and prisoner number, was his armor.

Touching it gave him an intense desire to go home. He'd been avoiding the feeling since well before being captured, but he'd stuffed it deep inside him much harder and more deliberately since he'd come to this place. Escape was a double-edged sword. It could keep him alive, but hope for it too much, and it would drive him mad.

It was very hard for Warren not to hope too much.

Markus' plan was solid. He knew the facility. He knew there were long-range shuttles, and best of all, he claimed he knew access codes and gate locations that would give them a fighting chance to cross Paragon space to get back to Terran-controlled territory.

With that, paired with Warren's knowledge of the camp, the kind of Green band they'd need to slip through the guarded corridor to the facility, and where to get the access cards once they were inside, they could pull this off. Markus could supply everything that had kept Warren from seriously considering escape: the means to slip off the planet-moon undetected and the chance to get to friendly space. They'd have to be damned lucky, and Markus would have to deliver.

Warren slipped his armor back into the crate and pushed down the nerves. He couldn't take it. It would be too bulky, stick out too much, and make him far too visible. This was goodbye. In terms of their escape, they would take one step at a time. If Markus was full of shit, it was a hell of a way to go out. Better than this shit hole.

He grabbed a pair of the thick overcoats the Greens got to wear, complete with head wraps that covered their faces and ears. Goddamn, they had it nice. Warren was toasty when he was all geared up. He took the other coat to Markus and told him to put it on.

"We have a problem," the old man said instead, peering out the window.

Skrill was still tied to his desk chair, so that wasn't it. Warren joined Markus at the window and followed his gaze toward the sky. His heart sank. Glinting in the sunrise, dwarfing the prototype ship by a factor of ten, if not twenty, was a massive new Paragon warship. It was slowly descending over the camp and research facility.

Warren knew it was the archgeneral's ship even before Markus said it. "Security will be doubled. And . . ." he turned and looked at their restrained Trew friend, "they'll be coming here for an update on all new prisoner intakes."

"You sure?"

"Ask him," Markus said, shaking his head. "It happens every time Hadras comes."

"It's true," Skrill said, that nasty smile returning to his face.

"How long?"

"Within the hour."

No time. Even if they knocked the Trew out or tied him

up and hid him somewhere, his being missing from his post would be sufficient to raise the alarm, and their escape plan was contingent on that not happening. They'd never get a shuttle off the ground. They would institute a lockdown.

"Maybe we wait," Markus hissed. It was as close to panic as Warren had ever seen him consciously display.

Warren shook his head. Not an option. Skrill would spill the beans on them without question. They'd sweep the camp looking for them. There would be no place to hide. No, they had to go now.

He fished in his pocket and pulled out the last three med pills. They were the only medicine either man had or would likely have from this point forward. If either was injured, it would be up to the stars and Markus' Divine whether they'd heal. He turned to Skrill. "You're gonna swallow these," he said, slapping them on the desk.

The Trew looked at him with wide eyes. "Now, w-wait a m-minute!" he stammered.

Warren rolled his eyes. "They're not going to kill you. Jesus. They're just going to make you sleep nice and sound until we're long gone from this rock." He hoped so, anyway. Like the others, the woman he'd gotten them from had said they were the sleepy ones, but who knew if that was true. In the corner was a jug of water and glasses. Posh indeed— water whenever he wanted it.

Warren motioned for Markus to fill and bring him a glass. "Take them," he commanded Skrill when Markus held the cup and the pills to his lips. Warren reclaimed the ore shard and poked it into the alien's chest for good measure.

The Trew swallowed the pills. Warren forced him to open his mouth and show him the pills were gone, then watched the alien intently. It wouldn't take the medicine long to kick in, especially not three of them. Markus dressed in his Green overcoat and head wrap, and each carefully tied on colored armbands as they waited.

After several minutes, the Trew was still conscious. His stupid smile was back and growing with each minute that passed. Warren stood, restless. "Maybe I'm immune," Skrill said with a cackle, loving how uncomfortable his two kidnappers were.

"Med pills work on everyone," Warren said. At least, that'd been his experience up to this point.

Skrill laughed again, a screeching sound. "What are you going to do if I—"

Smack.

The pills hit the small alien so hard he passed out in mid-sentence and splatted forehead-first on the top of his desk. Warren surged forward to check him. Pulse was fine. He forced the Trew's eyelids open to make sure he wasn't faking.

He wasn't. They were dilated like black holes, and there was drool coming from the corner of his mouth. It was the dead weight of his head that was the real giveaway. Nobody could relax their neck muscles that well without being toasted. Warren let his head go, and it smacked the desk again. What a satisfying sound.

"We'll untie him," Warren said, starting on one of his hands and legs. Markus started on the other. "This way, it looks like he just passed out here on his own, under-slept maybe, or had a bender. He won't be able to tell them anything until he wakes up, which won't be 'til tonight."

Markus nodded. The guards would be suspicious and alerted, but it might work. It probably wouldn't raise the alarm or initiate a lockdown or a search. It would give them the time they needed.

"The archgeneral's ship is stationary," Markus said after Skrill was free and they'd disposed of the twine they'd tied him with. "Guard activity will be doubled in the next few minutes as Hadras' contingent comes down." He looked at Warren, the near-panic creeping back in. "We need to go *now*."

Didn't have to tell Warren twice. He surveyed the room one last time for any sign that they'd been there. Even the storage crate with his armor, he'd carefully put back where it had been. If all went well, maybe he'd be able to come back and retrieve it. For that to happen, they'd need what came next to go well.

"Let's roll," he said.

CHAPTER EIGHT

ARCHGENERAL HADRAS' ship was even bigger than Warren had surmised. It filled the sky and towered like a monolith over the camp, which was abuzz at its arrival. It was the same tri-hull design as every other Paragon warship, but it was larger than any Warren had ever seen. He wondered if it was the perspective. Spaceships rarely hung in the atmosphere so close to the ground.

However, Markus confirmed it. It *was* bigger and meticulously maintained. There wasn't a rivet out of place or a porthole that was not crystal-clear on that ship. He'd spent a lot of time there. Its perfection was overwhelming. Ominous. Hadras clearly ran his operations on a massive scale and like clockwork.

If that were the case, how would Warren and Markus succeed in slipping past him? How could they pass such enormity when they were so small?

That was where Warren knew they had the edge. He'd always worked small, many of his missions being solo. He found the cracks to slip through, then wreaked havoc from the inside. He felt locked in as they walked swiftly, transitioning from the freshly fallen snow of the lesser-traveled paths to the stiff, icy sludge of the main corridor. He idly adjusted his green armband. It felt odd to be wearing one, but that was mixed with the thrill of turning the Paragon's willingness to hand out privilege in exchange for betrayal against them.

There were more guards than usual, but Warren saw opportunity in that. Given the hustle and bustle of the arriving cargo and troop ships from the behemoth overhead, there was far more noise in the air and far more activity to keep track of.

The guards were nervous. Distracted. Stick out in an environment like that, cause any sort of friction, and it was game over. Blend in? Roll up like a greased wheel? You might not even get a second glance.

The gate at the camp's fence line was their first test. They slipped into the facility at dawn with a group of early-shift workers. It wasn't a cold morning, and with dismay, Warren noted that almost nobody was wearing the head-wraps. Their first stroke of bad luck.

The guards waved them through without stopping a single worker for more than the second it took to ensure they were wearing a green armband. Some of them were glancing at the ship overhead as often as the prisoners were. So much the better.

At the second gate, however, the guards were far less distracted. The groups of workers sorted themselves at the end terminus of the fenced corridor leading into the facility into discrete lines, depending on where in the facility their work took place. Markus shepherded Warren toward the far-left line. "For the lower levels," he whispered. "Shuttle and loading bays are cliffside, down at the very bottom."

Uneasiness blossomed inside Warren as the line they

were in narrowed to single file. The guards at the gate were screening prisoners one by one, swiping their access cards on a hand-held reader as they passed through. No one else in their line was wearing the head wraps.

"Name and section," the Paragon guard asked when it was Warren's turn to step in front of him. Markus was right behind him. His hand was out for the access card.

Warren handed it to him. "Lower sections," he said with an outward ease that he'd long practiced in his former line of work. "Name is Warren."

The Paragon guard swiped the card and cocked his head when Warren spoke his name. The small gesture would have been enough to drive an untrained person mad. There was no face to read behind the opaque helmet the guard wore, only Warren's reflection.

What reaction was it? Did the guard do it all the time? Or had the name caught his attention? Did he work this post every day and know every person who came through, and he didn't recognize Warren?

The card reader beeped. It was not a pleasant sound, nor was it abrasive. Did the beep mean his card checked out? Or had Markus messed it up and something was wrong?

"Remove your facial coverings," the guard said abruptly, head back up.

Warren's heart skipped a beat, but he didn't show anything other than compliance. He smoothly removed the head wrap and stood with his face naked to fate. Did the Paragon know who he was? That he'd helped Markus, who was standing one step behind him? Were they looking for him?

"Is there a problem?" he asked, knitting his brow in a confusion as well-practiced as his all-business ease.

The Paragon guard paused, then let the silence extend. Any other nervous fool would have tried to fill that silence by preemptively explaining that there *must* be a mistake if there was any kind of problem. He was just a regular worker trying to get to his job, so please just let him pass.

Whatever it is, he's sure he has an explanation. No, sir, you don't need to call over any additional guards. Everything is fine. See, I have my card and my armband. More questioning? No, that's unnecessary. What are you doing? Wait!

Then that fool would have talked himself into interrogation, isolation, and perhaps even a plasma bolt through the back of the head.

Not Warren. He kept his mouth shut and never lost his look of innocent confusion.

"Your duties in Black section?"

Warren hoped that meant the lower levels. He licked his lips to make sure he didn't stammer. He and Markus hadn't gone over what jobs they were posing as having. "Janitorial and solid waste removal," he said—the most common, baseline, mundane level of labor, which was the same in every corner of the galaxy. Everybody pooped. Except for the Serm, but he doubted they worked down in the Black section. It also had the virtue of being undesirable to the point that nobody ever wanted details. Just do your job, and stay away from me.

"Proceed," the guard said and handed the card back to him.

Thank baby G and Markus' Divine. He was through.

The guard stopped Markus. He would have him unwrap his head, too, and from the scene Warren had witnessed when the old man was cast out and almost murdered by the guards in the middle of the prison camp, he couldn't imagine anyone in this facility didn't know his face.

He paused. It would be death. It would be even more suspicious if he spoke up for him. Why would any prisoner stick their neck out for another unless they both had something to hide and no authority of their own?

"Remove your face coverings, human," the guard said.

FUCK.

"Uh," Warren said to the guard without any idea what in the shit he would even say. "He's, uh . . ."

Warren was flailing. It was all going to be over in a second, and he was going down with the old man. From dumb luck, too. The one goddamn guard who wanted to check everyone's face. But then . . .

Markus did something remarkable.

He coughed.

It was a deep-in-the-chest croupy cough, the kind that made you recoil because it sounded so nasty. The guard took a step back without thinking. Markus did it again, even worse.

"He's got cabin cough," Warren said, seizing on the momentum. "Shift supervisor still needs him to spot-clean and polish for the archgeneral. Hence the head wrap." He covered his mouth as though the head wrap was a preventative measure for contagion.

It was a dangerous gambit. The guard could easily take Markus out of line and either march him back to camp or send him to the infirmary. But even though Warren had made up cabin cough on the spot, it sounded innocuous, right? Especially with all the extra hubbub of Hadras being here and things needing to look and work perfectly.

"Keep your head covering on for the duration of your

shift," the guard commanded, and he handed Markus his card.

Wisely, Markus didn't react other than to pass through the gate and join Warren on the other side. "That was close," he said breathlessly once they were out of earshot.

"That was goddamn genius," Warren said. Markus winced at the curse. Warren's eyes nearly rolled all the way into the back of his head. "Calm down," he said. "It's not even your god I'm talking about, is it?"

Markus sniffed the air. "There is only one god."

Warren shook his head. "Regardless, you've got some special ops steel in those veins after all. Which is good. We're going to need all of it."

THE FACILITY WAS A MAZE. All the signs were written in Paragon, a language Warren had never been able to make heads nor tails of.

It was all dots in sometimes insanely complex and other times minimal clusters. They weren't letters. He'd flunked every xenolinguistic course he'd taken in primary, secondary, or military school. He'd flunked most of his terrestrial language courses, for that matter. It was spoken language where Warren shined. Whenever an operation involved another species' written word, he'd had it uploaded into a voice recorder. He had the ear to pick that kind of stuff up. However, alien signs and directories meant nothing to him.

Thank the stars for Markus. He knew his way around the facility like the hallways of his house. Their first stop was a storage room, where they picked up the buckets, mops, and other accouterments of the janitorial trade.

Markus also had them don the gloves and booties of sanitation workers. Then they were off to the central elevators that would take them to the lower sections.

They moved quickly. Everyone in the facility was doing the same. Warren's bucket squeaked as it rolled, but no one seemed to notice. There was even more hubbub inside than outside, and again, they could use it to their advantage. People were so focused on the arrival of the archgeneral that no one took notice of two Greens walking around inside in full outside winter gear, head wraps included.

He took the opportunity to take images with his holoimager and people-watch, taking note of the assortment of people this facility held. There were other humans. Not many, but some. None looked like Markus. They were pale, malnourished, and downtrodden.

He'd picked well when he'd told the guard he and Markus were janitorial staff. That tracked inside the facility. There was also a variety of other species, including some Warren didn't recognize. Others he did, like Trew, some Zyyzzks, and more than a few Plenorians, which made sense since this facility was devoted to computers and other such technical research.

There were some Ooran too, which made Warren wonder why. They were mostly known for their biological work. Medicine. Integration between technology and living tissue. Warren hadn't heard anything about that.

"This way," Markus whispered to him, grabbing his elbow. He pulled them into an elevator and pushed one of the incomprehensibly marked buttons. The old man was more nervous than Warren had expected now that they were deep inside *his* territory.

"Everything all right?" he asked, taking advantage of their solitude in the lift.

Markus took a breath. "Those guards."

"Which ones?" Warren hadn't a clue which ones had stood out to Markus. He hadn't noticed anyone any different on the Paragon side of things, but then, he had not really looked at them.

"You'll see more of them. With the red streak on their helmets."

"Okay."

"Those are Hadras' guards." The old man swallowed, visibly shaken. "He's here. In the facility."

"Well," Warren said, not concerned, "we'll just have to make sure we don't run into him, then, shall we?"

The elevator chimed pleasantly, and the doors parted.

Standing in from of them, ringed by guards like the ones Markus had just described, was a towering man Warren had never seen before yet instantly knew.

Archgeneral Hadras.

CHAPTER NINE

THE ORNATENESS of his armor was unmistakable, as was the red plume on his helmet. Unlike the guards or the other Paragon soldiers, the archgeneral's helmet had an open slit across the eyes, and through it burned two ice-blue irises. They were the same color as the sensor dots that covered Paragon armor.

Paragon Blue. Their eyes were the same color. Who would have thought? The skin around them was snow-white, which made them stand out all the more. It was the first time, Warren thought, a human had eyes on what a Paragon looked like under the armor. It was a shock that they *had* eyes.

Warren was gaping. He knew it when the guards around the archgeneral snapped their rifles up to cover the two surprised men in the elevator and from Markus' sharp poke in his back. It pushed him into a deep bow, face to the floor. It was all enough to bring him back to the present, and his first thought was, *Shit. Did the archgeneral recognize Markus?*

For an agonizing moment, nobody moved. A standoff as

Warren and Markus stayed bent over, and the archgeneral stood outside expectantly with his guards. Waiting. Waiting for . . .

Warren mumbled a reverent apology and, with a reach back to tug on Markus' coat, shuffled out of the elevator, which he presumed His Greatness wanted to use while keeping his face pointing to the floor. It was tight enough in the hallway that they had to bump into several of the Paragon guards to avoid the archgeneral. They held their hands up when they did, apologizing profusely.

Warren's bucket squeaked with every step he took, sounding like a wounded animal. It was a nightmare. At any second, Warren was sure they were going to open fire or seize them and rip their head coverings off, exposing them as the traitors and escapees they were.

By some miracle, that didn't happen. The Paragon troopers closed ranks around the archgeneral as the humans shuffled away from him, eventually clearing to let them through. The archgeneral and his guards poured into the open elevator, clearing the cramped hallway. Just before the doors closed, Warren stole another glance at him.

Hadras was staring at them. Warren's stomach dropped.

He pointed. "Clean this," he said, then the elevator's doors closed, and he was gone.

Warren looked at where he'd pointed. The dark, polished stone floor they were standing on was scuffed with the archgeneral's and his posse's boot marks. He remembered the bucket by his feet and the mop handle he held in his hands to push it around. Hadras had given an order to two of his janitors: clean the dirty floor. Nothing more. No recognition. They'd met him face to face and managed to slip past him.

Behind him, Markus was shaking. "They're gone,"

Warren assured him. They were alone in the hallway, but he whispered anyway. Goddamn, that had been close. He waited a minute for the old man to catch his breath and calm his nerves. "I don't think they recognized us."

"I was sure he'd caught me when the doors opened," Markus whispered back, still gasping a bit for air but improving. "I had my face to the floor the entire time after that, though."

"He only saw a janitor when he looked at me," Warren said. He gave the old man's arm a squeeze. Markus nodded at him. He was better. They'd made it through. He could find his calm again.

Warren looked down the hall. They were at a dead-end to their right, where the corridor met the elevator. To their left, the hall ended in a 'T.' "Which way?" he asked.

"I'll show you," Markus said, breathing well again. "After we give the floor a quick scrub just in case anyone is watching, or the archgeneral comes back this way."

He wiped his face clean of the sweat it had collected during his panic and set off a step ahead of Warren.

THE PATH to the shuttle and the cargo bays cut through the heart of the research facility. It was much less busy down here, so Warren felt like he and Markus stuck out. However, the old man led them onward without hesitation. That was good. Walk confidently, and everyone assumed you knew where you were going and that you had a right to be there.

Also to Markus' credit, their access cards worked at every locked door or guarded checkpoint they passed through.

There were research labs down there, with people

working in white coats and thick gloves. Giant banks of blinking computers filled entire rooms.

They continued deeper into the center of the complex. "Are we going to see the AI?" Warren asked when it dawned on him how restricted the areas they were passing through were.

"Not quite," Markus said, not slowing down until they reached a junction where the hall split in four directions. They went straight, but Markus pointed down a long, wide corridor to their left. It terminated in a circular room that had several other hallways leading to it. At the center was something that chilled Warren to the bone, even though he had no context to make sense of what he was seeing.

It was a pitch-black cube, so black that it reflected none of the dim light around it. It perched on the tip of one of its corners. It had no entrance or exit and was the size of a large room.

"The AI?" Warren asked Markus. They were paused in the hallway, which was blessedly empty for the moment.

"The AI," Markus confirmed.

Warren snapped a few images. "How does anyone get inside?"

Markus didn't have time to answer him before the cube offered its answer. With the same shimmer and flash in which he'd witnessed the AI ship disappear and reappear not twelve hours earlier, someone appeared in the circular room from thin air.

Two someones, when Warren peered closely. It was a Paragon guard and a small figure in a mobility assistance chair. Warren recognized the small figure in the general sense because he'd seen someone like them not long ago. Warren snapped one last image, then stowed the small device.

"We must keep going," Markus hissed to him as the two figures started moving toward them.

Warren obliged after one glance back to confirm what he'd seen. "That was a Navid," he said to Markus once the hallway junction was past them.

Markus nodded. "They're part of the AI."

"Navigators?"

"No. The Navid don't have Navigators anymore."

Warren knew that was true, with one specific exception, someone he hoped was safe and sound far from this place. "Then why are they here?"

"I don't actually know," Markus answered. "That wasn't my department." He picked up his pace even more. The bum wheel on Warren's bucket was now squeaking so loudly that it sounded like it was going to fall off.

"We're almost there."

———

THEIR ROUTE to the shuttle bay was down one last set of elevators. No archgenerals to bump into this time, blessedly.

It now made sense why they'd had to get so close to the highly-secured heart of the research facility. Below the large, circular room the AI cube occupied was a massive central column that projected down miles to the thermal energy plant that powered the whole thing.

That column was also what affixed the facility to the mountainside, making it one with the rock. From that column, hanging out over the cliff's side, were the cargo and hangar bays, open to the free flow of air traffic. The final bank of elevators ran down the outside of the power column.

It was windy in the shuttle bay. Vorkut V had an

atmosphere, so the flight entrance of the bay could be left open all the time. There was only a weak thermal field in place over the deck plates to melt any snow that might waft inside. There were shuttles of different types and configurations along the walls on either side of the large opening.

There were no guards in sight.

"This one," Markus said and hustled them toward one of the larger craft. "Ditch the mop and bucket." Warren had become so accustomed to his squeaking companion that he'd almost forgotten he was still wheeling it. "No janitor gets access to a shuttle like this."

Warren nodded. This was the point of no return. There was no going back if they were seen. They'd probably be shot on sight or dragged to face the archgeneral and interrogated. Tortured.

Best to move quickly, then. They sprinted across the hangar bay's deck. It was so polished that Warren half-slid into the side of the shuttle. He caught Markus when he did the same. The old man straightened and turned his attention to the door panel.

A sound on the opposite wall of the hangar made them freeze. Footsteps. The two crouched instinctively, which was useless if whoever was approaching had come from the same entrance they had. There was no cover between them and that door, just wide-open hangar.

By a miraculous stroke of luck, who was out there had come from the other side, and the shuttle was blocking them from view. Heart racing, Warren squat-waddled to the rear edge of the shuttle and slowly peered around the corner. A Paragon trooper was in the middle of the hangar bay, walking toward them. Shit.

Warren looked around. There was nothing to grab, no weapons in sight, only his stupid bucket and mop. Those were thirty or forty paces away, back by the side entrance. He had nothing but his two hands. The guard called across the space, asking who was there in the singsong rhythm of the Paragon tongue. He'd heard them. Hiding in place would not work. Warren's two hands would have to be enough, and they'd better hope this trooper was alone.

"Get the shuttle open and working," Warren said, whispering into Markus' ear. He shoved the old man toward the hatch and crouched just behind the shuttle's back corner. He listened intently, gauging the distance to the soldier by the sound of his footfalls.

He was calling out again when Warren launched at him. He caught the soldier in the midriff where he had aimed and drove him down onto the deck with the force of his body weight. Through the helmet, Warren heard the soldier gasp as the wind was knocked out of him.

There was no sense in punching the trooper when he had that helmet on, so Warren swung his body around to lock him up in a wrestling hold that gained him leverage on the trooper's right arm. He grabbed it with both hands, then twisted, using his legs and the trooper's torso against him. The guard's shoulder popped, and he screamed in pain.

The pain seemed to waken him, however, and, lightning-quick, he twisted out from under Warren, slipping out of the hold, then used the strength of his legs to launch the human off him.

Warren slid back several feet on the polished deck before reorienting himself, gaining purchase, and hopping up in a crouch. The trooper was where Warren had left him, using the floor and his body weight to pop his shoulder back into place. He then rotated it and flexed his hand. Warren could tell it still hurt, but the advantage was lost.

Warren bellowed and rushed the guy, trying again to

catch him by surprise. Not this time. He raised a knee and smashed Warren in the nose as he was about to tackle him. It knocked Warren sideways, and the trooper used his momentum to fling him away. Warren landed like a sack of spuds, his right hand pinned awkwardly underneath him and hyperextending his wrist. It flared with pain.

There was no time to acknowledge the injury, however. The Paragon was upon him once again, throwing blows with fists, knees, and elbows at whatever parts he could reach.

Warren dove at his knees, and while he couldn't slam his shoulder into them like he wanted to knock them out of joint, he wrapped his arms around the guard's ankles and yanked him off his feet. He landed on the deck with a heavy thud, and Warren scrambled on top of him, grabbed his helmet with both hands, and repeatedly smashed it against the deck. Maybe he could give the bastard a concussion.

No dice. The trooper swung his legs up, scissored them around Warren's neck, and twisted them and his torso to slam Warren down on the deck. Warren separated, scrambled away . . .

And nearly fell through the hangar bay's opening. His heel teetered on the edge, and he looked down to see several hundred feet of cliff face disappearing into white and gray snow. The floor was slick here, shining with snow melted by the thermal field.

The Paragon trooper stood two meters away. He wiggled his helmeted head as if to shake off Warren's attack, then flexed his fingers and arms before tensing them into fists. The move said, "This is over."

Both fighters stood for a long moment, chests heaving from exertion. Warren was sweating. He was sure under all that armor, the Paragon was too. Or whatever their version of sweat was. Maybe they self-cooled by breathing through their mouths like dogs. He'd ask Markus about it if he ever got the chance.

The Paragon attacked so fast that Warren almost didn't have time to react. He came in low, sweeping a kick that Warren barely avoided by jumping forward into the trooper.

He must have anticipated that Warren would jump in that direction—where else could he move with the cliff ledge at his back?—and he was ready for him with a giant bear hug. He let Warren carry them both to the floor as he twisted so he was on top of Warren, legs gripping his torso like a vice and arms free to do damage.

And damage they did.

The first blow landed in Warren's gut, knocking the wind from him. Another to his face made him see stars. And another, and another. Blearily, desperately, Warren stopped trying to grapple the Paragon's armor and used his arms to try to cover his face to stop the crushing blows from landing.

The Paragon grabbed them and pried them away. Warren resisted and screamed in the bastard's face.

It was no use. The trooper had the advantage of being on top. He could push down while Warren was left with only his strength to push against all that body weight. It wasn't a battle he could win, but goddammit, he would fight as long as he could.

The Paragon trooper lowered his helmet to Warren's face as he pushed. It was a taunt, a move of dominance to say, "You are mine now."

Warren's heart sank since the Paragon was right. Then he caught sight of something in the reflection of the guard's helmet. It took him a second to figure out what it was because it was entirely unexpected. A goddamn miracle.

He looked back at the trooper. He didn't seem to have seen what Warren had. He was still focused on slowly, steadily, and mercilessly forcing Warren's arms back to the deck. Warren screamed at him and threw everything he had into resisting. He felt the Paragon tense, winding up to respond . . .

Warren let his arms go. The Paragon jerked, off-balance from the sudden loss of resistance paired with his extra exertion. Warren head-butted the motherfucker in the face.

Even through the helmet, Warren cracked him good. The Paragon's weight shifted, and Warren took the sliver of opportunity he had been given. He scrambled out from beneath the trooper and dove to the side in one motion. "Now!" he shouted, hoping Markus could hear him.

Markus had fired up the shuttlecraft while the two were fighting. They'd been so absorbed in their mortal combat that neither had noticed when he'd lifted it off the deck, flown it into the center landing/takeoff path, turned it around, and backed it to within three meters of the pair fighting near the cliff's edge, then set it down again.

There were booster rockets on the shuttle's stern, glowing blue and sending off waves of shimmering heat in the cold air. They were primed and ready to fire, and fire they did when Markus heard Warren's shout.

The hairs on Warren's ample beard singed as two fiery blue plumes roared out from the stern of the shuttle. They worked like an invisible kick as well as a blowtorch. The Paragon trooper burst into flames as he flew over the cliff's edge.

The shuttle screeched on the hangar deck as the sudden force propelled it forward, but Markus had already shut off the boosters. That allowed Warren to rush to the opening and look down. The trooper fell like a fireball with a smoke trail until he disappeared into the gray-white depths of the chasm. Paragon barbecue. Warren had never imagined he'd see the like.

"You okay?" Markus asked. He was standing halfway out of the shuttle's hatch, eyes wide.

Warren nodded. "Thanks for the assist." Then he staggered but managed to catch himself with a knee and an arm before he hit the deck. His head was swimming, and he was still perilously close to the opening. He felt a tug under his armpits. Markus. The man was hauling him back, away from danger.

After a few moments, his vertigo subsided, and Warren patted the old man's hand. "I'm okay," he said. Markus released him, and he stood under his own power. Wobbling, but better. He touched his forehead, and the fingers came back with blood.

"Remind me never to head-butt a guy in a helmet," he said ruefully.

"Noted."

Warren looked around, considering the hangar bay for the first time since the fight. It was still empty. No alarm had sounded. No troops had come to aid one of their own. He and Markus had managed to get to a working, fired-up, and ready long-range shuttle undetected. It seemed impossible, yet here they were.

"Let's go," he said wearily.

Markus agreed with a nod, and the battered men boarded the shuttle, strapped in, and fired the atmospheric boosters for real. They roared, and Markus guided them expertly out of the hangar opening, then angled them up toward the atmosphere and space beyond it.

They passed the prototype ship as they ascended, and Warren took the opportunity to snap more images. The prototype was swarming with drones and worker pods again like it was preparing for another jump drive trial. Beyond it was the archgeneral's massive ship, a thousand meters higher in the air. It bristled with weaponry, looking every bit the warship. It could destroy the entire surface of the Vorkut moon if it wanted to.

"Don't worry," Markus said, sensing his companion's tension. "We're coded as a high-priority materials transport on a tight turnaround. Nobody is going to bother us from here on out."

Warren took his word for it. Really, he'd had no choice from the moment he'd saved the old man's life. He'd tied his fate to Markus from that moment.

He sank back into his seat. His work was over for now. The next bit was up to Markus. He knew how the Paragon transponder codes worked to make them look like a vessel that was not worth bothering. He knew the gate codes to let them leave this system, and he knew the network well enough to get them back to Terran space.

Maybe. The last part was fuzzier. Markus had never been out that far on the edge of Paragon territory, but that's where Warren was fairly confident he could take back over. Those waypoint gates were his bread and butter. It was only a question of time.

Warren stole one last look at the two ships, now far below them as they rose into Vorkut V's upper atmosphere. "How long did you say it was before that thing was operational?" he asked.

"Weeks. At most."

"And how long to Terran space?"

"Days at least. Maybe weeks."

Warren nodded and closed his eyes. His head was pounding. A concussion, surely, from head-butting the

Paragon. He needed meds. And chow. Markus had insisted the long-range shuttles should have them stocked. There was a chance they could make it. How fat or slim, he didn't know, but it was there.

"We best make that the former, then," he said about Markus' time estimate. "Clock's ticking."

AEXON HUB

Terran Federation Space

CHAPTER TEN

"D-5 is drifting."

"I see him." Lieutenant Commander Eunice Carrol had to grit her teeth to keep the frustration out of her voice. She'd seen it already, but CAG had beaten her to the punch, something she was doing often these days. Carrol switched to her squad channel. "Lux, watch your z. You're dropping at point-7."

"Stick is doing that thing again, Commander," a squeaky voice came back. Lux. They said he was a lieutenant, and while she had seen the stripes herself, nobody could convince Carrol that he was a chin hair past sixteen. Same went for every pilot on *Providence*.

Carrol and CAG were on loan from *Glory*, who was parsecs away, getting repaired and retrofitted from her clash with the Paragon a couple months previous. Everyone's clash with the Paragon.

It had left the Fleet in shambles. But in those shambles were survivors. Only a few were from the Solar System, but many ships from the colonies and outer reaches were intact. The Paragon attack had been centered on Earth rather than a larger-scale assault. It had nonetheless been devastating, given that so many ships had been recalled to Earth on the promise of peace talks, but not quite a death blow.

Glory had ensured that, as had her crew, her captain, and her fighters. That was why Carrol was out in this distant place, teaching children to fly manually. Remote flight in sim couches, the standard for aerospace combat in the last two decades, had proven hackable in the Paragon assault. Through a stroke of insane misfortune-turned-fortune, *Glory's* fighters had been flown by hand, with Carrol in the lead. That had given her and CAG valuable experience much of the rest of Fleet sorely needed.

"It's not your stick, Lux," Carrol said, failing to keep the impatience from her tone this time. "It's you. You're pushing it too hard for too long." There was a snicker over the comms at that, and she wanted to roll her eyes. "Cut the bullshit," she barked. "We're two clicks out from the event horizon, and Lux, if you hit that membrane at the wrong angle, you're going to spin out on the other side and smash into one of us. So listen up!"

Silence on the other end.

"'Yes, sir,'" Carrol snapped.

"Yes, sir," came a chorus of responses.

"Lux, stop waiting for your HUD to register a change in axis. The ball is always going to be a split second behind. You have to feel it yourself, okay? Ease off on your stick right before the ball catches up."

"Yes, sir."

Flying manually was completely different than flying in a sim couch. It had its disadvantages, to be sure, like blowing yourself up if anything went wrong, an undeniable downside that had pushed the Fleet toward adopting sim couches in the first place.

The advantages were likewise undeniable. You could *feel* what you were doing out there. The reactions, even though sims had a purported zero latency, were faster. The experience of flying was visceral, the fighter tactile, an extension of one's body—once you had enough time and experience.

These pilots did not. Yet.

A gate loomed ahead of them. The fighter squadron was taking point in a mock escort formation several clicks ahead of the TDF cruiser *Providence*. They were about to pass through onto Aexon Hub, a waypoint complex on the fringes of Terran space.

Why so far from home? One, it was close to where *Glory* was being worked on, and two, it was where the majority of the Fleet that was still intact was based. It was where the pilots who needed help were.

Although a training exercise, it changed nothing about interstellar physics and spatial dynamics. Gates were tricky to fly through in a fighter, particularly by hand. Carrol's warning hadn't been an idle one. You had to do it right.

Passing through them safely in a small craft depended on what type of gate it was. A long-range gate like the one they were about to pass through, unlike local in-system gates, had significant gravitational sheer to deal with, and the longer the distance the gate took you, the more intense the gravity field was.

You had to ease off as you fell in, then gun it on the other side since both sides of the gate curved space-time inward toward them.

In the earliest days of interstellar travel, ships would sometimes get stuck in the event horizon of a gate, neither here nor there, a rock in the middle of a rapid for someone else to come and smash against. Lose power in that ether space, and you could get stuck forever.

That wasn't happening today. They were going to stay in formation, goddammit, slip through the gate like they were supposed to, and still be in formation when they came out on the other side at Aexon Hub. They were professional pilots and were going to act like it, even if they did look like they were only sixteen.

"Prepare to ease off," she called when the gate filled their view, blotting out the stars with its swirling maelstrom of pure energy. Every gate was bright white when viewed head-on, but when you looked at the edges, each had its own colorful hue, a mixture of the ambient matter caught in the event horizon and the strength of the singularity that powered it.

This one was blue. It would be a different hue on the other side.

Carrol's fighter pitched forward and caught the outer edge of the gravity well. "Feel it!" she called. "Just like in practice, kids, let the fall catch you and throttle back as it does. Keep your eyes on your lines!"

Carrol practiced what she preached and felt the rush of her organs catching the gravity just as her fighter did. It felt like diving over the top of a rollercoaster. What had felt like "ahead" seconds before gradually turned into "down" as the well asserted itself.

You always fell into a gate, then rose out of it. It never felt like stepping through, at least not in a small craft like a fighter. Very different from a larger ship that had gravity plating, where "up," "down," "ahead," and "behind" were fixed orientations. This was more fun. Over the comm, she heard someone get sick before they managed to cut off their suit mic. She smiled. Fun if you could keep your cookies down.

"Steady," she called to her baby pilots. So far, so good. "Hands off until you're through, then gun it!"

Right on her line, she fell into the bright white energy. Her perception of velocity went wild the instant before she passed through the membrane. For a split second, it felt like she was falling far too fast. She didn't panic. She lifted her hands off the stick and let the gate take the lead. It was straight down now.

Flash.

She was through. Her stomach floated as the feeling of down was suddenly behind her and her unpowered momentum ceased to be sufficient to propel her forward. She grabbed her stick in that rollercoaster moment and shoved it all the way forward. She slammed into the back of her seat and her fighter surged ahead, fighting gravity and winning. She eased off the acceleration as soon as her fighter started to pick up speed and rechecked her formation line. Right. On. Goddamn. Target.

A moment later, she was free of the gravity field. The gate felt like it was behind her rather than below, and she was in Aexon Hub. "Sound off," she ordered her squadron. Each of the pilots called in, some sounding the worse for wear in the nausea department.

When she checked their positioning, everyone was right where they were supposed to be. More or less. "Decent work," she said. Still some things to clean up, but the kids had done it.

"Aexon Control," she called next, switching to wide comm, "appreciate the smooth sailing." One of the constant jobs on a gate complex was keeping the energy membrane intact and smooth. Not an easy thing to do, and Fleet was maniacal about keeping it from getting out of shape, spiking, or otherwise being inconsistent.

It was customary for the commanding officer to thank them for their hard work, from a ship's captain down to a shuttle pilot. It was also customary for Control to acknowledge. The Fleet turned on such little exchanges, the comforting background hubbub that reminded one they were alive.

This time, however, Carrol got nothing but silence on the wide band. She frowned and checked her radio. Comm was five by five. "Control, do you read?" Still nothing.

She tried System Control next. It would have been watching their entry to the flight path of every other vessel in the planetary system. That comm channel was dead, too. Carrol tensed. Aexon was an outer system, tiny compared to Earth or the colonial systems, but this was more than strange.

"Weapons hot," she barked to her squadron. "Maintain formation and watch your scopes." She snapped to her ship-to-ship with CAG. "You guys getting radio silence there too?"

CAG confirmed it. "We're scanning."

There had been reports of Paragon activity in the outer systems. Skirmishes. Nothing of major significance, but they'd been numerous enough that the outer sectors were on constant alert. Carrol hadn't seen any of that. Neither had her squadron. That was about to change. Carrol knew it as certainly as she knew these pilots weren't ready for it.

The gate behind them seemed fine. Its platform windows were dark, but that wasn't out of the ordinary. Most of these outer gates were monitored and maintained from a central location. Carrol's HUD informed her that was ahead, near the terminator of the gas giant the whole complex rotated around and drew power from.

Aexon Hub was just that. There was no base, colony, settlement, or other installation of significance here. It was a series of four gates leading to and from other systems, not that many for a hub.

They were crucial, however, especially out in the outer reaches. Lose control of a hub like this one, and you were looking at massive disruptions in travel as other routes, often taking a ship weeks or months out of the way, had to be figured out to reach a system that had previously been at its fingertips.

They carried formidable weapons platforms, maintained short-range attack vessels on constant patrol, and had several dedicated squadrons of fighters. Thus, radio silence and zero activity were very concerning.

"Eyes on the horizon," she told her squadron as they, and *Providence* right behind them, picked up speed to round the terminator and get their eyes on the central gate. If there was any action going on, it would likely be there.

And it was.

"J-squad," the *Providence's* XO said over the ship-to-ship channel, superseding CAG for the moment. "We have positive Paragon contact bearing two-seven mark one-one, down 3-z."

"We see them."

The control tower was on fire.

More a sprawling complex than a tower, it was attached to the largest gate in the hub and housed the system's permanent personnel as well as having short-term military and civilian accommodations and amenities. Carrol assumed they were modest. These weren't well-traveled gates in comparison to the inner systems. Still, the complex housed more than a thousand souls who were currently fighting for their lives.

Carrol saw two Paragon cruisers. They were engaged in a firefight with the main weapons platform, which formed a secondary broken ring above the gate. It looked like a halo and had the station complex within it, a common design. Plasma and missile fire poured into and out of that halo, lighting up the starscape. Carrol switched off her long-range radio and instructed her squadron to do the same. They were about to enter the Paragon jamming area, and no one needed that in their ears.

"Tighten up, everyone," Carrol called over the short-range. She could see some of her squadron drifting, which indicated that her fresh-faced pilots were nervous. She gave them calm and measured practical advice to keep them the same and give them something to focus on.

"Stay close, and we'll be able to cut through the interference and hear each other. CAG has our six back there in *Providence*. She'll call in targets and attack vectors, get us set up for success. And then if things get dicey after that, group leaders will take point wherever you're at. Just like in your couches."

This was stuff they already knew. A reminder of the familiar. She hoped they were ready, and she didn't feel like digging deep to find her own answer to that question. They'd have to be.

"Adjust to B-line," CAG called from the ship.

A series of attack vectors flashed to Carrol's holographic HUD. They were projected on the inside surface of her cockpit bubble in real-time, attuned to every minor flight adjustment she made. A sophisticated system and a lifesaver.

One of the attack vectors was bright blue. Another was

red, the "R-line," and another yellow, the Y-line, and so on.

"Roger," she replied and sent that vector to the rest of her squadron. She further broke them out into four groups, wedge formation for each.

As they fell into their assigned approach, *Providence* erupted in a flurry of long-range laser beams, which were useful to blind scopes, and an impressive display of missiles, which were useful for blowing shit up. The offensive firepower ripped through the space her squadron had occupied moments earlier. A well-coordinated maneuver. Her squadron had gotten that right, but the real test was ahead.

Carrol counted enough Paragon fighters to make up three squadrons. It was impossible to tell ahead of them, but the numbers were right. If each Paragon cruiser had four squads, it either meant this battle had been raging for some time and the Paragon had taken their licks or that the Paragon were holding back reserves.

She was inclined to believe the latter, given the state of things on the Fleet side. Two-thirds of the weapons platform was space dust. Wholly destroyed. Through those sections, the Paragon had poured weapons fire onto the station and what appeared to be the fallback position of several small short-range attack vessels. Those were valiantly holding their ground and attempting to spare the facility from annihilation.

They'd succeeded so far. Much of the station was on fire, but it was still there. The firefight between the remaining defenses and the Paragon ships was in full force. It wasn't a fair fight. The Paragon's two cruisers overpowered the Fleet defenses two to one—until *Providence*'s first barrage hit home, forcing the Paragon to turn.

Now the odds were even.

"Attack speed," Carrol barked, adrenaline surging

through her as additional power surged through her fighter. It was *her* fighter from *Glory*. Both she and CAG had insisted upon that when the request came through to borrow their services. She'd fine-tuned the machine in the months following the attack on Earth, tweaking it with DLC—De La Cruz, chief mechanic on *Glory's* flight deck— to respond to every nudge and whisper she could throw at it like an appendage of her body.

Twenty Paragon fighters had broken off from the station assault and were turning to meet them. Carrol grinned at the numbers. One-to-one. A fair fight. Perhaps things weren't going as well for the enemy as it appeared. The Paragon never fought fair.

"Weapons free!" Carrol called. "Stick with your group leader!"

Then she dove. Her stomach flew into her throat, and her vision constricted from the acceleration. It was the closest one could get to flying in gravity out in space. She then jerked her stick hard right. Stars streaked as she reoriented and the Paragon fighters were dead ahead, enough at an angle now that they'd either have to break formation to intercept her group head-on or take crossfire.

They broke formation. In fact, they scattered. Carrol called target assignments, but it was a free-for-all by that point. The ensuing firefight was brief, not because J-squad was that lethal, but because as quickly as the Paragon fighters had rushed out to meet them, they turned tail and hit their boosters in an all-out burn back to their cruisers.

Carrol dialed up a long-range look on her HUD and saw why. The Paragon cruisers were breaking off their attack on the central complex. The fighters had never intended to engage them, only stall them. Buy time for their cruisers to get free and line up for a gate approach.

It would work, too. The first Paragon cruiser was disappearing through the gate as it fought off weapons fire to its rear with well-timed countermeasures. The other cruiser wasn't far behind, a steady stream of fighters and other smaller Paragon craft pouring into its open hangar bays in its retreat.

No, not retreat. A hit-and-run. *This* was the pattern of attacks Carrol had been briefed on. This is what the Paragon had been up to the past couple months: popping in to inflict damage at seemingly random spots, most of them on the fringes where help was slow in coming and local defenses weren't especially robust, then bugging out when things got heated.

Pinpricks. Body blows. It had been odd to hear about since these were not standard Paragon tactics, and it was infuriating to witness. Aexon was in shambles, and the fuckers were getting away without a scratch.

"Pick a target and gun it," Carrol snapped over the squad channel. They still had a chance to pick off the running fighters before they made it home.

She chose the fighter closest to her and followed her own orders. She slammed into the back of her seat and pushed the stick forward until she nearly blacked out from the acceleration.

It worked. She came in at nearly twice the fighter's speed when it was still several thousand meters from the straggling cruiser and landed a direct plasma-fire hit on its fuel core. It exploded as she streaked past it, knocking her off her line, but she compensated easily, then arced away to avoid getting into either the cruiser's rear firing solution or *Providence's*.

Through the radio, in fits and starts now that they were so close to the Paragon cruisers and their blanket jamming signal, Carrol could hear her squadron cheering themselves on, and she saw more than a few Paragon fighters bite the dust under their fire. It was mop-up duty, not representative of a real engagement, but for getting their feet wet, it was best. They were getting their Ks. Job well done. Almost.

Carrol spotted another Paragon fighter off from the main group, not moving toward the cruiser and looking lost. She sighted it and throttled up. No harm in a lion going after the sick gazelle. All part of a predator's day. She strafed the craft several clicks out, which seemed to waken it because it started to evade. Clumsily. Carrol realized it wasn't a fighter. It was a support craft of some kind. There was no return fire. Wrong place, wrong time, she thought. All the better for her to notch another kill. Die, you Paragon bastards.

The call signal on the craft changed as Carrol lined up a kill shot and pulled the trigger. An SCPE-7X Needletail erupted from her port airfoil. Its plasma trail lit up the space in front of her in a bending blue-white line as it homed in on its target.

"Shit!" The call signal on the craft she'd just fired at was now Fleet blue. She reacted without thinking, changing her plasma turret's targeting system lock, putting her fighter into a hard bank, and pulling the trigger again, this time firing at the missile she'd just launched. It was less than a second away from hitting home. Her plasma cannons erupted, bolts of pure energy flying at near-light speed.

An explosion lit the space in front of her, and she saw stars for several agonizing seconds before her eyes adjusted, as did the scopes feeding her cockpit HUD.

The craft was still there.

"Fucking shit," she murmured, leaning back in her seat and taking deep breaths to get her heart rate down to an acceptable level. She snapped on a broad-band ship-to-ship. "Call Sign Six-Six-Oh-Charlie-Two, you want to tell me what in the hell you're doing flying out there with a goddamn Paragon signal?"

And a Paragon ship, she thought when she flew in close enough to get a good look at the thing. It was a Paragon shuttlecraft, no question. What in the hell were they doing with a Fleet call sign?

She was about to ask again when a response crackled over the open frequency. "Delta Wing, we are carrying two Fleet MIAs in a stolen craft. Requesting permission to dock. Somewhere. It's . . . been a long time getting out here. Would really appreciate it if you didn't shoot us down after we came all this way to find you."

Carrol was gobsmacked. The voice sounded human. The Fleet code they were flying was current enough that her onboard computer recognized it. But it had to be a trick.

"Let 'em in," CAG said after Carrol had radioed in, weapons still hot and trained on the Paragon shuttle. Several of Carrol's squad had joined her since there was nothing else to do at the moment. The rest of the Paragon were gone. "Captain says we'll do it by the book, under full guard. But yeah. Let's see who's in there."

"Acknowledged." Carrol switched to her open comm. "You'll follow me," she said. "Fifty meters on the dot. We have eight other fighters flanking you on all sides. You deviate from my course so much as a millimeter, and we'll blow you to hell, you got that?"

"Crystal," came the response, as well as a cough.

What a human phrase to respond with. She'd heard many things in the dark reaches between the stars, but she'd never heard a Paragon cough.

The shuttle stayed on its prescribed heading and flew

into *Providence's* main hangar bay. Carrol felt the gravity field take hold of her craft by way of her organs settling down inside her body. Not a feeling she enjoyed. Same went for feeling them float when she left for the vacuum, but it meant she was home. Well, not home. Home was sitting several gates away, getting an overhaul. *Providence* was only home for now.

She was out of her cockpit and standing on the deck when the shuttle landed. Her sidearm was in her hand, cocked and ready for whatever newfangled Paragon trap was about to be sprung.

Providence's security forces agreed with her skepticism. They were out in force, also with sidearms cocked, loaded, and ready to fire at whatever came out of the Paragon craft should it be anything less than polite. The shuttle hatch clanked, then hissed as it swung open. A figure was inside.

"Hands up!" one of the security detail called, and everyone's weapon, Carrol's included, swung toward it.

The figure raised its hands.

"Exit slowly."

The figure stepped out and onto the hangar deck, blinking. It was a human. A large one. Male. Insane beard, and from the way his cheekbones stuck out like mountain peaks and his clothes hung loose, particularly around his waist, Carrol guessed the man was starving.

"You, too! Hands up, and exit slowly."

There was another figure inside. Also tall, but this one was rail-thin, even thinner than the first man who'd stepped out. He had scars on nearly every inch of his visible tightly drawn skin, and when the overhead light in the hangar caught his face, he had the craziest, most colorful eyes Carrol had ever seen. He nearly fell when he missed the step but managed to recover in time. Barely.

"I'm Lieutenant Henry Warren," the first man croaked. His voice was raspier than it had been over the radio, a gut-wrenching mixture of relief and desperation. His arms shook above his head as if the effort to keep them there was the hardest thing he'd ever had to do. He'd clearly been through hell. Both men had.

"Terran Defense Force Serial Number 4478-C26. We urgently need to speak with your captain."

FREEPOINT SHIPYARDS

Terran Federation Space

CHAPTER ELEVEN

DRAKE HATED THESE THINGS. He drummed his fingers impatiently on his thigh, stopping every so often to scratch at the itchy wool fibers of his pants.

The dress uniform was the worst part. Tight. Hot. Stuffy. It matched the Admiralty to a tee. Doc stood beside him, reaching over every so often to adjust the captain's collar or brush back a stray hair. Drake had to swat him away like a gnat. "You're fussing."

"When entering the lion's den," Commander Lazare "Doc" Broussard said in his clipped English accent, "it is best to have the most impressive mane one can manage."

Drake frowned. "Is that even a turn of phrase?" Doc was well-known for quoting literature, poetry, and history when he felt it suited the moment. He was also well-known for making shit up.

"Don't worry about it," he answered with a smirk, straightening his shoulders. He nodded forward. "We're on."

Doc and Drake were standing in the holoprojection room of the Freepoint shipyards, a facility as far from the

Fleet Headquarters on Earth as you could get and still be within Federated space. *Glory* was at Freepoint, undergoing the repairs and retrofitting she couldn't get at the Jupiter facilities.

Those had effectively been wiped out during the recent Paragon assault. The attack had been several months ago, and in Drake's idleness as he waited for his ship to be restored—upgraded, really—he'd been paying attention to what the Paragon were up to. Nothing good, as usual, but he saw some disturbing patterns that he'd pointed out to the Admiralty in the form of a report and a request.

Now, apparently, the Admiralty wanted to talk to him about it. It was the first time he'd been called before them since his return to service, and before that, the first time since he'd been up for a court-martial and he'd instead opted to "retire."

Not a pleasant memory.

Drake shook off the painful past and his nerves to focus on the present. The image of a startlingly pretty young woman had materialized in front of them, looking like real flesh and blood after the projection room was finished rendering her. Holotechnology had improved by leaps and bounds since Drake had last seen it. Her hair was pulled back in a perfect bun, and her bright white smile screamed "top brass."

"Gentlemen," she said with no preamble. "If you'll perform the test, please, I can transfer you over to your session."

Drake nudged the good doctor with a parade-rest elbow. That was his cue. Doc mumbled an apology and flashed an awkward smile, then pulled a small zipped case out of his black medical bag.

Doc was nervous too. With a flourish, he unzipped the

case. On one side of its interior was a series of small metal capsules. They looked like oversized pills with small cutouts in the center—windows to a suspension liquid inside—and two lines etched on the exterior. On the other side of the case were syringe cylinders and a pneumatic gun to load them into.

Doc took the gun and clicked one of the syringes into it, then slid one of the capsules in.

"Best not to anticipate it," Doc whispered to Drake as he pressed the syringe gun to the captain's neck.

"I have done this—" Drake started, and Doc pulled the trigger without warning. A needle from the cylinder plunged into his neck an inch or so below his left ear.

For an instant, there was a painful feeling of suction as the capsule filled with Drake's blood and microscopic amounts of other tissues. Then the needle retracted with a hiss and a click, and it was over. "Before," Drake finished. He rubbed his neck and grimaced. The test was not pleasant.

With a flourish, Doc turned to the holoprojection of the HQ aide and jiggled the capsule. The liquid inside sloshed, and one of the lines etched on the window slowly turned bright green.

Drake was clean.

The process tested for the presence of the mind-controlling creature the Paragon had used to infiltrate much of the Terran Defense Force, including Drake's ship in the body of his second officer Commander Eunice Carrol.

Such infiltrations had been shockingly widespread, uncovered after the Paragon attack, but thankfully, this test had been developed very quickly. The Paragon creature left very distinct genetic residue all over its host body. That was particularly true in the bloodstream and at the base of the skull, where it liked to wrap itself around the brain stem and feed off the nutrients and oxygen supplied to that organ. People tested positive even several months later, and the extent to which the civilian population had been infiltrated was still largely unknown.

In the military, the test was a game-changer. Drake's concerns about the Paragon had nothing to do with the type of leaks the Fleet suffered in the Paragon attack on Earth, and what a relief. Drake was certain there were many ways the Fleet and the Terran Federation at large were falling apart because of what had happened, but if the creatures had been allowed to continue wreaking havoc, it would have been the end of everything. The apocalypse had again been held off, if only for a little while.

"And you, Doctor?" the aide asked Broussard. The fake smile never left her face, apparently. Doc flashed a fake smile back and, keeping his mocking cheer, shot himself in the neck. His test came back bright green as well. "Thank you, sirs," she said, satisfied, then looked down at an unseen control panel. "I'm transferring you to your drone, Captain."

Drone. Great. Drake was going to appear in HQ via a robot.

The room around him flickered. The woman disappeared, and after the projectors settled and were fully rendering the new surroundings, they were standing in the halls of Fleet Headquarters.

Holoimaging like this worked off the Quantum Entanglement network and was instantaneous. The technology had improved dramatically since Drake had last used it. It was like he was there. Even the sound was three-dimensional and immersive.

This drone, whatever it looked like, tracked his head

movements. The effect was seamless. For all intents and purposes, he was, standing outside one of the many briefing rooms at HQ, thousands of light-years from here. Incredible.

"Captain?" a man called. Drake realized he wasn't alone in the hallway. There were a dozen people standing around. Drake frowned when he realized that no one else was in uniform. Someone was approaching, and Drake could tell from the cut of his civilian suit that it was a politician well before he caught sight of his laminated VISITOR badge. "Captain Drake, is that you in there?" The man flashed a billion-watt smile.

Drake remembered he was a drone. He wondered how sensitive the audio pickups were in the projection room and the same for the speakers his drone had on the other end. "This is Captain Drake," he called.

Given that the man winced, the system was very sensitive. "We read you loud and clear, Captain," he said, the hint of a Southern Americas drawl softening his voice. "Let me see if I can get your imagers on."

Drake realized the politician meant the projectors on the Earth end of the connection that would render him into the space there like it appeared for him at Freepoint. He realized that too late for him to protest; the politician stepped back with a satisfied look before Drake could open his mouth again. Drake saw a projection of himself flicker to life, reflected in the man's eyes.

The man stuck out his hand. "Name's Purdy. Freshman on the Federated Security Committee." Drake couldn't help but frown. The fuck was the council doing here? Purdy kept his hand out, and the open, friendly expression stayed on his face through Drake's pause, making it all the more agonizing.

Embarrassed, Drake stuck his hand out to grab Purdy's but only waved through light and air. The councilman chuckled. "I guess I kinda set you up for that one. My apologies, Captain." He lowered his hand. "It is such a pleasure to meet you, though. I'm very much looking forward to hearing your thoughts about what those Paragon are up to out there."

He knew about Drake's report? What in the ever-living hell was going on here? Outwardly, Drake tried to stay neutral; he mumbled something along the lines of "The pleasure is all mine, Councilman." His head was spinning. He wanted to sit down. Or better yet, leave. Get some air.

Purdy got even closer, however. "Just so you know, Captain," he said with a none-too-subtle glance at the assembled company, all of whom wore the same VISITOR badges and iterations of the same expensive suit and even more expensive smiles. "I'm on your side in there. I think you're a goddamn hero."

That snapped Drake's attention back to Purdy. "Thank you," he said slowly and deliberately, narrowing his eyes. A self-professed ally implied there were enemies.

Purdy nodded agreeably. "And I tell you what; I'm not the only one. Don't let them fool you." He indicated the others around them with a nod. "If you ever decide to go into politics, and you should, come to me first. It'd be my pleasure to take you under my wing and show you the ropes." Drake lost the composure war and blanched visibly at the suggestion.

Purdy guffawed. The sound made Drake's skin want to crawl off his body. "Oh, come now! We're not all that bad. You ever change your mind, you let me know. See you inside." He winked and moved off.

"Who in the blazes was that man?" Doc asked in a whisper. He wasn't being broadcast, just Drake. The captain could dismiss him, but it was reassuring to have him around.

"No idea," Drake whispered to his friend softly, then shot him a look to communicate what he didn't dare say out loud. He didn't trust Purdy, and he was rapidly losing trust in this meeting.

Drake had a job to do. His observations of Paragon activity were time-sensitive and demanded immediate action. This security committee Federation council stuff felt like theater, and that was the last thing Drake had time for.

WHEN THE DOORS to the meeting room finally swung open, everyone began to filter inside. Drake wondered if he needed to walk in with them. His drone moved by itself, however, floating to a prescribed seat at the head of a long table. The Admiralty representatives were seated nearby. Six of them, three chairs on either side of the table nearest his seat, with one missing.

Drake was dismayed to realize the missing seat must belong to Admiral Jack Sturgess. Jack had been instrumental in corroborating and supporting Drake's theory on what the Paragon were up to and had recently provided additional intelligence that had all but made up Drake's mind that the threat was imminent. But he wasn't here.

More concerning, however, were all the politicians. They filled the rest of the seats down the table, and a haughty-looking man took the chair at the far end.

"Please be seated, Captain," one of the admirals said. Hawkins. Drake knew her from before. The ornate stripes and braids on her uniform told him she was C-in-C now.

Good for her. She'd always been one of the good ones. As good as an admiral can be, anyway.

Drake sat. Doc shuffled to the side of the projection room, out of the way. Drake was grateful that he didn't leave. Lion's den, indeed.

"We've received your request for additional support at Freepoint Station," Hawkins said, getting down to business. It was one of the reasons she was a good one. "And your report indicating you believe there is the imminent threat of Paragon attack there."

"I . . ." Drake couldn't help but be distracted by all those VISITOR badges. He forced himself to focus on Hawkins. "This is a security level-4 briefing, ma'am?"

"It is. Proceed." She looked perturbed, whether by him or all the civilians, Drake couldn't tell.

Drake swallowed. "Then that's correct, Admiral." Hawkins' brief summary was accurate. In a nutshell, Drake's analysis of the recent Paragon hit-and-run attacks and Jack's recent confirmation of a suspicion Drake had held since the outset of his investigation had led him to the simple conclusion that they were planning an attack on a major Fleet target.

There was only one major Fleet target in that region of Fringe space: Freepoint Station. "With the destruction of the Jupiter shipyards in the Paragon attack on Earth, Freepoint is our only high-capacity shipbuilding, repair, and retrofitting facility. If the Paragon were to destroy, or even worse, seize the shipyards here, which I believe is their intention, Admiral, I...

"Well, I don't have to tell you how catastrophic that would be. It is my recommendation, Admiral, that we fortify our defenses here in anticipation of an imminent attack."

"If I may, Admiral," the politician said at the far end of

the table. His voice matched his haughty expression. Words slipped from his mouth like oil. "I think you misunderstand the purpose of this meeting."

Drake stared at him. "Oh?"

The man folded his hands together smugly, elbows on the table, and leaned closer to the microphone in front of him, even though the room was small enough to easily carry his voice. "We're not here to discuss your request for ships. A ludicrous suggestion, by the way, when we barely have enough ships to patrol Earth and the colonial worlds as it is."

"Who are you?" Drake asked, trying unsuccessfully to keep defiance out of his voice. He could see Doc tensing from the corner of his eye, wanting him to get his rising blood pressure down. Drake would try.

"Councilman Henri Laurent." He said the name like Drake should recognize it. He could tell the man was from southwestern Europe from his name, but that was it. The lack of recognition amused the councilman, and he smiled at Drake. "I'm head of the security council."

"With all due respect, Councilman," Drake said, "there won't *be* anyone to defend Earth or the colonies if we can't build and repair ships."

There was a chuckle from the Admiralty people. It didn't make Drake feel better, but at least he knew he had allies there. Maybe they hated this, whatever in the hell "this" was, as much as Drake did.

The chuckle drove Laurent's smug smile off his face, and he reddened. "You are here, Captain," he said too loudly for how close he was to his microphone, "to answer questions regarding your role in the attack on Earth that caused the destruction of those very same Jupiter shipyards you're being so cavalier about, along with dozens of Fleet ships, the entirety of the planet Mars, and very nearly Earth itself. Your role in the precipitation of that attack, the events that followed, and in how on the very brink of peace, Captain, Earth now finds itself plunged into war."

Drake frowned. "My role?" He was caught off-guard. What role?

Laurent pressed on. "Is it not true, Captain, that you were pulled out of self-imposed retirement, a matter which we will certainly also be discussing shortly, and sent on a clandestine mission to obtain and install a weapon to be used on the Paragon *before* the attack occurred?

"And is it not also true that a Navid by the name of...of . . ." The councilman paused to leaf through several sheets of printed paper. "A Navid female by the name of Idri, an illegal Navigator trainee, was taken from the Navid home-world in another clandestine operation and sent to *Glory*, directly to you? An operation which led to the destruction of the TDF cruiser *Ulysses*, again *days* before the Paragon attack on Earth?"

"I . . ." Drake didn't follow. What was this bastard getting at? He looked at the empty chair where Jack was supposed to be sitting, then at Admiral Hawkins. Surely these were questions for them, not him. Hawkins' face bore a grimace. She had no help to offer.

"Don't look at them," Laurent spat. He was in a lather by this point. "You look at me, sir, and you answer me. Is it not also true, Captain, that you were the commanding officer in charge of the Dagus Massacre, an event which nearly plunged us into full-scale war twenty years ago and a stain on Terran-Paragon relations that has hindered peace talks ever since? An event that you have yet to stand a court-martial for *even to this day*?"

Jack's empty chair mocked Drake. So, that's what this

was—an ambush. Why, Drake still didn't understand, but some of what that politician Purdy had been alluding to in the hallway and the sickening feeling Drake had felt building in his stomach was starting to make sense. "If the councilman could explain what this has to do with the current situation at Freepoint," Drake said through barely controlled rage, "perhaps I could speak to his concerns over my report more clearly."

"My *concerns*, Captain Drake," Laurent said, slowing his speech very deliberately for emphasis, "lie in the fact that a member of our military who very nearly caused a war two decades ago seems to have been part of a pre-meditated and secret plan to derail a peace process right on the eve of its breakthrough, very nearly destroying this planet and plunging us into an all-out conflict with the Paragon, and currently seems intent on ensuring full-scale war with the Paragon continues! How that man is sitting in uniform at this table asking for *more ships* rather than in a courtroom is inexplicable to me."

Drake felt like he might explode. Burst into flames right there in the meeting room, then find Laurent and wrap him in a giant bear hug so he burst into flames too. There hadn't been a question from the man. Nothing to answer. And whatever Drake had expected this meeting to be, it was not. It was a farce. What was the point?

"Chairman," someone else said. It was Purdy. "If I may interject?" Red-faced, Laurent snapped a look at the younger man. Purdy didn't wait for him to say yes. "I grant you that the circumstances leading up to the Paragon attack on our Solar System are worth investigating, but surely, we can all agree that the actions of Captain Drake *saved* Earth.

"This room we're sitting in would not be standing were it not for the actions of *Glory* and her crew. I personally propose a resolution to decorate the captain and would like to thank him from the bottom of my heart for his service."

The meeting room descended into madness. All the assembled politicians were out of their seats now, some hunched over their microphones, others just screaming across the table. Even the admirals were out of their seats, trying to calm the room, but it wasn't going to work.

This wasn't a meeting. It was a circus.

Drake wondered if this was being broadcast. It had that kind of feeling of theater. And goddammit, if this was going to be the state of affairs, the Paragon had already won. It was over.

Drake couldn't accept that.

"How did that tech say we could make adjustments to the feed?" Drake asked Doc, trying to remember the two-second interaction they'd had with the young man who had set the projection room up for them. Everything had been preset, he'd said, but just in case, there were ways to change settings like volume.

"Voice-activated, I think, Cap," Doc said, raising his eyebrows.

Drake nodded. "Increase broadcast volume to maximum," he called toward the ceiling, hoping that was the right way to do it. There was no response. Drake inhaled; either it had worked, or it hadn't. "QUIET!" he bellowed with every ounce of authority he'd picked up as a ship's captain.

The room projected around him fell silent, and two dozen blinking eyes turned to stare at him. Good. His volume was on full.

"The chairman has asked me several questions. Allow me to respond." His heart was still pounding, and he knew his face was still flushed with rage, but he delivered his words calmly and concisely. The silence continued, which Drake took as tacit acceptance.

"Everything I have ever done has been in the service of protecting Earth and her colonies. You can litigate my effectiveness in doing so as much as you wish, but the fact remains that both of them are still under dire threat. The Paragon are not gone. They never have been, and I submit to you, Chairman Laurent, that they used the peace process itself to perpetrate what was very nearly a fatal blow to all of humanity—something *you* are complicit in, as are all of us. Now they are preparing a new threat which I've detailed in my report to the best of my ability."

From the side of the room, a sliver of light caught everyone's eyes, including Drake's. Admiral Jack Sturgess stepped into the room. The bastard. Drake gave him his nastiest look and was met with a nod. *Continue.* Thanks a lot for the help, asshole.

"Furthermore..." Drake took a deep breath and got to the point he'd been attempting to bring forth from the start. The admiral's appearance had helped him remember that he was there to share news. "I can confirm another development that I've suspected for some time, ever since the pattern of hit-and-run attacks began."

Drake called to the voice activation system, and asked it to display an image over the feed. It popped up in front of him, hanging in midair. It was a man—or rather, a Paragon—tall, impressively dressed with a shining gold helmet, and flowing red, gold and white robes.

"This image was taken three days ago during an assault on our outpost at Kreeva." Drake paused, scanning to see if there was any recognition from the assembled. "That is Archgeneral Hadras."

There was the news. Hadras was back.

Drake watched as the information flew over the head of the civilians, but landed with the admiralty. Good. They remembered.

Hadras was perhaps the greatest tactical mind the Paragon had ever employed. The Fleet had faced off against him several times during the Third Conflict and its aftermath; Drake, personally, had battled him several times. He was brilliant. Deadly. And always unorthodox.

When the Paragon had started making hit-and-run attacks, probing defenses and weakening them bit by bit with the minimum of losses while hiding their numbers and randomizing the locations, it screamed Hadras. The arch-general never acted without a meticulously constructed plan that was very often cleverly disguised and always deadly.

Drake had gotten in his licks against the tactician, but he'd taken them as well. Too many times. The mention of Hadras' name was enough to raise Drake's blood pressure, and he was relieved to see it did the same for most of the top brass he recognized.

"Is that name supposed to mean anything?" Laurent was speaking again. "Or assuage our concerns over you, personally, Captain?" Somebody really needed to shut him up.

"It should mean everything to everyone here. Hadras is the single most accomplished tactician I have ever faced in my career, and he is planning to attack the Freepoint ship-yards. I am absolutely convinced of it.

"By using his hit-and-runs, he's already weakened our defenses to get within two gates' access of the only way in and out of this facility. Enough, I think, for him to launch a large-scale attack and succeed in reaching here within the next few weeks. Without the immediate dispatch of reinforcements, the Fleet could very well lose our only remaining high-capacity shipyards to the Paragon.

"*That* should scare you, Councilman. It certainly scares me."

Laurent opened his mouth to speak again, but Drake slammed his hand on the arm of his chair. The increased sensitivity of the microphones in the projection room made it sound like a thunderclap.

"As for your concerns about me," Drake said, letting the fury edge back into his voice. "Fine. Go through the declassification process with Headquarters and serve me a goddamn subpoena if you want. I'll answer every question you ask of me but know this. There will never be peace with the Paragon.

"They are *intolerant.* They believe they are superior to all other life in the galaxy. They have no concept of peace with lower life forms, or of coexistence, or diversity in any shape or form. Purity is, quite literally, their religion, and they will never, ever seek peace in any meaningful way."

Drake lost his voice before he voiced his next thought, and he had to cough to recover it. "What I have seen . . . The things the Paragon have done, gentlemen and ladies, in my years of military service; it boggles the mind, the depths of their contempt. Their peace entreaties were a ruse from the start. My actions, and that man's standing over there."

Drake pointed at Admiral Jack, who was rooted by the door. "They weren't about heroism or conspiracy. They were desperate. And they barely, *barely* worked. You have absolutely no idea how close we came to annihilation. Please, I beg of you, do not let us be so foolish as to let that happen again."

Laurent shook his head, finally backing away from his microphone and leaning into his chair. Drake wondered if, impossibly, he might have gotten an inkling of truth or sense through to the smug bastard.

"I'm not surprised," the councilman said, voice oily as ever, "to hear that peace has no chance from a man who manages, over and over again, to put himself in the middle of Paragon bloodshed."

Nope. Not an ounce. Fuck him.

"You are dangerous, Captain. Rest assured, you *will* be called to answer our questions." Laurent stood, signaling that the meeting was coming to an end. "And in regards to your request for more military support to be assigned to the Freepoint shipyards . . ."

His mouth curled into a smirk. "We have your report and will take it under advisement."

CHAPTER TWELVE

"SON OF A BITCH, JACK."

Drake seethed. He was back on *Glory* in his quarters, with the admiral on the more-traditional video QE network. Drake wished it was still a hologram so he could wrap his hands around the man's throat and give a nice squeeze. "What in the starry fuck was that? It was an ambush; that's what it was, god*dammit.*"

Doc put a hand on Drake's shoulder, trying to calm him. It only succeeded in Drake shoving him off and resuming his pacing in the small space. He really wanted to hit something. Throw a book or maybe a person. Do some damage. But he didn't.

Even as he raged, there was a voice in his head telling him to keep it together. More than anything, he wanted Jack to explain why. Why had he thrown him to the wolves like that?

Jack, for his part, simply sat there on the screen, presumably waiting in silence for Drake to calm down. Cold, steely silence.

"Talk, you bastard," Drake said, using every ounce of command technique he had in him to stop pacing and focus.

"Things are changing," Jack said simply.

"No shit."

"I don't think you're aware of how much things are in danger of falling into chaos here on Earth. The Paragon incursion has the entire Federation council trying to eat itself, a small taste of which you encountered today.

"Laurent is their attack dog, and the 'security committee' is their means of exercising more direct authority over the Admiralty. I'm sorry to say that our names are being thrown around at the heart of it, both by those who would like to gain power by discrediting what we did and those who would call us heroes."

Jack stopped to rub the bridge of his nose and looked down. "That is to say, your ignorance and your absence are by design." He looked up. "I don't want you here. I want you out there doing your goddamn job, to use the type of language you seem to employ so often."

"Putting me in that meeting sure seems like an odd way to help me do my job, Jack."

The admiral grimaced. "Yes, well, I obviously hadn't planned it that way. The committee must have forced their way in last-minute. I honestly don't know how; I'll have to look into it. A leak in the Admiralty, probably."

Drake could tell that was a new thought for the admiral and that it set the spymaster's part of his mind spinning. A new mystery to solve, another little conspiracy to unravel. What an exhausting existence it must be to live in a world of incessant paranoia.

"Regardless," Jack continued, "I was detained, the attendance of the meeting was changed, and you were caught unaware."

There was a beat. That was as close as Drake would get to an apology from Jack. Fine. He leaned back in his chair and fixed on one small part of Jack's non-apology. "You were detained."

Jack smirked. He appreciated that Drake had heard that and picked it up without further prompting. He had something for him. "I was," he said and tapped on some out-of-view controls. On the screen, the image of Admiral Jack sitting in his HQ office was replaced by an image of two men Drake didn't recognize. He didn't recognize their names, either. "Two escaped POWs from a Paragon labor camp were picked up several days ago at Aexon Hub."

That name Drake recognized. "Carrol and CAG are at Aexon Hub with *Providence*."

"Not anymore. They're en route to Freepoint as we speak with the POWs in tow."

Interesting. "You said, '*Paragon* labor camp,' Admiral?"

"Correct."

More than interesting, astounding. Drake wasn't aware of a single case in which POWs had escaped from a Paragon labor camp and made it back to Fleet-controlled space. These two men must be something else.

He glanced at their names: Warren and Markus. Warren was a lieutenant. His mission list was pages long, all of it blacked out CLASSIFIED. "One of yours?" Drake asked knowingly.

Jack didn't even have to answer. His ignoring of the question confirmed it for Drake. "They claim to have first-hand insight into what Archgeneral Hadras has been up to."

Well, goddamn. That *would* be incredible intelligence. Jack had Drake's undivided attention.

"Debrief them. Report back to me."

"Yes, sir," Drake said. His anger over the meeting was

subsiding, replaced by intense focus. He had a mission now. Something to do.

"You're lucky to be all the way out there," Jack said after another long pause. With the business portion of the call completed, Drake could see how exhausted he was. He was slighter after the Paragon infection he'd suffered that had nearly taken his life a few months prior, nasty synthetic parasites eating his body from the inside out.

However, Drake could tell it was more than that. The admiral was starting to look old.

"No, I'm not," Drake said about his luck in being out in Freepoint. He leaned toward the screen. "He's coming, Jack. Hadras wants this shipyard." The Paragon had been as decimated as the Fleet after the Earth attack. "They need it just as much as we do."

"I know you're right."

"The Admiralty looked like they might, too."

Jack nodded. "Won't help much now that the committee is involved." Jack mirrored Drake's posture and leaned toward his monitor, becoming larger on the screen so that Drake could clearly see his face.

His eyes belied his body. They were strong, clear, and determined. "But you don't worry about that. I will work on finding some goddamn ships. You find out what these POWs know. Report back to me."

"Yes, sir."

Jack ended the call.

CHAPTER THIRTEEN

FREEPOINT STATION WAS a marvel of nature and modern technology. Even before the destruction of the Jupiter shipyards during the Paragon attack on Earth, the majority of the Fleet's shipbuilding, repair, and retrofitting operations went through Freepoint in spite of its relatively distant location.

Why? Freepoint was unique in that it had a supermassive gas giant upon which a far-reach gate could be constructed, and it had a mineral-rich asteroid belt six or seven times as large as Earth's, not that Earth's asteroid belt was that large. It wasn't, but there was a comparison to be made.

The yellow star around which it all orbited held not three, four, or five but six rocky terrestrial-type planets, three of which were in the goldilocks zone and required no additional life support to mine. With the marriage of a gate that had the distance to make it not as remote and the richest system in Fleet space for the materials necessary to make starships, voila! You had the largest, most extensive yards in the Terran Federation.

Carrol viewed it sprawling ahead of her as she exited Freepoint's one and only gate. Massive, yes, but singular. There was no hub here. One way in, one way out, and heavily mined for defensive purposes. The mines were Carrol's first concern as she flew in ahead of *Providence* in her fighter with the squadron behind her in escort formation. As she waited in the safe zone while her call sign and transponder were verified by System Control, she took in the complex.

It was easier to build ships in space than it was on the ground. Thus, most of Freepoint was a space station. The station took many shapes and forms over its endless-seeming expanse, but the most predominant was like honeycomb. The hexagons had facilities on the inside and docks around the outside.

Making up the latter were drydocks, landing bays, fueling depots, and retrofitting hangars buzzing with the manual/EV variety and the robotic arms of automation.

The insides of the hexagons displayed thousands of dotted lights denoting quarters, workrooms, labs, machining facilities, manufacturing plants, quarters, gyms, promenades, movie theaters, pools, restaurants, all run by civilians since there were so many contractors involved in making starships that there was an entire non-military wing of Freepoint.

The station had everything. It was in the middle of nowhere, but it sparkled with life like a casino in the desert.

Carrol wasn't looking at the station to take all that in, however. She was looking for one tiny part in particular—a drydock. She couldn't remember which one, then she spotted it, or rather, she spotted what the drydock held.

Glory.

The warship was far away enough to be nothing more

than a dot, but the HUD on her cockpit had directed her eyes to it and put an orange ring around *Glory* to confirm that was home. It was dead ahead.

CAG's voice crackled in her helmet radio. "Designated flight path coming to you."

Carrol acknowledged, her fighter chimed, and a green flight path lit up in front of her—their route through the minefield. The mines were in constant motion. No flight path was the same, even minute to minute.

Providence's path would be different from Carrol's since System Control took that motion into account.

The mines were tiny, made of a material so non-reflective that you couldn't see them with the naked eye until they were exploding on top of you. Spheres six inches across, Carrol thought she remembered, pure black and packed with explosives to drive expanding hardened metal coils that could breach an armored warship. Deadly little bastards.

"D-Wing actual," called a new person over the open comm.

It was a voice Carrol recognized. CAG, too, from her response. "That you, Zed?" she asked.

"That's a roger-affirmative." Carrol smiled. *Roger-affirmative.* Zed was making up words, overdoing the jargon for a laugh. Punk hadn't changed a bit, had he? "Actual, you have clearance once free and clear to launch your designated personnel transport with D-wing Escort Dash-Four-Seven on the following transit lane to rendezvous with *Glory* and transfer all duties from *Providence* at that time."

"I think I got about half of that, *Glory* Control," CAG snorted, "but I can acknowledge receipt of the transit lane to you. We'll see you in a bit, passengers in tow."

The trip through the minefield would take them almost

an hour. It was an agonizing amount of time for someone who could see their destination on the horizon after days of deep-space travel, but Carrol could take it.

Then she would say her goodbyes to her borrowed squadron, break off from *Providence*, and escort a transport shuttle with CAG and their passengers on it to *Glory*. Hopefully, the pilots around her were now better equipped to handle whatever the Paragon were fixing to throw at them. They seemed as though they were.

Carrol settled back in her seat.

Almost home.

XO was all business when Carrol crawled out of her fighter and stepped onto *Glory's* flight deck. He watched the personnel shuttle as it touched down, brow furrowed, massive sloping shoulders tense. He acknowledged the second officer with a grunt as she sidled up to him.

The full gravity of the ship was hell on her tired muscles. She felt as though she might collapse right on the metal grating, bones turned to mush. The tedious flight through the minefield had been longer than expected, a nice cherry on top of twelve straight hours of flying.

The main hangar bay in which they stood was in chaos, which didn't help. It was, however, exactly what Carrol had expected. She'd been with *Glory* for the first couple months of her massive retrofit and knew just how extensive an overhaul the old girl had been slated for.

There would be an almost entirely new set of exterior hull plating, the replacement of almost fifty percent of her hull bracing, including a brand-new hectoton supersteel central beam, a full overhaul of the power and propulsion systems, and a gut job on the central computer and networking stations. The life support systems would undergo the same—ah, the prospect of fresh filtered air!—and the defensive systems would get new plasma cannons, an upgraded laser array, and a retrofit of the missile silos to allow for the newer models the Fleet had moved to in the decades since *Glory* had last been out there strutting her stuff.

She was almost going to be a new ship. Almost, but not wholly. The grating below Carrol's feet had been freshly painted, but that paint was rounded from the layers upon layers that had stacked up over the years. Bulkheads would show the same if you stopped to look at them. Dents. Blemishes. The slight dip in the most-traveled corridors that were scuffed to a shine just from the foot traffic.

No amount of retrofitting or repair would take away the imperfections that were all around if you knew where to look for them, which was as it should be. Those kinds of things took time and there was no replacement for them, just like there was no replacement for *Glory*.

Stars, it was good to be home. Exhausting but good.

"Let's see what these two are all about," XO said quietly enough for only Carrol to hear.

It drew her attention back to the shuttle, whose large port-side hatch had swung open. The two passengers stepped out, as they had a week earlier on the flight deck of *Providence*. They looked less haggard now, especially Warren. He looked taller and even bigger, and he had been big before.

It made Carrol think of Smith, *Glory's* towering Marine, though Warren was much scruffier, an uncouth grump. Smith was a model warrior in every way.

"Gentlemen," XO called across the flight deck and

started to walk toward them. Carrol followed. "Welcome to *Glory*."

Warren blinked. Recognition flashed across his face.

"I'm to take you straight for debriefing," Oh continued.

Warren offered a salute. Everyone, including the old man, Markus, returned it. "Thank you, sir," Warren said to XO, who now stuck out his hand in greeting, first to Markus —they shook—then to Warren, who did the same. "I'm sorry. Did you say we're on *Glory*?"

That elicited a smile from Oh. "Indeed I did, Lieutenant." He turned and gestured for them to follow. "If you'll follow me, please." Warren gave Carrol a nod, made sure Markus had his bearings, and the four of them set off together.

Carrol had to give herself a shake to try to wake up her body and mind for the meeting ahead. How she would make it through sitting still in a room for longer than a few seconds without nodding off, she didn't know. Then again, it didn't matter, did it?

XO, however, put a hand on her shoulder to hold her back and let the two guests walk ahead a little. "Hold your horses," he told her. He fished something out of his pants pocket and handed it to her. It was a small bracelet made from silicone with an intricate series of metal lines and dots on the inside.

"Wrist Computer," he explained, slipping it onto her wrist. "Part of the new security measures that work with our shiny new computer system. Personal transponder, communicator, computer interface, etc., all wrapped into one. Everyone's been calling them 'wristcoms' for short.

"Fancy little things. No more running about unsupervised, and no more needing to find a panel for intraship comm." He tapped the bracelet, which was surprisingly comfortable to wear. A holographic display popped up from it, with a menu that had all sorts of things on it, including vitals, comms, and an interface for her personal console in her quarters. "They'll trigger an alert if your vitals go south, ping a final location if removed or destroyed, and can even be rigged to transmit person-to-person—voice or haptic.

"You have a message waiting for you," XO said, pointing at a notification icon in the corner of the holographic projection. He tapped it for her, and the notification expanded into a message box filled with numbers. When Carrol recognized what they were, she flushed.

"Neat," she said, closing the message as quickly as she could without catching too much of XO's attention.

XO nodded, then winked at her. Apparently he'd missed it, thank the stars. "I put you on the next C shift. Get some rest. You look like hell."

Carrol frowned. "But the briefing?"

He shrugged. "Eyes-only anyway. If I need you before your shift . . ." he tapped her bracelet, "I'll call you." He left.

She watched him lead Warren and Markus through the nearest hatch. She was disappointed that she wasn't going to hear what those two had to share. That *Providence* had immediately been rerouted here from Aexon Hub in the wake of a Paragon attack told her it was important. Sensitive.

On the other hand, she was so tired while just standing that she could have curled up and passed out right in the middle of all the hubbub.

Sleep. She was gonna get her some of that. When she was sure she was alone, she brought up the message with the numbers again.

Yeah . . .

CHAPTER FOURTEEN

WARREN'S IMAGES WERE GRAINY. Projected onto the main screen in the command deck briefing room, it was hard at times to make out what they were looking at.

Drake sat at the end of the table in his customary seat, flanked by XO on one side and Chief Engineer Fredrickson on the other. Markus sat next to XO, and Warren stood at the far end, explaining the images he'd managed to take during their escape.

Their tale was astounding, and even more astounding was what they were saying they'd seen on Vorkut V.

"You can see here," Warren said, narrating as the grainy stills advanced with a jerking motion, "the ship is tethered. They use that cable as a hardwire for the AI while it's docked with the facility."

The images advanced again, another shape coming into view. "And that?" Drake asked, squinting to see if that would improve the fidelity. It didn't. "You're saying that's Hadras' flagship?"

"That's correct, Captain. Here." Warren bent to a set of controls built into the briefing table and advanced the slides. "It was easier to see once we were at a higher altitude."

From farther away, the graininess was not as noticeable. Drake recognized the warship he was looking at instantly. He'd seen it before. A big, hulking thing in the tri-hull design that almost all Paragon ships had, but bigger. Its angles were more severe and sleeker. Less upright. More menacing and sharper. Apparently, the archgeneral was up to more than just hit-and-runs.

"That's the *Scythe,* all right," XO mumbled, naming the archgeneral's flagship. He, too, knew the ship on sight.

"Can we go back to the prototype?" Drake asked. It flashed back up on the screen.

"You're saying that it's controlled via that . . . tether?" Fredrickson asked, frowning and leaning forward with intense, incredulous attention.

"Only while docked," Markus answered for Warren, finally speaking up.

He was another incredulity-inducing aspect of this briefing. Similar to Hadras' flagship, Drake instantly recognized what he was: something that wasn't supposed to exist. Not anymore, anyway. However, his kaleidoscope eyes, impossibly advanced age, and the web of small scars that covered every inch of his tightly drawn skin were unmistakable.

A Blaspheme. A human forcibly combined with Paragon DNA. The Paragon had denied they existed since the end of the Second Conflict, but there had always been rumors. POWs taken and never accounted for, descriptions of the labs they were taken to and the experiments that were done on them. The physical results, what they looked like, and their eventual decline from favor and wiping out. No photographs.

No holovids or scans, only stories. Stories of some who'd volunteered, who'd sought it out, drawn by a sick, deranged belief that maybe the Paragon were right. They *were* superior. They *were* gods, and after the purification of their dirty blood, they could touch the Divine too.

Drake wondered if Markus was one of those. He'd been working with them for the past five decades, hadn't he? That was what the records said.

Warren clarified Markus' statement about the tether. "Otherwise, it's controlled via a system very much like our QE. The artificial intelligence is housed inside the facility." A new picture flashed onto the wall, slightly sharper than the shuttle's images but still rather grainy because of the extremely low light.

They were looking down a hall at a solid cube balanced on one of its points and half-buried in the floor. There were no entrances or exits, and it was a pure, unreflective black much like the prototype ship. "I managed to take an image of it from a distance during our escape."

"How do you get inside the damn thing?" XO asked.

"The AI jumps you inside or out," Markus said. He seemed impressed by that, which grated on Drake.

"Because the data connection between the AI and the ship is quantumly entangled," Warren said gravely, "the ship's range is unlimited. Whether it's within a hundred meters and tethered or it's on the other side of the galaxy, the AI's control is instantaneous."

"What about the range of the displacement mechanism?" Fredrickson asked, brows furrowed even deeper. "In the ship?"

"Still theoretical," Markus answered. "But we've jumped the ship just over two hundred light-years, so the distance of a far-reach gate."

It felt like the air had been sucked out of the room. Nobody spoke for a long, tense time.

"That's impossible," Fredrickson said finally. He leaned back, shaking his head, then looked at Drake incredulously. "It's absolutely impossible for this thing to do what they're claiming it does, Captain."

Markus snorted. He looked at Warren as if to say, "I told you so." Warren flexed his jaw.

"No fucking way," Fredrickson said, seeing the exchange but not backing down. "First off, nobody has even entangled the kind of complex data transfer you're talking about here over *any* distance, let alone a persistent enough pairing to exist outside space-time.

"Secondly, for a computer to be able to do what a Navid does... I mean, not only would that be taking computational capabilities thousands of years into the future, a literal status-quo-shattering feat, Captain, that probably borders on full-fledged sentience if not even surpasses it entirely into the realm of something entirely more advanced.

"It would *also* mean the Paragon have managed to break down into concrete physics what those people do intuitively: peek inside a black box that physicists in every corner of this galaxy have been trying to crack since the dawn of interstellar travel. Not even the Navid know how they do what they do. It's...it's . . ."

Fredrickson's voice trailed off; he was at a loss for words. He tossed his arms up, then folded them over his chest. A beat later, he found his words again. "These two are saying the Paragon have made a breakthrough that changes *everything* about the limits to the known universe, Captain. Literally everything." He shook his head again. "I don't believe it."

"I assure you, gentlemen," Markus said, not hiding his

defiance, "the prototype ship is very real, as are its capabilities. Just because you cannot conceive of the rules being rewritten does not mean they haven't been. It does mean that maybe you, in fact, have misunderstood the rules from the start."

It was Fredrickson's turn to snort. "I think you've misunderstood what that ship's capabilities are, then."

That raised their guest's hackles. "You were not there," he said to the engineer, cold.

"But you were," Drake called, putting some boom into his voice to retake command of the conversation. Markus turned to look at him, face red. "You were there because you worked on the ship, correct? In fact, you were instrumental in this breakthrough in AI for the Paragon, right?"

Drake's question wasn't innocuous. It was an accusation, which was how he meant it.

Markus swallowed. "I was one of the lead researchers on the project, yes."

"So, you fully admit to collaboration with the Paragon?"

"I do." Markus drew himself up ramrod-straight into his seat, still defiant. "I might remind you, sir, that under the Pretext Accords of the Second Conflict in which I was taken, no prisoner of war may refuse work."

"You can cut it with that bullshit," Drake said, allowing his anger to peek through. This man was a petulant, arrogant asshole trying to see how much he could get away with, and Drake was having none of that.

"The accords apply to *very* limited circumstances that don't lead directly to military advancement, not to mention they were abandoned by both sides during the Third Conflict."

Markus didn't have a retort for that. Good. Drake

pressed further. "Have you taken the Paragon rites? Do you despise your own flesh now?"

Markus swallowed again and looked at Warren. The other soldier looked at the deck as if they had known this moment was coming but had no good response for it. The old Blaspheme then turned back to Drake with a blink of his insane eyes and said, "All flesh is to be despised, Captain."

Right out of the Paragon holy texts. It was a chilling admission. The two had been right to hesitate over it, though Drake supposed Markus had told the truth. If he'd lied, Drake wouldn't have believed him. That would have been much easier because he could have just thrown this collaborator into a cell and wiped his hands clean.

As it was . . . "I can't trust you," Drake said to him finally. He shook his head, thoughts swirling. "How did you even manage to escape? I've never heard of anyone escaping from a Paragon POW camp, ever."

Again, Markus bristled. "You're insinuating I'm some kind of...of spy? Or plant? After everything we went through to get here?"

"You're a collaborator of the worst mind-boggling kind by your own admission. You've been helping the Paragon hand-in-hand for decades. How can I believe a single word out of your mouth?"

Markus stood, shaking. He looked at Warren. "I told you this was a mistake," he said, and he slammed his hands on the table. That caused XO to stand and adopt a defensive posture. Markus jabbed a finger at Oh, then Drake. "I told you they would never listen."

Warren finally spoke up. "Captain, please." His tone turned softer, pleading, and he pointed at Markus. "I owe that man my life. I, too, had my reservations at first, as

Markus is well-aware. But Captain, at every turn, in every instance where I doubted him or there was an opportunity for him to mislead or betray me, he has proven himself to be trustworthy at incredible risk to himself.

"Yes, he is a collaborator, but, sir, it is *because* he has worked so closely with the Paragon over such a long time that we're even able to be here and warn you about this weapon." Warren switched the view on the projector back to the image of the AI ship with the *Scythe* hovering next to it. "And he's not mistaken about it."

Warren made sure he met Drake's eyes so the captain could see what haunted him. "I've seen it myself. I saw the ship jump with my own eyes."

He pressed a control on the table and brought up a new video. This one was shot from the ground. It was like the others: grainy. Drake could make out the prototype ship, untethered, and higher in the atmosphere.

Warren pressed play, and the ship on the screen shimmered. Despite himself, Drake leaned forward in his chair. He'd seen that shimmer before or something like it. It was different from a Navigator's shimmer. He couldn't place how but it was, and the discrepancy was strange. Cold. Uncomfortable. The shimmer intensified. In a blink, it was gone from one place, and flashed into existence in another. Even though the crude imager with which the video was taken had trouble re-focusing on the ship's new location, it was clear to everyone what they'd just seen.

"There is no mistake," Warren said. He pointed at Markus. "The mistake, Captain, would be to ignore this man and let Hadras deploy it in battle."

Silence.

Drake found it hard to breathe for a moment. The meeting resumed shortly after he regained his wind.

Everyone was seated again. He only half paid attention. His mind was racing.

These images of the AI ship had been taken weeks prior. It had taken Warren and Markus that long to finally reach Fleet space on the back of Markus' access codes and limited knowledge of the Paragon gate system out that far. The ship should be ready to finish its trials and be deployed. They had only days, Warren estimated. And they were willing to go back there, he and Markus, to lead a mission to destroy the thing. Drake's back was against a wall with an inevitable mission that was not of his liking.

"Lieutenant," Drake said to Warren when the meeting was breaking up. He motioned for him to stay behind. XO glanced at Drake, wondering if his commanding officer wanted him to remain too. Drake sent him off with a shake of his head. He wanted to be alone with the man.

Markus left without a word, just another skeptical glance at his fellow escapee. Fredrickson mumbled his way out, and then they were alone. Drake squared with the fellow soldier. "How can you trust that man?"

"I had to, sir."

Drake asked him to elaborate. Warren shrugged. "After what I saw, I figured I didn't have any other choice. If I did nothing and he was lying, I'd die in that prison camp. If I did nothing and he was telling the truth, I'd die in that prison camp, and so would everyone else I care about.

"If I trusted him and he was lying, I'd die trying to escape. Better. Not great, but better. And, sir, if I trusted him and he was telling the truth, well, there was a chance I could live up to my duties as a soldier in this Fleet and protect everyone I care about. So, like I said, sir, I didn't really have a choice, did I?"

Drake nodded. *Damn.*

"If I may?" Warren asked, a request to speak freely. "I don't see how you have any other choice either."

———

"HE'LL USE it to jump past the minefield."

It was the last piece of the puzzle that Drake had been searching for. Although everything inside him was screaming that Markus, a man who'd turned his back on his own flesh and blood to embrace the Paragon ethos, could not be trusted, Drake's mind screamed just as loudly that this made sense.

It all made horrifying sense. The reports of Hadras' numbers were not wrong. He didn't have enough ships to take that minefield head-on. He simply had a way to get around it.

Drake turned to Admiral Jack, who was on the QE monitor, looking similarly disturbed. "That would mean Freepoint is far more vulnerable than we'd anticipated."

Drake nodded.

"It could also be a trap."

Drake nodded at that, too. "To what end?"

Jack was at a loss. "Your guess is as good as mine. Do you think this Markus can be trusted?"

Drake shook his head. Goddammit. "But I don't see how we can run the risk of ignoring this, sir." Warren was right. "If it is true, we have a window right now and only right now to head this off. I think we have to take it, Jack."

"Agreed."

"We can't leave Freepoint any less defended than she already is," Drake said, shifting into practical mode. How could they pull this off?

Jack furrowed his brow. "Also agreed. Proposal?"

"*Glory.*" It made sense in every way. With their jump capability, they were the only ones who could get deep into Paragon territory without being seen and quickly enough to meet the timeline given by Warren and Markus as to when the ship would be fully operational.

Jack nodded. "Permission granted."

"You don't need to check with the security committee first?"

That got a smile from the weary admiral. "I'm sure the formal request is around here somewhere, just waiting to be sent over."

"Of course, sir."

Jack grunted. "One other thing. The raid on Aexon Hub. Paragon took a QE codex. By the time you ship out, all our current codes will be compromised, including this one, and codices will have to be changed out Fleet-wide. But you can't wait. Go."

Drake nodded. That would mean no comm. A true blackout. Maybe that was for the better if they were to slip in and out undetected, which they would have to do if they hoped to survive such a mission. "That means Hadras is close," he added. A tried and true tactic from the old nemesis, taking away their comm. His attack was imminent, so the ship must almost be ready.

"Unless you can stop him first," Jack said.

"Yes, sir. Thank you, sir."

Jack would catch heat for this, especially if it went sideways. After the earlier meeting, Drake knew that for certain, given that the Federated Security Committee was so deeply involved. Might even cost the old spymaster his job, though Drake would believe that when he saw it. You didn't tangle with Jack and succeed. *You* walked away. Drake knew that very personally.

"And, Captain?" Drake focused on the admiral again. "*Don't* trust this Markus fellow. Keep your wits about you. Get to know him better and find out why he had a change of heart."

"Understood."

"Good luck." The transmission ended.

Drake tapped his wristcom and routed a call. "XO, report to my quarters, please."

CHAPTER FIFTEEN

CARROL WASN'T where she was supposed to be.

A hand slipped from her chest to her navel and gently rubbed there. It wasn't her hand. It pulled her closer to the naked body behind her, which formed a perfect half-circle to her own: bare thigh to bare thigh, stomach and chest to back, and a face that nuzzled into the nape of her neck. Carrol grabbed the hand and pulled it back up to her beating heart.

"You're hot, Pilot," she said.

"As in attractive?"

"As in fucking sweaty."

"I might point out I'm not the only one leaking heat at the moment, Pilot."

Carrol peeled away, threw off the sheets covering her, and turned to face her fellow furnace. Zed's face looked flushed from physical exertion. Her heart skipped a beat at the sight of him in that position, looking at her the way he was.

The two were in his quarters on Freepoint Station—the series of numbers she'd received on her wristcom. Most of the berths on *Glory* had been cleared out for refit. She'd tried to sleep; she really had. She had come straight here from the flight deck.

She'd laid still for all of five minutes before she couldn't take it and peeked her head out to see if there was anyone who'd see her sneak off. There hadn't been. All the onboard berths had been cleared out. Sneaking into Zed's had been a much riskier proposition, but if you put a towel over your head and looked like you had just come from the gym, nobody paid you any mind. He'd been waiting for her. Weeks since they'd last seen each other.

Carrol swallowed to collect herself, remembered what he'd just said, and arched a disapproving eyebrow. "Leaking?"

Zed's expression remained deadpan, but his eyes sparkled with a laugh. "I choose all my post-coital words very carefully."

"Oh, you do?"

"For maximum sexiness, yes."

"Of course."

"And pilot puns kill in present company."

"Pilot puns?"

Zed bit back a stupid smile and doubled down. "Absolutely. I regret to inform you that you are leaking heat *all* over the place." He made a circle with his fingers and held it over his eyes. He looked up and down with a serious frown. "Jesus fuck. IR scope is blown out, there's so much heat coming off you right now. You better come back to the barn."

Carrol tilted her head and squinted skeptically. "My . . . Is my body the delta wing in this scenario?"

Zed dropped his hand. "Obviously."

Carrol gestured to her chest and spoke in a mocking tone. "I suppose these are my landing lights?"

He frowned. "God, no."

"Oh?"

"Definitely not."

"Okay. Then what are they?"

Zed considered, looking down, then up to her eyes, then back down, ultra-seriously. "I, uh, those are . . . sensor—"

"If you say 'pods,' I'm going to punch you in the dick." He paused. She raised her fist. "See if I'm joking."

"I would never say those were pods."

"'Cause you sounded real close."

"Weapons turrets, maybe, but definitely not pods."

"*Turrets?*" She flung her fist toward Zed's nether region.

He blocked it just in time. "Boom! Cockpit shielding activated." Emphasis on the syllable one would expect.

Carrol laughed and swung her fist again. Not hard, but Zed didn't expect this one, and she got a satisfying groan from him. "Serves you right," she said righteously.

"Serves *you* right because *I* have checked the manual."

"Oh, you have?"

"I have. Cover to cover. Those...those are not in the manual, so you and I are definitely going to have a conversation about unauthorized upgrades."

Carrol scoffed. "Upgrades?"

"Big-time."

"I'm starting to think you don't know your way around a delta wing, Pilot."

"Okay, fine. I can tell you this because it *is* in the manual, which I have read cover to cover, remember. It very clearly states that this right here," he reached for her backside, "a hundred percent without a doubt is your tail!" He got a nice big handful and squeezed.

Carrol laughed out loud. Zed wrapped himself around her. She protested at first, pushing against him, then relented. She kissed him, felt him hold her, and then laid on his arm, staring into his face.

This was relatively new. It had started back on Earth during their blink of a shore leave before *Glory's* refit had picked up in earnest. Or rather, *re*-started. Carrol flashed back to seeing the lieutenant in the pilots' Ready Room for the first time, the recognition, and then Efremova, *Glory's* current command master chief, clocking it.

"*You two have history?*" she'd astutely asked. Carrol had said no, but that had been a lie. They did have history. Quite a bit of it, though it had long been dormant at that point. It wasn't dormant anymore.

Zed had reached out. Dinner? Why not? It's just dinner. Of course, it had been more than dinner that very night. It hadn't stopped once duty resumed, which was the riskiest part of all.

Back when they'd first tangled in the sheets, Zed and she had been equals—trainees in the same program. Fraternization was not allowed in the Fleet under any circumstances, but it happened all the time. Humans would always be humans with very human needs and desires. No reg was going to change that.

Discipline was usually reserved for the most egregious cases, which was what the two of them had become. Carrol was Zed's commanding officer. He reported directly to her. Oops.

As she gazed into his eyes, however, Carrol didn't care. Not even a little bit. "You make me laugh," she said, flushing as he held her tighter and his hands moved over her back. She gripped him in return.

Zed smiled. "That's good?"

Carrol nodded. It was very good. Better, even, than she remembered from back in flight school. Maybe the end of the world had something to do with it. Besides, it was just sex. It wasn't like it was serious. If things got hairy or compromised, they'd break it off. They'd talked about it.

Those were her excuses, anyway, for the sneaking around and the breaking of regulations, which she would never have dreamed of before. Not like this.

"The sneaking is good too though, isn't it?" Zed asked, reading her mind. Carrol didn't know how, but it wasn't the first time he'd done it. He used his free hand to push her hair back from her face, and she nodded.

It *was* fun. It was hot, in fact. And dangerous. It made her want him again. She kissed him. Just sex. The risk just made it better, that was all. Pilots lived on the adrenaline surge of risk. Easily explained. She melted, giving in.

Her wristcom chimed. Somewhere.

Carrol shot up, straight as a rod. Someone was calling her. "Shit." She scrambled from the bed and dove for the pile of clothes nearby, half hers, half his. But that was only underwear and socks. The rest of their attire was strewn from there to the door. Neither had made it far inside before the disrobing began.

Had she put the bracelet in her pocket? Carrol followed the trail, scrambling as it chimed again. It sounded even more urgent. Louder. Insistent after being ignored. "Shit!"

Zed got off the bed and helped in the search. Each chime from the tiny device sent Carrol's blood pressure through the roof, but it also helped zero in on where the damn thing was.

Zed found it in the sheets. Must have fallen off during their . . . activities. Carrol snatched it from him and slipped it on, hands shaking. "Carrol here," she said, trying not to sound breathless.

"Where are you?" It was XO. "Why are you on Freepoint?"

The wristcoms had location tracking; he'd said that when she landed. *Fuck.* "Just went for a walk, sir."

A pause on the other end. She wondered how much the first officer had looked into the data. If it was more than a cursory look, if he were to dig into its history, he'd see she'd been in the same set of quarters for the past . . . Damn, Carrol didn't even know how long she'd been there. What she'd just said was a lie, and it wouldn't take more than looking up the berth assignment for this cabin to figure out who she was with.

"Well, get your ass over here," XO finally replied. "Captain wants to put together a department heads meeting ASAP."

"I'm on my way."

The bracelet vibrated in her hand, indicating the voice call was over. She looked at Zed, who was sitting on the edge of the small bunk now. "You think he's suspicious?" she asked him. The other pilot shrugged. She stared at the offending bracelet. Damn. "He sounded fine." Maybe too fine, which was suspicious. *Damn.*

"What's going on?" Zed asked as she hurriedly put her uniform back on.

"I don't know. Probably something about our visitors."

"Visitors?"

"Two guys we picked up at Aexon Hub."

Zed waited for her to elaborate, then gave a knowing smile. "Can't tell me about it, huh?"

"Can't tell you what I don't know." Her clothes were back on now, sans boots. She stepped into the closet head and used TP to wipe off the crusty mirror so she could fix her hair, then shot him a look. "But yeah, Lieutenant. I couldn't tell you even if I did."

Zed shook his head and stood, then sauntered over to the doorway and leaned against it. "See," he said with a tilt of his head, "that's hot too, you know? Sleeping with the big shot."

Carrol pushed him aside and hid a smile. She grabbed her boots, sat on the edge of the bunk, and struggled to put them on. She swallowed. "We should stay away from each other. For a while."

"Sure."

She looked at him. His expression was unreadable. "Good."

"Good."

Carrol nodded, then bent to tie her boots. When she stood, Zed kissed her. It was deep, much more so than she'd expected. Sincere. She was flushed when he let her go. "All right then," she said and paused to catch her breath. "See you around."

"See you," he said.

She left abruptly, cheeks burning. Just sex, she told herself. *Just sex.* Right?

Damn.

CHAPTER SIXTEEN

"How are you doing in there?"

Assistant Engineer Sudan's voice echoed down the long maintenance tube. She was a pinprick of light several meters away. Idri grunted and repositioned herself to face that direction. "Slowly!" she shouted back.

This was all the result of what Sudan had called "being stir-crazy." Idri had shown up in the engineer's shared quarters two weeks earlier, complaining of headaches, anxiety, and a maddening combination of exhaustion and sleeplessness. She'd been to Sickbay complaining of the same, but Doc had patted her on the head in that infantilizing but still endearing way he treated everyone, no matter their rank, age, or gender, and told her she was fine. Stick to rest. Heal.

She felt fine, though. Healed already. So, it didn't work. There was only so much rest she could get, only so many thousand times a day Idri could practice her recitations or study the Tome. In desperation, Idri had gone to Sudan.

'You're clearly going stir-crazy!' the young engineer had said. An indecipherable phrase for a Navid, but Idri had decided to accept her assessment as well as her prescription. "Get out there and *do* something."

Fine, but what the heck to do? That was another human word Idri had picked up—heck. Sudan said it. Idri had noticed that much of *Glory's* human crew liked to curse with strong, abrasive language. She'd also noticed that Sudan preferred to stay away from such words. Heck, she'd been told, was a more archaic, less aggressive and offensive word to use.

Sudan had advice in the "what to do" department as well. Idri had no engineering or maintenance experience, but she and Sudan had seen that as a plus. Why not learn more about the ship? If you knew how to fix things, you'd never be bored on a starship.

Now, Idri was stuck in a maintenance tube barely larger than she was with a battery-powered melting and re-sealing tool in hand, trying to swap out a tiny circuit board no bigger than her palm. She was rethinking saying yes to such a thing. She wasn't claustrophobic, but she was cramped. That made it hard to work.

She'd cut the little hole too wide, outside the marked lines in the plastiform. Thankfully, upon inspection, it didn't appear as though her torch had damaged anything besides the circuit board she was trying to swap out.

Glory still used bolts, rivets, and screws on its metal components, as space- and seafaring vessels had for centuries, but much of the ship's interior structure was plastiform, a material that was far lighter than steel or even titanium but just as strong and very easy to heat, form, and then let cool with the right mixture of heat and electric current. Fasteners were hardly necessary, hence the torch.

She had the small circuit board out and was carefully

putting the new one in its place when Sudan called down again. "Idri. You'd better come out."

The Navid frowned. The call had startled her, and the circuit board was askew. "I've almost got it!" she shouted.

"Come on out," Sudan insisted.

Idri ignored her. Just a slight adjustment. The circuit board wouldn't budge from off-center. A couple well-placed nudges and a grunt or two, and the darn thing popped into place. "Darn." Another Sudan-word. "It's in!" Idri shouted gleefully. "Let me just close it back up, and I'll be right out!"

Idri held the plastiform cover in place, clicked on the torch, and began to seal it. Her original jagged lines disappeared as the plastiform re-molded, reverting to its stronger-than-steel room-temperature self after the torch passed over it.

It was almost impossible to burn yourself in the process unless you tried to. Amazingly safe. Pretty, too, after she was done. The cuts were gone and the panel was back in place, covering the swapped-out circuit. As far as she could tell, a job well done. Idri beamed in pride.

She carefully and meticulously returned the plastiform torch and the other tools she'd used to the small canvas roll-up wrap she'd taken them from. Sudan's wrap. These were her tools, but Sudan was larger-framed than Idri, which was why Idri had gone inside this maintenance tube.

Sudan would have fit since she was small enough to get anywhere she needed to go, but by her own admission, it wasn't comfortable. Idri'd jumped at the chance, and even after finding out just how tight and uncomfortable it really was, no regrets. She grabbed the tool wrap and shimmied back out of the tube. "All done," she said as she plopped onto the deck with a satisfying *thunk*.

Sudan was standing next to Commander Oh. Idri

frowned. *Uh-oh* was her kneejerk reaction. Had she done something wrong? No, the XO's expression wasn't scolding or upset. "Department Heads meeting," he said.

"Of course," Idri responded, still confused. They could have just rung her on her wristcom.

"Someone wanted to come say hi, however, at the first opportunity."

Idri's frown deepened, and XO pointed down the corridor. Someone was standing there, mostly hidden in the shadows. Like the maintenance tube Idri had just come out of, corridors in the lower decks were tight, and none were well-lit. She hadn't noticed a person standing there.

It was a man, a human, so tall he had to stoop in this section of corridor so as not to hit the low overheads when he stepped forward. The light finally hit his face, and Idri gasped.

"Warren!" she screamed. It was so loud that she startled XO, Sudan, and Warren, but Idri could not have cared less. She flung herself on the hulking soldier and hugged him hard.

Tears came to her eyes, and she didn't try to stop them as she held him. She lost it when he hugged her back, close and strong. He was real. It wasn't a mirage or a dream or a mistake.

"You're alive," she said finally, looking up at his face and doing her best to blink away the tears so she could see him. He was gaunt and far more haggard than Idri's memory of him. The past several months had clearly taken their toll on him. His eyes were kinder than she thought she'd ever seen them before. Grateful. He was happy to see her too, and that realization made her sob again as guilt slammed into her.

She'd left him on Corvus, her in a long-rage shuttle, him

standing on the fiery hangar deck of the dying *Ulysses*. He'd arranged it that way, sacrificing himself so she could escape the Paragon attack designed to stop her from reaching Earth and *Glory*.

The last thing she'd seen before completing her first-ever deep space fold had been his gleaming armor. His voice had been in her ears, telling her over the radio to go. Now. It had been a mistake. She should never have left him. She should have found a way.

His eyes were shining too, and he nodded. She didn't even have to say it. He knew. "It's okay," he said, and he hugged her as tightly as she held him. "It's okay."

Idri cried for a while. How long, she didn't know, and she didn't care. When she was done, she stepped back from Warren, still holding one of his giant arms. She wasn't going to let him go lest he turn into an apparition and dissolve. Irrational? He was solid and real, so why run the risk?

"I made your shirt wet," she said. Then she looked at XO and Sudan, who were still standing there in the cramped corridor, looking awkward. "I'm sorry."

XO smiled and shrugged. Sudan just beamed. Warren just shook his head. "It's not even my shirt."

Idri realized she'd never seen him without his armor. "Thank the stars you're alive," she said, still trying to wrap her head around it. "What happened? How did you escape and even find *Glory*? Where *is* your armor?" A million questions exploded into her mind, impossible to contain.

Warren held her back. "Slow down, kid. I promise you and I can sit down and talk about all of it." He smiled. "Short version, I'm alive, I'm happy to see you too, and we can catch up later."

Catch up. It meant explain. Sudan had taught her that one, too. "I have so much to tell you as well!" Her journey to the armory where *Glory* found her. Becoming a Navigator. Saving Earth. She grinned. "I almost died!"

"I heard that," Warren said, shaking his head but smiling despite himself. "I also heard you are supposed to be resting right now and healing from all that. What are you doing crawling around in the walls?"

Idri kept the grin and looked at Sudan. "Keep from going stir-crazy."

XO chuckled. "I feel that." He straightened and glanced at Warren. "Though we might all be relieved of idleness' burden sooner than we thought." He looked at Sudan. "I'm afraid I must pry our Navigator away from you, Crewman."

Sudan nodded curtly. "Of course, sir." It wasn't a formality one usually accorded to one of her rank and position, but XO was classy like that. It was one of the reasons everyone loved him, from enlisted to officer.

XO looked at Idri. "On the double, then. I'd imagine we're late already."

CHAPTER SEVENTEEN

"Is this really necessary, Captain?" Markus asked unpleasantly as Doc stuck a syringe gun to his neck. "We were screened once on the *Providence*, and then again when we landed here. Do you think we managed to pick up a Paragon mind-control parasite in the past couple hours?"

"This is a classified briefing," Efremova, *Glory's* command master chief and former head of security, called from the far end of the conference table. Her Russian accent was heavy with reproach. "You test, you *like* test, or you get out."

"It's necessary, Mister Markus," Drake said, biting back his own forceful retort. He gestured at Broussard, and the doctor pulled the trigger to draw the old man's blood. The capsule filled with inhumanly shining, red blood. Drake wondered if that would throw the test.

"Clean," Doc said a moment later when the capsule showed green. Apparently not.

It was Drake's turn next. He was the last one to be tested. He stood at the head of the conference table, which was filled to the brim down both sides with Doc, XO,

Markus, Warren, Carrol, Smith, *Glory's* new master-at-arms and head of security, Idri, Chief Engineer Fredrickson, DLC—which was short for "De La Cruz," the ship's flight deck officer—CAG, and Efremova.

Every seat was occupied. The gang was all there.

"Clean," Doc said when Drake's test came back green.

Good. Everyone was who they said they were. "Let's get right to it," Drake said. He dimmed the room lights as Warren rose from his seat and took up position at the far end of the table by the projector controls.

Images of the prototype ship, the interior and exterior of the facility, and Hadras' ship flashed by as he explained the situation they were in. Then he played the holoclip of the ship making its jump, which Drake still found uncomfortable to watch.

He'd seen it several times, and with each successive viewing, it made his skin crawl worse. There was something so off, so wrong with the way it shimmered. Even the light was wrong, but why, Drake couldn't put words to beyond "unnatural."

From the looks of the rest of the room, he wasn't the only one. Idri looked shaken, her pale-blue skin more ghostly than normal.

"I still don't fucking see how that's possible," Fredrickson muttered from his seat, hand on his chin, rubbing.

"We've tabled that discussion for now," XO reminded him as gently as Drake had ever seen him address the hothead engineer. The two of them hadn't liked each other from the jump in the Jupiter scrapyards *Glory* had been resurrected from, and not a ton had changed since then.

Or maybe it had. Fredrickson had no retort for the first officer, only gave a deferential nod.

"It doesn't matter anyway." Warren spoke from the front, eyes on Drake, and repeated what he'd told him during their last conversation.

"The Admiralty agrees with you," Drake said in response. "The possibility that the Paragon have developed an AI capable of folding space is not one we can ignore. The threat is to be considered real, clear, and time-sensitive."

There was an audible exhale from Warren. Even Markus slumped in his chair and rubbed his face in relief. Drake watched him carefully. It seemed genuine, as did the glance the old man shot him a moment later that clearly said, "Thank you."

Drake nodded, then addressed the room. "We've been ordered to the Vorkut system to deal with the prototype ship, which will be operational in . . ." He looked at Markus again.

"Days, now, surely. If it isn't already."

"This is Olle Markus," Drake said and indicated the old man.

He blinked at the mention of his first name, which Drake had only recently learned while digging through ancient Fleet records. He seemed surprised.

Drake noted that and moved on. "Mister Markus has been a Paragon prisoner for the past several decades and was a lead engineer on the prototype ship's artificial intelligence. He is to be considered the foremost authority on the craft."

The captain left out the collaborator part. He'd resolved that it was best to table *that* now that the decision had been made to take him at his word. Drake's crew took him at his and respectfully nodded at their guest.

"If I may," Efremova called from down the table, her

arms folded, and her Russian accent thick, "where did images come from?"

"I took them," Warren answered.

"How?"

"I bartered for an imager in the camp."

Efremova chewed on that. Drake could tell she was impressed. She indicated the prototype ship. "And how do we destroy that thing?"

"For that," Drake said, "The floor is yours, Mister Warren." He'd planned the next part.

"We're not," Warren said of the ship. "Our target is the facility where the AI is housed." He changed the projection on the wall to show the odd black cube in the center of the research complex. "Even then, we're going to see if it's possible to steal it rather than destroy it. If that's not possible, we'll blow the whole thing from there. Everything special about that ship is inside that cube. Take it out, and the ship is useless."

Drake's crew leaned in to get a better look at the mysterious object. Several of them muttered to each other. Carrol asked the most pertinent question. "How does one get inside?"

"They are folded inside," Idri immediately answered. She was still looking pale and was sweating. She turned to Markus, her big eyes wider than normal.

"That is correct," he said.

On Warren's slideshow, the image advanced to the pair he'd captured coming out of the cube. "It should be noted," Warren continued, pointing, "that QE is likely useless close to the device. Markus says it gives off considerable quantum interference."

"Short range radio?" Carrol asked.

Warren nodded. "Which is why we go down with a

shuttle rather than trying to call for one. But . . . even short range will likely be spotty. Those walls are thick."

The images Warren had taken in the corridor continued, meanwhile, to advance. Idri jerked up straight in her chair when she saw the figure being wheeled by the Paragon guard had enough fidelity to be recognized. "That's a Navid!"

"Also correct," Warren answered. "Not a Navigator, we think."

"No," Idri said with a shake of her head. "No they are not." Drake wasn't sure how she could know that from just an image, but there was no room for doubt in the way she'd said it.

"I'm not sure to what use," Warren said, "but there are Navid in the camp."

"You're not sure?" Carrol asked with a frown.

Markus interjected, getting her attention with a shake of his head. "I was only privy to the AI side of things. I never worked with the Navid prisoners."

"And I never had a chance to speak with any of them," Warren added.

"Just how many prisoners are there on that ice block?" CAG asked, speaking up for the first time in her signature drawl.

"I'd estimate two or three hundred," Warren answered, and he changed the image to an overhead view of the sprawling labor camp. "All different species, including humans."

"How are we planning to get in there?" Carrol asked.

Warren clicked his slideshow forward to a graphic of the Vorkut system. The moon was highlighted next to its gas giant, and just beyond that, a region of space was lit up.

But it wasn't space, was it? "Vorkut is surrounded by a

dense, active asteroid cloud. Markus and I actually hid inside it until the opportunity to leave through the gate presented itself. With a precise-enough jump, *Glory* can hide inside it too." He changed the image to a recording from their shuttlecraft showing a mess of tumbling rocks as far as the eye could see. Its haze blotted out the stars.

CAG let out a low whistle and looked at Idri. "You have your work cut out, young lady."

"I can do it," she said impassively.

"Great," Efremova said in a tone that indicated anything but. "We can jump in. But how can we possibly get to moon without entire Paragon fleet seeing us and pouring through gate?"

"Another gift from the asteroid cloud," Warren said. "Vorkut V is frequently inundated by meteor impacts, so much so that the penal colony has an automated defense system with which to shoot them down and/or deflect them."

CAG snorted. "Y'all are nuts," she said, and everyone turned to look at her. She was focused on Warren. "You want to ride one, don't you?"

Warren half-smiled. "Hollow one out, line it with crash metal, stow a shuttle and ops team inside, and send it down, yes."

"It could work," Fredrickson said, lips pursed and eyebrows raised.

"What about moon's meteor defense system?" Efremova asked.

"It's likely designed for common elements and compounds, not crash metal. We land, and they never know the difference."

"You mean crash," Carrol pointed out.

"Which is what the crash metal is for."

CAG chuckled and shook her head. "Like I said. Nuts."

"Small landing team," Warren continued, addressing Drake directly. "They'll pick their way from the crash site up and over the ridge, infiltrate the facility, and gain access to the AI cube. Then the shuttle flies in, picks them up, returns to *Glory,* and we jump out of here before Hadras and his ships catch us."

It was the first time the Paragon archgeneral's name had been mentioned in the briefing. Most of those in attendance didn't know who he was. Drake could see the name pass over them without a blink. A few did know the name. Doc, of course, plus Fredrickson and Smith. Those who were in the dark sensed from the others that it was a name that should be recognized.

Drake cleared his throat. "Archgeneral Hadras is an old *friend,*" he said with a wry smile. "He's the commander behind the AI project and someone to be taken quite seriously." He paused, then moved on. "Thank you, Mister Warren. The team will indeed be as small as we can make it." Drake addressed the rest of the room. "The Lieutenant here has indicated to me that's he's willing to forgo the discharge he is due in order to participate in this mission. I'd suggest you all take the opportunity to thank him for that, as I have." Drake turned back to Warren. "It'll be you, Mister Smith, an engineer of your choosing, Mister Fredrickson, one with expert data-extraction experience—"

"We're not taking this Markus guy?" Fredrickson asked with a raised eyebrow. "He obviously knows the AI far better than the best person I can send."

Warren cleared his throat and gave his fellow escapee an apologetic look. "The hike from our crash site to the facility will be rugged in the extreme. I'm afraid Markus wouldn't possibly make it in his physical condition."

It was a reasonable objection to the old man being with the landing party, but the truth was that Drake wouldn't have agreed to let him go, regardless. There was still too much to learn about him before he could be trusted like that.

Markus, for his part, only nodded in agreement. "I concur."

"You'll consult," Drake said, then continued the team list from where he'd left off. "CAG, choose me a pilot for the escape shuttle, and Commander Carrol, you will be leading the group." He glanced at Warren to see if there was any resistance to the last bit. "I hope you understand if we want one of our own in command."

If the soldier was upset, he didn't let it show. "Of course, Captain," he said, his voice perfectly measured.

"In addition to her piloting skills, she has ops experience, isn't that right, Commander?"

Carrol cleared her throat. "Uh, yes. That's right, sir."

Drake gave a small smile at the embarrassment. His Second Officer's resume was lightyears long. The classic over-achiever. If one didn't know the officer, one might think it was borderline indecisive. Drake knew better. Carrol wanted to be the best. She wanted to reach the very top. Command, and beyond. That was hard to do in the Fleet when you came from nothing and knew no one; she'd toiled in obscurity for a long time. Far too long. Until she came to *Glory*. He couldn't think of a better person to lead their team.

"Captain," Smith called, speaking up for the first time. "I'd like to request the addition of our Marine K9 to the team." He meant Cheddar.

"Considered on the team as soon as we decided to send

you," Drake said with a nod. The e-Marine nodded back, satisfied. That addition was a no-brainer.

Warren, however, looked unconvinced. "I'm sorry, captain, you're . . . referring to a dog?"

"I am, yes," Drake said. The dog had been found living on *Glory* in the Jupiter scrapyard. She was enhanced like Smith and just as deadly, and the two had become inseparable.

The K9s were the best early-alert and attack systems an ops team could get, and her recently-returning abilities—which had only continued to grow since what Drake had seen back on Earth—only increased her value. She alone would increase their chances of a successful mission two-fold. Drake explained as much to Warren.

"If you say so, sir," Warren said, still looking skeptical.

"What about getting inside the cube?" Idri asked, breaking in. "How are you getting folded in there?"

Warren looked to Markus, jaw working. "We're not exactly sure. Yet."

"I've never been inside myself," Markus admitted. "But I am reasonably sure the material from which it is constructed is crash metal or crash metal-like."

"The working theory is that we can burn through with a plasma cannon," Warren said.

Fredrickson whistled long and low. "That could take a while. Could the AI be tricked, perhaps, into jumping you inside?"

"Or that, though Markus is doubtful on that point."

"Sounds fuzzy," Carrol observed with a scowl.

"It's a risk," Warren admitted.

"An unnecessary one," Idri said with a shake of her head. "I can fold the team inside."

"Absolutely not," Drake said, and he slapped his palm flat on the conference table for emphasis.

"Agreed," Warren said. Idri snapped a surprised look at him. "It's too dangerous," he told her.

"Your greatest value," Drake continued, "is right here on *Glory*. Besides, you're going to need recovery time from jumping the ship."

"My recovery time has improved dramatically." She turned insistently to Doc, who was directly across from her. "Is that not true, Doctor Broussard?"

Doc had been deep in his thoughts, and the question surprised him. He cleared his throat, uncrossed his legs, and leaned forward. "Uh, that...that is true, but . . ."

"Captain," she said, returning to Drake. "I am the only guarantee for the team to get inside that cube and to get them out. Safely. Not to mention those are my people being held captive in that facility. That is where my greatest value is. I must be a part of the team. I must."

"You still can't jump in there blind," Warren reminded her.

Idri's nostrils flared in his direction. "So we use the cannon to burn a pinhole through. I'm assuming that would take a fraction of the time it would to create a doorway?"

"Sure."

Drake held up his hands to stop them both. "There's no need to discuss it," he said. "My answer is final."

"But, Captain!"

"The answer is no!" He slapped the table once more and stood. The room went silent. Drake took a breath to let the tension ebb, then turned to Warren. "You will have to find another way inside," he said evenly.

Warren nodded. There was an uncomfortable silence.

Doc cleared his throat. "Far be it from me to pile on," he

said with an apologetic smile to Drake, "but Idri does raise at least one, if not several, good points. This cannot just be a black ops mission to destroy or capture the AI. There are prisoners on that moon, suffering, just waiting to be collateral damage. Our plan must take them into account."

At the front of the room, Warren sighed heavily. "He's right," he said with a grimace. "I'm not particularly fond of many of them, but it's a foregone conclusion the Paragon will liquidate the camp whether we're successful or not, given it will have been compromised."

"Most certainly," Markus agreed grimly. "I'd imagine they'd abandon the facility and just leave them there to starve or freeze to death."

Goddammit.

Drake put his head down. He'd considered that and rationalized that they would have to swallow certain unsavory elements, like leaving some of the prisoners behind. It was too much to ask the team to take on one impossible target, let alone two.

That had been in his head. Here in this room, when he heard the voices he trusted the most, he knew he'd been wrong. They were right. They couldn't leave those people to die.

He raised his head. "Doc, you can coordinate a rescue plan with CAG and XO?"

Both of them nodded.

Drake's stomach was in knots. This was precarious. Far too complicated and extensive. For a black ops mission, that was a death sentence, but they would have to make it work. Had to.

"We must all keep the stakes of this mission in mind at all times," he said to his people. "If Hadras is allowed to complete this project and deploy the prototype ship, I am convinced he intends to bring it here to Freepoint and use it to jump past the minefield and take this facility."

The group gasped as that dawned on them.

"Virtually every defense strategy available to us here is predicated on the minefield. If we lose that advantage, Freepoint is lost, we can't make or repair our ships at scale, and the Paragon have a decisive upper hand. So . . ." He stood. "We must be successful."

There were nods all around. Good.

"We're underway in six hours. Disseminate to your departments accordingly. Mister Carrol, you and your team will train en route to Vorkut. Understood?"

Another round of nods.

"Dismissed."

The crew filed out of the room except for Markus, who lingered. When he was alone with Drake, he finally spoke. "You don't like me, do you?"

"I don't trust you."

"Reasonable. You don't know me." His eyes glittered in the low light of the conference room, still dimmed for Warren's holoimages, which remained up on the far wall. "You should, though," Markus continued. "I'm the only one who can help you."

"So it would seem."

A beat passed. There was something in the old man that felt familiar. It was the way he spoke infrequently, his haughty yet reserved demeanor, not tipping his hand in any circumstance, or giving any indication what he was thinking. It reminded Drake of the past, and the old soldiers of his youth. Scarred. Haunted. And tough. Their air of superiority was earned, mostly. They saw combat that few others had. The recognition was uncanny, and Drake's inability to read him, unsettling.

"Was there something else you wished to say?" Drake asked.

Markus nodded. "Let the Navid go on the mission. It will fail without her."

Drake gritted his teeth and flexed his jaw. "We'll see," he said, though that was the last thing he wanted.

CHAPTER EIGHTEEN

CARROL GRABBED the closest flight deck crew member she could find, which wasn't hard. There were hundreds of them running in every direction, easily visible in their jumpsuits. They were color-coded to their departments and bright enough to hurt your eyes if you looked at them for too long. An overstatement, that last bit, but they were damn bright by design. It *was* the flight deck.

The hubbub had ticked up by an order of magnitude since Carrol had last been there as *Glory* prepared to disembark from Freepoint. That *and* get the ball rolling on this rescue mission Doc had shoehorned them all into.

A steady stream of personnel transport craft lined up to land in *Glory's* main hangar, and teams of jump-suited crew tractored them over to the elevators for stowage in the smaller hangers and cargo bays on the lower decks. They'd have a fleet of them, Carrol realized. Made sense if they were to pick up several hundred POWs. That was not Carrol's concern.

"You seen CAG?" she shouted to the young man she'd snagged by his orange collar.

He pointed.

She was in the middle of the massive room, standing on top of a piled-high crate pallet with De La Cruz at her side, barking orders that were impossible to hear over the din of the landing spacecraft. She looked as happy as a pig in slop; she was in her element. Carrol nodded and let the crewman go.

"Excuse me, Lieutenant!" she yelled when she got close enough to the pile of crates for her voice to carry over the noise.

CAG looked down at her and grinned. She didn't get down, though. She yelled instructions to a group of multi-colored jumpsuits, leaned close to DLC and talked into his ear, then finally hopped down. "Project Airlift," she shouted with a grand wave at the whole affair.

Carrol nodded. "Impressive," she shouted back.

CAG smiled from ear to ear. "What can I do you for?"

Carrol swallowed. "I wanted to talk to you about the op. You're choosing a pilot?"

"Yes!"

Carrol swallowed again. "So, about that. I had some suggestions about who might be a good fit."

"Oh," CAG said with a laugh, "that's 'chosen,' Commander. Past tense." Carrol's face went slack. CAG patted her shoulder. "Knew you would be stressing about it, and I'm nothing if not efficient!"

"Um, who did you choose?"

"Lieutenant Zed! Figured you'd want the best, present company excluded, of course."

"Of course." Carrol struggled to keep her face neutral, worried she was failing miserably.

"What do you think?" CAG pressed, hands on her hips. She was proud of herself.

"Yeah," said someone behind Carrol. She turned to see Zed. Naturally. "What do you think, Commander?" he asked, a rakish smile on his face. He was in coveralls, though they were a dull blue, made duller by the grease that covered him from head to toe. "Already working on our own little transport," he said by way of explaining his appearance. "One of the new Class-7 armored shuttles. Should be a fast little fucker."

"I think that's great," Carrol said, putting on the happiest look she could muster. She did not think it was great. The entire reason she'd come down to talk with CAG had been to avoid this, but she was too late. Raising a ruckus about it now would draw more attention and prompt questions. "I'm looking forward to having the lieutenant on the team."

Zed just smiled at her. Damn him.

"Well, you're welcome," CAG said.

"Thank you." Carrol indicated Zed. "Mission training is on Deck Twenty-two, Gamma cargo hold, twelve hundred hours. Don't be late."

"I'll be there," he said with an unnecessary salute.

Carrol left before either of them could see her expression crack. She could feel Zed's, CAG's, and everyone else's eyes burning into her as she walked, or that's what she imagined. Impossible to tell.

Great.

So much for staying away from each other. So much for keeping it on the down low. This was why fraternization was frowned upon. She was losing, and she hadn't even started playing this new and dangerous game yet.

WARREN LUXURIATED in his giant quarters. A few months ago, he would have considered them to be small. Older ships like *Glory* were spacious in many ways but cramped in others. Crew bunks and quarters fell into the latter category, and this ship was no exception.

However, terms like "giant" and "small" were relative and depended upon perspective. Warren had just spent weeks in a single-cabin shuttlecraft, which meant every-thing—*everything*—was done in the full view of another human being. For weeks. In deep space.

To Warren, this five-square-meter bunk with a retractable head and step-in shower was the Taj Mahal. He'd used both minutes earlier in that order and felt like a king.

It was a boon that Captain Drake had taken them seriously. He had no doubt it was his sway that had the Admiralty approving this mission. And although returning to that icy hellscape made his stomach knot, that had been the point of his and Markus' escape from the beginning.

Just being around other humans buoyed him, as did real, solid food. In the trash bin under his bunk was a protein and rice bowl that had real chicken in it, which he hadn't tasted since the *Ulysses*.

He looked in the mirror and straightened, still just in his towel. He was damn thin. He'd have to work on that. But he didn't look like he was dying anymore, and that was progress.

There had been times, particularly in the long spaces between their last few gates toward Fleet space, that Warren had wondered if they were going to make it, he and Markus. Boredom, darkness, and starvation had threatened the two of them physically and mentally. The latter had been the most dangerous. Those times had included moments of madness. Despair. And so much silence. One of Warren's biggest worries was that he wouldn't be able to handle the noise of civilization if they made it back. That after all the silence, it would be too much.

It wasn't. The noise was a welcome relief. Thank God, it felt like home. He turned away from the mirror, satisfied with the reminder that he was alive. The silent darkness had not consumed him.

He was half-dressed when he heard a knock on his cabin's hatch. "Just a second," he called and reached for a uniform undershirt to cover his torso. It left him barefoot but otherwise covered. He opened the hatch.

Idri stood in the corridor.

"Idri," Warren said, surprised. "What are you doing here? Shouldn't you be in the fulcrum, preparing for our first jump?"

"That is not for several hours," she replied, and Warren detected no small amount of edge in her tone. "May I enter?" she asked. "I would like to speak with you."

"Sure," he said and stepped back from the hatch to allow her to come in. He closed the door behind her, then stooped to pick up his towel and the previous set of clothes, which were still on the floor. "Took a shower," he mumbled as he tossed them onto the bunk, then sat next to them. Damn, he could use a nap. He wondered how he was going to sleep on *Glory*. Sleep on *Providence* had been spotty.

"Do you think I'm a child?" Idri asked with a blink of her oversized eyes.

Warren blinked back. "What?"

"A young human. Is that what you think I am?"

Warren didn't follow. "No?"

"I am aware that my features, such as the ratio of my eyes to my head, in addition to my stature, are similar to those of a young human. Relatively speaking, for a Navid, I am certainly in the earlier years of my lifespan, as well as relative newness of my position on this ship as Navigator, but I am not a child."

She was upset. Clearly. And she wasn't a child, even if she looked to be around nineteen. Idri was older than most of the crew on this ship in non-adjusted years. The average age of a spacer in the Fleet was twenty-five, and Idri was forty-two in Earth years. In Navid years, adjusting for their lifespan in comparison to humans', she was closer to twenty-three, but her point stood. She was not nearly as young as she appeared to be.

Warren decided to choose his words carefully. "I am aware of all that."

Her nostrils flared. "Then why do the officers on this ship, you included, treat me like one?"

Warren was at a loss for words.

"I am a full member of this crew," she pushed on. "I have proven myself in battle, just as you predicted I would all that time ago when we were together on *Ulysses*. I helped save Earth. I have proven myself at every turn thus far, and still, even when I can be of assistance, I am sidelined."

Well, goddamn. She was spitting fire. Making sense, too, not like the adolescent backbone that had been so grating to Warren on the *Ulysses*. She was different now. It was plain to see. There was gravitas in the way she spoke, an assuredness and confidence that hadn't been there the last time he'd spent much time with her.

And a larger vocabulary. "Where'd you learn a term like 'sidelined?'" he asked.

Idri's nostrils flared again. "Assistant Engineer Sudan has taken it upon herself to teach me a certain amount of

Fleet lingo. I would remind you as well that just because I am still learning Standard, it is no indication of my maturity or lack thereof. Just as I would not consider you to be an idiot for not being fluent in Navid."

Touché. And still spitting that fire. He folded his arms over his chest. "It's not up to me," he said, understanding what this was really about. "Okay?"

Idri pressed. "Does that mean you concede I am right? That I should be a part of this landing team?"

Warren didn't answer. He didn't need to. Idri took it as a yes, which it was.

She nodded and defiantly straightened, then delivered her ultimatum. "Then *you* need to convince Captain Drake to let me go."

GLORY'S COMMAND deck was the heartbeat of the ship. All one had to do to get a sense of what shape she was in—if she was strong or wounded, sleeping or awake, bored, quiet, or loud—was to step up to the center console and listen. Every sound, every reverberation on every deck from stem to stern, could be heard or felt there.

In the Jupiter scrap heap, filled with mothballs, she'd been deathly still. Drake remembered wondering if she'd ever move again, but even then, at that moment between oblivion and resurrection, Drake could feel it. There was something there, dormant but waiting.

She was fully awake now. Bright-eyed and bushy-tailed. The command deck had its own cacophony, but what Drake found most reassuring as he ran his hands over the center console was how alive the entire ship felt. It was now filled to the brim with a seasoned crew.

There had been challenges in that, given that this would be their first underway together, but retention had been high from their last cruise. Drake's Dogs, as the holdovers called themselves, would initiate and train the newcomers. The process would be much smoother, led by XO, who'd done that many times before. Drake could feel that too from the way the ship sounded. Her crew was happy to be there. Excited.

She had been retrofitted from bow to stern, which was Fredrickson's domain. Everywhere Drake looked, he saw upgrades. Many were grafted onto the old structure, so the fits weren't seamless, and their brand-new shine was contrasted in several places with *Glory's* patinaed bones, but that would mellow in time and become seamless. The point of a refit wasn't to make a new ship; it was to keep an old one going.

Drake's real pride, however, was in the crew. What had once been a scrambling mess of stressed-out, overworked, undertrained, and overwhelmed kids was now a seamlessly functioning unit. Everyone strode with purpose. It was loud but never overly so. No panicked shouts, no clueless cries for help or frustrated profanity. It was professional and practiced, with the appropriate quips and verbal jabs that came when a crew was tight.

"Quite the improvement, eh?" XO said, stepping up next to Drake. "Been drilling with this A shift all month. Chomping at the bit to show you what they can do, Cap." The first officer tapped the command console, which had a two-dimensional display of *Glory* as seen from each of her three axes. Alongside each view were status indicators for systems, crew, and supplies. "I reckon she feels just about the same way."

All systems were green. Power, engines, armor, weapons

and defense, environment, structure . . . It was almost enough for Drake to forget how dangerous the mission ahead was and soak it all in. *Glory* was a proper warship again, and arguably in the best shape she'd ever been in. Ready to knock the piss out of anyone who crossed her.

"You and Mister Fredrickson have done a bang-up job," he told him.

XO shifted his weight and gave an "aw, shucks" shrug. "Freepoint had a big hand in it too, sir," he said, deflecting as was his way.

Drake gripped the edge of the command console. "Glad to see they left this one, though." That console had been there since Drake first took command decades earlier. Through all their battles, repairs, refits, and mothballs, that one piece of equipment had stayed put and working. He couldn't recall if he'd told XO to make sure it stayed. He probably hadn't. It was one of those things he implicitly knew the first officer understood.

"Of course, sir," XO said with a serious nod. "Heart of the ship right there."

"I'd agree," Drake said.

"New innards, of course," XO added, giving the bottom part of the console a soft kick. "Fredrickson couldn't help himself. I think you'll enjoy the new holoprojectors, though, and a much better tie-in with our new computer."

Drake smiled. That was fine by him. *Glory* felt the same, and that was what mattered. "Status, Mister Oh?" he said, straightening and calling XO by his surname. He allowed his voice to carry, which had the effect of bringing a hush to the command deck.

"All systems reporting go, Captain," Oh responded, allowing his voice to do the same.

Motion in the room stilled, then crew members settled

seamlessly into their assigned positions. The air was expectant, poised. Ready. "Take us out, Commander," he ordered with a satisfied nod.

XO swelled his ample chest and bellowed, "Ship the gangways, secure from external power, seal the locks. Damage Control to stations. Report green when secure for movement."

With practiced chatter, his commands translated to the various stations on the command deck, and a chorus of voices swelled to forward those commands to the appropriate locations throughout the ship. Drake could feel the minute vibrations as the exterior gangplanks and causeways were removed and the hatches closed off from the drydock. He also felt the deep thrum as Engineering began the final spin-up of their core, readying to be cut from their power umbilical, and propulsion systems were primed and ready to take over once the ship was released and moved into the void of space.

Communications relayed their departure readiness to Dock Control, and the response was, "Go." With a series of heavy thunks in quick succession, *Glory* was released from Freepoint Station's magnetic clamps. Inertial compensators kept the deck from dipping with the movement, but the telltale flicker of the lights as her power core took over all systems told Drake they were free. *Glory* was once again whole, a self-contained world.

"Helm, ahead one-quarter maneuvering," the XO said matter-of-factly.

"Ahead one-quarter maneuvering, aye," Helm returned. Drake could see it was a familiar face. Shannahan. They'd battled the Paragon planet-killer together. Helm had high retention. It was good that they'd kept the young man. He slid *Glory* out of the drydock like she was butter.

"Free and clear," the young man called with a glance at the command station. He was proud of himself. Drake gave him a slight nod of recognition that said he felt the same. Within minutes, they glided into the minefield, ready to slowly work their way through the complicated, ever-changing maze. It had been effortless. What a contrast to the last time they'd left drydock.

"We'll be through to the gate in just under an hour," XO said, his voice lowered for only Drake to hear.

The captain nodded. Good. From there, they'd burn under full power to their first jump point.

Then they were on their own.

UNCLAIMED SPACE

CHAPTER NINETEEN

"To the right, to the right!"

Warren's insistent shouts hurt Carrol's ears, and they were unnecessary. Their person-to-person comm was state-of-the-art. It could pick up sub-vocalizations with ease and project them with sufficient volume to be heard with ambient noise interference over a hundred decibels. Screaming into the radio was unnecessary.

Granted, Carrol *had* missed her fucking turn.

The corridors of the Paragon facility stretched before her, dark and still. They, unlike Warren, were quiet. For now. Carrol knew it wouldn't last. "Your shouting isn't going to help my memory," she hissed back at a more reasonable volume as she doubled back down the corridor and went left the right way at the crossing. "Nor is it going to help us stay away from Paragon troopers."

"The alarm has already been raised," Warren shot back, though his voice was lower in volume now. "They're going to find us anyway."

He wasn't wrong about that, and Carrol's little blunder had just cost them precious seconds. The cube room was close. Warren was there already, but he and Sudan, the engineer Fredrickson had selected as their data-extraction specialist, had been separated from Carrol, Smith, and Cheddar when they'd scrambled to avoid a group of Paragon guards. And Warren only had half their plasma cannon.

"Hurry!" Warren said. He was back to shouting.

"I am!" Carrol shouted back. *Fuck this all upside-down and backward.* He was right. With the alarm raised, an unfortunate consequence of their security run-in, it was no mystery to the Paragon where they were headed. That was the assumption. There was only one thing in this facility that really meant anything: that AI and the cube it was in. It was a race.

Cheddar barked from somewhere. Carrol whirled in mid-stride to see a handful of Paragon skid into the corridor behind them, weapons already firing. "Your six!" Carrol shouted to Smith, but he was already returning fire from the pair of shoulder cannons built into his Marine armor. He didn't even have to turn around.

A sharp kinetic sting to Carrol's shoulder twisted her into the corridor wall, and she stumbled. Smith caught her and kept her from falling. Carrol's momentum was halted, however, so she took the opportunity to squeeze off several shots from her plasma rifle . . . and missed. Three remaining Paragon troops bore down on them, and with deadly accuracy, they shot out Smith's shoulder cannons. Carrol and Smith shuddered as the weapons exploded, momentarily blinding them.

Bolts of plasma ripped through the space around them as the Paragon closed. Carrol fired back. It was blind, but so were they. Maybe she'd get lucky. Her vision cleared, and she knew she hadn't been. The three troopers were only a few dozen meters away, aiming for a kill shot. It was over.

'And then it wasn't.

Cheddar, the crazy beast, appeared out of nowhere, dropping her invisibility and pouncing. She took the nearest trooper by surprise. Its white blood splattered the corridor, then turned a smoking black. Wordlessly, Carrol sighted on one of the remaining troopers, and Smith did the same. They fired in almost perfect unison, and the last two troopers fell.

Damn right. They were clear again. For the moment. Carrol didn't know how, but Cheddar had bailed them out. There wasn't time to dwell on it, only to keep moving. It wasn't until she felt another sharp sting in her leg, however, that Carrol realized she had another problem. She looked down. "Goddammit," she said. She'd been hit in the knee. Her shoulder too, but the real problem was the leg.

"I'll carry you," Smith said, dipping his shoulder to grab her behind the knees.

"No," she said, wriggling him off. She tore her pack off her shoulders and handed it to him. "You run," she commanded. "With this." It was the other half of their plasma cannon. "Go," she insisted, pulling herself up on her damaged leg. Goddamn, it hurt. "I'll be right behind you."

The giant Marine obeyed, and his dog was right behind him. "I'm sending Smith up ahead," she called and grunted in pain as she tried to walk. She got static back, then winced when the Paragon battle cry screamed over the channel at a volume that would make Warren's shouting pale in comparison.

She shut the radio off. It was useless now. Carrol just had to hope Smith and Cheddar would reach Warren in time to set up, burn a hole through the cube, and get inside.

Extracting the AI was off the table now. To be honest, so was blowing the thing up. There were weapons out there with sufficient force and energy to melt or smash crash metal, but you couldn't carry them, so Carrol and her team didn't have them.

They had the conventional kind that had to be placed *inside* the cube if they were to do any damage. As Carrol limped down the corridor, praying her team would have time to punch that hole through the cube, she knew it was a foolish hope. They were screwed.

She was right. When she finally arrived at the cube, Smith and Warren were frozen on the floor. Cheddar and Sudan were nearby, also frozen. The plasma cannon lay next to them, not fully out of the carrying pouches. They'd failed.

Again.

Carrol let out a frustrated half-shout, half-curse, ripped off her headset, and punched the reset button on her wrist-com. Her view returned to the dark, dank lower decks of *Glory*, and her paralyzed team members unfroze. Smith and Warren both sat up wordlessly, though Warren ripped his headset off in frustration. The Marine was the picture of calm. Down one of the side corridors, she heard Sudan groan.

Over the radio, which was independent of the headset, a final voice joined the pity party. "At least your time was down, guys," Zed called apologetically. "A little." But not enough. The pilot was in their makeshift huddle room, running the simulation, recording it, and keeping time for the after-action review. So much had gone wrong, like it had every time they'd done a practice run thus far.

From memory, Warren and Markus had programmed the layout of the research facility into the training simulator.

They'd determined the lowest-risk and highest-efficiency routes to the AI cube and selected portions of the lower decks that matched them the closest. Add the fancy new holographic processing capabilities of *Glory's* upgraded central computer, and it looked like the real thing when you put those headsets on. Felt like the real thing too, given the simulation suits they were wearing under their normal gear. Electric shocks when you got hit that paralyzed your muscles to simulate loss of mobility, including locking you up if it was a mortal wound.

The training was as immersive and realistic as they could make it. That wasn't the problem. The problem was that they were getting their asses handed to them.

"Perhaps holding the lieutenant back at the crash site with the shuttle is unwise," Smith offered. He was sitting up, with Cheddar panting next to him.

"And blow our only route of escape?" Warren asked with a shake of his head.

"Agreed," Carrol said. It was too early to call this a suicide mission. Whatever their fortune, good or bad, while they got into the facility, there would be no hiding or surprise after they blew the cube. The only way to survive was a very quick exit, which was why the plan was for Zed to stay at the crash site with their escape shuttle primed and ready to fly in and pick them up the second they got free. Take that away, and it was curtains.

No, they had to find another way, or at least try.

"Another mission failure," Warren said, standing with a groan.

"The commander took a wrong turn," Smith said honestly.

Carrol shook her head. *Thanks, bud.* He was right,

though. "Not sure, in the end, how much that cost us, but I did. And it did. And here we are, all dead."

"Cost you sixteen seconds and five points of success probability," Zed said over the comm.

Carrol sighed. "You capture the whole run?"

"That's what you pay me for, Commander," he quipped.

"Then roll back the tape. We're coming to you."

Exhausted, her team gathered their gear, including their fancy holosim helmets, and trudged back to the starting line, where Zed was waiting to show them the tape of their last failure. Maybe they'd see something obvious that had gone wrong. Maybe cleaning up those measly five percentage points of mission success would push them over the line next time. Maybe Cheddar's newfound magic trick would come in handy. Carrol wasn't sure, and she still had a sinking feeling in her gut. She looked at Warren, who'd fallen into step beside her, and they locked eyes. He had the same sinking feeling. She could see it in his expression, plain as day.

This wasn't working, and it wasn't *going* to work.

CHAPTER TWENTY

WARREN FOUND Idri practicing in the fulcrum. Preparing. She was focused in the extreme, hands on the pitch-black globe in the center of the roughly spherical room. She didn't hear him until he let out an impressed grunt as he took in the surroundings.

It was dead quiet. Not quite the bottom of the ship since it would be foolish to place a vital facility close to the outer hull where it could be easily destroyed. It was buried in the loud-machinery areas of the lower decks, but you could hear none of that once inside. Warren wondered if it was the shape of the room that did it or special insulation.

And the stars... Good God, you could *see* them, particularly as you got closer to the center of the room. The walls seemed to disappear. Warren tilted his head back and forth, shuffling his feet at the same time. It didn't look like holograms, either. These were the stars as they appeared outside *Glory*.

"It's a complex series of light tubes and reflective channels, all of which are aligned to concentrate here at the fulcrum," Idri said. She was now watching him.

Warren nodded. Made sense. "I remember you telling me that you needed to see the stars in order to jump." That felt like so long ago. A lifetime. There was no anger there, however, or regret. Warren had meant every ounce of what he'd told Idri when he saw her again. It was okay that she'd left him behind. It had been necessary, which was why he'd set it up not to give her a choice. What he felt as he stood in this large room that touched upon infinity was pride. And gratitude. And perhaps an apology.

Idri could sense that; he could tell. "You want to ask me something," she intuited.

Warren nodded.

Idri folded her arms, more the adult than Warren remembered or expected. She waited.

"Can you shoot?"

She blinked. "I . . . have not." Navid were pacifists. That was well-known.

"Well, you're going to need to be able to shoot if you're on the team."

Her eyebrows shot up. "*Am* I on the team?"

Warren shook his head. "But if I'm going to convince the captain that you should be, you're going to have to be able to defend yourself." When Idri frowned, Warren pressed. "Is that going to be a problem?"

She straightened, hardening. "No."

Warren nodded. *Okay, then.*

GLORY'S FIRING range had seen better, more-polished days, but it would do the job. There was rust on the metal-grated floor, and the crash metal that lined their bay was pitted and graying at the seams, but it was intact, floor-to-ceiling. One could use any portable weapon here, miss wildly, and be in no danger of damaging the ship. That was all they needed.

Warren had checked out several weapons from the armory. They were arrayed in the bay he currently shared with Idri. The metal walls on either side and the hip-height shelf in front of them smelled of fresh paint and sparkled pure white. It was lipstick on a pig in contrast to the rusty floor, but *Glory's* refit had reached even here. Warren grabbed a hand pistol. "Let's start you with this."

Idri looked at the gun and frowned. "Is that what your team will be using?"

"No." It was too small to inflict much damage in a real firefight, nor could it carry enough of a charge. It *was* small and easy to use, which was why he'd picked it.

Idri was having none of that. "Give me what the team will be using."

Warren chewed his bottom lip, then set the pistol down and picked up one of the assault rifles. It wasn't the heaviest or the biggest, but those weren't desirable traits when they'd be hiking over a mountain range and speed was of the essence. "This right here should do the trick."

Idri took the weapon and its weight surprised her. Her arms sagged. To her credit, she recovered quickly and glared off his help. She was roughly holding it correctly, with the stock toward her shoulder, one hand near the trigger and the other on the base of the barrel. Okay. Warren told her to sight on her target, which was a hanging plastiform plate ten meters out. She lifted the stock to her shoulder, placed a finger alongside the trigger, aimed the barrel toward the target, and lowered her face to the side so her eye was along the sight.

Warren raised his eyebrows, which Idri caught and gave him another glare. "I have been studying," she said.

"I can see that."

He only had a few corrections for her, a nudge on her elbow to keep it close to her body, a tilt to keep the barrel on a straight line. Back the chin up a bit and widen the stance. Idri was a good student. She took each adjustment in stride and listened perfectly.

"Keep your eye a bit away from the scope," Warren counseled. "This is an energy weapon, but the plasma releases are mechanical, so it kicks. You keep creeping up close like that, and you're going to get a black eye."

"Understood," Idri responded.

"Loosen up. Your shoulders are starting to bunch."

"It is heavy." It was. She'd have to build up her strength over the next few days.

"I'm supposed to hit that circle ahead?" she said, indicating the target with a stare.

"Yup. You see the little display inside the sight?"

Idri squinted, closing one eye so only the other was looking into the scope. "I do." This rifle had a powered scope with a holographic overlay and target recognition and tracking. The latter wasn't on yet. Warren wanted to see how she did with her own eyes.

"Use that to find the target."

"Okay."

"Keep your eye back from that scope."

"Okay."

"Get the middle right in your crosshairs, right in the middle where the two lines cross."

"Okay."

"Then, when you're ready, when you feel steady and it's right in the center, move your finger to your trigger, exhale, and squeeze."

Idri fired. The recoil of the weapon nearly knocked

her over. The shot went wild, a white-hot streak of plasma that buried itself in the ceiling a few meters away. Flushing, Idri refused Warren's help to steady herself and re-gripped her rifle. Her knuckles were whiter than the rest of her skin as she clutched it. Her nostrils flared in frustration.

"You need to hold the rifle," he said gently. "Not crush the thing." She nodded, let out a quick, short breath, and adjusted her grip. Her knuckles regained some color. Good. "Take your time this time."

"Will I be able to take my time during the mission?" she asked through gritted teeth as she lowered her head to again sight on the target.

"No," Warren answered honestly. "But first things first. Learn how to fire with accuracy. You just saw what firing wildly accomplishes."

Idri fired again. This time, there was a resounding *ping* that echoed over the range as a plasma bolt sheared off the edge of the plastiform target. It wasn't the center, but it was an improvement. Idri let out a surprised whoop and grinned at Warren. A decent shot. Warren tried to hide that he was impressed by grunting, but he knew he'd failed. *The kid picked things up quickly*. He reminded himself that she wasn't a kid.

Warren paused to consider their next step before asking her for the rifle and clicking a switch on its side, then handing it back to her. "Okay. Let's try with the auto-targeting on, then."

Idri raised the rifle to her chin and frowned. She was seeing much more in the scope than crosshairs now. If it was working properly, the scope was picking up the objects around them: the walls, the floor and ceiling, wind direction and intensity numbers that were zero in the range, plus distance, temperature, and the target hanging down the range.

Warren asked her if the target had an orange box around it. Idri confirmed it did. "Sight it in the crosshairs, then give the trigger a half-squeeze to confirm target lock. You'll feel it give a little click and then resist a bit more. Keep it right there. Helps to not fire by accident before you have a target selected."

Idri did as she was told and squeezed halfway. "The box is green now."

"Good. Move to get the crosshairs green, then fire. Squeeze the trigger all the way. Don't jerk it."

Idri hesitated, moved back and forth, then fired. The shot went slightly wide. She gave a frustrated grunt and lowered the weapon. Warren was about to encourage her by telling her to try again and try to relax when Idri let out another sharp exhalation, raised the rifle, and took a deep breath. On the exhale, she let her body relax, most notably her shoulders, gave the trigger a half-squeeze, and then with a small, fluid correction in her aim, pulled the trigger back.

A plasma bolt erupted from her rifle, streaked down the range, and punctured the plastiform target dead center. A perfect shot. Idri whooped again and lowered the rifle with a giant sigh of relief and pride.

This time, Warren didn't try to hide that he was impressed. "Good shot!" She'd picked it up very quickly, and she had a lot more fight in her than he would have imagined. Maybe this would work.

Maybe. Speed was her friend, but strength wouldn't be. She wouldn't be able to hold the rifle up for long. Lift, acquire, lock, fire. Lower and move. Save her strength for the next target.

He stepped out of their firing bay and fiddled with the

range controls. Downrange, the available targets shuffled. He selected three of them this time and set the closest two in motion. One swung back and forth from the ceiling, and the other did the same and also moved up and down. Idri frowned.

Warren gave a knowing chuckle. "Now, let's see how you do with something that moves."

CHAPTER TWENTY-ONE

In deep space, the one thing that could hold a candle to the importance of faster-than-light travel the gates offered was their ability to let the Fleet *see*. Nearly as much as the network of portals let ships, personnel, and goods flow among the stars, the gates allowed one to know what in the hell was going on out there. Where there was a gate, there were eyes, and where there were none, it was dark.

Long-range scopes, long-distance probes, and all manner of infrared, ultraviolet, gamma ray and gravity wave, and dark matter-detecting sensors existed too. Even though such technologies had been around for centuries and had been improved to look farther into the universe around them, much could be missed at such great distances. Especially small things on the cosmic scale, like a waiting warship or several of them.

Such were Captain Drake's thoughts as *Glory* approached the gate that would take them beyond the Fleet network. Out here, on the edge of the Fringe, everything was automated, even the gates. The one they were about to pass through was so remote it didn't even have a name, only the designation EX447. It would take them from the Perseus system to a star that likewise had no name, EX447-Alpha. Very creative.

Whoever had come up with the cold, calculating catalog system ought to be commended. It matched the mood of being there in person.

An automated gate had scopes and was tethered to the same QE network as a manned gate. If anything odd showed up on those scopes or its sensors, it was recorded and instantly sent to the rest of the Fleet. However, automated scopes searched in deliberate programmed patterns and had unavoidable blind spots. They were woefully incomplete, and they could be fooled. A blind gate was always dicey, and they put Drake on edge. He'd rather just jump since that had the element of surprise. Gating, like automated scopes, was predictable.

"Status?" Drake asked XO for the dozenth time in the past ten minutes. He fidgeted with his uniform jacket for probably the same.

"Still five by five," the first officer answered. "Shall I tell Helm to slow?"

Drake shook his head. He could detect no reason for them to delay. "Just keep Tactical on alert."

"Of course, sir."

There wasn't any reproach or annoyance in Oh's voice. His response was entirely deferential and professional. It was a magical quality he had, the presence of mind and trust in his commanding officer to follow orders without question or fatigue when they were the *right* orders.

He also questioned or pushed back when they were the *wrong* orders. Drake trusted his XO without reservation. It made their command of the control room frictionless and often impenetrable to outsiders since much was communicated without words. Oh knew Drake was anxious, but it was the right mindset. Justified, given the danger of the unknown ahead of them. Why fight it?

Drake took a deep breath. "Thank you, Commander," he said, though no thanks needed to be given. "Take us in."

"Helm," XO called with a single nod of acknowledgment. His eyes had not left the command console and the course that was displayed there. *Glory* on approach to the gate. "Adjust z up point-three degrees and slow to one-half."

It was the perfect adjustment. *Glory* hit the gate nose-first and dead center. As the command deck passed through the membrane, Drake felt the nausea that accompanied gating. Doctors and physicists had debated for a century if that microsecond was even detectable or whether the sensation was a placebo effect or the body responding to the space-time rending process that was taking place.

Drake felt it every time. Most people did. It wasn't pleasant, but it passed quickly. *Glory* was now on the other side, several dozen light-years from their previous position. They were in the EX447-Alpha star system.

"Tactical," Drake called the second they were free and clear. "Anything?"

The ship was on alert. A fighter squadron flew escort, weapons primed, propulsion engaged, and the ship's every scope and sensor was looking in every direction for the slightest movement. They were days from another Fleet ship. Out on the Fringe, maddeningly close to the Paragon space's border, they were truly alone.

It wasn't just the Paragon out here, either. It was pirates and unallied races. Anyone with the means to look for the opportunity to take what they wanted. The Fringe was wild and blind.

"Nothing, sir," one of the tactical department heads

called. They were pacing behind the several manned stations feeding real-time information from various parts of the ship.

Drake nodded. It was from just outside this system that they would jump. There was a dark matter nebula a few hours away at full burn they would hide in, then have Idri take them to their next jump point. If they were spotted by the Paragon or anyone else, it would be in transit there.

"Take us into the polar magnetic field," Drake said to XO, referring to the green gas giant that powered the gate they'd just emerged from, "and hold there." He wanted to get a good long view of the system before they went elsewhere.

They'd been in high orbit for less than ten minutes when Navigation reported an anomaly farther in-system. There was something in close orbit around the EX447-Alpha star.

"Put it on my display, please," Drake called.

The three-dimensional holographic display projected by the command console shifted from a wide view of the star system to a close-up of the star. Its light had been heavily filtered, which made a tiny dot barely visible between them and it. The projection adjusted as the sensor crews worked to get them the clearest view. The scopes were able to zoom closer in.

The dot was a mere million kilometers from the star. According to the readouts, that was on the edge of where metallic compounds would melt unless they were specially shielded. That gave him a sinking feeling and set off an internal alarm. What was the chance that something large enough to be visible at a half-AU was circling a star at the very boundary of where it was safe? Not bloody likely, as Doc would say.

"It's generating a gravity field!" one of the analysts in Tactical called just as Drake saw that information on his projection.

Drake and XO exchanged looks. It wasn't natural; it was constructed. It was another gate, drawing its power from the star and placed close so it would be invisible to long-range scopes or sensors. A second later, their scopes zoomed in and gave them enough detail to confirm what gravity detectors had told them.

It was a secret Paragon gate, which was confirmed by the design and the energy signature. "Put the ship on alert," Drake told the first officer. "Let everyone know there's evidence of Paragon activity in the area and look for more." Gates like these almost always came in pairs if not threes or fours. They were transit hubs designed to get the Paragon from star system to star system fast.

"Shall I relay this through the QE as well?"

Drake considered it. This was massive news. The Paragon had built a gate hub right under the Fleet's nose, although EX447-Alpha wasn't Fleet-controlled territory. This was Unclaimed Space. The Fleet defended and maintained its gate, but these systems were used purely as pass-throughs, corridors through which ships could get from A to B.

Sometimes there were local settlements or authorities unaligned with the Terran Federation, and those gates were leased to the locals or set up and maintained by the Terran Defense Fleet for shared use. Others, like EX447, were in systems nobody seemed to want.

The Paragon placing a gate here wasn't tantamount to an invasion. They didn't claim this space either that they'd announced, but it was an expansion onto humanity's doorstep. It was a precursor to a new invasion. One didn't hide a gate for no reason.

This is it right here, Drake thought. This was how they'd launched their surprise attacks on Fleet positions over the past several months, and it was how they were going to get close enough to Freepoint to do the same.

He knew this gate wasn't the only one the Paragon had snuck under the Fleet's nose. This one led to another, and probably another, each deeper within Terran space and closer to Freepoint. With a star powering it, even a small gate could qualify as a far-reach and tunnel through thousands of light-years. They wouldn't need to have set up that many of them. This was bad, but . . .

"No," he answered XO's question. "We're not breaking radio silence, Commander."

The Paragon would crack their QE codes soon if they hadn't already. It was too risky. Anything that might tip them off that *Glory* was going to Vorkut was off the table. But the information was still too important to just sit on. "Prepare a coded message beacon and send it back through the gate. Put a hefty delay on it, too"

XO nodded. By design, it would take days to get picked up, but at the least it would get back to Jack, and it wouldn't blow *Glory's* position in the process.

"Activity!" Tactical called.

Drake's eyes snapped to his tactical display. An energy signature was emerging from the gate. They didn't yet have the fidelity to get a good look, but Drake knew what it was. A Paragon warship.

"Hold," he called to the bridge, sensing their alarm as the images of the new ship clarified. It was a Paragon cruiser all right, now free of the gate. Drake shared the same instinct he felt from the rest of his crew; to call for battle stations and rush the ship before it could get its bearings. But its appearance didn't necessarily mean they'd been spotted. Prudence told him to stay as concealed against gas giant as they could manage. He would let the Paragon make the first move.

He glanced at CAG, who was seated at her station, in constant communication with the fighter squadron outside. "We've seen them, but we have no idea if they've seen us." She gave him an affirmative. Her fighters weren't going anywhere without his say-so.

Good. They'd hang tight and see what these bastards did.

"Navigation," he called, calm and steady. "Find us a spot on the gas giant's edge we can decay to, and helm, restart station-keeping once we get there." Better, even, than the magnetic field was the planet itself. They could slip behind it, peer around, and wait.

It turned out to be excruciating. The Paragon cruiser just hung beyond the gate for what felt like an eternity, not moving a meter. As it did, or rather didn't, it slowly dawned on Drake that it was doing what *Glory* had done when she'd first entered the system: staying put to scan her surroundings carefully and cautiously.

That interpretation boded well. It meant they hadn't yet been seen. What remained to be determined was whether they would be. The combination of boredom and tension was painful—the curse of being a soldier.

"It's moving," Drake called when he saw the vessel change position.

The ship didn't beeline toward them. It didn't launch fighters. They likely would have burned up that close to the star. The cruiser must have intense shielding since even *Glory* would burn up after a few minutes that close. It turned around, backed up, went forward, turned, and then started moving from side to side around the gate. The maneuvers were not defensive in any way. If Drake had to guess, he'd say they were examining the gate, perhaps making sure it was operating properly.

On the most important level, that was a relief. On another level, however, it was a complication. The ship certainly didn't look like it was going anywhere, and they had no idea how busy this gate was. Even if the cruiser left, what was to keep it from coming back or another ship from emerging from this gate or the one that was likely on the opposite side of the star?

"Tactical, do we have eyes yet on any other gates in the same orbital plane?"

The answer was no. That either meant there wasn't one, which was unlikely, or that there was, but it was on the opposite side of this one, which was the easiest configuration from which to tap a gravity well and construct two or more stably orbiting gates. They balanced each other out. It was possible to do it other ways, but they were far more complicated and unnecessary in almost every circumstance.

"Navigation," he called. "How long until this gate rounds the terminator?"

There was a brief pause as the crew ran the numbers. "Looks like just under two hours, Captain."

Two hours until the Paragon ship was out of sight. "And it'll be on the far side for how long?"

"Sixteen hours."

Damn. EX447 was a pretty big star. That was good. Drake nodded. "We should get a view of the other gate by then, and if it's clear, we'll burn out of the system then."

It was still a risk since the Fringe was clearly crawling with Paragon. However, their nebular hiding spot was only two hours away at full burn, and it would offer the same cover the star was affording them in their current position once the gate orbited around the terminator curve. They would make a run for it and hope no ship came through the paired gate.

They were going to have to be very careful out here.

"Navigation?" Drake called again.

"Yes, sir."

Ensign Travers. That was who he was speaking with. The young woman had short blonde hair and a warm personality. She was new, but Drake could tell she would fit in nicely. "Wristcom Idri and let her know you'll have updated scopes and coordinates for her to go over for her jump."

Travers nodded. "Of course, sir."

They were going to have to thread the needle. He hoped Idri was up to it. They'd be jumping further and more frequently than they ever had. Four jumps was what they'd planned. That was what the charts they'd dragged out of the old Fleet database from when Navigators had been in use decades ago indicated.

However, Drake knew from experience that you couldn't rely on charts. You had to jump, then pause and recalibrate and scope out the next one, then adjust from there. *Good God, what in the hell were they doing?*

"It's a shame," XO said, sidling up next to Drake and breaking him out of his spiraling train of thought.

"Shame?"

Oh nodded. "That we're so close to this gate without the ability to tap it. Map whatever network it is the Paragon are building out here."

Drake hadn't considered that, but the first officer was right. Gates, although they were a physical network of micro black holes punching through space-time, were also a computer network of coordinates registering locations on each side. If one had access to that network, even tangentially, you could ride the data stream and see where in space-time that data was going. You could map where the gates had been set up. The only downside was that the data stream connection could just as easily be traced back to you —unless you had someone who knew the system and how to hide in it.

"Markus?" Drake asked XO, raising one eyebrow.

XO shrugged. "Worth a shot, right?"

Drake nodded. Hell, yeah, it was worth a shot.

CHAPTER TWENTY-TWO

EFREMOVA and her security detail were probably overkill. Markus wasn't a prisoner. By all accounts, which now included Carrol's in addition to Warren's, the old Blaspheme was being exceptionally helpful in the ops mission prep and training, particularly in his ability to map the Vorkut research facility and look for efficient routes that avoided congested areas, patrols, and the like.

But—and Drake couldn't shake this—until all the shit had come down upon them and every card had been put on the table and everything Markus had done, told them, and helped them with had proven to be true, Drake wouldn't trust the man. Not someone who'd willingly helped the Paragon for so long. Who'd taken their practices and beliefs as his own.

Not someone who shared their DNA. Efremova and her guards were *probably* overkill, but Drake would rather err on the side of caution when it came to Markus.

Drake knocked on the hatch of the old man's assigned quarters. There was no answer. Drake knocked again. Still no answer. "Unlock it," he asked Efremova, frowning.

Markus was supposed to be in his quarters. He did not have clearance to be roaming about the ship without an escort.

It was dark inside when Efremova opened the hatch. She entered first, hand on her hip where a sidearm was fastened, but she relaxed after she stepped inside. She gave Drake a nod to follow her, and her hand dropped away from her weapon. Drake went in.

His small room was little more than a single bunk, a desk, a closet the size of a school locker, and a door to an enclosed head. Downright spacious for *Glory*, if not for anything else. Markus sat cross-legged in the center of the small room, shirtless, with one of his hands in a tight fist to the center of his chest and the other hand on a short rod that had a string attached; it looked like piece of charge-cord from engineering he'd rigged to a battery wand. The man was muttering to himself. No, not muttering. Drake recognized the softly-spoken words as Paragon recitations. He was praying.

Snap!

He'd whipped the charge cord over his shoulder. It flashed an electric-blue in the darkness, and Markus winced before continuing his whispered prayer.

Drake recognized what he was seeing. The Paragon did this, bruising, scratching, even cutting their skin during holy rites and day-to-day penance. Flesh was to be despised. It was full of sin and imperfection. Life, as the Paragon saw it, was a waystation on the path to an immaculate afterlife.

As Drake understood it, one day, that perfect afterlife would merge with the physical world, and all the ugliness, death, tragedy, and sadness would forever be wiped away by bliss and joy, but only once the physical realm had been purified. To them, anything other than Paragon was an imperfection, a sinful stain that must be washed out and exterminated. It was the only reason to exist.

Seeing Markus speak holy words to that effect with conviction and reverence was deeply unnerving. At the same time, watching what was meant to be an intensely private and personal practice, Drake felt shame as well. He wasn't supposed to be standing there. No one was.

Snap!

Markus whipped his back again in a flash of blue. Drake saw a welt form where the whip had made contact with his shoulder. It must have been excruciating. Markus muttered more Paragon verse, took a deep breath, then lowered the fist he'd held to his chest, let go of the rod, and opened his eyes. Their kaleidoscopic colors shone brightly, even in the darkness of his cabin. Drake wondered if the old man could see better in the dark. If that shine wasn't just added color but one of the enhancements the Paragon experiments had given him.

"Can I help you?" he asked flatly.

Drake cleared his throat. "My apologies," he said, shifting his weight awkwardly. "You didn't answer when we knocked."

"I would have answered when I'd finished my recitations." His tone was still flat, but Drake saw annoyance flash across his eyes.

Drake was still uneasy about having Paragon prayers performed on his ship. "The apology was sincere," was what he decided to say. He meant it.

Markus inclined his head, indicating it was acceptable, then bristled again when he caught sight of Efremova standing by the hatch with several of her security team behind her. His eyes narrowed. "Am I going to be arrested for praying?"

"No," Drake answered quickly. "No, they're here to escort you."

"Escort me where?"

"To the forward sensor cluster."

Markus raised a thin eyebrow. "Shall I take that to mean that you've encountered an unmapped Paragon gate?"

Huh. Drake raised his eyebrow. "You know about the hidden Paragon gates?"

A smirk played over Markus' face. "Whichever, specifically, you're referring to? I doubt it. But I *am* aware that the Paragon have a vast network of unmapped gates all across their space."

"This one isn't in their space."

"And other species' space as well." He paused. "I assume you wish me to assist you in mapping them undetected."

"Yes. If you are able."

"I believe it was part of our debriefing that Mister Warren and I manually mapped several gates in order to find our way back to Terran space, and we were not caught doing so. So yes, I am able."

"Good. Then if you'll follow Mister Efremova, her team will escort you to the forward sensor room."

Markus didn't move, just eyed the security detail with suspicion. "Am I being asked or told?"

Drake flexed his jaw. "It is a request." He couldn't help adding, "You asked me if I trusted you. Well, here's an opportunity."

Markus' face was unreadable, and he let the pause in the conversation drag as Drake waited for his answer. "I will assist," he finally said. "Of course." His expression hardened so slightly it would have been easy to miss, but Drake didn't. "Next time, however, knock and wait for me to respond."

He then stood, opened his closet/locker, and took out a simple pullover shirt he'd been given by the onboard quartermaster. It read *Never say die* on the front, the motto of this new crew. Drake had no idea if it would stick. You never knew about such things.

As Markus turned to pull the shirt on, Drake got a good look at his back and torso. The man's skin was a spiderweb of scars, welts, and self-inked tattoos. He'd never heard of the latter being a Paragon thing, but then no one had ever *seen* a Paragon out of their armor. Their organic material combusted the second it was exposed. All of it looked ancient, layers deep, with decades of scars on top of decades of scars. Well, not all of it was ancient. There were fresh welts too, including the two Drake had seen him inflict just now. Markus hid it all with the shirt and then straightened, chin up.

He was proud, Drake realized. That spiderweb on his back was evidence of his piety and proof of how devoted he was to the Paragon and their Supreme, who was god incarnate. Drake shivered, involuntarily. The devotion was . . . unsettling.

The old man clocked the scrutiny and waited for Drake to step aside so he could exit. The captain obliged after shaking off the moment. When the tall old man was walking down the corridor with his security escort, Drake leaned close to Efremova. "Make sure you keep a good eye on him," he said, voice low.

The Russian woman nodded. "I'll keep both."

CHAPTER TWENTY-THREE

"GOD*DAMMIT!*"

Carrol threw down her headset so hard it cracked. She was drenched, stinky, and dead. Her team was the same, strewn around her on *Glory's* dank lower decks. The thing people didn't tell you about starships was how *hot* they got. And moist. As long as your power plant and insulation from vacuum were working, the biggest issue in maintaining life support was heat dispersion, not retention. You had to find ways to radiate it outside.

Glory's systems to do so were in the lower decks, and Carrol felt every goddamn degree of it.

They couldn't get over the hump. They'd finally achieved consistency with getting their asses to the cube. It took every ounce of speed, effort, and ingenuity to do so, but for the life of them, they could not get close to boring a hole large enough in the AI's crash-metal cube shield to enter through. Not even ten percent of their estimated needs— and it *was* an estimate, the kind that you wanted to err on the conservative side of.

In that regard, they kept failing spectacularly. It was

taking far too much time. The rest of her team was just as frustrated.

"My apologies," she said as she stooped to pick up her headset and inspected it for damage. She *had* cracked it. The holographic imagers inside were flickering and askew. She'd need a new one.

She pulled her greasy hair back and let out a frustrated grunt. What were they going to do? She didn't know. "Reset," she called finally. What could they do except try harder? She felt no small amount of pride in how her team picked themselves off the deck without the smallest groan or protest. They were handling this better than she was.

Warren spoke up as Smith and Sudan picked up the half-assembled cannon and other equipment. "Commander."

"Yes, Lieutenant?"

"Perhaps we should take a break."

Carrol arched an eyebrow, but he was looking past her. She turned. Someone was standing in the corridor.

"Idri!" Sudan called, a giant smile of recognition spreading over her dripping face.

The Navigator was dressed in garb that was unusual for her. Rather than her usual flowing robes, she wore the same simple all-black under-suit Carrol and her team were wearing. She also held a simulation body rig and helmet. "I am in the right place?" she asked tentatively.

Carrol turned back to Warren, agape. "Did the captain approve this?"

Warren shook his head but added, "He might if we're able to get a successful run."

Carrol paused, unsure of how to proceed.

"Just to see," Sudan chimed in, stepping over to the Navid. It was clear to Carrol that the two had become close.

"Can't hurt to see, right?" Warren piled on.

He had a point. "You recovered from your last jump?" Carrol asked Idri. They were only four hours from the last time she'd folded the ship deeper into Unclaimed Space. Carrol knew that Idri was getting much better at handling jumps. She was much stronger and recovered faster.

"I'm cleared by Doc."

"Doc knows?" Carrol found that hard to believe.

"Not that I'm here," Idri said. She shook off her embarrassment. "But I'm cleared for any activity, including jump, so..." She shrugged. "I'm ready to help."

All eyes were on Carrol. Even Zed crackled on the comm, "How about it?" He must have been the one to give her the sim equipment.

Fuck it.

"Can't hurt to try," the commander said. "Let's get you suited up."

THE SIM SUIT WAS CUMBERSOME, particularly the helmet on her head that made *Glory* look like the Paragon research facility and provided realistic projections of enemy soldiers, but Idri handled it. Beneath her black operations suit, she'd worn her thinnest robes. It was only a few days, but she'd been practicing with her rifle to get the stamina to hold it. Running along with the team, she realized she'd have to do the same with her legs to keep up. She handled that, too.

Carrol's team was a practiced unit now. That much was obvious. Several times, Idri got underfoot or was out of formation and exposed. Warren had a minor freakout about every time it happened. However, she was also a quick study and acutely aware that she needed to fit in with *them*, not vice-versa. *She* had to make the adjustments, so she did. By the time they were approaching the AI cube, she'd learned enough to go for several minutes without bumping into anyone or getting shot at.

Resistance had been minimal. That which they'd encountered had been eliminated within seconds. No alarm had been raised. However, Warren told her this was where things always turned: when they stopped to burn their hole into the cube.

But this time, the cannon was only burning a hole for Idri to look through. It took less than a minute.

"You two," Warren said to her and Sudan, wiping sweat from his brow. "You're up."

Idri knelt next to the plasma cannon, radiating heat. They'd used real crash metal and real plasma; those weren't just holograms. The ship's computer extrapolated them into the simulation, but they'd actually burned through real stuff. Peering in her headset, Idri could see there was a hole in the holographic cube, about the size of a finger, and she could see inside, beyond.

"Will . . . the simulation know how to handle me jumping inside?" she asked. "What do I do?"

"It knows you're standing right there," Carrol answered. She pointed at the cube. "It knows where the cube is. Just do a real jump. The computer will know you're inside."

Idri nodded and took a deep breath. Simple enough. The group huddled around her. "You have to stay close to me," Idri told them.

Sudan, who was closest to her, nodded and took her hand. "Okay."

"I'm ready," Idri said to Carrol.

"Good," the commander said, looking over the rest of the group. They were pressed in tight together.

. . .

"Incoming!" Warren shouted, looking behind them.

Troops had appeared at the far end of the hall. Lots of them. The corridor around them lit up with plasma fire. It was remarkably realistic.

"Go time!" Carrol shouted, crouching in even tighter.

"Jump," Warren said.

Idri gripped Sudan's hand tight. It was comforting that it was her on the team. Pure luck if you believed in that sort of thing, which Idri didn't. It was right. It made her feel like the two of them becoming friends over the past several weeks had been for a reason, and perhaps this was it. Idri eyed the cube in the headset and noted its distance, then closed her eyes and felt where she was on *Glory's* deck. She compared that with the distance projected on her headset. It wasn't going to be perfect. That would have to wait until they were there in the flesh, but this would be close enough. This was a jump into a puddle compared to what Idri was used to.

"Here we go," she said to everyone and jumped.

The space around her and Sudan expanded into infinity for a moment. Idri let it. Nearly. With her sense of self, she held onto the image of the AI cube. Where she had been, she let go, and she let the image in her mind become her new anchor, the new place where she existed, and she was singular instead of plural. A point rather than all points.

As she did, another place pulled at her. A cold, dark place. Ice. It was strong. It was like gravity, that dark, cold place, affecting her fall to the spot in *Glory's* corridor, bending her straight line to it into an arc. The arc got sharper, and the new place started to come into focus. Her fall into the singular was in danger of veering off-course, and

Idri got the chilling sense that this cold dark place *wanted* her to appear somewhere else. In a place Idri could not see or locate, behind a barrier.

The barrier looked familiar. Idri allowed herself to get a good look at it . . .

Snap.

The dark, cold place was severed from Idri's perception and not by her. It was so abrupt that it nearly sent Idri flying off into everything around her, losing her anchor to the real world where she occupied one point in space and time and not all of them. Idri held onto the image of the place where the simulated AI cube and *Glory's* deck met in her mind.

Sound, taste, smell, and sight returned to her in a rush. Sudan was still holding her hand tightly. The engineer was shivering. So was Idri, and the entire rest of the team, despite the humid heat around them. They were back, and their headsets were beeping triumphantly.

"Hell, yes!" a voice called close by. "Hell-fucking-yes!" It was Carrol, sharing an exhausted high-five with Warren.

They'd done it.

Idri took off her headset. Sudan was struggling to do the same, so Idri helped her. In the young engineer's eyes, she could see the same haunted expression she knew was in her own. "You felt it?" Idri asked her. Sudan nodded. Idri wondered if anyone else had. From their excited reactions, she guessed not.

"First time," Carrol said, beside herself with relief and excitement. "Next step, obviously, is to add on extraction to the sim and us getting the hell out of here, but goddammit, that's the first time we've been inside!"

Idri nodded, wishing she could share the commander's happiness. She did share the feeling of accomplishment, but all she could think about was what she'd seen in the jump.

When she'd focused on the cold, icy darkness that was pulling on her, she'd seen the same thing her simulation headset was showing her: the AI cube. However, it wasn't a simulation assembled from holoimages or sketched from the memory of someone who'd worked on it. It was the real thing, out there on Vorkut V, cold, unfeeling, and methodical. It was unlike anything Idri had ever sensed. It was not Navid, though it tapped into the same powers and abilities Idri possessed. She was drawn to it, and it to her, but someone had deliberately severed that connection.

The AI cube was real and horrific.

And someone was trying to keep it hidden from her.

CHAPTER TWENTY-FOUR

"Vijay was over yesterday to check up on the yearlings. They all seem pretty good. Couple of the males are starting to look a little . . ." Ellen's voice trailed off, and she chuckled. "Well, frisky, I guess. Vijay said they might need to be separated from the rest soon, so it's time to go and re-install the southwest fence. Hopefully, the grass there has had time to recover. Think so . . ."

Drake closed his eyes and let her voice become a soothing drone. He'd meant to go through her taped messages before. He had dozens of them from the months they'd been at Freepoint. Things had just been so busy. Still were busy, even between jump points, as *Glory* was currently.

XO drilled the crew to their limit shift after shift. CAG was doing the same with her pilots as well as pulling double-duty with XO to make sure their "rescue convoy," as they were calling it, was ready for Vorkut. Fredrickson had his team checking and re-checking every inch of the ship's systems, new and old.

It was a lot to supervise. There was a pile of reports

sitting on his desk, waiting to be looked over and signed off on. Nothing needed to be done right then, however, and Drake missed the voice of his beloved. He'd record his own message for her, to be sent back once they were in the clear for Fleet comms to send it to her. But that wouldn't be for a while.

There was a knock on the door of his quarters.

"Yes?" he called, straightening in his chair.

The hatch opened. Carrol poked her head inside. "Can we speak with you, Captain?"

Inwardly, Drake sighed. He'd been ready for a longer moment of peace, but a starship had a nose for such things and a penchant for mucking them up. "Of course."

Into his cabin spilled the second officer, along with Warren, and then Idri behind him. The Navid got his attention. He arched an eyebrow as Carrol walked over to him and handed him a small stack of papers that summarized their training runs. They hadn't been going well. Page after page documented their failures.

"I think you might find our most recent set of training runs to be the most illuminating, sir," Carrol said, indicating that he should flip to the end.

Look at that. A few successes. They'd managed to beat the simulator into the AI cube. "Let me guess," Drake said, putting down the printout. He pointed at Idri. "Those last few runs were with her on the team."

"That's correct," Carrol said, looking like she was bracing herself to be chewed out.

Drake had half a mind to do that, but he didn't. "No." He shook his head, put the report down, and pushed it back across his desk toward his second officer. "The answer is still no, Commander."

Carrol flexed her jaw. She was fixing to fight this.

"We've failed every simulation without her, Captain. We don't even get close to the thing."

"Well, keep at it."

"We've kept at it. Enough to know, sir, that we don't have a chance without her. We've run it that many times."

"It's too much of a risk, Commander. You're going to have to find another way." Drake held her gaze, but she was firm in her resolve.

"What if this is the only way?" Warren asked, coming forward to stand shoulder-to-shoulder with Carrol. He too had the hard set in his jaw of someone who was looking to fight. He glanced at the report and tapped it. "Sir, with all due respect, as planned? We will fail without Idri. And this is the best plan. The *only* plan."

"Idri is the single most important member of this crew," Drake countered. "With her abilities, she's probably the single most important member of the entire Fleet, and you two want to send her onto a hostile planet and into an enemy facility? I think we all know it's going to get hairy down there. You made that clear yourself, Warren. How would she even defend herself in a firefight?"

Idri stepped forward like she'd been waiting to hear that. She shimmied to bring something she had slung over her shoulder swinging up to her chest. It was a plasma rifle. On cue, Warren reached into his uniform pockets and tossed three objects into the air. It took Drake only a split second to realize they were target spheres. Idri fired her weapon in three precise consecutive shots, and the target spheres were reduced to dust that trickled down through the air and onto Drake's desk.

"I can defend myself," Idri said. She let the rifle fall back on its sling to rest behind her back.

Drake didn't bother to hide that he was impressed. But .

. . He turned back to Warren. "Can she do it with auto-targeting turned off?"

Warren shifted. "That's going to be our second lesson," he said honestly.

Drake nodded. His mind was a whirlwind, and he let silence fall over his cabin just to marshal his thoughts.

"Captain," Idri said, finally, "please, if there was any other—"

Drake held up a hand to stop her from going further. There was only one real choice. It wasn't the one he wanted, but it was the right one. "She's on the team." *Fuck.* "But she gets herself out of there and back onto the ship if it gets hairy. She must not be captured, and by all that's holy in this damned universe, you will *not* let her get killed."

Carrol didn't smile. She didn't rub it in, nor did Warren. Drake imagined Markus would have, the smug bastard, but he had been right. All of them had. Idri needed to go. "Thank you," she said with a smart nod, then she and Warren left the room.

Idri remained. Of his three visitors, how had Drake missed that she had the most fight of any of them? Her eyes burned with ice-cold fire. They accused him.

"It's not that I thought you weren't capable," Drake said, cringing at how that sounded. Maybe he *was* guilty of over-protection, but Idri needed to be protected.

Or did she?

"This mission will succeed," she said, eyes still burning. "I will guarantee that, Captain."

Drake couldn't help but believe her. "Of course." He couldn't let her know about his doubt. She already knew his fears. Without another word, she left.

CHAPTER TWENTY-FIVE

THE STARS WERE unfamiliar to Drake. Subconsciously, the eye looked for familiar patterns, trying to find the groups and constellations it was used to seeing either on Earth or from any of the various colony worlds in the Unified Federation.

Out here on the Fringe, the comfort of familiarity was missing, and the eye was left to wander aimlessly. It had produced so much anxiety that most of the early human vessels to venture into deep space lacked windows or portholes. Interior screens could be filled with light and color and were better than searching endlessly for something that wouldn't be found.

It gave Drake the heebie-jeebies. He shook it off and forced himself to focus on the information the command console was giving him. They were in position for their last and final jump, hiding in the magnetic field of an intense pulsar a handful of light-years from the Vorkut system and deep inside Unclaimed Space. The pulsar masked them from detection. Each of their stops along the way had been carefully and meticulously chosen to offer them the maximum cover and be as far off the beaten path for any gates, Paragon or others', as they could plan for. They were using the Fleet's charts of Paragon territory and what Markus provided as he was down in the forward sensor cluster, working on figuring out what they didn't know. It had worked so far. They hadn't been seen.

Yet.

This last jump, however, would take them out of the general sparseness and fuzziness of Unclaimed Space, a Wild West where anyone and everyone could set up shop if they wanted to. It was mostly a desolate wasteland where you could go a millennium without bumping into anyone and plop them down deep into Paragon territory. They'd skirted along the fringes of Paragon space until now, dipping their toe, so to speak, several times into the edge of it. Now they'd be all the way in. If they were caught, it was over. There would be no one within a hundred light-years to come get them out. Of all the steps they'd taken thus far, this was the one that could not be taken back.

"All departments report secured and ready," XO said, sidling up next to Drake.

The captain nodded and enlarged the holographic display he'd been poring over to show it to his first officer. It was as detailed a representation of the Vorkut system as they could manage from a combination of Warren's and Markus' memory, data from the shuttle they'd escaped in, and the imagery they were currently receiving from their long-range scopes.

Drake had three possible points for them to jump to, each with its own pluses and minuses. Jump into open space, and chances were high that someone or something would spot them the second they arrived. Jump too deep into the asteroid cloud, and they risked returning to the realm of space-time with a rock in their belly that shouldn't be there. Pop! They would be one of Idri's patented explosives. It was impossible at this range to track individual asteroids. They were going to have to rely on Idri's senses and spatial awareness in the moment to avoid disaster. Their job was to give her room to work with.

"Here," XO said, jabbing a large, stubby finger at the innermost jump point. Drake raised an eyebrow, which Oh ignored. "Trust the kid," he said without hesitation.

He was right. Again.

Drake nodded. With a tap on his console, then a swipe, he sent the coordinates to the fulcrum chamber. It would give Idri as good a view of that spot as the ship could muster. "What's our time to the moon passing on the other side of Vorkut?"

"It's behind it now. Peeks back out in eight hours."

Drake inhaled and let it out slowly. He looked at his friend. They were as ready as they'd ever be. "It's yours to call, Commander. It's now or never."

XO nodded and got on the ship-wide comm. "All hands, prepare for jump." He then toggled the fulcrum. "Navigation, we're ready when you are."

"I'm ready," Idri came back, loud and clear.

"Jump."

The reality around Drake began to bend, twisting and folding him and everyone else into it until they disappeared.

VORKUT SYSTEM

Paragon Imperial Space

CHAPTER TWENTY-SIX

IT WAS QUIET.

There was a brief flurry of activity after *Glory* appeared in the Vorkut system as she was made battle-ready, re-tuning her scopes and weapons, priming fighters to launch, and giving the crew time to rouse from the disorientation of the jump. Then . . .

Silence, then a collective inhalation as everyone aboard waited.

Nothing happened. The tactical display on Drake's readout remained the same. There were no intercepting ships, no incoming missiles or torpedoes, no energy weapons directed their way. There was only the asteroid field churning slowly around them. Idri had dropped them right in the middle of it. A perfect jump.

"Tell our Navigator she is to be commended," Drake finally said to break the silence. It was also the first breath he'd allowed himself to let out, something he hadn't realized until he did it. The entire command deck crew exhaled with him. XO knew the command was meant for him, so he walked softly over to the Nav station and told the supervising officer to relay the message. "Keep us looking like a hole in the void. Nothing to attract attention."

Glory was as dark as she could be while maintaining battle readiness. Main power and propulsion were on standby with the vents closed. Weapons were primed, but behind tampions for the energy cannons and breech doors for the torpedoes and missiles. Their scopes and sensors had come in hot. Otherwise, they wouldn't be able to see around them, but Drake had those switched to passive, too.

Now that she was here, *Glory's* mission was to stay hidden. Ready, but hidden.

"Here," Drake said, tapping a portion of the three-dimensional map of the asteroids around them. It was a cluster of particularly large ones. He showed them to XO, who nodded.

"Helm," he called. "Take us to thirteen-point-seven-seven by two-point-zero-zero, range sixty-three kilometers at one-quarter thruster only."

Even thrusters were a risk for short-range scopes. Any movement was. You could catch light and reflect it into someone's eye just rolling in place, and that would be enough to get the wrong entity to take a closer look. It was also risky to maneuver that close to the asteroids. Those rocks were at least five times the size of *Glory*, but that was what made them worth it. They were perfect cover for the ship to sit behind and stay hidden long enough to let the mission play out.

Drake felt the almost imperceptible vibration of the thruster array firing and the subtle shift in gravity from the acceleration as they got underway. Good. Everything was going to plan so far.

"How long until the Vorkut V moon is in our launch window?"

"Just over seven hours, sir."

"Call down to Fredrickson," Drake told XO. "Tell them his engineering team is up, and they have four."

———

SITTING in the middle of *Glory's* main flight deck was a rock. A giant, craggy, dull rust-and-gray *rock*. "We're flying in that thing?" Zed said for the entire operations team as they took it in. "You have *got* to be shitting me."

Carrol had known this was the plan. They all had, but a vague concept and seeing something in the flesh, so to speak, were two different things. In concept, hurtling through space in a rock didn't sound that bad. Standing there looking at it, it sounded nuts. The thing was the size of a house, if a house had been built like a giant russet potato.

"It looks like a turd," Zed said, again speaking for the group. It did look like that, but Carrol preferred potato. It also looked like the durasteel beams supporting the flight deck were bending under its weight. And it was just not flyable-shaped.

"Over here!" a voice called. It was Fredrickson. The chief engineer waved at them from the right side of the rock. Carrol swallowed her hesitation for the benefit of her team and accepted Fredrickson's summons.

The front of the potato—Carrol refused to think of it as a turd—was slightly more encouraging, emphasis on "slightly." Fredrickson and his team had been busy in the hours since they'd jumped in-system. Not only had they hauled this lump onto the flight deck, but they'd managed to hollow the damn thing out, going in from the nose of the roughly oblong shape. Inside, the hollowed-out asteroid was pure black, but not naturally. Carrol recognized the material as crash metal. In the center of the makeshift crash-metal bunker was a shuttlecraft. A light troop carrier designed to hold ten people.

"Shuttle is secured, primed, and ready for flight checks," Fredrickson said, hands on his hips and chest puffed out so far it looked like he might topple forward. The engineer was beaming with pride. He pointed at the asteroid's interior. "That's an unbroken seamless six-inch layer of crash metal. We're going to torch it when we seal you inside, so there's not a crack in it even then."

"Well, how in the hell are we getting out?" Carrol asked, alarm rising.

Fredrickson walked to the sliced-off nose of the aster-oid/potato and slapped a small round silver sphere embedded in the crash metal. "Explosive bolts, tuned to this metal's frequency." He then pointed at the shuttle. "Which you have programmed into that as well, just in case something doesn't fire. I wouldn't leave you guys hanging."

"And how, exactly, am I supposed to fly this thing?" Zed asked. It was the next pertinent question on everyone's mind.

Fredrickson laughed. "Oh, there's no *flying* this thing." He pointed at a rectangular seam in the deck below them that ran around the perimeter of the spud asteroid. Carrol hadn't noticed it when she came in, but she did now. The asteroid was perched on top of a flight deck elevator. "This is going to load you, your team, the rock, and everything into a custom-built ship-length rail cannon." Fredrickson made a fist to represent the potateroid, laid his palm flat, presumably to represent the rail cannon, and then cried, *"Whoosh!"* The fist flew off his palm. "You're on your way. Aerobrake on a half-revolution around the Vorkut gas giant, and—" *Smack!* He made a splat with his fist again and re-opened his palm. "Impact on the Vorkut V moon a couple hours later."

What. The. Fuck.

Fredrickson grinned at the shocked silence. "Gnarly, huh?"

"Disturbing," Smith responded with narrowed eyes.

Fredrickson chuckled again. "Oh, don't worry about it. We've rigged some aerothrusters on the asteroid's exterior for minor course corrections en route, but I doubt they'll be necessary. The math all checks out. We should be able to land you dead on within a couple kilometers of the labor camp."

"How are we going to make course corrections if we're on compression drugs?" Carrol asked, frowning.

"Oh, no compression drugs, I'm afraid. We figured you guys can't afford the hangover. Plus, if something does go wrong with your course—which, again, it won't—you need to be conscious to correct. We'll have no control over you once you're launched."

"And how many gees will we pull on that rail cannon?" Zed asked, scratching the top of his head.

"Eight, maybe nine. Doc's rigged a stim shot for anyone who passes out."

Fuck.

"Come *on*, man!" Zed griped.

Smith pointed at the chunk of asteroid from the nose of the spud that had been lasered off to hollow out the core. "That will be re-attached as well?"

Fredrickson nodded. "Torched back together like nothing ever happened to it. *That* you may have to blast open a bit once you get the crash metal open, but I doubt it. Personally, I think most of the asteroid will burn up in the atmosphere on your way down. Or get shot off by the camp's anti-meteor system."

He slapped the black crash metal again. "Which is what this is for. They could have a Level Six plasma cannon on that moon, and this stuff could handle it. The whole meteor could burn up, and the crash box would be left behind. You'd just be a fireball at that point, so no one would be the wiser."

There was silence as Carrol and her team took that in.

Fredrickson sensed their hesitancy, and he sobered. "You'll make it," he said earnestly. "I guarantee it. Two-hour trip, and you'll be on the ground."

Carrol nodded. It would have to be good enough. "All right, everyone, load in," she commanded. The team grabbed their gear and headed toward the shuttle, which was open and waiting. Carrol held Warren back. "*Do* the Paragon have crash-metal-rated cannons down on that moon?" she asked him in a low voice.

Warren shrugged. "Would certainly seem like overkill for a meteor defense system."

Carrol nodded. It would. That was the bet they'd made when they came up with this plan, but now, standing on the flight deck and staring at how crazy a plan it really was life-sized and real-time . . . "Wouldn't it be like the Paragon to embrace the overkill, though?"

Warren grimaced. "Then we'd be fucked, wouldn't we?"

CHAPTER TWENTY-SEVEN

"Insertion team reports they are secure and ready for launch," called someone from the bank of Operations consoles.

"Rail cannon is primed," another person called from the engineering stations.

Drake acknowledged both reports with a quick nod and a thank you. "Have we loaded the vehicle . . . asteroid into firing position?" It was still crazy to say, but here they were, about to launch their ops team in a *rock*.

"Locked and loaded," XO reported.

"And Nav has double-checked their math?"

"Double-checked would be quite the understatement, sir."

"Vitals are coming in nice and clear," Doc reported from the other side of the command console. He'd insisted on remaining on the command deck for the acceleration phase. Drake assumed he'd insist the same during landing. It was nice to have him on hand.

Okay. It was go time. "Tell Mister Fredrickson he may fire when ready."

Drake brought up a holoimage from the highest elevation of the stern of the ship. It had a nice view of the rail cannon, a long magnetic-levitation-driven accelerator they'd hastily built down the spine of the ship from stern to bow. It followed the footprint of the super-cannon they'd used against the Paragon planet-killer a few months earlier. The impact of that weapon was still visible on the ship's structure if you knew where to look: indentations in the hull from its bracing and dark streaks of charred and melted hull that fresh paint couldn't cover.

They had discussed keeping the super-cannon assembled on *Glory*, but it hadn't worked on the planet-killer, which was its sole purpose. It would work on smaller targets like Paragon cruisers or other less-armored or smaller targets, but it had the downside of being a one-shot weapon. It took everything *Glory* had in her to fire it a single time. After that, she was dead in the water. It didn't make tactical sense to use it on smaller targets, so why keep it? The technology was there, saved and cataloged. They'd dig it out again if they ever needed it.

The rail cannon that was about to launch their insertion team toward Vorkut V would leave no such mark. Its power needs were minuscule, and it was easy to assemble and tear down. Centuries-old technology. Fredrickson reported that the asteroids around them were so naturally high in ferrous metals that the rock they'd chosen hardly had to be modified to work with the cannon. It was a simple solution, if not an elegant one.

After a final adjustment to align the ship on the designated flight profile, the XO gave the order to fire.

That brought Drake back from his musings to the projected image from the stern. It was just a blur as the asteroid jumped off the rear of the ship, flashed down its length, and was ejected into space, where it was swallowed by the darkness. Drake changed his console view to a graphical representation of the space around them when the asteroid appeared as a blue-green dot tracking away from the ship. Ahead of it was a dotted yellow line, along which it was moving precisely.

"Telemetry is within safety margins," Nav reported. A young officer there turned from leaning over their crewman's chair and beamed. "It's right down the line, sirs." Nyota was her name. Drake would have to remember to commend her and her group for their work when this was all over.

"Thank you, Ensign," he told her.

He looked at Doc, who was carefully watching the readouts on the well-being of the team. "Vitals are steady," he finally said with no small amount of relief. "Everyone's conscious and stable."

Drake let his relief show. It wasn't over yet. The aerobraking wherein the asteroid used the friction of the Vorkut gas giant's upper atmosphere to slow down was going to give him fits of anxiety, not to mention the crash landing. Yeah, that part...

"Good luck," he whispered to the blue dot, which got tinier on his three-dimensional tactical display as it got farther away and the magnification scaled out to follow it.

He gripped the edge of the console and took a deep breath. The plan had been to remain on the command deck for the duration of the two-ish-hour flight of the asteroid, but as Drake stood there watching it hurtle through space, he knew that had been folly from the start. There was nothing to *do* here. He would just exhaust himself watching, or worse, fuck something up from the deadly mixture of boredom and anxiety. He straightened and addressed XO. "Track their course," he said, knowing the command was unnecessary. He gave it, nevertheless. "Keep tactical scopes on full alert, weapons and fighters at the ready."

"Yes, sir."

"Notify me when they're approaching the landing site, or . . ." His voice trailed off. He didn't want to say, "If there are any problems." There weren't going to be. Why speak such a thing into existence?

Two hours. Goddammit, it was going to be hell.

"Coordinate with CAG, too, to have your transport teams at the ready for when all the shit goes down."

XO nodded like he'd started that process already. Drake was sure he had. He didn't need the captain to tell him his job. "Where will you be, sir?"

"I'm going to pay our guest in the forward sensor cluster a visit." He rapped his knuckles on the tabletop. "Try to keep myself from going crazy."

MAYBE SPENDING time in close quarters with someone he didn't like wasn't a brilliant way to kill time. The forward sensor cluster was not large, maybe a hundred square feet, with a bank of controls in the center that cut the small space down by half. There were four workstations, which was the implied capacity of the space. Add one anxious captain looking over the shoulder of someone he didn't trust or particularly enjoy, and the room was very full. It also had the same downside for Drake that the command deck did. There was nothing for him to do down here except look over people's shoulders.

There was one silver lining. Markus and the crew members assigned to assist him were making progress. Slow progress, but progress nonetheless.

"The data won't come in any faster the closer you get to the screen," Markus said without looking away from his readout as Drake hunched over him, watching.

Smartass. "Perhaps," Drake countered in the same dry tone. "But said data will certainly be easier for these old eyes to see."

Markus shifted. It was obvious that he didn't want the captain there. Drake's kneejerk reaction to that was to suspect the old man of something nefarious. Maybe his annoyance was a cover to get Drake off his back so he could do something malicious.

Drake quickly dismissed that notion. The other crew members in the small room also seemed perturbed that he was there, not that they'd show it as explicitly as Markus was. They were too well-trained. However, Drake had been a captain for a long time, and he could tell when he was stepping on toes.

The other reason Drake had to consider that his suspicions of the old man were misplaced was the data they were getting back. Markus had managed not only to hack into the Vorkut gate, but he'd also gained access to a regional hub that had stacks upon stacks of number strings, some of which they'd determined contained the locations and access codes of more gates. It was spectacular.

"There," Drake said after straining for a long, uncomfortable moment. He pointed at Markus' screen, tracing a set of numbers and symbols. "That's another one. Right?"

Markus frowned and leaned forward. After a moment of careful consideration, he nodded. "Yes." He tapped his console controls and a new display came up, this one a graphic representation of their region of space. There were half a dozen dots in bright colors on that screen, and after Markus fed the new string of numbers into a data field, a new bright dot appeared. Another gate. Markus half-turned to Drake. "Well-spotted," he said grudgingly.

Drake kept leaning over the man's right shoulder. "Eyes might not be what they used to, but they still do the job." Markus grunted in acknowledgment. Drake stood. No point in pushing the guy to the edge. Give him his space. As far as Drake could tell, he was doing his job.

"You still have perfect vision though, huh?" Drake asked Markus after a prolonged silence. "A gift from Paragon genetics?"

"Astoran, actually," he replied, not taking his eyes off his screen. "Paragon have limited eyesight compared to humans."

Drake arched an eyebrow. "Something humans do *better* than the Paragon? I've never heard of such a thing."

Markus turned. "The Paragon don't believe they're perfect, Captain," he said haughtily. "That would be stupid."

"Humility is certainly not a quality they project."

"Not outwardly. But the Paragon would not be so formidable a foe if they believed themselves to be superior to their enemies in every way."

"Really." It was just about the most verbose response Drake had ever heard from the old man.

"There are many things you humans do that demands respect."

Drake cocked his head to the side. "Don't you mean 'we' humans?"

Markus reddened. It was a telling slip. "Excuse me," he

said, pushing his chair back so he could stand. "I need to make some adjustments."

Drake stood aside to let him pass, which was awkward in the tiny space, then watched him go. The forward part of the sensor cluster, which was situated in the nose of the ship, got direct data readings from the scopes. Behind them, where Markus was escaping to, was a small antechamber that had additional controls that wouldn't fit in the single room. On the other side was a hatch that opened into a corridor leading to the rest of the ship. It was a cramped place to work, and it heated up quickly. Drake made a mental note to make sure that XO's duty shifts in this area were well-cycled, so no one got stuck there for too long.

He forced himself to focus on Markus. He didn't want to push the old man. It was natural, after working with the Paragon for so long and taking on their religion, their DNA, *all* of it, that he would see himself as one of them. However, at some point, it needed to become past tense, and that point should come sooner rather than later. He wasn't Paragon anymore. He was helping *Glory*. If Drake was ever going to fully trust him, it needed to be "we humans," not "you."

Drake's wristcom chimed an incoming call, which the tiny display showed was from XO. He tapped it. "Yes?"

"Port showing movement."

"Hold, Commander," he said loudly into the bracelet. It wasn't necessary. The microphones embedded inside it were sensitive and adaptable enough to capture sound with perfect clarity no matter where or how loudly their wearer was speaking. Getting through shielding interference, on the other hand, was another matter, and the front array was shielded like a mother.

He stepped outside the front room into the

antechamber with Markus, who looked at him question-ingly, then excused himself to go back into the forward array. They were avoiding each other now. Great.

"Can you hear me?" Drake asked over the wristcom. The hatch to the interior of the ship was closed, but Drake rested a hand on the locked wheel that would open it. He'd get farther away from the array shielding if necessary.

It wasn't.

"Yes, sir," XO said, his voice loud and clear. In the fidelity of the transmission, Drake could hear the tension in his voice.

"What is it?"

"Picking up movement to port," he said. "Something small and closing."

Drake's heart rate spiked. "Send it down here," he said and stepped to one of the control stations so he could toggle a screen to take the feed. "Station Four in the front array antechamber."

The screen in front of him flickered, then changed to a tactical readout akin to what he'd see on his console on the command deck, albeit in two dimensions. 2D was more than enough. It was a Paragon craft, all right. "Can we get visual on it?" Drake asked.

"Not without going active," XO replied.

It was small, whatever it was, and it was moving slowly toward them in an odd back-and-forth pattern. Not odd. "Search pattern," Drake said. It hadn't spotted them yet.

That relief lasted all of a half-second. No sooner had Drake uttered those words than the slow, sweeping movements abruptly changed, and the Paragon craft reversed course and hightailed it away from *Glory*. "Fire!" Drake heard XO shout over to Weapons. "Helm, ahead full in pursuit."

"Belay that!" Drake shouted into his wristcom. Now that the game was up, the full power of *Glory's* sensors were tracking the Paragon blip. Drake saw that it wasn't a vessel but a drone. A fighter at full speed couldn't chase it down, let alone *Glory*. They didn't even need to. "Jam it," he shouted. "All frequencies!"

A moment later, the image on Drake's screen showed the drone had stopped dead in its tracks. Excellent. XO had heard the command. The drone was indeed remote-controlled, and the jamming signal had severed the connection.

But something was wrong.

In the array room, Markus was shouting.

Drake looked up to see him running toward the threshold.

Markus kept shouting, "Don't!"

His warning, beyond Drake's ability to decipher, had apparently come too late, however. There was a high-pitched whine in the sensor room as *Glory* broadcast noise across every outward-facing transmitter she contained. Drake's screen flashed white. Pure static.

Markus, stood in the doorway with a wild look on his face. They'd fucked up, but Drake didn't know how.

"Incoming!" XO yelled over the open channel.

And then an automated warning blared from the front control room that took Drake a split second to recognize It consisted of three words. No, letters. The computer said, "E ... M ..."

"Markus!" Drake yelled when the realization hit him like cold water. The old man was standing somewhere he shouldn't—the threshold. Drake lunged for him, grabbing him by the arm, and yanking him back. The motion was so uncontrolled, it sent the two of them crashing to the deck, Markus landing on top of him.

Drake felt a sharp pain in his left shoulder. It was the last thing he was aware of before everything around them exploded with a shriek.

CHAPTER TWENTY-EIGHT

Everything hurt.

Carrol's eyes fluttered open, and even that was excruciating. She panted to get a breath, but those small movements sent hot knives stabbing through her chest. With each breath, the pain cycled through her body in a perpetual loop of agony. The air she managed to pull into her tortured lungs didn't taste like air, and she coughed. That was by far the worst pain to that point.

Good lord, it fucking hurt to cough. That made her cry out in agony, which also hurt. Her existence became nothing but pain, but she couldn't accept that. Her eyes stung, but she forced them open to take in her surroundings. She'd rather do anything besides focus on the waves of agony that coursed through her body. She realized there was smoke swirling around her, and the pain in her chest was probably caused by hanging upside-down, twisted up in her shuttle chair's harness. Jesus fuck, the thick material was carving a trench across her ribs and sternum, or it felt that way.

She grasped for the harness buckle. It was somewhere

in the center, she thought. Probably. Yes, it was. She found the metal with her fingers and pawed at the release buttons.

Click.

"Fuck!" she cried when she fell hard to the shuttle's deck. That was what happened when you suddenly had nothing holding you up.

Scratch that and reverse it. The deck of the shuttlecraft was above her, and she was lying in a near-fetal position on its ceiling. She lay there for a long moment, dazed. The smoke was thinner down there, and she was able to suck in a few gulps of air without the restraints keeping her from taking a full breath. It was thinner, too. There was a breeze, a cold one. *What the fuck?*

Everything was wrong.

As her head cleared, it dawned on her how much was wrong. The last thing she remembered was hitting the upper atmosphere over Vorkut V. They'd been on their calculated vector for the entire ride, just as Fredrickson had promised. No adjustments had been necessary. Right down the line.

It was dark after that. She must have passed out. Everyone had. Carrol looked up, and in the dim light coming in the front of the shuttle, she could see the rest of her team dangling upside-down like she had been, still unconscious. Well, Smith was rousing.

Wait, what was that light from the front of the shuttle? Power was down. That much was obvious. So where were the light and the breeze coming from? It took Carrol every ounce of strength and pain tolerance she had to roll over and push her body into a kneeling position. The shuttle ceiling was pitched at a sharp angle sloping down to the left, which made it even harder, but she did it. What she saw shocked her to the core of her being.

There was no front to the shuttle, nor was there crash metal or stone. Not anymore. Carrol was peering up through a mound of smoking dirt and rock into a featureless gray sky. Snowflakes filtered through the opening, carried by the cold breeze. "Holy hell," she said aloud, surprised by how raspy her voice sounded. They were down on Vorkut V all right, but not according to the plan that had been drawn up.

"Are you okay, Commander?"

Carrol turned to see Warren on the ceiling with her. He was reaching up to assist Smith, who was also awake. "I'm fine," she croaked, hoping to speak her well-being into existence rather than express how she really felt. "How is everyone else?"

Smith clunked down next to Carrol, then shined a light on Sudan. Where in the heck had he been stowing a light? The dude was like a Forest Scout. Always prepared. Idri squinted painfully with the light in her face. Sudan and Zed did the same. They were rousing.

Cheddar whined from her secured crate in the back. Smith got her out while Carrol assisted Warren in getting the rest of the team down. Idri was last, more tangled up in her seat harness than the rest had been, but in fairly short order, everyone was free and testing their limbs and joints to see if there were any serious injuries.

There were none. That was a major miracle.

They climbed up and out of the rock, dirt, and ice hole they were in.

"Ho-ly shit," Zed said as the pilot looked at the site of their crash landing.

Forget the landing part. This had been a *crash*. the crash-metal box was half-buried in the frozen dirt and still smoldering. What was left of it. The front, which included the shuttle, had been blasted off, exposing the inside. There was nothing left of the asteroid.

"What happened?" Carrol asked, wondering if anyone remembered more than she did, which was nothing.

Nope. Nobody else could recall either, but it didn't matter. Warren pointed at the melted edges of the crash metal, which were still burning. It was generating most of the acrid smoke that wafted into the back half of the shuttle. "Plasma blasts," he said, not getting too close to the molten shell.

They'd been shot down by plasma weapons powerful enough to cut through crash metal. It must have sent them spinning end over end, and they'd blacked out as they came down over the mountain range. The g-forces could easily have been enough to rip their heads off their shoulders, to say nothing of the uncontrolled impact with the ground. "Ho-ly shit" was right.

Looking at the smoldering crater, it was inconceivable that anyone had survived. They'd been completely exposed. If the g-forces hadn't been enough to rip them apart, landing with the opening facing the ground or the trees around them should have crushed or impaled them. They'd gotten very lucky.

"You think they saw us?" Idri asked, looking back the way they'd come.

Behind the crater was a long, impressive line of charred and smoldering forest. They'd been a fireball coming in, lighting anything up that was in their way. It was like a giant arrow pointing at them. They probably hadn't been spotted since, like Warren had said in their brief, meteors hit Vorkut V all the time. The defense system was designed for them, and it was automated. Even if someone had been watching as they'd crashed, the smoking line leading toward them indicated that Fredrickson was right; they'd been a fireball at that point. It was unlikely that anyone had recognized something amiss with the streaking meteor, but why take the chance?

"We should move regardless," she said, taking the opportunity to fully survey their surroundings as Smith and Warren waded back down into the hole to check the back of the shuttle for their gear.

In the direction of their fiery trail through the trees loomed a mountain range. Carrol recognized it from the hours she'd spent pouring over the terrain maps of the area that Warren and Markus had been able to provide. They weren't very detailed, but the ridge formations around the camp had been pretty distinct, and that was enough to get their bearings. They were in the right place, for the most part.

"The good news," Warren said as he was helped out of the crater by Zed. Idri and Sudan helped Smith. "Is that all our gear was stowed in the very back of the shuttle. Most of it is fine."

"The bad news is that the shuttle I was supposed to fly is cracked like an egg," Zed said, surveying the crash.

"That," Warren said with an agreeable nod. "And . . ." he looked toward the mountains that Carrol had been eyeing, "we're twice as far from the labor camp as we're supposed to be."

Carrol's heart sank. The forest was thick with ever-green-type trees and mounds of underbrush that were covered in a deep layer of snow. Traversing it was going to be slow. Same with the mountain range. That, in particular, would be difficult, which they'd known going in, but the added time and effort to get there would compound that.

"How far do you think it is?" she asked him, putting a hand over her eyebrows to blot out the gray sky.

"Two days."

Not so bad.

"We'll have to overnight at least once."

"We have the gear for it?" The question was for Smith, who had their packs from the shuttle strewn about him and was methodically opening them one by one. He nodded to her. They had the gear.

Carrol let out a relieved breath. Not the end of the world, but they had to get moving. There were no signs of the Paragon in the sky or in the forest that surrounded them, but that didn't mean there wouldn't be. "Let's pack up and move. If I remember your briefings correctly, Warren, temps are going to plunge at night, so we need to haul ass before we have to stop and conserve our heat."

"What about the shuttle?" Zed asked.

"Obviously scrapped, so you'll come with us."

"I meant are we going to leave it here? Open like that? Makes it pretty obvious it wasn't a meteor should anyone come looking."

Carrol looked at the smoldering crash site. It was cooling, and snow was sticking to the charred wreckage. The same was happening with their scarred line through the forest. From the color of the sky above them, Carrol didn't think the snow would let up anytime soon. Quite the opposite. "We just leave it the way it is. Better to go now and get distance than try to rig up something to move it, bury it, or whatever. I think it's going to be covered in snow pretty soon anyway."

Zed nodded, as did Warren. It was a risk, but so was staying where they were. Best to get moving.

The team assisted Smith in getting everyone's packs

filled with the necessary available gear, shouldered them, and set off with Warren in the lead. Carrol looked at the sky one last time as they left. It was impossible to see through the thick cloud layer, but she thought about *Glory* and wondered if the crew knew they'd made it.

She hoped the ship was safe. They were going to need a new escape plan.

CHAPTER TWENTY-NINE

"Captain. Can you hear me?"

The voice came to Drake as if from the end of a long tunnel, accompanied by a pinprick of light. He tried to respond but was unable to do so. The pinprick of light was coming closer, and the voice along with it. "Captain?" it repeated. He focused on it with great effort.

With a rush to all his senses—sound like the roaring wind, light with blinding brilliance, the bitter smell in his nose and the taste of smoke on his tongue, and sharp pain all down his left side—Drake regained consciousness.

"Don't move." The voice belonged to Markus. He was standing over Drake, or rather kneeling. The captain realized he was lying flat on the deck of the antechamber. Around them was a horrible hissing, the air was thick with smoke, and it was hot. Sweat was pouring from his brow and pooling in his ears. Drake wanted to sit up, but Markus put a hand on his shoulder. "You are bleeding," the old man told him.

Grunting in pain, Drake felt his left side. His shoulder was on fire. He'd messed something up inside it. When he hit the floor, he remembered. It felt dislocated. Made it hard to move, so he stopped and reached across his body with his good arm to finish checking himself out. He found something warm, sharp, and rocky sticking in his side just below his ribcage. His hand came back wet with blood.

"What happened?" he asked.

Markus moved to the side, out of Drake's field of view, grunting in pain as he did. There was a shard of rock buried in his thigh, and the wound was oozing blood.

"You're bleeding, too," Drake said to him. The old man's blood was impossible to miss. It practically glowed in the dim light, filled with glittering, metallic-looking flecks.

Markus nodded in distaste, then pointed toward where the horrible hissing was coming from. And the heat. In place of the port-side bulkhead of the antechamber, he saw a giant, craggy rock glowing dull red, with torn and melted metal and plastiform surrounding it. On the deck around them were shards of glass-like rock, some embedded several inches into the control consoles.

"What in the hell?" Drake asked, again trying to sit up. Again Markus put a hand on his shoulder to stop him. It would be unwise with the shard in his side, Drake realized. Good advice. Better to stay put for now.

"The drone," Markus started.

Ah, yes. The drone. Drake remembered now. The sudden flash of white and XO yelling, "Incoming." The alarm from the sensor room. "It fired off an EMP, didn't it?" he asked Markus.

The old man winced and nodded. "Before destroying itself." He looked at their surroundings. "Explosively." He glanced behind Drake at the front compartment. "You pulled me from closing bulkhead," he said as if he were still processing what had happened.

It was all coming back now and starting to make sense. Drake had heard the sensor alarm for an incoming EMP and realized the ship was about to lock down critical systems behind crash-metal-shielded bulkheads that would protect them from the circuit-frying pulse. One such bulkhead would have smashed Markus. Drake had acted on instinct.

"You saved my life," the old man said, blinking at him. He didn't look happy about it. In fact, he looked downright upset.

"Don't mention it," Drake responded, dryly. How that could possibly upset the old man, Drake couldn't fathom, but there were more pressing mysteries to solve at the moment.

He his attention to their surroundings. The EMP systems had activated, cutting them off from the front compartment to protect the sensitive equipment there, but that didn't explain the giant fucking rock that had smashed through their hull.

"The drone's explosion was close to an asteroid," Markus added, noticing Drake's interest in their intruder. "The damage to *Glory* could be extensive."

"Yes it could," Drake said. He looked at the bulkheads. They should already be back up. Operating properly, they came down to protect the ship's vital areas, then retracted to allow systems to be reconnected. That hadn't happened. Something was wrong. "Help me up."

Markus shook his head. "You really shouldn't move."

"I can hardly see anything, and if I sit up, you'll have a much better look at how to pull out the damn thing. Help me up."

Markus considered for a half-second, then nodded. He grabbed Drake by the bad shoulder, let the captain gain purchase with his good arm and his legs, and on the count of three, they hauled him to a sitting position against the crash-metal door that led to the forward compartment. It was surprisingly cold.

Drake reacted to it. Markus gave him a knowing look. "I believe the forward compartment is in a vacuum."

Damn. Three of his crew had been in there.

Drake filed that to mourn later. Here and now, his main concern was making sure he and Markus didn't join them in the Great Beyond. It was dark in the antechamber, save for the dull red glow of the intruding asteroid and a pair of overhead glow strips.

"We appear to have battery power," Markus said, following his gaze.

Drake shook his head. "Those are luminescent. Not connected to power of any kind. We're completely dark."

"Do you think the rest of the ship is?"

"I don't know." Drake tapped his wristcom. Incredibly, it came back to life. Its power must have been cut just in time to avoid being fried by the pulse. Hopes were dashed only a few seconds later, however, when the tiny device registered a long series of error messages: its connection to *Glory's* central computer was dead. Made sense. The computer was a critical system, so it was behind crash metal, now. Hopefully, those bulkheads had also dropped in time to cut power to the ship so nothing important had been powered on when the pulse ripped through everything. But if they were also still down like they were in this forward compartment, if the ship overall was still without power because those mechanisms had failed, well that was a problem ...

Just looking at the equipment around them, it was hard to say. Everything had been ripped up by asteroid shards, many of which had burned what they'd impacted. Impossible to tell if the smoke and black streaks he saw everywhere were from the frying of powered circuits or because they'd been pummeled by red-hot asteroid hail.

The condition of the rest of the ship would have to wait. Of primary concern was the giant glowing rock poking through their hull. The hissing, Drake realized, was atmosphere escaping. To boot, the red glow of the rock was fading. That was the only thing keeping them and their diminishing air warm. When it faded completely, and/or the last of the air escaped around its imperfect seal with the hull, whichever came first, they would suffer the same fate as the three crewmen in the forward compartment. Damn rock had probably saved their lives.

"We must get out of here," Markus said, speaking Drake's thought.

"Agreed." Drake looked at the shard in the old man's thigh. "Which means we have to get that out of your leg."

Markus shook his head again and got in position, squatting by Drake's injured side. He eyed the wound with obvious distaste, something Drake was starting to notice, whenever exposed flesh or fluids were around. The old man swallowed it, however. "You first," he said. "Your wound is bleeding more than mine."

Drake nodded. It was getting harder to breathe. They needed to move. "Fine," he said.

"Brace yourself," Markus said flatly. "This will hurt."

CHAPTER THIRTY

CARROL and her team made terrible time. Other than surviving, they had met with little luck. Crash landing early in the Vorkut day had been one good stroke, but the rest was bad. The valley they'd landed in was like a giant bowl, good for collecting anything that fell into it like snow. Tons of snow. The drifts were meters high in places, and the team had to pick their way carefully around the worst of the drifts so as not to fall into one and suffocate while forcing their way out.

It was exhausting, and they had to change out the person on point every fifteen minutes. They did not walk single file to hide their numbers should someone run across the trail. They walked that way to conserve energy.

Idri never took point. The willowy Navid couldn't push the snow out of the way, plus Drake's last order to Carrol had been to protect Idri at all costs.

Eventually, they realized that getting to a higher elevation would be better since the drifts didn't seem as severe there, but the hiking was still not easy. The slopes were full of boulders and steep. When the sun started going down, they'd made it barely half the distance Warren had wanted, and this was the easy part of the hike. The mountains towered above them, wind-whipped and ominous. Snow-shoes would have been smart.

She paused, panting, taking a break.

The forest was breathtaking. It stole your breath because it was hard to walk through, but it would do the same from how impressive it was. The trees looked like jumbo versions of the pines you found on Earth, akin to the sequoias of the American West. Their limbs were laden with snow and had frosted tips straight out of a holiday holoimage.

Beyond the occasional distant crash of a branch breaking under the weight or snow sliding off when it was piled too high, it was silent in the forest. The combination of the snow and the density of the trees and underbrush muffled every sound. It was the most peaceful place Carrol had ever been to.

Beneath the snow, in the patches where it was thin enough that her boots touched the ground, Carrol could see green. Moss, she guessed, but maybe it was grass. Whatever it was, how it could perform photosynthesis under the snow was beyond her. Tunnels ran under the bottom layers of snow, the size of a mouse and even larger, like a house cat. The forest, for all its silence and pristine, unchanging surface, was teeming with life. That enhanced the peace Carrol felt rather than detracted from it.

Something rustled behind her. Carrol whirled, battle-ready, with her plasma rifle on her shoulder.

Zed stood in the snow, hands raised. "Just me."

Carrol rolled her eyes and lowered her weapon. "The fuck is wrong with you?" she asked. "Sneaking up like that."

"Thought I heard something," he said, looking off their trail of trampled snow into the darkening forest.

Carrol stood there with him in silence for a moment, then said, "Heard something like what?" She looked behind them. The portion of the scar their landing had wrought on the landscape was nearly covered in snow. Even the smoke column that had been rising from the crater, a veritable beacon shouting "Hey! Over here!" was gone now, the fires finally extinguished by the cold, the snow, or both.

Zed frowned and shook his head. "Not Paragon," he said. "Something like—" Carrol heard an animal cry. "That." Zed shouldered his rifle.

The two silently waited for the sound to repeat so they could get a bearing on distance and location, but it didn't. Zed looked at Carrol, but she shook her head.

It had been smooth working together thus far. Carrol had expected Zed to make comments and needle her in front of the others. Play games, try to embarrass her, or otherwise dance on the edge of getting them both court-martialed. Everything Carrol knew about him indicated he was an insanely good pilot and a fucking terrible soldier. It was why he'd been stuck on *Glory*. In their brief Academy romance days, Carrol's need to follow the rules and do what she was told had been a horrible pairing with Zed's inability or resistance, whichever it was, to do those things. He still was like that.

Well, he hadn't transformed into a grown-ass adult, but he *was* acting differently in some ways. He'd been as serious as anyone about this mission. He hadn't said a word to Carrol about their . . . whatever it was that was going on. *Had* gone on. That shit was done.

Zed caught her looking at him too long. He smiled at her.

Carrol looked away from him, focusing back on the forest. There was a tree not far off with the most interesting bark pattern. It was dead quiet.

"Where you planning to bed down tonight?" Zed asked, his question a whisper. Just like that, the bastard made Carrol regret even *thinking* anything nice about him. She shot him a murderous look, and he threw up his hands with a rakish grin. "What? It's cold, is all I'm saying."

He'd been so good. "Zed, I swear to you, I will shoot you in the face right fucking now."

The bushes ahead rustled. Carrol and Zed whirled toward them, weapons trained, adrenaline pumping. Silence, then more rustling. Carrol silently motioned for Zed to take one side of the bushes, and she took the other. They split left and right, stalking slowly. The snow was so light that virtually they could move silently.

Carrol approached her side in a crouch, rifle up. Zed was on the other side, even with her. Another couple steps and whatever was around the corner would be visible. They exchanged looks and silently agreed to move the last few feet quickly and in sync. Carrol evened out her breath, set her feet, and coiled her legs. When she nodded to Zed, they sprang.

Warren was standing thigh-deep in the snow, well off their beaten path. He didn't respond to them, which indicated to Carrol that he'd known they were there the entire time. "Jesus, Warren," Carrol said, breathing deeply to slow her racing heart. "Why didn't you—"

The giant man held a hand up to quiet her. Carrol obliged. The three stood in silence for a long while before Warren lowered his hand. He turned to look at them. "Wolves," he explained. "Or whatever one would call pack-hunting quadrupeds on this ice block. The dog tipped me off."

"We heard them, too," Zed offered. "A minute or so ago."

Warren nodded. He pointed at the snow at his feet, and Carrol crunched forward to see. An indentation penetrated through the layers to the icy ground, and a medium-small animal of some kind lay inside it, eviscerated. Among the blood and bones, Carrol could make out tufts of white-brown fur, which indicated it was a mammal, likely one of the animals who'd made those tunnels through the lower layers of snow she'd seen. "Hasn't frozen over, which means the kill is pretty fresh," Warren said grimly.

"How big do you think?" Carrol asked him.

Warren pointed at tracks that led to and from the kill site. They looked like paw prints with a neat "x" shape in the middle of a central pad and four clawed toes. Big ones. In total, they were nearly the size of Carrol's hand.

"I'd say pretty large," Zed said with a low whistle, examining the prints.

Carrol turned back to the forest. It seemed much less serene now. Warren shouldered his rifle and trudged back toward the path. He needlessly cautioned them over his shoulder as he left.

"We're going to have to be careful."

CHAPTER THIRTY-ONE

THE BULKHEADS REMAINED STEADFASTLY DOWN.

There was good news: the asteroid was cooling, and it was a *lot* less uncomfortable in the antechamber. Drake's sweating had stopped. In more good news, his shoulder was mobile again after being popped back into its socket, and he could move around with the shard out of his side. It looked like it had been hot enough when it pierced him to have cauterized the wound, though Drake hadn't let Markus dig to find out. His breathing was still labored, but all things considered, it was about as positive an outcome as one could hope for.

It was the same for Markus' leg wound. It had turned out to be deeper than Drake's but in a much less vital area, and the bleeding was less than expected. They'd bandaged each other and called it good.

The bad news, however. The downside of the asteroid cooling was things would very quickly get much *colder*. They had zero life support. That much had been made clear over the past half-hour, although the timespan was a gut-level guess since there were no readouts in sight. No life support wasn't a guess, though. There was no air coming through the vents in the small compartment, and as the giant rock in the bulkhead cooled, so did everything else. The air leak thankfully hadn't worsened, but Drake wouldn't take that for granted. Now that he could move, there was only one thing on his mind.

"We cannot stay here," he said to Markus between grunts as he wrestled himself into a standing position.

"Agreed. What do you propose?"

He pointed at the bulkhead covering the hallway hatch. "There's an airlock just about five meters back that direction."

"I thought that section of the ship was vented."

"It is, but unless the airlock itself was punctured, it will be sealed off like this compartment."

"Will it function without power and life support? Surely not."

Drake nodded. It would. "Every airlock stores a single compression charge in an isolated tank. We'd just have to get in there and cycle it by hand. The process is mechanical, not electrical."

Markus chewed on that, then nodded skeptically. "Okay, but how do we reach the airlock? You indicated these bulkheads cannot be raised."

No, they couldn't. Drake hobbled toward the giant rock embedded in their hull, and reached toward it when he got close. It wasn't glowing anymore, but he wasn't in any hurry to get burned, so he approached it slowly, feeling with his hand how hot it was with every step forward. When it seemed safe, he touched it using the end of his uniform jacket's sleeve. It was only warm, so he reached out with his bare hand and withdrew it quickly but received no burn.

The rock was cool enough to touch. Barely. That meant it was cool enough to move.

"You can't be serious," Markus said, his eyebrows rising in alarm.

"Dead serious." He pointed beyond the asteroid. "There's a power conduit just outside. Shot now from the pulse, I'm sure, but that's good because we'd be able to grab it safely. It runs back along the hull and terminates right at the airlock hatch. We'd just have to follow it."

"How?"

Drake unbuttoned his jacket and draped it over his right side and planted his boots on the deck grating, then leaned into the rock and gave it a tentative shove. It shifted more than Drake had expected. The whisper of the air leak turned into a shriek. That was not good. Drake stopped pushing the rock, and it tipped back to where it had been. The shriek faded. It still sounded louder than it had been, but it was better. He shook his head. "Whatever we're going to do, we need to do it fast."

"What *are* we going to do? Last I was aware, vacuum is still quite deadly to humans. I can assure you it is just as deadly to human-Paragon hybrids."

"I assumed so," Drake said as he looked around the room, mind spinning. He spied something up above them—an air duct. He reached up to grab it and was able to find purchase on the grating with his fingertips. It wasn't enough to do anything with, so he dropped his hands and continued to look around, this time for something to stand on. There wasn't anything, except . . . "Can you give me a boost?" he asked Markus.

The old man frowned.

"A place to put my feet." He pointed at the duct.

"I don't—"

"Just crouch down here and bend your good leg or cup your hands. Whatever, just so I can—" Drake maneuvered the confused man into position, careful to keep his injury out of the equation. "There. Thank you."

"From the lack of airflow, would that not indicate the duct is sealed by the same bulkheads that we are behind?"

Drake nodded as he put his foot in the crook of Markus' good leg and his hip and used that to boost himself up to the air vent. "That's correct." A twinge of pain stabbed him from his wound and another from his shoulder as he reached over his head, but he gritted his teeth through both. He grunted as he yanked the grate off, then turned his attention to the hood. "But everything I'm looking for is right . . . in . . . *here.*"

The hood came off so abruptly that he nearly toppled backward. He gripped the edge of the duct frantically and tightened his fingers on the metal. Thankfully, it wasn't sharp enough to cut him. He'd lost enough blood. He steadied himself once more and let the grate clatter to the deck. Behind it, with an elbow bend and then running the width of the room, was a tube, and surrounding that tube, now visible in a completely artificial bright yellow, was insulation. The fibrous stuff came out in puffy chunks when he pulled on it. He got down and showed it to Markus. "You think you can grab the rest of this along that duct?" He pointed at the path it took along the room.

Markus nodded. He was taller than Drake, and with the insulation exposed, he was able to pull it out easily.

As he did, Drake hobbled over to the supply cabinet they'd retrieved the first aid kit from. There were supposed to be other supplies in there, too, and Drake sent up a silent prayer that it wasn't just first aid kits that XO had made sure were fully stocked. His prayers were answered a couple seconds later when he fished out two full rolls of multi-bonding tape. "Commander," he said to the ceiling, "you deserve a goddamn raise."

"Sorry?"

Drake held up the rolls of tape. "Our tickets out of here." Markus was standing beside a tower of bright yellow insulation. "Is that all of it?"

Markus nodded, then shook his head in confusion. "I don't understand."

Drake didn't blame him. His plan was certifiably nuts, but it was better than none.

He pointed at the insulation. "Start wrapping that around your body." He punctuated the command by gripping the bonding tape's lead edge and pulling a length off the roll. It extended with a satisfying *riiippp*. "Then you're going to seal it up by wrapping this around it."

What Drake was proposing slowly dawned on the old man. "It will be airtight."

Drake nodded. They were going to wrap themselves from head to toe in as much insulation as they had, then cover that with tape. "Makeshift EV suit," he explained.

Markus blinked for a moment, stunned, mind swirling like Drake's had not long ago. He ran through the pros and cons and the permutations of their predicament. Apparently, he came to the same conclusion Drake had because he reached for the pile of yellow insulation and started wrapping it around his bad leg.

"Hand me the tape." He reached for it.

CHAPTER THIRTY-TWO

Night on Vorkut V was cold, and it was *dark*. When the planet-moon fell into the shadow of the Vorkut gas giant, as it did every thirteen hours, the temperature plunged, and there was nothing but the starry sky to illuminate the frozen landscape. When you could see them, that was. The cloud layer was persistent, which served to hold in some of the heat.

That night, as Carrol and her team set up camp, it was clear, freezing, and beautiful. The stars were brilliant. Brighter than on *Glory*, which Carrol knew had something to do with the way the atmosphere filtered light.

They'd made up time by moving up the slope and using that to traverse the less heavy snowfall. Warren estimated they were a half-day's climb from the top of the ridge, and the camp was probably about another half-day's descent from there. Not bad, considering their crash. Considering *everything*, really.

"Camp" was a hole they dug into the snow. Each had a full expedition pack with a thermal mat, a sleeping sack, a tent, and anchors if they needed to hunker down on a cliff face. Carrol shuddered at the thought. The thermal pads, in particular, were handy to keep them off the frozen forest floor, as were the tents to keep out wind and falling snow. When the group huddled together for a collective meal, they used neither since it was clear and calm.

They couldn't make a fire since the smoke would be a dead giveaway. They did have thermal capsules that worked like an extreme version of the sleeping pads. Smith cleared the foliage that could catch fire out of a nice spot, cracked open a few capsules, and busied himself by taking his fellow camper's rations one by one and heating them up. Cheddar, meanwhile, circled their perimeter and stopped next to Smith every so often to be tossed a morsel of steaming food, which she never failed to catch in the air. She'd gobble it down, then make another round of the camp while Smith heated more food.

"They seem quite in their element," Zed said, sidling up next to Carrol, who was standing at the edge of the warmth the capsules were giving off. "Don't they?"

She nodded. The capsules gave off light too, which was one reason why they'd buried themselves in a snowdrift. It encircled them at Carrol's chest height and mostly obscured them. Smith, like Warren, knew what he was doing. The two clearly had ops experience. She didn't, only training. Simulations, but nothing close to the real thing. She'd always wanted to. She'd always felt as though she'd be good at it if someone gave her the chance. Before coming to *Glory*, she'd been relegated to a desk, ignored and belittled for a long time.

"So do you," Zed said.

She tensed. She'd forgotten he was there. "What?"

"You seem to be in your element," he clarified.

"Ah." He seemed to mean it sincerely, which surprised

Carrol in an entirely different way. A lump formed throat. She had no idea why. He noticed, which embarrassed her, but he smiled and looked at the sky to give her space.

"You see the thunderstorms?" he asked after a long, silent beat. Carrol followed his line of sight. "You stare long enough so your eyes can adjust, and Warren says you can see them on the gas giant. Constant lightning. See?" He pointed at a part of the night sky.

Carrol couldn't see anything but darkness where the planet blotted out the stars. She glanced at him.

"I'm not pulling your leg, I swear," he said.

Carrol shook her head. "What do you want, Lieutenant?"

He shrugged. "Warren wanted me to ask you about first watch."

Carrol cleared her throat. "Let me guess; he's volunteering."

Zed nodded. "Smith too. In the same breath."

Of course. "Tell them both I want them to get some rest. Let someone else take first watch."

"He also had an idea about a new escape plan."

"Oh?"

"We steal a Paragon shuttle. The facility has several of them in the lower docking bays, down on the cliff face."

Not a bad idea. "Tell him I agree."

"Sir." Zed gave her an overly formal response and a quick salute. Fucking dick. He turned to leave.

"If we're doing sniper checks," she called after him loud enough for the whole group to hear, "might as well bring me some chow."

"Yes, sir!" he said.

When Carrol was alone, she looked toward the Vorkut gas giant and stared like Zed had said. Goddamn if she didn't see flashes of light in the dark half-circle. There were hundreds in greens, blues, and yellows, flashing as they did across the North American plains.

It was beautiful.

———

IDRI HAD WON despite the predictable protests from almost everyone. She was on first watch. She took her warmed rations, unfurled the heavy coat from her backpack, put that on, took out the small bag of personals she'd snuck inside, slung her rifle over her shoulder, and trudged out to the snow a few meters from camp. Cheddar joined her, intuiting what she was doing without a command.

They set up toward the mountainside and dug into the snow to make a little hide. The Paragon camp was over that ridge. If they were going to come in the middle of the night, it would probably be from that direction, so that was where she trained her rifle's scope. The weapon still felt foreign in her hands, but she got more used to it the more she held it. That was one reason she wanted to take a watch. They would likely go into battle tomorrow. She wanted to be ready.

In the distance, the wolf-creatures Warren had told the group about howled. Cheddar went rigid, ears up. It was a haunting sound, and it made her shiver far worse than the cold of the night. She was on edge; they both were. Cheddar let out a low growl and stayed in an ears-up, crouched position. When she got tired of staring along with the dog, Idri checked the systems on her rifle, which were fine. A minute later, she checked them again, then set it aside and dug into her bag of personals.

"You get enough food?" Warren asked when he joined

her a short time later. She'd heard his plodding footsteps, but Cheddar hadn't stirred from beside her, so she'd figured it was him.

"I'm fine, thank you," she responded.

He crouched in the snow next to them, nodding in approval at the little mound she'd settled onto. In front of her, propped up in the snow, Idri had set a book she'd intended to read from. "Is that a *Tome*?" he asked, surprised.

"I have a small copy. Doctor Broussard made it for me."

"Huh."

They were silent, but Idri waited for him to say more. When they'd spent time together on their journey from Navid, he'd taken exception to her constant reading and recitation of the Navigators' holy book. "You're not going to ask me to stop?" she finally asked, eyebrows raised. "Or tell me it's annoying?"

He shrugged. "You aren't reading it so far as I can tell."

Idri turned away. She wished he would leave her alone. "The commander told you to rest, I believe."

He didn't leave. And he was right about the reading; she was failing in that regard. Her thoughts were elsewhere. Troubled.

"Have you ever killed anyone?" Warren asked.

Idri swallowed. It was the one thought on her mind. How had he known? "No, but it's simple."

"Oh?"

"Sure. You taught me; just let the muscles take over. Aim. Squeeze. And then it's over."

"It's not that simple."

She didn't imagine it would be, and she felt foolish for saying so. She looked at him, and where she was expecting to find judgment, disdain, or annoyance, she found compassion. That threw her. "It's not that simple."

"Navid are not supposed to kill."

She shook her head.

"But you're not Navid anymore, are you?" He smiled as if he were reminding her.

"No," she said.

He nodded. "Good." He stood and gave her an awkward squeeze on the shoulder that was meant to be reassuring. "You just remember that it's not simple, and you'll be just fine."

And then he left.

Cheddar let out a sigh as his footsteps faded. It was quiet in the forest now. The howling was gone. The large dog leaned into Idri and tucked her legs in tight to conserve heat. She laid her giant head on Idri's lap, ears still twitching at sounds Idri couldn't hear, eyes and nose scanning for sights and smells beyond the Navid's senses. The young woman bent and gave the top of the dog's head a kiss, something she'd seen Smith do. Cheddar sighed again and nuzzled closer. She wasn't going anywhere.

"We're going to be just fine," Idri said, echoing Warren's parting words.

She hoped he was right.

CHAPTER THIRTY-THREE

THE BIGGEST DOWNSIDE of Drake's makeshift suits was that they weren't going to be able to see. Not a single inch of their bodies could be unsealed or uncovered, which unfortunately included their eyes. Rupturing a lung was a very real, very dangerous risk if the pressure in their suits dropped enough, hence sealing them and their insulation with bonding tape, head and all. But no matter. Drake knew his ship, and they had a pair of safety measures to make sure they didn't get separated.

While their wristcoms were useless in terms of communicating with the rest of the ship, Drake had figured out how to rig them to maintain contact with each other. With a tap, either of them could initiate a haptic homing signal that would either decrease if they were drifting further apart or increase if they were getting closer. The second safety measure was a bundle of wires Drake had yanked out of the sensor controls in the antechamber, braided into a makeshift rope, and tied them around each of their waists so they tethered together.

"Just follow my lead," Drake told Markus as he helped him seal the last bits of exposed insulation. Bonding tape was magical stuff since it adhered to anything. Just expose it to the air by unrolling a strip, then place it on a surface—any surface, including the tape's backing—and let it sit for twenty seconds. The tape's glue could probably bond in less time than that, but five minutes was a safety measure because after twenty seconds, bonding tape was not going anywhere without taking the surface to which it was bonded along with it. As long as Drake and Markus covered each other in full, their seals should be perfect.

It took a little figuring out since the last piece had to be done blindly, but the two wrapped each other from head to toe except for a tiny hole over Drake's right eye and their mouths. The last thing each would do was take a big breath. Drake gave Markus one last check as the old man had just done for him, then tore off the strip that would go over the man's mouth.

"You're set," he said, voice muffled by the insulation. It was nasty stuff to talk through. Fibers kept getting into his mouth. "Remember," Drake stressed, "if you rupture your suit and you feel that pop in your ears, exhale *immediately*. Do you understand?"

The captain didn't tell him that if that happened, he would pass out in seconds. It didn't matter. He wouldn't *die* in seconds, and Drake would haul him into the airlock.

If Drake lost pressure, they were fucked. Markus didn't know how to operate the airlock when he could see, let alone blind.

It was a shit plan, but it was all they had. It was far better than hope, which was even more of a shit plan.

Through the pinhole by his eye, Drake saw Markus nod

to the instructions. "Loud and clear," he said. What a distinctly human phrase. Drake wasn't sure he'd ever heard him say such a thing.

"Okay," Drake replied. "Let's do this."

The two shuffled toward the asteroid shard, and Drake checked their tether one last time to make sure it was tight around their shoulders and torsos. The asteroid was cool to the touch, so it was now or never. Drake covered his eye hole.

"Inhale," he shouted. They'd have that breath, plus maybe one more from the buffer of the insulation. It would have to be enough.

He sucked in the biggest breath he could, held it, and placed his final strip over his mouth. The hole the strip had to cover was far smaller than the strip, designed to be overkill and to leave nothing to chance since each had to complete this step blind. Even if it wasn't placed perfectly straight or smooth, there would be plenty of extra surface and margin for error. Drake counted to thirty, ten seconds past the bonding time for the tape just to be sure, then gave a yank on the tether. It was time to push.

The asteroid shifted as soon as they started pushing but then stuck. Panic gnawed at Drake. They had two minutes, three tops, to get outside, crawl along the power conduit, and get to the airlock before they passed out from lack of oxygen.

The average person could last ninety seconds without training. Drake *had* trained in oxygen-deprived environments. Every member of the Fleet did, but that had been years ago. He had no idea how much of that ability he'd lost. Of necessity, they'd allowed thirty seconds to let their last strips of tape bond. They couldn't afford to encounter more obstacles like the asteroid getting stuck.

Drake pushed hard since he was desperate. Markus did the same. In sync, the two men rocked back and then shoved with everything they had.

The asteroid fell out almost too fast. Drake pitched after it and careened toward an unknown void. He grunted when he blessedly landed on something flat. He could just barely make out the grate pattern of the antechamber deck through the insulation and the tape.

The tether was slack between him and Markus. He reached around carefully, feeling for his companion, and found him on the deck to his right. On the other side, where he'd been searching with his left hand, he found the jagged edge of the hole the asteroid had punched through the ship's hull. Jagged was an understatement. From its saw-toothed edge, Drake pictured it looking like broken glass. Whether it was sharp enough to cut through their bonding tape, Drake didn't know, and he wasn't going to find out. He let go of it the instant he touched it. They were lucky to have fallen onto the deck. If they'd fallen on one of those shards, it would have been game over.

Getting through the jagged opening was an exercise in terror. Drake led, moving much slower than he wanted to. His lungs were starting to burn. It had taken another thirty seconds, maybe longer, but this was the most dangerous part of the escapade. Once they were outside on the hull, Drake knew he could find that power conduit quickly, and it was a straight shot from there to the airlock. The extra time spent being careful not to rip their suits open on the hole was justifiable if they got through.

Drake felt gravity give way as he carefully swung a leg through the hole. Good, he was outside the hull. He searched with that leg, tapping along until he found what he was looking for.

The conduit! It was round and exactly where it was supposed to be.

He wanted to shout, but he resisted the urge since it would expel the last bits of oxygen his body was extracting from his last breath. Instead, he hooked his foot underneath it, wedged it securely, and carefully pushed himself off the deck. He swung through the hole, miraculously not catching his suit on anything as he did, and let his momentum carry him around the fulcrum of his foot until his hands were close enough to grab the conduit by where his foot was.

Ooomf!

Searing heat met his fingers. Drake couldn't help his surprised exclamation of pain. Then he realized it wasn't heat; it was cold so extreme that his nerves couldn't tell the difference. Although Drake had been exposed to the frigid temperatures of vacuum when that asteroid had been dislodged, vacuum was a terrible conductor. It didn't efficiently rob one of their body heat. However, metal did, and Drake had apparently not insulated his hands sufficiently.

Didn't matter. He had to move. It had been over a minute. His lungs were starting to burn almost as badly as the uninsulated portions of his hand. Drake adjusted his grip to where he did have insulation, and he started crawling along the conduit. When he felt the tether tighten, he backed up, then waited. They'd unspooled two body lengths of tether on purpose. Drake knew he was now clear of the opening, so Markus could execute the same maneuver he had.

His lungs were starting to bark, but he wanted to push his inhale as far as he could before using the residual air in his suit.

Waiting with nothing to do except hope Markus was figuring things out without getting impaled or otherwise breaching his suit, all Drake could think about were his lungs. He was getting lightheaded. They needed to move. *Goddammit*. Why was it taking Markus so long? How long *had* it been?

Hurry the fuck up! Drake thought.

Drake felt a tug on the tether. It was faint, so Markus was probably fading as fast as he was, but it was there. He didn't tug back in acknowledgment, just scrambled forward on the conduit, no longer being careful about where he put his hands. They had to *move*.

The airlock was five meters from the antechamber along the conduit and away from the nose of the ship. Drake had traversed about a third of that, so there should only be three meters left. Cake. However, he had lost all sense of distance, speed, and orientation as his lungs starved and his body suffered. Brain fog threatened to overwhelm him, so he focused on the only thing he still could: putting one hand over the other.

He couldn't feel the tether anymore, either. Had Markus been cut free? Was he floating into the void, doomed by Drake's insane plan? For fuck's sake, the airlock might not even be viable. It might have suffered the same fate as the sensor room or its antechamber and been blasted open by asteroids or twisted metal that would prevent it from opening ever again.

The siren's call to take a breath sang to him. It would be okay. There was air within, circling around his body, the siren reasoned.

One hand over the other.

His hands were now numb, which was better than stabbing pain. Drake felt like he'd been crawling forever. He was sure they weren't going to make it. This had to be too far, right? Something was wrong.

One hand over the other.

They needed to turn around. Go back. He was convinced he'd remembered incorrectly and the conduit *didn't* end at the airlock. It must go past it, and they'd now climbed too far. Maybe it had been part of the retrofit. Goddammit, why hadn't he paid closer attention to the ship's changes?

One hand over the other.

Drake's hand hit flat hull instead of round pipe.

Frantically, he wrapped his legs around the conduit and flailed with both hands, desperately looking for the grip-hold that would open the airlock's hatch. He found it, clutched it with his lungs screaming—not yet; he didn't want to take his last breath yet—and pulled with every ounce of strength he had left. It opened.

Drake wanted to scream in joy. He didn't wait for the door to finish opening. He grabbed the edge and hauled himself inside with a pump of his legs against the conduit.

Mistake.

Rrrrriiipppppp. His suit caught on something. Probably the door—a hinge or a lever.

Drake felt his ears pop and he exhaled; the action was pure instinct, drilled into him by decades of training. Normally, one could expect a few seconds of consciousness with empty lungs, but Drake's bloodstream was so depleted from holding his breath that he wouldn't get that.

Darkness started closing in on him.

Damn was his last thought. He should have used his last breath when he had it. Markus didn't stand a chance, fumbling blindly around an airlock he didn't even know top from bottom. They'd made it to the place that could save them, yet they were going to die. It didn't seem fair, but dying never did. *Damn!*

The darkness came for him, swallowing Drake in its merciful embrace.

CHAPTER THIRTY-FOUR

Huddled together at the top of the mountain ridge, Carrol and her team peered onto the labor camp and research facility below. It was a lot farther down than she'd expected, perhaps a thousand meters. They had to cross boulders and ice sheets until they met the tree line, and deep snow drifts from there. They had quite a hike ahead of them.

Looking through his rifle's scope, Warren frowned. "What is it?" Carrol asked him, shuffling toward him.

"It's . . . different," he said, not taking his eye off the scope and continuing to sweep it back and forth. "I see no prisoner activity in the camp or over in the mine." He waved his hand at the places he mentioned.

"It's been weeks since you were. Maybe they've shut down that operation?"

"Maybe."

Carrol sighted her scope on the target and studied the research facility. It seemed to be teeming with activity. Dozens of Paragon troopers going in and out, equipment strewn everywhere, and the prototype ship was right where they expected it to be, hanging a few hundred meters over the sprawling complex. Its umbilical cable hung below it and disappeared into the building. "Facility seems as expected."

Warren grunted an affirmative.

"Maybe not," Zed called from down the line of team members. "Lieutenant, you said shuttles were kept in those lower hangars along the cliffside?"

"Yeah."

"Well, those hangars look sealed off to me. I'm seeing shuttles on that upper plateau instead." Zed pointed at a flat area on the cliff face directly above the research facility. There were two rows of a dozen shuttles each on the ledge, staked down and covered by tarpaulins. A single elevator ran from a staging area at one corner of the facility up the cliff to the ledge. It was the only way up or down from the facility. Conspicuous as fuck; mission-failingly so, if they were going to steal one of them.

"We'll have to split up," Carrol realized. They couldn't ride that elevator from the facility up to the shuttles. They'd be seen in seconds. They had to drop down on them from the top instead. "Zed and I can break off to the left, follow the ridgeline down from there, and drop onto the ledge from the top." She pointed at the rest of the team. "You all will head straight down from here as planned and approach the camp from the forest."

"I will accompany you," Smith called from beside Warren.

Carrol shook her head. "I appreciate the vote of confidence in our ability to protect ourselves," she said with no small amount of sarcasm, then pointed at the facility, "but the truth is that your skill set is most needed down there. You're sticking with the insertion team."

He accepted it. Good, because she was right. They all wanted to fly off this rock after all the shit when down, but *causing* said shit was far and away the top priority. It chafed Carrol to reduce the numbers of that team, but it was foolhardy to send anyone off to do something alone, and both she and Zed were pilots. That gave them twice the chance of success in securing them a ride home.

"We're not going to make it down before dark," Warren said with a shake of his head, tacitly agreeing to the decision.

Carrol had assumed that. "We shelter before nightfall, then each proceed on the complex at 0500. Sunrise. We just have to make sure we're in position to arrive at the same time, so wherever you make camp, ensure it's close enough to get there by sunrise."

Warren nodded. That would work. As long as each team was close enough to their target, they'd be in the correct positions at the same time. No need for comms until the job was done and Warren's team was ready for extraction. Not if everything went according to plan. "You make goddamn sure you two are in one of those shuttles, waiting for our signal," he said.

"You make goddamn sure you blow that AI cube and get everyone back out of there for us to pick up."

Warren again grunted an affirmative, but not a happy one. "I don't like it." He put his rifle down and bundled into his jacket against the whipping cold.

"You have another plan?" Carrol asked him.

He shook his head. "Not that. The whole thing. It's weird. Just a feeling."

"I'm open to any suggestions, Lieutenant."

He shrugged, continuing to shake his head. "We move

at sunrise. 0500, like you said. Just keep eyes in the back of your heads because *something* is up."

Carrol stared while she contemplated life and the decisions that had led them to this point. Okay, then. It was decided. "Zed." She gestured. "You're with me."

CHAPTER THIRTY-FIVE

DRAKE REGAINED consciousness with the smell of stale air in his nostrils. It was wretched. And cold. It hurt his aching lungs to inhale, but he was able to do so. How had that happened?

He cracked his eyes open. They felt like eggshells. He could dimly see. As his vision cleared, it was hard to make out where he was, but gradually, his eyes adjusted. He was staring up at a pair of luminescent lighting strips in a small room. He was inside.

The airlock! His previous moments of consciousness came back in a flood: crawling along the outside of the hull, his aching lungs and brain fog, finding the airlock hatch, opening it and entering too quickly, getting caught, his suit ripping . . . His suit!

It took every ounce of his strength, but he lifted his head and looked down the length of his prone body. The bonding tape had been ripped open down his side, presumably where it had been breached coming inside the airlock. The tear stretched to his head. His helmet had been ripped open and pushed down behind his neck, which was what was allowing him to see, he realized. And breathe so freely. How had *that* happened?

Drake's answer lay on the ground near his feet. Markus had passed out on the airlock floor, his own suit torn open around the neck and head so he too could breathe. And he was breathing. Drake could see his tape-covered chest moving up and down.

Somehow, Markus had managed to do what Drake had failed to: get the airlock hatch closed and cycle the emergency air supply inside, which was what they were now breathing. How he'd done that blind, Drake couldn't imagine. The airlock controls were on the other side of the room. Granted, it was just one lever to pull, but that lever was behind a panel and alongside two other levers that wouldn't do anything with power out.

Markus had figured it out, then had the presence of mind to open his and Drake's suits so they could get full breaths. The rips in their suits had allowed the vacuum to pull air out but allowed some in as well. It wouldn't have been enough.

What had served them so well to hold their breath out in the vacuum was certain death inside the airlock. They'd die from not being able to take another breath, even with the air they needed on the other side of the barrier of bonding tape and insulation.

Incredible. Drake was impressed and grateful. Markus had saved both their lives. "Markus," he called. His voice sounded like a bag of rocks scraping across the deck. He coughed, then tried again. "Markus?"

No answer.

With his lungs and shoulder screaming, Drake hauled himself into a seated position. He remained there for a long while to regain his breath before making another herculean effort to crawl over to his companion. The old man was face-up, with only his makeshift helmet torn off. The bonding tape must have made contact with his skin because there was a nasty gash on his forehead that hadn't been there before, a tape-sized strip of skin that had been ripped off. The upside of bonding tape was the same as its downside when it came to skin contact. It bonded with everything, even skin.

Blood pooled over the wound, still a fresh, wet, sparkling crimson. Drake realized the wound was healing before his eyes. From the edges of the gash inward, Drake could see cellular repair happening. It was like he was watching a time-lapse of the normal human healing process. The blood started to disappear, absorbed back into the skin.

Also incredible.

Drake wondered if he'd judged the old man too harshly because of that blood. It would be the height of hypocrisy if he had, wouldn't it? That was something the Paragon did. The Fleet welcomed all who pledged to fight, and despite all the conflict and resistance and perhaps even regret and second-guessing, Markus had pledged to fight. He was here. He had helped. He'd saved their lives after Drake had saved his. Drake mused as he looked up and around them, taking in the state of the airlock that he might be instrumental in saving more lives. He might have to be.

"Markus?" Drake repeated for what seemed like the thousandth time, but there was no answer from the old man. He was out cold. Deeper than sleep. Drake put a finger to his neck. He couldn't find a pulse, yet every few seconds, Drake saw his chest move up and down. It was the damnedest thing.

He started counting the length of time between breaths. What had started at around ten seconds was getting longer.

Twenty. Thirty. When it reached a minute, Drake figured he needed to intervene.

"Markus!" he shouted and shook him by both shoulders. That had the unwanted side effect of smacking the back of the man's head on the deck. "Shit," Drake said, bending over to see if he'd hurt him.

A gasp.

Drake looked into the Blaspheme's face.

Markus was awake. His kaleidoscope eyes were wide and wild. He wasn't in the airlock with Drake; he was somewhere else. Somewhere terrifying. With a yell, he grabbed Drake by the neck and squeezed hard.

"Markus," Drake wheezed as he brought his hands up to pry Markus' away. "It's . . . me!"

With a double-fisted chop, Drake smacked off one of Markus' hands, which enabled him to roll away from the old man. He landed on his bad shoulder and bellowed in pain. It was all he could do to crawl back to the bulkhead and seat himself against it, wheezing.

Markus screamed and thrashed, trying to get to his feet while fighting off unseen assailants. He looked like he was in a fever dream.

"*MARKUS!*" Drake yelled, miraculously finding his voice for one moment.

It worked. Markus stopped, half-standing, and blinked several times in rapid succession. His face was covered with sweat, and he was shaking. Drake had seen that look many times: post-trauma. "You're in the airlock with me," he said soothingly. "On *Glory*. We came here through the hull breach, remember? Together?"

Still shaking, Markus locked his gaze on Drake, blinked again, and then nodded. He collapsed against the opposite bulkhead, closed his eyes, and took deep, calming breaths.

When he opened his eyes again, they were steady and rooted in the here and now. "My apologies, Captain," he said, and Drake could tell he meant it. He was deeply embarrassed. "I was . . ." He paused, at a loss for words.

Drake looked away to give him some privacy. "No need to explain."

"It's a Paragon healing response," Markus said, anyway, albeit begrudgingly. "If an injury is serious enough, I will lose consciousness to speed up the process."

"Ah," Drake said, biting the tip of his tongue. "I hope I didn't hurt you."

"No." The old man shifted uncomfortably. "I hope I did not hurt *you*."

"I'm fine," Drake said. There was more to how Markus had awakened, the terror he'd seen in his eyes, and the fighting for his life, but if there was trauma there, it was Markus' story to tell. He would let him tell when, or if, he was ready.

Markus nodded appreciatively at the discretion.

"In fact," Drake added with a cough, "I am more than fine." He gestured at the airlock. "I'm *alive*, thanks to you."

Markus inclined his head. "We are even," he said, sounding more relieved about that than being alive.

"Is that also some Paragon thing?" Drake asked him, thinking back to how the old man had insisted it be acknowledged earlier that he'd saved Markus' life, how upset he'd seemed about it. "'Owing a life?'"

Markus nodded. "A life can only be traded for a life," he said seriously. "You saved mine. I had to save yours."

"Well, thank you."

Markus shook his head as if Drake didn't understand. "In order to reach the afterlife, one's ledger must be balanced. It is sacrosanct. To leave such a debt unpaid mean eternal damnation."

"Wouldn't want that."

Markus bristled. "You make light of it."

"Well, with humans, we look out for each other no matter what, sacrosanct or not. Particularly fellow soldiers."

"An odd philosophy."

"You should remember it. It's an ancient concept called 'no man left behind.'"

Markus inclined his head. "If I were taken, Captain, by the Paragon, would you come for me?"

"I would," Drake answered, without hesitation. "For any fellow soldier."

"Is that what I am?"

"I hope so." There was a pause. Markus clamped up, thinking. Drake shook his head and shifted subjects. "How did you manage it, anyway?" he asked. "The airlock?"

"You'd already done the hard work and opened the outer door. I just hauled ass and pulled every lever I could find. One of them had to be the manual release."

"Hauled ass, huh?" Drake repeated. He smiled. "That a Paragon thing, too?"

Markus frowned, then smiled back wearily. "No."

It was a Fleet term and an ancient one at that. A fascinating slip. And not the first one. "Maybe you're still a little more 'soldier' than you want to admit," Drake said. "That's the second time you've done that today."

Again, Markus frowned.

"It's not bad thing, right?" Drake said. "There's more than one heaven out there."

Markus shook his head at that. "There is not."

"Seems like you better hope there is. You're picking a side, here, you know."

That seemed to make Markus exceedingly uncomfortable. Silence hung in the air for a long beat.

"And it's that right there that makes me not trust you." Drake said, finally.

Markus looked pained. "I understand," he said. He looked, for all intents and purposes, like someone who was trying to be neutral; to do the right thing but remain uninvolved. Well, that was bullshit. He was involved. Heavily. But how did you make someone see that when they didn't want to? "Would you still come for me?" Markus asked, his expression earnest. "Even then?"

What an interesting question. "I . . . suppose I would."

Silence.

"Perhaps you can assist me in shedding my suit?" the old man asked of Drake, wanting to move on. The captain nodded and stood. Deep down, Drake knew there was a lot Markus had to decide and atone for . . . but at the very least he'd proven that he'd act in his own self-interests, which included surviving their current predicament.

With great difficulty, they took turns ripping off the exterior tape layer and tearing out gobs of insulation. "Leave those," Drake indicated when it came to freeing their hands from the makeshift gloves. Both he and Markus had bits of tape bonded to their hands. "When we get to Doc, he can remove that stuff without taking off our skin."

Markus nodded. "And how *are* we getting to the doctor?" he asked.

It was a good question, and one Drake had already started considering. Overhead, the airlock had only luminescent lighting. They'd had to pressurize it manually, with only the emergency air reserve to fill it, so that meant it had no power. Not a good sign, not after the length of time since the EMP. Beyond the inner airlock door, Drake could see that the corridor was a dark, twisted mess. It was clearly breached, which could explain their lack of power by itself . . . but it was also possible the entire ship was still down. Either way, there was no opening the inner airlock door.

He winced and directed Markus toward the lockers on either side of the airlock. "You take that side," he said, pointing. "I'll take these."

Drake flung open one of the lockers, revealing an EV suit. He rifled through the pockets of the suit and indicated that Markus should do the same. "We're looking for little white tabs," he explained and held up a hand for reference. "About palm-size with a colored dot in the center. Should be somewhere in the pockets of the suits."

"Like this?" Markus asked a moment later. He was holding a small plastiform square. It had a red dot in its center.

Drake swallowed. "Yup." A moment later, he found one in the second suit he went rifling through. It too had a bright red dot in its center. "Damn," he said and gave a knowing nod. It was what he'd expected and feared.

"These are radiation tabs?" Markus asked.

"Good guess."

"What color indicates high levels?"

"Oh, I'd bet you can make another good guess, Markus."

"Red."

Drake nodded grimly and leaned against the lockers for a moment to catch his breath and think. Power had not yet been restored to this section of the ship; they knew that from being in the airlock. Curiosity about the rest of *Glory* had driven Drake to look for the radiation indicators. In the event of an incoming EMP, resistant bulkheads closed over every exposed critical system on the ship, like the forward sensor pod they'd just escaped from. There was no power after that; everything was disconnected. The vast majority of the bulkheads on the ship retracted as power was restored, lifted electronically, but the most critical first step were those bulkheads that shielded the power core. Those worked on a mechanical system, non-electronic and automatic, which raised the shielding once the pulse had passed.

If that didn't happen, however—if that automatic system was damaged—the power core began to overheat from plasma buildup that had nowhere to vent, and radiation levels started to increase. Those bright red radiation tabs that he and Markus had just found indicated radiation was high, which told Drake that the crash-metal bulkheads around the power core had not been raised.

Why had Fredrickson and his crew failed to address the issue? There were manual release controls on both the port and starboard hull. Damage from the explosion, probably. Lack of access. Whatever the reason, those bulkheads needed to be raised, or radiation would poison the ship and its crew, him and Markus included.

Drake explained that to Markus. "Any significant radiation concentration also increases the chances of us being detected by the Paragon," he pointed out, adding yet another dire consequence to their predicament.

"We have to get those bulkheads up," the captain said. It was as simple as that. "Flush the plasma system and restore power."

"How do we do that?"

Drake looked at the EV suits they'd uncovered while looking for the radiation tabs, then back at his companion. He sighed deeply. "We're going back outside."

CHAPTER THIRTY-SIX

WARREN AND COMPANY made camp on the outer edge of the valley floor. It was about an hour from the labor compound, so they'd have to pack up before dawn, but he figured that was ideal. Moving through the forest in the dark would be difficult, to be sure, but it would provide ample cover as long as they were quiet. That would be critical for their survival this close to the camp.

Idri had once again volunteered for first watch. He was proud of her. Thus far, she'd been a perfect fit. As had Sudan, their engineer, whom Warren hadn't known anything about before she'd reported to training. She handled her shit, too, no fuss, and that sourpuss of a chief engineer Fredrickson had said she was the best computer person he had. His actual words had been, "best-at-every-thing person I have." Her real test would come when they got into the research facility. Idri's too.

All of them would be tested.

First, however, food and rest. The climb down the slopes had been arguably more difficult than the climb up. Warren had once heard that over the history of Earth's greatest peaks, it wasn't summiting that was so deadly. It was the climb down that killed you. These peaks weren't that high, but they were cold, rocky, and difficult.

He was glad Carrol had taken his advice and planned for two full days' hike from the crash site. They'd covered maybe a tenth of the distance this second day as the crow flew, but in number of footsteps taken, today had been longer. Everyone was exhausted, freezing, and hungry. The coming darkness wouldn't help the temperature part of the equation, but Vorkut V's long night would afford them some decent rest.

Smith again made them all hot food, then he, Sudan, and Warren set up their single-person tents while Idri and the dog tromped off to make a lookout hidey hole nearby. Even the dog had been an excellent companion. She certainly was handy as a guard with her heightened senses. Warren wasn't sure how helpful she would be when they got to the facility, but Smith had assured them of her stealth and attack capabilities. They were probably superior to the rest of team's. She could full-on disappear.

The howls of the wolf-creatures serenaded him to sleep.

CRACK!

Warren jerked awake when gunfire echoed across the forest. A single shot. He bolted from his tent, grabbing his rifle and not bothering to don his warm clothes or even put his boots on. Smith was out of his tent as well, and they followed the sound of the gunshot together.

Idri was standing in the middle of a small clearing, bathed in a mix of silver and blue light from the gas giant. Her gun was slack in her right hand, and she was looking at the smoking carcass of what she'd just shot lying in the snow.

It wasn't a wolf or any other creature native to Vorkut.

"Shit," Warren murmured, raising his rifle to sweep the rest of the forest, looking for movement or heat. Smith did the same. Idri had shot a Paragon trooper.

"What's going on?" a voice called from the camp. It was Sudan, shivering in the snow, looking wide-eyed.

"Paragon patrol," Warren hissed. He lowered his weapon when he was satisfied that their immediate surroundings were clear. "Start packing up," he told her. "And keep your weapon on you."

The engineer nodded. She'd brought her rifle like she was supposed to, even though she was only half-dressed. Good for her. Warren addressed Smith as he shouldered his weapon. "Cover us."

"Yes, sir."

"Idri," Warren said, reaching out to her. She was still standing stock-still, eyes wider even than Sudan's. She was in shock. "Hey, Idri! I need you to step back, okay?"

"He was going to find the camp," she said, still staring at the dead Paragon in the snow. The soldier had been twice her size. Then she looked at Warren, dazed, and started to shake. "I didn't see him until he was almost on top of me."

Warren gripped her shoulder to steady her. "You did good. Look at me. Hey." She met his gaze and he squeezed her, willing calm and clarity into her. "You. Did. Good."

"Others will have heard," she whispered, eyes still wide.

He nodded and gave her a grim smile. "That's why I need you to step back, okay?" She nodded. "Shoulder your rifle and help Smith sweep the forest." She nodded again, still shaking, but did as she was told. Warren let her go. "Where's the dog?"

"Here," Smith said. Cheddar was at his side. Warren hadn't seen her and figured she must have gone invisible. They were all going to have to do that.

He pulled a Ka-Bar from his belt, flipped it, and plunged it into the dead Paragon's chest. He'd never cut through their suits before, and it took every ounce of strength he had to get the blade to slice the stuff, but they cut just like every other living creature. Or dead creature, in this case. The owner of the suit decayed into ash as Warren did his work—the Paragon self-incinerators were intact, as they always were—but that didn't matter. This would accomplish his aim.

He took gobs of the ash, some of it still wet, and flung it around the clearing. Streaks and splatters of Paragon blood soon glistened on the snow, along with the blobs of dark tissue that had self-destructed. It made quite the scene, particularly when the former turned into the latter with a telltale sizzle and a burst of smoke.

Warren stood when he was done, covered in the black stuff like the clearing. He nodded. "Hopefully, it looks like the wolves did it," he said to Smith and Idri.

The Navid looked on in shock, her face twisted with horror.

More patrols were coming. That much was certain since someone had to have been close enough to hear the sound of Idri's plasma rifle, or they would look for a lost colleague. If Warren's display was convincing, however, it just might buy them enough time to slink away before those patrols showed up, set up camp somewhere else, and wait for dawn. But they needed to move fast.

"Let's pack up and make ourselves scarce," he said to the other two.

They gave affirmative grunts, Idri included. She looked like she was regaining her nerve because the others were going about their duties in such a workmanlike manner. Focusing on the mission was the treatment for what ailed her. It was not a cure since she might never be cured. No Navid had taken a life as far as he knew, but here she was with a smoking rifle. Still, it had to be done. She hadn't just volunteered; she demanded to be brought along. Warren had told her there would be consequences.

The three rushed back to join Sudan, who had much of the packing done.

Idri had pulled that trigger when she needed to. Warren would find time later to say how proud he was of her.

In the meantime, so much for rest.

———

ZED and Carrol made their camp in an ice cave at the head of a small canyon that was about a half hours' distance from the shuttle plateau. Its entrance was just large enough for them to crawl inside with their packs on, then it opened into a large room. No one would come looking for them unless they'd been seen going in. The two huddled together in the darkness, watching the dusk's light fade from the entrance for a solid half-hour before Carrol let them pitch camp just to make sure they didn't have to run for it. This close to their target, she didn't want to take any chances.

Zed didn't complain. He hadn't during the entire trip, Carrol realized as they ate cold meal packs. The cave was solid ice; no way to block light when the undulating blue-white facets reflected it every which way. They'd decided the heat capsules were too risky, thus cold food. The only illumination they opted for were super-low luminosity glow sticks they hung around their necks that lit their faces in an eerie yellow-green. Those, hopefully, weren't strong enough to show through the ice to the outside. Carrol didn't think so, given the reflections and refractions of the ambient light.

"You've been so good," Carrol said to Zed as she munched on a mushy stew consisting of re-constituted proteins, fats, and carbohydrates. They were wrapped in their sleep sacks, trying to get warm.

"What do you mean?" His head was a floating blob of color.

"I dunno. I kind of expected you to make more jokes or, like, grab my ass or something."

"Are you saying you want me to grab your ass?"

"No."

"Because if that's what you want, Commander, all you need to do is maneuver said ass on over here into my sack. I can take care of that for you."

"I was expressing gratitude."

Zed harrumphed. "Sounded like you were expressing surprise."

Carrol arched an eyebrow. "I guess I was."

He shook his head and pointed his utensil at her in a playfully accusatory manner. "You know, I have the same training as you. I know how to take a mission seriously."

She shrugged. He had shown her that. But . . . "I remember that being an issue, though," she said, thinking back to when they'd first met. "Not taking things seriously back then. I remember that was one of the reasons we broke up."

Zed's expression became sincere. "We didn't break up because I didn't take you seriously, Eunice. From what I remember, it was quite the opposite, actually."

Carrol put her head down. "I meant taking the Fleet seriously."

Zed had been the delinquent in the pilot program, constantly on the edge of being kicked out because of his disdain for the rules. His extraordinary talent for flying kept him in, which had always grated on Carrol. There were a lot of pilots like that. They were not as invested in making a difference or a career out of the Fleet like Carrol was. That was one of the reasons she'd decided to drop out of the program.

Zed was right. The only indication he'd ever given her when they were together for that brief time—months, she figured; maybe six? That was a long time in your early twenties—was that he was devoted to her. He hadn't strayed that she'd known about, and though he'd had the hardest time showing up for class or on the flight deck, he'd always been where he said he would be when it came to sneaking off somewhere for a quickie or hitting the local bars for a night out. The fact that he *could* be responsible but chose not to when it came to flight school had grated on her, eventually too much, so she'd left. Without telling Zed, as she recalled.

She wondered how long it had taken him to show up for class and realize she wasn't there anymore and had dropped out of the program.

"I am sorry for that," she said after a prolonged silence. They hadn't talked about the past yet. Not really.

"For leaving? Or for not telling me?"

"The latter."

Zed shrugged it off, the lightness returning to his manner. "Ancient history," he said, and he wrapped up his meal pack with the utensil, then set it aside to snuggle down inside his sack. He was acting cavalier about it, but Carrol could tell there was still pain there. She was surprised to find it was the same for her. She'd blamed Zed when it came to the reasons their relationship had failed, but she now realized that wasn't entirely true. A lot of it had been her. She'd run. From what . . . she didn't fully know.

Zed covered his glow stick, and Carrol heard him lie

down to sleep. She finished her meal, wrapped it up, and tossed it aside, then covered her glow stick and settled into her sack to sleep as well.

"Good night, Commander," Zed called. Goddammit, she hated it when he used her rank.

"Night. *Lieutenant.*"

There was no need to have a watch with this setup. They would have had to go outside to see, exposing themselves to what they were trying to hide from. That would be more dangerous than staying inside. There was nothing left to do for the next day. No plans to make, equipment to check, or targets to assess. It would all be there in the morning, ready to go. They were both free to get a good night's sleep.

Yeah.

A full, good, quiet night's sleep.

"Holy fucking balls," Zed yelped when Carrol kneed him in the back a few minutes later, trying to find the opening of his sleeping sack. "What the fuck?"

"Shut the fuck up."

"You scared me."

"Well, move over."

"What?"

"It's fucking freezing! Move over!" Zed wriggled aside enough for Carrol to slip inside his sack with him. It was warm in there, thank the gods. She wrapped herself around him, shivering. "You're like a furnace," she said through clenched teeth.

"And your feet are like coolant rods."

"Sorry," she said. She hadn't realized she'd been rubbing her feet against his. "I have my socks on."

She reached down to slip them off, and Zed yelped again. "That is *decidedly* worse. Fuck, you are cold."

"Why do you think I came over here?" she said, then ran her fingers over his chest, pressing against him as tightly as she could, small spoon to big spoon but in reverse.

They lay like that for a long time.

"I am sorry," she whispered into his ear.

"Is that why you came over here?"

She nodded, her chin on the curve of his neck. She moved her hands from his chest along his torso.

"I see," he said when she'd gone far enough south.

He turned over to face her.

"I wanted to tell you I'm sorry," she said.

Zed swallowed. "You're going to tell me I'm sorry with your clothes on?" She laughed. "Because that sounds great, but this," Zed put his hand on the button of her stiff and poky standard issue underlayer pants. "Christ almighty, whatever this is is pushing right up into my junk. Painfully."

She laughed again, then ran her hands up the back of his head and through his hair and kissed him. "Well, maybe you can help me with that."

CHAPTER THIRTY-SEVEN

HOLY FUCK, it was so much easier to go EV when you could see what you were doing. Drake reveled in having a proper suit with creature comforts like a visor, fabric that was not only a perfect seal but was made to move freely, and luxuries like *air*. He only got to drink it all in for a moment, however, because what he saw through his visor was not great.

Glory was in rough shape, far worse than Drake had expected. Giant shards of rock bristled from her port side like quills on a porcupine, and there was a massive spike near the stern, right around where the engineering sections were. Drake had a sneaking suspicion that Fredrickson's crew, if they were still alive, were stuck behind it, which was why they were still in this predicament.

He and Markus walked down the hull, feet hum-clicking with each step, verifying the magnetic charge that kept them from floating off into space. *Glory* had a slight gravity field projected onto its hull to prevent that from happening, so-called "skin gravity." It was ten percent of Earth standard, but it wasn't anything to trifle with and was more of a failsafe than a guarantee. The gravity boots safely secured them to the metal exterior.

It wasn't the only thing they secured to. More than once, Drake accidentally stepped on a small shard of asteroid and had to stop and pry it from his boots. The asteroids were full of ferrous metals. Even in the dim light of the Vorkut star, Drake could see them glint a shiny gray. No wonder the asteroid shards had proven to be so deadly; they were practically solid iron or some other hard metal. Who knew? They had been strong enough to pierce his ship in many places.

"Careful not to step on them," Drake called to Markus after getting the millionth shard stuck in his magnetic boots. They had radio now, too. That was nice.

"I'm aware," Markus replied with a frustrated grunt. Drake turned to see that he had stopped to remove rock chunks from his boots.

If it weren't for the destruction and mayhem around them, Drake might have thought it was beautiful out. The Vorkut gas giant was close enough and at the right angle to reflect much of its star's light, which lit the asteroid field around them. It was thick and constantly moving. Every so often, thankfully in the distance, a pair of rocks would come together and shatter. Vorkut was a brilliant blue, and Drake would swear he saw the fifth moon slowly swinging around in its orbit. His team was down there, counting on him. It was not like he needed any further resolve, but Drake used their situation anyway. They were going to succeed or die trying. They were all in on this mission.

Making good time, especially compared to their previous blind tape-covered crawl, Drake observed an answer to at least one of his mysteries—why they were alone on the port-side hull. The main stretch of mid-ship airlocks, the ones where a rescue mission to access the exterior bulk-head and plasma manifold releases could most easily have launched from, were gashed open in an almost perfect line. Dumb bad luck.

The main airlocks on the starboard side of the ship were probably fine, but that was a hike, especially through a ship without power when you had to open every door by hand. Drake and Markus had been the closest hands to the problem. At least, that was what Drake hoped. It was also possible that everyone inside was dead. Freak catastrophic atmospheric venting or poison.

Or maybe the radiation levels were already lethal. All those tabs did was tell you when levels had risen above normal. They did not indicate the actual severity. He and Markus could be marching toward their deaths at this very second.

Drake pushed all the worst-case scenarios from his mind. As dark as it was inside *Glory*, he had faith. It hadn't been that long. They would restore power and get the radiation under control, and she would be fine. Everyone would be fine.

They reached their destination a short time later. Drake, panting, stopped to stand over a panel the size of his torso with bright yellow letters that said MANUAL SHIELDING RELEASE. "This is it," he called to Markus, who was huffing over the radio. "Help me with it, will you?" he asked after he made sure he had one magnetic boot firmly planted on the ship's hull. He kneeled down on the other leg, and Markus did the same without being prompted. He either had EV experience or was a fast study.

There were two handholds, one on either side of the panel, and the men pulled it open on the count of three. They felt a thunk through their suits as it came free. Drake guided it next to them and let it settle onto the hull, secured by the ship's skin gravity.

"Um, Captain?" Markus called while Drake was doing so.

Drake turned. Under the panel were four levers that had to be pulled in sequence to trigger the internal mechanisms across the ship that would raise the EMP-shielded bulkheads in a reverse chain reaction to what had dropped them. What Markus was pointing out made his heart sink. The four levers were intact, but they were glowing with heat and radiation.

"What do you suggest?" Markus asked through a burst of static. The radiation was getting to their radio.

Drake gestured that they should back off. Their suits had radiation protection, but only for the stray solar flare or the odd gamma ray. They couldn't handle a pummeling like what was coming off those levers for more than a few seconds.

He shook his head. This meant the buildup was considerably worse than he'd thought. They couldn't wait for the power circuits to be restored. The ship was in a critical state with its plasma stuck in the venting system, getting hotter and hotter and more and more radioactive. The pressure had to be released, but those automatic systems were stuck closed, probably even melting by now. "We have to vent the plasma manifolds," he replied to Markus' question. *Damn.*

"It's going to take two of us."

"You GOT IT?" Drake asked Markus for the millionth time. The old man was annoyed, perhaps even insulted, but it was critical that he follow the instructions to the letter.

The manual plasma release wasn't far away. It was on the other side of the colossal asteroid shard sticking out of the engineering section. However, it was an all-or-nothing proposition. Nicknamed the "blowhole," once you threw it open, there was no closing it. It would drain the plasma system if left to its own devices, plasma and coolant blowing out into space in one giant plume.

It was designed to be a failsafe fuel dump to protect the ship from a core meltdown. It would also cool those levers almost instantaneously, and once those were thrown, the automated systems would take over. They'd register that the core was *not* in imminent danger of a meltdown and close the manifolds to keep from dumping further plasma. Then *Glory's* remaining fuel would be safe. But the levers had to be thrown. They were here, and the manual release for the blowhole was just past the asteroid shard. Drake couldn't be in both places at once.

"In sequence," Markus repeated, not bothering to hide his annoyance.

"Soon as you see the plume. It'll be as bright as the sun. You can't miss it."

"I know what a plasma looks like."

Drake pointed at the levers. "One, two, three, four soon as they stop glowing."

"Captain," Markus said, stopping him. "I understand."

Drake nodded. It was just that if Markus didn't do this, *Glory* would be disabled. A sitting duck, waiting to be blown away by the Paragon when they inevitably found her, or they would sit in this asteroid field until she became a frozen tomb. Drake didn't say that to him. He could see by the old man's face that he didn't have to. He knew what was at stake. "I'm trusting you here," he told him. This was it. No more beating around the bush or dropping subject.

Markus was either rediscovering his humanity or not. "You're picking a side. Okay?"

Markus' eyes were steely and steady. "Okay."

"Okay."

The static on their radios was bad, and it would get worse with distance and the additional radiation between them. "Don't wait for me to signal. I doubt we'll be able to hear each other over the interference. You just throw these after you see the plume."

Markus nodded. He understood.

Drake inhaled and set off without another word.

Ahead of him loomed the shard. 'Colossal' would have been an understatement of a descriptor for it, as was 'shard.' It was a whole-ass asteroid. From the way it glinted, Drake could tell it was almost entirely metallic, like the smaller shards. Iron, if he had to guess. Up close, he could see where it had slammed into the ship. Several major cross-beams were warped or broken and curled inward around the edges, which complicated things. Those were structural. They'd have to be replaced if the asteroid was to be removed, but that was an interesting thought. Drake tucked it away in his brain for later.

He reached the other side of the shard and saw the blowhole about thirty meters dead ahead. He'd never done what he was about to attempt to do, not from the outside while standing right next to the damn thing. It could very well kill him. The manual controls were precariously close to the vent, ten meters away at most. That was *not* far, considering it was about to release energy equivalent to a small sun. Very small, but still a *sun*.

It also occurred to Drake that the all-at-once venting would produce the exact type of hey-look-at-me energy plume *Glory* had worked so hard to avoid.

Maybe he'd get lucky and survive. Maybe they all would.

Drake prayed for luck as he knelt and wrapped his fingers around the two grips that would open the blowhole. He shot one last look in Markus' direction and hoped the old man was good for his promises. Once these grips were pulled, there was no going back.

It was a simple swing from their closed position down to their open one. They moved much more easily than Drake had expected, and at first, the venting was much quieter. Silent, in fact.

Drake started running the second he flipped the switch. He felt the deck under his magnetic boots rumble about two steps after that.

On his fifth step, the hull beneath him exploded.

CHAPTER THIRTY-EIGHT

THE MORNING WAS the first time Carrol had seen sunshine on Vorkut V. The dawn light made it riskier to pick their way from the ice cave down into the small canyon, given that the sun made everything more visible than the usual gray-white haze, but Carrol would take it. They'd found a canyon seam to climb down that was out of sight, and they were covered in the closest replicas to prisoner garb that Markus and Warren could describe to the ship's stores.

They were also making good time in the warmth. Carrol didn't know if it was because of their night together or despite it, but Zed and she were moving in sync. Their communication was silent, instantaneous, and precise. They found routes through the rocks and ice without a word, seamlessly taking turns, one going first and helping the other where necessary. It took them about a half-hour to descend to the ledge.

Down in the snow and trees, it was the same as they advanced toward the shuttle plateau, stopping every so often to listen for Paragon patrols or point out a buried branch or uneven terrain that might cause them to fall or make noise. They were quite the team. It made Carrol think about their flying together during the attack on Earth. They'd been quite the team, hadn't they?

The small canyon started to narrow, and as they rounded a particularly sharp bend, the two froze. They'd reached the plateau, and not more than ten meters ahead was a group of Paragon troopers in all-white powered suits with bright blue dots covering them.

Shit.

Carrol slowly moved back around the bend and gestured for Zed to do the same. When the rocks were between them again, she let out a sigh of relief. The troopers hadn't moved. She doubted they'd been spotted.

They'd backed themselves into a corner, however. Carrol had seen seven troopers. Far too many for them to take out quietly, and whatever moves they made here early in the day needed to be quiet until the fireworks started. By then, it was go time. She'd thought about this a lot. Too many variables to consider before they got here, but now they were getting a clearer picture.

"We'll have to observe the guards' patterns," she whispered when she and Zed were sufficiently back into the underbrush to speak. "Start picking them off, or better yet, find a hole and try to make it into one of the shuttles. Hide out there 'til it's go time."

"How many guards?"

"I saw seven in that group. Who knows how many total?"

Grim. Zed leaned against the bush they'd hidden behind, and Carrol adjusted her pack, which was hidden under the ragged prison overcoat each was wearing. It wasn't a good disguise, particularly up close. Beneath the worn brown-gray material, they were in full Fleet gear, packs on their shoulders and rifles in hand, things a real prisoner wouldn't have. The coats *would* let them blend in from a distance.

"As long as they don't send any patrols into this canyon," Carrol said, considering their prospects, "I'd think our chances are okay."

"Commander?"

"Maybe, if worst comes to worst, we can try a diversion. Blow something up."

"*Commander?*"

Carrol turned at the urgency in his voice. Zed had his hands up, and he was looking behind them. Carrol followed his gaze, and her stomach dropped to her toes.

Four Paragon troopers were standing in the snow behind them, weapons raised and ready to fire. One made a singsong noise that belied his mean, faceless look. He gestured at her with his rifle, and she didn't need a translator to understand. He was telling her to drop her weapon and put her hands in the air like Zed.

She did. Apparently, the Paragon did patrol the canyon.

THE LABOR CAMP was way too quiet.

What Warren remembered from mere weeks earlier as a massive, bustling, chaotic mess of life was now, by all outward signs, mostly abandoned. The mine pit was still as well, no dust rising from the conveyors, no crunching of wheelbarrows on the narrow winding paths, no loaders churning and clanking as the sorted stone moved down them in plastiform containers for shipping off-world. He didn't understand. The mine had been operating for decades from the age of some of that equipment, and

Warren had personally seen that the remaining magnesite deposits were plentiful. There was no reason to shut the operation down.

He felt like a prisoner again, regardless. Perhaps it was the camp itself, these trees, the snow, the cold. Perhaps it was wearing the nasty-ass overcoats, which *Glory's* threads department had dutifully replicated for the team to wear in sight of the camp—perhaps a little too well. Maybe it was that it hadn't been that long since he was on the other side of that fence, and he didn't like it.

The quiet of the camp had him on edge. As he, Smith, Idri, Sudan, and Cheddar wove through the trees along the fence line, they saw neither hide nor hair of *anyone*, guard or prisoner. It was like the Paragon were opening the front door and inviting them inside. Either that or the camp had been abandoned. Warren liked neither scenario.

He halted the group at an out-of-the-way corner of the fence line that was shielded from view by the backs of several prisoner huts. Sudan had the wire cutters, and she moved forward with them in hand to create an opening, but Warren halted her. He took out his dagger, made sure his hand was only touching its rubber-wrapped grip and none of the metal parts, and tapped the fence. He was greeted by a shower of sparks.

Okay, the lights were still on. It made the quiet even more disconcerting.

They'd planned for this. Sudan produced a wire and a pair of insulated gloves from her pack, then took one end of the wire and wrapped it around the nearest current post. She unspooled the wire across the post on the other side of where they wanted to get through and secured it there as well. Then she went about slicing the existing fencing from top to bottom on both sides as they'd planned. Warren didn't know if the electrified fence was rigged so that if power was interrupted in a certain section, an alarm went off somewhere that indicated exactly where the breach was, but why take that chance? With their wire running from one post to the other, keeping the current alive, they wouldn't trip the alarm. It was Engineering 101.

Each team member slipped under the active wire, careful not to touch it, and when everyone was on the other side, Sudan closed the breach. It was obvious that the fence had been cut if a guard looked closely, but it might pass muster from farther away if they hadn't tripped the alarm.

"Let's move," Warren whispered to his team.

He slung his rifle over his back, hidden under the prisoner overcoat but ready to slip into his hands and ready to fire at a moment's notice. Everyone else did the same and they set off, using the prisoner cabins for cover.

They were empty, and not because they were the derelict, abandoned kind he and Markus had hidden in. These had been teeming with inmates the last time Warren had been in the camp. Now, there wasn't an individual to be found. The same held true as they progressed to the center of the camp and the central pathway. From around the corner of an administration building, Warren observed the chow hall. Empty.

He finally spotted some activity by the research facility. A small group of guards was unloading equipment from one of the dozens of transport containers that littered the landing field to the right of the pathway. The central gate was wide open, nothing like the guarded bottleneck through which he and Markus had snuck to get off this rock.

Then Warren spotted the intake office. "This way," he whispered to the team, and he diverted them toward the shack.

"What the heck?" Sudan hissed. "Facility's that way."

"Unfinished business," he shot back. If the camp was this quiet and abandoned, he was going to take advantage of that and recover what was his.

The door to the office was ajar. He followed procedure and carefully cleared the room with Smith, Idri, and Sudan, but he knew it was empty well before then. Papers were strewn about the floor and over the intake desk. The chair had been overturned. It looked like they'd left in a hurry. Warren shrugged off his overcoat, then set his pack and his rifle down as well. "Watch that," he said, pointing at the front door. Bewildered, his team nodded, but they didn't protest.

Warren hustled into the rear storage area of the shack and sent up a prayer to the stars that his armor would be where he thought it was. He pulled out the bin he remembered and saw his armor, neatly folded and untouched since the last time he'd seen it. Its power core even clanked around inside the helmet when he lifted it. "Goddamn right," he muttered. *Now* was the time to put it back on.

"Aren't you going to stick out like a sore thumb?" Idri asked, frowning as he rejoined his team in the front office. He was wearing his armor like the warrior he was.

"We're not going in through the main gate," he answered, clicking his suit on. It hummed to life, thank the stars. It made him feel whole. "We'd stick out like sore thumbs even with our coats on since there's nobody here to blend in with." He ran his armor through the startup tests for its systems: weapons, life support, and mobility assist. Everything was working, which was a goddamn miracle. He felt whole again. For the first time in ages, he felt like himself.

"So, what do we do?"

"There's a whole mess of transport containers along the right side of the field. We can use those for cover and find a side entrance. I know they exist. We have to stay hidden as we move anyway, so why not move as armed and powered up as possible?"

Idri agreed, not that he needed her to. He was back in his armor, and nobody was getting him out of it. She did, however, convince him to put his prisoner overcoat back on, which had some wisdom to it even if the coat barely covered him now. It would be worthy of a double-take, and sometimes that was all the edge you needed in combat.

Warren inhaled as his dopamine high of getting back what was his faded. This was the diciest part of their mission: getting into the facility. Plan A had been to blend in with the workers as he and Markus had. They'd manufactured access cards to Markus' specs and green armbands to go along with their overcoats. The former might still come in handy, but the rest of that plan was out the window. They would have to get inside the facility the old-fashioned way: sneak in and bust heads.

Guards didn't seem to be plentiful from the outside, and the prototype ship was still in the sky. That meant that whatever else the Paragon had pulled out of this facility, what they were there for, what they wanted, was still there. He was beginning to wonder if that uneasy feeling in his stomach was just his innate pessimism. Maybe this was exactly what it looked like, an incredible stroke of good luck.

"Lieutenant," Smith called from just outside the door to the shack. Warren raised his head to look at him. The Marine was looking at the sky. "I think you should see this." Warren walked out to join him, Idri and Sudan in tow.

In the clear morning sky, pushing through the faintest wisps of thin cirrus clouds at the top of the troposphere, a massive ship was descending toward the complex. Warren's blood pressure rose just looking at it, and his chest constricted.

"What is that?" Idri asked, picking up on the change in body language.

"That," Warren said, "is Archgeneral Hadras' ship."

Peering farther up, he saw other ships, glinting specks in high orbit. Pretty soon, the system would be crawling with Paragon. The complex, too.

"We need to move." He went back inside to grab his helmet and clip it to the back of his armor beneath his pack.

He felt like this was retribution for entertaining the brief moment of optimism earlier. A cosmic smackdown for thinking things were breaking their way. They weren't. It hadn't been good luck that the camp was empty. Shit was going down. That was the only reason the archgeneral would be here. They had to get their job done before that happened, whatever it was.

"Stick together," he whispered to his team. "Hands on your weapons, ready at all times."

They all nodded. Even the dog looked poised and ready to go.

Warren led them out of the shack and back into the snow.

CHAPTER THIRTY-NINE

THE BLOWHOLE WAS TEARING the ship apart.

As Drake was launched into the vacuum, he got a bird's eye view of how compromised the structural integrity was in this rear section of the ship close to where the massive asteroid shard had pierced it. Several beams beyond those in the immediate impact area were exposed as the plasma release shook off loose hull panels. The longer the plasma fountain raged, the more the hull cracked and buckled in concentric circles.

Where was Markus?

Of more immediate concern to Drake, however, was how he was going to stop himself from spinning out into space. Lucky for him, the buckling hull had ejected him on a trajectory not out into deep space but toward the asteroid shard. When he smacked into the rock, Drake reconsidered the "lucky" part of that thought. He hit back-first, which knocked the wind out of him, and the back of his head hit the shard. The force of the impact sent him hurtling back down toward the ship.

That became Drake's new primary concern.

The hull was warping and splintering from the heat and force from the plasma. Still, it roared out into the darkness, looking like a geyser. Drake didn't know how long it had been, but it should have shut off by now. Markus should have thrown those levers, and *Glory* should be returning to full power. The plasma still blew like fury.

Drake hit the hull even harder than he had hit the asteroid shard because of that low-gravity field. He skidded along, sliding god knows where before catching a protrusion with his feet. He felt the *thunk* of the magnets in his boots latching on. A ring of superheated metal was expanding from the exhaust port and becoming molten as it went. Drake was just beyond it, but not for long

Still the plasma belched into the cosmos.

Where? Was? Markus???

He'd abandoned him, Drake realized. He'd been playing him the whole time, gaining his confidence and waiting for an opportunity of real vulnerability to present itself so that he could strike a deadly blow. Drake had been a sucker. They all had, but especially him. He should have gone with his gut from the very start. The man, or whatever he was, couldn't be trusted.

Except that was not what Drake's gut told him anymore. As he slowly slid toward the expanding pool of molten metal, Drake's intuition told him that Markus hadn't betrayed him. He was probably dealing with some unforeseen complication or was in danger. If they failed and this all went south, it wouldn't be from some nefarious design or sabotage. They had simply run out of luck.

The plasma flare shut off.

Blessedly, the fountain of energy ceased to tear into the hull and spew into the vacuum. Was it because the ship's energy stores had been emptied, or was it because Drake's gut feeling was right, and Markus had managed to help him save the day?

Drake gingerly picked himself up off the hull, taking care to make sure his magnetic boots were secure before standing. "Markus?" he called over the radio. In return, he received only static. "Markus?" he tried again. Nothing. The radiation must still be too thick.

Orienting himself with the asteroid shard, Drake hustled as fast as he dared back to the release controls.

It was deserted.

Drake's pulse quickened and he picked up his pace. From a few yards out, he could see that the levers were thrown. Markus had pulled through. Goddammit, he'd actually made his choice. But then . . . where was he? "Markus?" Drake tried again, breaking into a jog. "You did it! Where are you?"

Still no answer. Only static.

When Drake finally arrived at the controls, he started to piece it together. Several hull panels were missing. And right above the levers, where the stenciled letters MANUAL SHIELDING RELEASE had read just minutes earlier, was a gaping, still-glowing hole. The release valve wasn't the only place the ship had spewed plasma. It had probably blown up right in Markus' face.

Drake whirled, looking out up into the starscape. "Markus?!" he shouted. Dammit. Static, still.

His head swam with a torrent of thoughts and emotions. The old man must have been ejected into space. Could be dead already, but maybe not. Without the radio, how was he going to find him?

The answer was snug around his wrist. *The wristcoms.* They'd programmed them back in the antechamber to act as a homing signal for each other. Goddammit, why hadn't he thought of that sooner? Every second Drake wasted, Markus was out there somewhere drifting farther away.

His hands were shaking as tapped the small device, activating the signal.

Nothing happened.

Then . . .

Tap-tap, tap-tap-tap.

Drake yelled in satisfaction. The haptics against his wrist were unmistakable. Tap-tap, tap-tap-tap. He waved his arm around in deliberate patterns, feeling ever so slightly where the signal was the strongest.

There.

Toward the shard. Drake looked up in that direction.

A dot against the dark glinted back. These EV suits were basic. They, unfortunately, did not have an internal computer or a heads-up display of any kind. Vision was down to the naked eye alone, but that was enough. Drake saw Markus. His body looked limp, and he was rising steadily away from the ship, already twenty meters out and climbing. There was nothing in the way of his trajectory to stop him from floating all the way out into the void. But he wasn't far enough out that he was higher than the shard.

Yet.

Drake hauled ass—yes, in honor of Markus—out away from the shard. It was counterintuitive at first, but by the time Drake got to where he wanted to be, he'd created a nice angle between the shard, Markus, and he. It was eye-balled. Imprecise as fuck. No time to second-guess it, however.

Drake launched himself off the hull plating.

His stomach floated up into his throat as the gravity field fell away, and Drake contemplated whether or not this was crazy. It most certainly was. But as he floated steadily toward the old man's limp figure, the better and better his makeshift trajectory was looking. Like a quarterback on a football field—a game still played at colleges and universities across Earth and her colonies—you had to aim not where your target was, but where it was *going* to be. Drake had managed to do that rather perfectly. And from his angle with the shard, they would hit that, too, rather than careen off into empty space.

Thunk.

He made contact with Markus right in the chest.

It spun them both around, however; something Drake hadn't anticipated. As his field of vision twirled, he tried to get bearing on the shard. Tricky. A humbling reminder that he was an absolute idiot for doing this.

Smack

They hit against the shard butt-first, much as Drake had just minutes earlier when he was thrown off the hull in the plasma explosion. This time, however, he wasn't so lucky as to have hit at the right angle to send him back from whence he came. They skittered along the surface of the metallic rock, still traveling *up* and away from the ship.

"Aaaaaaaah," Drake yelled, churning his feet and trying to get a hold. He didn't dare let go of Markus, so he couldn't use his hands. But his boots; his magnetic boots. If only they could catch . . .

They did. By a toe.

It was only for the briefest of moments, but when Drake felt it, he slammed his heel down as hard as he could. It caught, too, and Drake did the same with his other boot.

With a jerk that nearly tore Markus from his grasp, their momentum finally stopped.

Drake hung there, panting for a good long minute, not daring to move his feet a millimeter. Once he got his bearings, he dared to look down. If he were a more expressive man, he would have screamed. They were right on the tip of the shard. Inches—literally one or two of them—from the very edge of the asteroid. It had been that close.

Carefully, with an aching precision, Drake crouched and maneuvered himself and Markus to aim back down toward the ship. Once he was absolutely sure they were pointed in the right direction, Drake kicked off the shard, and they were finally, blessedly, drifting toward home. It was going to take them awhile to get there, but so long as neither of them did anything rash, all they had to do was wait.

"You with me, old man?" Drake said, turning his attention to his companion. He was holding him from the side, with a partial view of his helmet, and more of his back. Markus' face was turned away from him, so he couldn't really see how he was doing, but at the very least, Drake could tell the suit was intact.

His nearest glove was another story. It was a charred and smoking mess, still wisping into the vacuum. Drake couldn't see the state of Markus's hand, but he wondered if his Paragon blood would be sufficient to heal it. It must have been the hand he used to pull levers, because the other appeared to be okay.

He stirred just before the two of them reached the edge of the hull's gravity field. "Take it easy," Drake told him. The radio was still laden with static, but he could hear him breathing. "Can you hear me?"

The old man squinted, clearly in pain, but he nodded.

Relief flooded Drake. "I've got you. Just stay still."

Markus nodded again. "Safe?" he choked out as they clunked softly against the ship's hull. Drake planted a boot, and then helped Markus do the same before letting him lie down against the metal. Beyond him, Drake could see lights flickering on all over the ship, and relief washed over him anew. *Glory* was coming back to life.

"We're safe, yes," Drake said, and he tapped Markus's faceplate. "You did it. Thank you." It was still impossible to tell what his hand looked like under the char and the bits of fabric, but it was obvious the old man was in incredible pain. Anyone else would be screaming. He moaned through clenched teeth.

"Guess I'm on your ledger again, huh?" Drake said, trying to make him smile. "That's twice in one day I've saved your life!"

Markus heard him. He didn't look happy about it. Again.

"Sorry," Drake said. "You'll have to heal up so you can pay me back."

But Markus was having none of it. Instead, he was trying to say something Drake couldn't make out. Drake leaned closer, thinking that if watched his lips move, maybe he could decipher it. "Danger," Markus gasped, finally clear.

He was distraught. About what, Drake didn't know. "No, we did it," Drake said, trying to reassure him. "You, Markus. *You* did it. Power is on. You saved the ship. You made your choice, and you chose us."

Markus wouldn't accept it. He grabbed Drake with his good hand at that last sentence, and he shook him with surprising strength. As he did, his eyes stilled, and he became lucid.

Haunted was what Drake saw. Regret. And fear. It stopped him and made his blood run cold. This was different, and he had to pay attention. "Danger," Markus repeated. There was blood on his lips, and Drake sensed that he was seconds away from unconsciousness. He shook Drake with his handhold on his suit fabric. "Idri."

Then his eyes rolled back, and he collapsed, out cold. His body had taken over, forcing him under so it could heal.

But not before the confession. It was the moment Drake had both been wanting and dreading from the moment he'd met him. It satisfied the feeling inside him that had gnawed since he'd laid eyes on him and Warren in the briefing room, which had grown as the details of their mission had unfolded; something wasn't right. Something didn't quite add up. This was it. That was what he'd been looking for.

The man beneath him *was* a traitor. Something he'd known about, been privy to, or maybe been part of and had withheld was up. They were in grave danger. All of them. The entire Fleet if Idri was involved, which was what Markus had just told him.

Drake looked into space beyond the ship to where he thought he could see the Vorkut V moon sliding along its orbit around the gas giant and wondered what the Paragon had put in motion. He wondered if his people would manage to get out of it. He wondered if the old man would find the redemption he sought or if he would end up the same as he'd arrived, just another enemy.

Had he warned them in time?

For everyone's sake, Drake hoped he had.

CHAPTER FORTY

THE ELEVATOR from the shuttle plateau down to the main facility was a lot bumpier than it had looked from the ridge. It was also a lot smaller than she'd expected. It barely held her, Zed, and their two Paragon guards. She thought briefly of trying to jump them since the jostling of the elevator offered the opportunity, but she decided against it. Not only were the Paragon troopers a full head taller than even Zed, but even if they did manage to overpower them by some miracle, there were more guards waiting for them at the bottom of the rickety elevator shaft. There was nowhere for them to go. Not yet, anyway.

She caught Zed looking at her, clearly thinking the same thing she was. She shook her head, and he nodded. Their training told them to wait for the right moment, not to rush. That was what she would do.

"This thing is so old-fashioned," he said, looking at the small windows in the rear of the compartment. Cables ran up and down there, which confused Carrol until she saw a counterweight shoot past. Old-fashioned indeed; the elevator was mechanical. Centuries-old technology. Practical, but not what she expected from the Paragon. Then she caught sight of the ship descending toward the facility.

"Holy shit," she blurted. It was massive. It dwarfed the all-black prototype ship tenfold. She recognized the design from Warren's and Markus' mission briefings and turned to one of the guards. "I see the archgeneral is paying us a visit."

The trooper just grunted and poked her shoulder with the tip of his rifle. He wanted them to ride in silence.

The elevator clunked to a stop at the bottom of the cliff. "Out," the guard said clearly.

Carrol turned toward him and raised her eyebrows. "I didn't know you spoke Earth Standard."

Smack.

It got her a rifle butt across the back that sent her out through the open elevator doors to sprawl in the snow.

"What the fuck?" Carrol heard Zed yell at the guard. She turned in time to see him shove the guard, who sprawled in the snow next to Carrol.

"Zed!" she shouted when he looked like he was about to follow the trooper down and try to take his head off. He froze, stopped by his name. If he'd followed through, he'd have been dead. The other trooper and his six friends on ground level had their weapons trained on him, muzzles glowing and ready to fire.

Carrol raised her hands and indicated that Zed should do the same. His face was flushed, and while she appreciated the support, she needed him to stow that protector shit and save it for later.

He got it. He took a deep breath and raised his arms to match hers. The Paragon fell on them and grabbed them with two on each side. They were then hauled roughly toward a side entrance to the research facility. As they entered, Carrol stole another look at the archgeneral's flagship and shivered. It was ominous and oppressive, hanging up there. She didn't like it.

Once inside, they were hustled through a long series of twisting corridors. None were marked, and Carrol knew that if they were ever to get out of this facility, she had to pay attention so she could find her way back. She tried, but she was distracted by how empty the facility was. They passed room after room with equipment, desks, laboratories, manufacturing and refining, computers—everything one could think of involved in the building of war machines like ships, guns, and fighters, all abandoned. There wasn't a soul in any of the large spaces except for Paragon troopers dumping various items into large containers.

They were pulling out.

The guards stopped so suddenly that Carrol nearly crashed into the one in front of her. There was an open door to their left. "Inside," another guard said in Standard.

It was a medium-sized space, about the size of *Glory's* conference room, and they were hurriedly ushered inside. Like everywhere else, it was empty except for them. Equipment was strewn about the room. If Carrol had to guess, she'd have figured it for a server room. Maybe it had something to do with the AI. There wasn't much to learn from the debris, so she focused on their guards. They didn't talk to each other, not that Carrol could hear, and she briefly wondered if they were telepathic. But no. Every so often she heard one vocalize, like the grunt she'd heard the guard make in the elevator. That and their small physical gestures and body language. Carrol figured that was all they needed to communicate. This was a unit. They'd trained together, deployed together.

Even their uniforms, she noticed, were slightly different from a regular Paragon's. They had gold woven into the contoured seams and a red streak across the tops of their helmets. Carrol guessed this was an elite unit. They were special. They didn't speak because they didn't *have* to. Their body language was almost all they needed, and it told Carrol they were nervous. Extremely so.

A moment later, Carrol figured out why. A tall, hulking figure stepped through the door to the conference/ex-server room. He was dazzlingly ornately in glittering golds, reds, and whites. Where the normal Paragon troopers had blue dots of light affixed to their suits—presumably to see; that had always been the working theory—this dude had gemstones. His headdress took the cake, however, when it came to ostentation. It was solid gold with a thin slit across the middle where the eyes should be and a giant red plume of the Paragon homeworld's version of feathers. It matched the red streak and the color scheme of the elite unit's uniforms. This was their boss, and they were his. He was taller than any of them by a few centimeters, and his glittering, ice-blue eyes burned imposingly behind the thin slit in his helmet.

Archgeneral Hadras.

He gestured wordlessly to one of the troopers, and they stiffened, bowed, and rushed over to Zed and Carrol. After a whack to the backs of their legs, the two dropped to their knees. Two more troopers rushed behind each. The sound of their plasma rifles whirring let Carrol know they'd been primed and aimed at their heads. She put her hands up, wondering if she would have to try to negotiate for their lives or if this was the end of the line. Again, why bring them here to do what they could have done up in the canyon by the shuttle plateau? Something in the giant man's demeanor told Carrol something different.

He regarded them carefully, two ice-blue eyes burning

behind the blank mask. He reached toward Carrol and she flinched, but it wasn't a strike. He grabbed her overcoat, the drab, dirty disguise they'd donned that morning to cover their tactical threads and packs. He flung it aside to reveal those undergarments. He then stared Carrol in the face for several seconds before straightening and turning to his guards.

He shook his head, then swept from the room.

The weapons behind them powered down. They were hauled to their feet by the troopers, then tossed outside the room to a waiting group of normal guards without the gold woven into their suits or the red streak on their helmets. The new guards hustled them down another corridor, heading somewhere else.

"Was that who I think it was?" Zed asked her, speaking in a low voice when they were some distance from the elite unit.

Carrol nodded.

"You notice he wasn't surprised by us being here?"

Carrol nodded again. He hadn't looked surprised. Hadras had been waiting for them. But not them *specifically*.

This was a trap, and it had been laid with someone else in mind.

———

IDRI HESITATED at the side entrance to the research facility.

They'd gone around to the far side of the complex. The entry was alongside the cliff face that dropped thousands of feet into an unseen misty valley. It had cost them time, but it was worth it. There'd been plenty of cover as they went, lots of storage containers brimming with equipment, and when they reached their destination, only three Paragon were standing guard at the side entrance. Warren and Smith had felled them with three perfect kill shots and tossed them over the cliff. Their access cards had worked, the ones programmed from Markus' memory, and the door was now open, with everyone inside save Idri.

Warren looked at her and frowned. He held his suit helmet with both hands, in the middle of putting it on. It was halfway down his forehead. "You good?" he asked as she steadfastly remained outside.

He was asking about the night before; her taking a life. But that wasn't what paused Idri at the door.

It was hard to articulate beyond that it was *dark* in there. Not dark as in the forest at night or the vast lightlessness of space. Dark as in she couldn't feel what was in there. It was the same feeling she had gotten from her first practice jump on *Glory* when they had been training for this mission. It was a purposeful darkness and the cold of something not quite alive. The feeling was intense beyond that door. Something lurked.

"I'm good," she finally responded, trying to fight off a feeling that wouldn't go away. Everyone was waiting for her inside, tense and ready to go. "Everything is okay." If there was a monster waiting for her, she wanted to face it. That was what they were here for. Warren nodded, believing her. He made room for her to come in past him, then shut the door with a loud clank.

CHAPTER FORTY-ONE

"Status," Drake called the second he stepped foot on the command deck.

He'd hauled his ass and Markus' far enough away from the manual release controls and its residual radiation to get his radio working again and called for help. They'd responded immediately, thank the stars—*Glory's* crew was indeed relatively unharmed—and had the two back inside within a few minutes. Drake had gone with Markus to Sickbay, filled them in on his regeneration process, got stitched up himself, and given strict orders to be told the second Markus regained consciousness. Then he'd bolted for the command deck, much to Doc's chagrin.

"Main power is still being restored, and we have significant port-side hull damage from the drone explosion, but systems otherwise appear to be coming back online. Our actual EMP damage is negligible, sir."

That was good. "Tactical status on the Paragon."

XO swallowed. "We have company."

He brought up a 3D wireframe display of the Vorkut moon and pointed at a half-dozen blinking dots, all of which were moving slowly away from the planetoid. "Six Paragon cruisers entered orbit around the moon about five minutes ago."

"Where did they come from?"

XO shook his head. "We were blacked out from the EMP measures, sir. We didn't see them until after they got here."

"Have they spotted the plasma field?"

"If they haven't yet, they will shortly. And sir," he reached down to the console and tapped in quick commands. The wireframe display of Vorkut V zoomed in until they were looking at the portion of its surface where the labor camp and research facility were located. There were two ships hovering over that locale now, and Drake recognized the newcomer.

"Hadras," he said. XO nodded. Shit, there it was.

"Raise the landing team on QE."

XO's face registered surprise. "Sir?"

They were on total comms blackout with the ops team. That meant they didn't have their radios turned on, but there were QE failsafes in those radios, and while those QE bands were now considered compromised by the Paragon raid on Aexon Hub, Drake would be able to get hold of them, at least. There was the added benefit that in the absence of a radio signal, it wasn't going to give away their location to the searching Paragon cruisers.

None of that answered XO's implied question, however. Why in the hell would they blow their ops team like that?

Drake leaned toward his first officer, tried to arrest the gnawing sensation in his gut, and spoke as softly as he could while still being audible. "I believe the Paragon already know we're here and that our tactical team on the ground is in grave and *immediate* danger."

XO blanched. "Sir?"

"Markus. He wanted me to know Idri was in danger."

The color drained from Oh's face. Neither man spoke for a good, long moment. "Opening a QE channel," the first officer finally said, keeping his voice low. The message he sent was a squawk, a simple request for a friendly response.

No response.

"Try by voice," Drake said with a nod. It meant the Paragon would hear them if they were listening, but that probably didn't matter anymore.

"*Glory* to Tactical Team, do you read?"

Still no response.

Damn.

"I'm not getting a response back from the QE system at all," XO said, which wasn't necessarily bad news. There were few things that could cause interference on the quantum entanglement spectrum, but a Navigators' null field was one. They'd gone over this in the briefing. It probably just meant the team was where they were supposed to be: in the facility.

Goddammit. Drake had no way to warn them.

"What do you propose we do, sir?" Oh asked, still ashen.

That was *the* question, wasn't it? It was impossible to determine what the Paragon did and didn't already know, but despite the non-response from the team's QE, Drake was willing to bet they didn't have Idri and company in hand. Otherwise, they'd be bugging out of the system.

By the same logic, and he didn't know how beyond plain luck or incompetence, he was reasonably certain they hadn't yet spotted their radiation field, or those cruisers would already be burning toward them at full power, guns blazing. Drake hoped those two very slight advantages would be enough. There was some time. How much, he didn't know, but there was some. And while they didn't have numbers on their side, sometimes surprise could count for just as much.

"Battle stations," he said, a fire sparking behind his eyes.

If the Paragon were playing games, *Glory* would play too.

CHAPTER FORTY-TWO

ESCAPE WAS the only thing on Carrol's mind as she and Zed were processed as prisoners of the Paragon Imperium. The intake was done hurriedly in a small foyer to a cargo bay. Along the walls were stacks of the plastiform containers she'd seen littering the grounds outside the facility. The two were told to strip to their undergarments. Then they were given loose-fitting, scratchy-as-fuck inmate clothing that matched the garb they'd donned earlier to infiltrate the camp. This time, it was the real thing.

"Thanks," Carrol said sarcastically as a Paragon trooper handed her an overcoat that was the spitting image of the fake one she'd just taken off. That one had been bundled up with her Fleet threads and the rest of her tactical gear and tossed into the nearest transport container. Everything, it would seem, was being packed to go.

The two were then pushed at gunpoint through a double-wide cargo door. It creaked open, and beyond it was a mesh wire cage with more Paragon guards inside. Carrol and Zed were handed off to them when they crossed the threshold, and the guards behind them hastily moved off. It confirmed what Carrol had suspected, that something was going on in the facility, and wherever that was happening—or was about to happen—it wasn't here.

The cage was opened by one of the guards, and they were tossed into a cargo hold . . . full of prisoners. Close to a hundred, and they were all craning their necks to get a look at the newcomers.

"So, this is where everyone is," Zed said as they stared at the welcoming party.

Carrol was more concerned with what was behind them. Above the cage in a second-story room that over-looked the cargo bay was another guard. The observation/control room had had its windows smashed out. You could still see the glass in jagged sawtooth shapes around the edges. In one of those former windows, a plasma cannon had been mounted, and another guard stood behind it, hands on its trigger. It looked like an automatic weapon, and it that could waste the entire room in a matter of seconds.

Hmmm. Three guards in the cage. They had rifles, but the biggest challenge would be figuring out what to do with the fourth guard up top and his plasma cannon.

Zed intercepted Carrol's gaze and, without saying a word, indicated that he knew what she was thinking. He moved away, and she knew what he was thinking, too. He waded into the crowd of prisoners, who were starting to go about their own business again now that the disruption was over. Carrol hung back, letting him go, and drifted toward the cage's doorway.

"Oh, I'm so sorry," she heard Zed say in response to a snarling grunt. She moved closer to the door, making it look like she was trying to get a look at her companion. He'd plowed into the biggest, meanest-looking prisoner in the hold. A Friar, from the looks of it, giant brown-fur-covered bipeds from the far side of Paragon territory. Carrol had never seen one up close, but goddamn, they lived up to their reputation of being huge.

Zed had knocked the creature flat on its back with a hard shove. "Let me help you up," he said, extending his hand.

He never got to complete the gesture because another prisoner—this one looked like a human, though he was so heavily covered in body hair and skin ink that it was hard to be sure—barreled into Zed and returned the favor of knocking him flat on his ass. "Sorry," the man hissed to him as he held out his hand.

Zed grabbed it before the man could rescind the sarcastic gesture, yanked himself up using the man's body weight, and planted a roundhouse punch on his face with his other hand.

The fight was on, perfectly executed. It was so obvious that Carrol wondered if the Paragon guards would anticipate the next part of the classic trap, but these were not elite forces. With Carrol standing a body length from her target, the door to the cage was flung open, and a Paragon guard burst through it to stop the prison-yard violence.

She dove through the opening just before the door swung shut. The two guards inside froze in shock since they were now sharing the cramped space with the enemy. The cage was about three meters wide by two meters deep, and the guards hesitated to use their rifles in such close quarters. That was what Carrol had been hoping for. She grabbed the closest guard's rifle barrel and shoved it toward him hard. The rifle butt slammed into the trooper's head, or helmet, with a satisfying crunch. Without missing a beat, Carrol jumped to plant both her feet on the soldier's chest and yanked in the other direction, using her body weight as she fell to try to rip the rifle from his grasp.

It worked. The rifle tore free of the guard's hands, and Carrol tumbled to the floor. She rolled to her feet and found that she was face to face with the other guard. She dove to the side as he fired. A plasma bolt sizzled past her head so close she could smell burning. She didn't have a proper grip on the rifle to fire since her hands were still on its barrel, but as she rose, she swung the weapon, butt out, in a wide half-circle. She caught the second guard in the side of his head, and he fell.

Carrol was flipping the rifle around to shoot him when the first guard grabbed her from behind. He was on her back with his hands around her throat, and his weight drove them both toward the floor. As they fell, Carrol realized she would come down on top of the rifle barrel, so she twisted to avoid impaling her midsection, then reached down to the trigger and pulled it.

The rifle blasted a hole through the first guard's stomach. He slid off Carrol's back onto the cargo bay floor, spewing blackened, smoking gore from what remained of his core.

Above them, Carrol heard the whine of the plasma cannon spinning up. Without taking the time to check if the second guard was still dazed from the blow she'd delivered, she wheeled the rifle around and squeezed a couple shots up through the metal cage, aiming at the control room. However, she missed both the cannon and the guard manning it. Before she could line up another shot, she was again grabbed from behind by the throat. Apparently, the second guard was *not* still dazed, and this time, the grab was a forearm chokehold rather than a wild pair of hands. The bastard stayed on his feet, refusing to be pulled down.

Carrol fired as close to behind her as she could without pointing the barrel at her face, but it was no use. The guard smartly stayed directly behind her, squeezing his forearm across her windpipe. This was no sleeper hold, and he was far stronger than she was.

She did the only thing she could. She kept writhing against him, and she kept firing wildly, rifle pointed in the direction of the plasma cannon. Her vision started to constrict, but still she fired and fought the hold. She poured shot after shot into the space above them until finally . . .

A scream.

Carrol and the guard paused in their mortal struggle to see a body fall from the control room and slam onto the metal roof of the cage. The cannon was on fire, though it was still charging itself to unleash its fury on the cargo hold prisoners.

BOOOOMMMMMMM.

One of Carrol's wild shots had hit home, and the cannon was on fire. The concrete wall it had been affixed to crumbled and began to fall, following the trajectory of the guard who had preceded it . . . toward Carrol and her opponent.

He released her, and without a plan for where to go or the safest place to land, they dove away from each other as chunks of concrete from overhead slammed into the pitiful roof of the metal cage. Yelling for no reason other than it felt like the right thing to do, Carrol huddled in the back corner of the cage as metal tore, concrete chunks shattered on the floor, and fiery remnants of the plasma cannon rained down like lava.

When it was over, there was silence in the hold. Carrol realized it, which meant she was alive, and she lifted her head out of her arms to see that the cage had been smashed, along with three Paragon guards, the two in the cage and the one who had manned the cannon. Carrol sprang to her feet and picked up the closest rifle, which involved kicking away a molten piece of metal, shouldered it, and sighted on the last guard. He was standing in the middle of the cargo hold, stunned, with his rifle pointing at a bloody-faced Zed and his two assailants.

Carrol smoked him through the head. One shot.

Zed grabbed the rifle from his dead hands before the Paragon guard's body hit the floor. He looked at Carrol like she was so goddamn hot, he could have taken her right there on the smoking floor.

Silence again reigned in the cargo hold as the prisoners took in the newcomers. Carrol put her rifle against her side and cocked her hip before addressing them.

"Who wants to get the fuck out of here?"

———

WHILE THEY WERE in the facility's corridors, Warren felt as though he finally, fully appreciated how helpful the dog could be. Cheddar was far more sensitive than the scopes in Warren's suit, to say nothing of a human's limited ability to see, hear, and smell compared to that of a super-dog. She served as their advance scout, often trotting dozens of meters ahead, scoping out the opposition. Because she could become invisible, the Paragon troopers didn't see her coming. His reservations, which he'd mostly kept to himself, had been entirely unfounded. It was something he couldn't be happier to have been wrong about.

The team had encountered only small teams of guards as they slipped deeper into the facility. They patrolled two or three troopers at a time; sometimes as many as six or seven. With Cheddar's advance warning, each time they ran into a group, the team hid and ambushed them quickly and quietly. It was remarkably easy, which meant Warren didn't trust it for a second. He kept waiting to run into an ambush of their own, manned by a garrison of troops around the next corner. It would make sense if the heavy security was close to the cube.

However, the garrison never appeared, and before Warren expected them to reach it, his team was staring down the long corridor that led to the AI cube.

It was deathly quiet.

"Nice and slow," he whispered to his team. If there was a trap, this was where it would be sprung.

They silently crouch-walked down the hall, listening intently with their weapons up. Warren had his suit's weapons out and charged and his plasma rifle in hand, as did Smith, and they'd donned their helmets. Idri moved as one with the team, weapon up and ready for whatever was out there, waiting to jump them.

Nothing did.

They entered the main chamber, which looked like a wheel with the pure-black cube at the center. The cube was just how Warren remembered it, tilted and slightly submerged, with a corner plunging into a cutout in the floor and a thick cable rising from the top corner and disappearing into the ceiling. Spokes left the central chamber in the form of corridors like the one they'd just entered from. Not all were straight; some took immediate turns. Warren and Smith checked each of those two turns deep. Empty.

In the main chamber, Sudan and Idri had their plasma cannon half-assembled. They'd be up and running in seconds. Good.

"Lieutenant," Smith said quietly, gesturing at the cutout

in the floor in which the angled cube was partially buried. He pointed at a gap in it that allowed them to see what was underneath.

Energy pulsed. Warren knelt on the stone floor and took a good look. He saw miles of power-transfer conduits going down forever, all plugged into the cube.

"Power looks to be sourced from geothermal," Smith said, and Warren agreed. That was an interesting development. Much more power juiced this cube than he'd expected. That meant blowing it wasn't likely to blow only the immediate structure.

He glanced at his fellow warrior. "We'll have to use timed charges." That would give them time to run. From the amount of energy vibrating under their feet, they'd need as much time as they could get.

"Cannon is ready, sir," Sudan called from a couple meters away.

Good goddamn job, he thought, and he stepped away from the cannon's sights. "Fire her up. Sooner we get in and out of that fucking thing, the sooner we get the hell out and blow it." He shuddered. Maybe it was the vibrations coming through the floor. It struck him as odd that Markus had never mentioned that the AI cube was sitting on top of enough energy to launch an orbital bombardment. Maybe it was how quiet it was in there, but whatever it was, Warren didn't like it. "This place gives me the creeps."

The plasma cannon's fire started burrowing into the cube's seemingly impenetrable matte-black surface. Warren turned his attention to the corridors that surrounded them, waiting for the Paragon to show up. They would.

It was just a matter of when.

CHAPTER FORTY-THREE

"Carrol to Warren. Do you read?"

The first thing Carrol had done after she fished her tactical gear and Fleet suit out of the cargo container was turn on her radio. Static. QE was dead, too. She gave a head shake to a watching Zed. "Same for me," he reported a couple seconds later.

As expected, the comm was not working this close to the AI cube, though "close" was just a guess and the real root of their problem. They were in the corridor outside the hold's antechamber, re-dressed and with their new pair of rifles strapped to their chests, trying to figure out what to do next. Behind them, the mass of prisoners was tearing through the rest of the cargo containers, looking for personal items or things to steal. Carrol didn't care which.

The curving corridor was quiet. Their guards in the hold had been the only ones assigned to them, it seemed.

"Should we try to find them?" Zed asked, reading Carrol's mind.

She shook her head. She wished they could warn

Warren and his team that Hadras was here and looking for them, but there was no effective way to do that. The radios were useless. She had no idea how to get from this section of the facility to the AI cube. Hopefully, Warren and his team were already inside or, even better, getting the hell out. Warren would have to take care of himself and hold up his end of the bargain. Carrol and Zed needed to do the same.

This corridor was very wide. She recognized it as a cargo-loading accessway. She couldn't see farther than twenty meters or so, but she knew there would be a double-wide door leading outside at the end of it.

"We stick to our mission," she told Zed. They needed to get to a shuttle.

Shouting erupted behind them. Two groups of prisoners were brawling over rags, it looked like to Carrol, but they clearly held significance to the warring parties.

"Hey!" she yelled, emphasizing the word by firing into the ceiling. The prisoners ducked in unison. She had their attention, and she thanked her lucky stars that only two weapons had been viable after the firefight and cave-in that had freed them. She and Zed had them; the rest of this rough-looking bunch did not. They'd make sure they kept it that way. They were vastly outnumbered, and many of these prisoners looked murderous. Desperation would do that to you.

Projecting her voice over the crowd, Carrol said, "We're from the Terran Defense vessel *Glory*. While his and my mission here is not to rescue you, help *is* on the way to evacuate you all to safety." She pointed down the curving corridor. "This accessway should lead us outside. I suggest you follow Lieutenant Zed and me to somewhere you can hide until the evacuation transports from *Glory* arrive."

There were grumbles among the crowd, but not many. You did what the people with the firepower told you to do, and "outside" and "rescue" probably sounded good.

"This way," she called, then started down the corridor. Zed fell in beside her, and soon, the passage filled with the sounds of dozens of footsteps. "Watch our six," she said to him, voice low.

He nodded his understanding.

Shortly, Carrol's guess was proven correct. When they rounded the curve that had blocked her view, a pair of double doors appeared at the end of the corridor. Next to them was a single door. Carrol approached the latter. One of the rougher-looking prisoners started fiddling with a control panel on the opposite side, which would presumably open the larger doors.

"We don't know where this opens to," she shouted to him, or it. Whoever it was, they looked more like a rock than a person. "Leave it alone for now." It turned its black-brown head toward her and appeared to stare her down, even though no eyes could be seen, then turned back to the panel and continued to tap it, ignoring her command.

Brrraaappp.

A plasma bolt sizzled past the alien's hand. "Hey!" Zed shouted, his rifle on his shoulder. "She said to leave it alone."

It worked. The rocky creature stepped—or crawled, it was hard to say—away from the panel.

Carrol glanced at Zed in a silent thank you, then turned her attention to the side door. There was a keypad and a card reader. Carrol remembered Markus had briefed them that cards were used for security access, and she had one. She fished in her pockets, wondering if the Paragon had snatched it. They hadn't. She produced it with a flourish, and Zed smiled. Good. Now to see if it worked.

Carrol slid it into the reader. It processed, flashing symbols that Carrol recognized as Paragon but could derive no meaning from. She had no idea if it was accepting the security card or telling them the reader was going to self-destruct in their faces.

The little screen flashed a brilliant white and made a pleasant-sounding chirp. Carrol grimaced, hoping she was doing the right thing, and pushed the door open.

And immediately closed it.

"Shit."

The sky was crawling with Paragon activity. Troop transports were as thick as gnats in the gray and darkening sky. The sunshine hadn't lasted long, nor had their good luck.

"Transports," she explained to Zed. "Everywhere."

"Coming here?" he asked.

Carrol opened the door just a crack and peeked outside, hoping she wouldn't be seen. The transports were not coming to their corner. Beyond the doors was a landing area that would hold several of the large transports, but it was empty. She didn't see anything lining up overhead to land on the plateau, either. This side of the facility was not the focus of the incoming activity.

That was good. Even better, she saw the elevator that ran up the cliff face to the shuttle plateau a couple dozen meters to the left of the landing area. It was sitting where they'd left it, at ground level. The stretch of landing area between them and it was wide open, without any cover, but their transportation was waiting to take them back up the cliff. She didn't see any troops guarding it.

Zed saw it, too, peeking over her shoulder. "We can

make it," he said, reading her mind again. It was becoming annoying.

"What about them?" she asked, indicating the crowd behind them. The prisoners were growing increasingly restless with all the sounds outside.

Zed shrugged. "Tell them to hole up here. It's safe as anywhere."

That was probably true. "Okay," she shouted after she closed the door. "Lieutenant Zed and I are going outside. It's crawling with Paragon troopers, so you all are best off staying right here." The last proclamation elevated the grumbles to full-fledged shouting, which Carrol should have anticipated. "Listen!" she shouted, trying to keep the unrest from escalating. "Listen, where we are going is too small for a group this size, but I promise you, transports from our ship *are* on the way. If you just . . . just remain calm."

It was too late for that. Several of the prisoners got in their faces, shouting and pleading, and a mass of bodies built up behind them. Carrol couldn't blame them. They'd been incarcerated here against their will. Now something big was going down, and they were scared. Vulnerable. They were not going to stay calm.

"Back up," Zed bellowed, and he fired some shots into the floor just ahead.

It worked. Briefly. The line of people scrambled back, which tangled them into the crowd behind them. Several fell, which made others fall, and the mob's line faltered. Carrol took advantage of that. With a single fluid motion, she shouldered her rifle, sighted up the control panel for the large doors on the far side, and blasted it. It shorted in a satisfying shower of sparks. The double-wide doors now could not be opened from the inside. "Time to move," she barked at Zed, then grabbed him by the shirt to haul him through the side door. He kept facing the crowd as they backed out. Some people wailed as they realized what was happening. Others snarled in fury.

Carrol kicked the side door shut the second they were outside, then fried the edges with a steady low-intensity beam. The metal melted into the frame and cooled quickly in the freezing air. By the time the crowd had returned to their feet and reached it, it was effectively welded shut. They were trapped, but they were safe. At least, Carrol hoped that was true. She hoped, too, that they would do as they were told: stay there and wait for rescue. She'd make damn sure *Glory's* transports came for them when it was time.

A Paragon transport flew overhead, low and loud. Zed and Carrol instinctively ducked, but it wasn't heading for them; it disappeared over the facility. Carrol figured it was heading for the main entrance. They'd come out of the facility where they'd been taken in. Convenient except for the lack of cover.

"Let's go." She pointed at the elevator, and he nodded in vigorous agreement.

Carrol and Zed were no longer wearing their prisoner overcoats. Whatever cover the coats would have afforded them was now lost. A prisoner heading up to the shuttle pad would be shot as surely as a Fleet soldier in black ops threads, so why carry around the extra bulk? They just had to move quickly and hope the commotion at the front of the facility kept eyes away from them.

They reached the elevator without being fired upon, but after they rushed inside and turned to face the doors, Carrol locked "eyes" with a Paragon soldier twenty meters away. Its blue dots glowed brilliantly against its white suit and the snow. Beyond it were dozens upon dozens of troopers pouring out of the transports and streaming into the facility through the main doors. This one, though, was looking right at her.

Carrol slammed the elevator door shut and stabbed a simple large "up" symbol on the interior control panel. Dutifully, albeit creakingly, the elevator started moving upward.

"Sonofabitch saw me," she murmured, going to one of the front corners of the lift and looking through the dirty windows. Zed joined her in the corner.

Back at ground level, Carrol spotted her trooper. He was talking and gesturing to a group of other troopers. He pointed at the elevator, and the other troopers walked toward it. As they slowly rose, the predicament they'd put themselves in dawned on Carrol. They were trapped in a slow-moving elevator with nowhere to go.

"Dammit!" she said, mind racing.

The troopers fired.

"IDRI, GET READY," Warren called from over by the plasma cannon. "You're up."

Idri acknowledged that and came over to stand behind him and Sudan. They'd been firing at the cube for the past several minutes. The blowback from the hole they were cutting, which was barely an inch in diameter, had heated the chamber. Everyone was sweating. The simulators had not prepared Idri for that, one of the many details they'd missed in training that made the current situation that much more real. The danger, too. Idri thought that was what she'd missed before. Get shot in training, and you waited for the reset. Try again.

Here? You got shot, and it was over. There was no reset. Sometimes that sharpened Idri's mind, giving her a hyper-focus she'd never before experienced. Things were slowed down, vibrant, and she felt like she was aware of every second as it ticked past. Other times, like back in the forest after shooting the trooper, the danger felt overwhelming. Gaps in time. Missed words. Numbness and terror. It was hard for her to reconcile that the same stimulus could make her react differently, but here in the chamber, with their pinhole about to puncture the AI's mysterious, protective cube . . .

At this moment, she felt focused like the most intense laser known to humanity.

Warren stepped aside to let her kneel next to Sudan, who was manning the cannon while the others watched the corridors for intruders. She bent until she was looking down the barrel of the cannon and straight into the hole. She would jump after she got her first glimpse of the inside.

"Through," Sudan said loudly enough for the entire group to hear. They all huddled close to Idri, Smith, Warren, and Cheddar included, and waited for her to jump them inside.

Idri peered through the long but tiny hole. It was still shimmering with heat, glowing from the plasma that had burrowed through it. She couldn't see anything yet, but that was expected. She waited.

"The second you see something . . ." Warren said. He was too close and breathing into her ear.

She shook it off and refocused on the cooling hole. It got darker as the temperature dropped, then the light and heat from the plasma faded, and there was only darkness inside. A pure black that seemed infinite and mysterious, like a hole with no bottom, until . . .

A light.

Something in the cube was flashing like a console. "I have something!" she shouted to the group. "Hold on."

She mentally latched onto the light inside the cube as the group around her closed in and jumped them.

CHAPTER FORTY-FOUR

Chief Engineer Fredrickson stood with his hands on his hips, shaking his head amid the chaos. Drake stood next to him as a team of engineers shouted to each other, plasma torches in hand, trying desperately to support one of *Glory's* massive transverse beams and weld it to the giant shard of rock that had pierced six of the ship's lower decks. The beam groaned and screamed and would not stay in place, which was a large problem for puny human arms, legs, and fingers when it weighed several metric tons.

On Drake's orders, *Glory* was moving. That was necessary to execute his tactical plan, but it was wreaking havoc on the repair efforts, which Fredrickson had called him down to see. His crew had cleared away the damaged bulkheads, conduits, wires, and pipes, so only the naked skeleton of the ship and the hole the shard had torn in it were visible. Angling his head, Drake peered up several decks and down several more. Fredrickson had teams of his people around the intruding rock on every deck it crossed, trying to do the same thing they were here.

"Even just an inch shift," the engineer said, shouting

over the other voices, the rending metal, and the hisses and sparks of the welding torches. "It throws off an entire weld, Cap. We're making no progress down here."

Drake nodded. It had been his idea to take advantage of the asteroids' metallic properties and weld the largest shards to the ship rather than try to extract them, which would leave gaping holes. Fredrickson had agreed. Theoretically, they'd have near-full structural integrity when everything was bonded together, a necessary element in the battle that Drake was in the process of precipitating. Now, the repair challenges were threatening to derail his plans for that battle.

"I need a dead stop," Fredrickson said. He gestured at his team, not only those on the same deck as them but the ones several decks above and below them. "Or this isn't going to work."

"How long?"

Before Fredrickson could answer, Drake got a hail on his wristcom. "Captain?" squawked XO.

"What is it, XO?"

"Paragon cruisers approaching our plasma field, sir."

"I'll be right up." Drake tapped his wristcom to close the channel and turned back to Fredrickson, grim. "I'll give you your dead stop as long as I can, Chief Engineer."

"We need a good hour, sir, maybe more." Fredrickson was exasperated. Not that long ago, the abrasive man would have raged at Drake over a situation such as this or perhaps thrown his hands up and quit. Those days were behind them, buried in the Paragon assault on Earth. He was still cantankerous, still haughty at times, and liable to push insubordination right to the edge, but Drake didn't find that to be a fault. He wanted his officers to have opinions and express their thoughts and particularly their disagreements freely. He made the final decision. Fredrickson had made incredible strides in doing just that.

It wasn't an accident or a mystery that the engineer had changed. Through the fire that was the Paragon invasion, the two had found trust in each other. Nobody knew how to use the ship better than Drake, and nobody knew how better to keep the ship useful than Fredrickson. Acknowledging that had let them pull off miracles.

"I'll give you as long as I can," Drake responded, hoping they could pull off yet another one. "Do your best."

"Yes, sir." Fredrickson wanted to say more, but he didn't. "We'll get it done, sir."

Good man. What a ways they'd come together, indeed.

———

SLOWLY, cautiously, two Paragon cruisers approached the plasma field *Glory* had belched out during the system purge Drake had executed to save the ship. It was impossible to miss, a giant mass of supercharged particles that even the naked eye could see, let alone scopes and sensors. To those, it appeared as a giant sign flashing, "Look at me! I'm right here!"

That was why *Glory* wasn't in that plasma field anymore.

Drake had taken them out of the plasma field as swiftly as he could, first deeper into the asteroid field so as not to be seen by their propulsion trails, then in a long, curving arc back toward the leading edge of the field, close to the Vorkut V moon that was their eventual destination. It put the two cruisers and the plasma field they were investigating several minutes from *Glory*. There were four other cruisers to contend with, but three of those were farther out on their own slow search patterns, and the archgeneral's flagship was down in the Vorkut moon's atmosphere, which Drake suspected wasn't going to change anytime soon. Not until Hadras had what he wanted.

If things went to plan, *Glory* would have the element of surprise and maybe even a straight shot at rescuing their team.

"No squadron activity?" XO called to CAG.

"They're sitting tight, XO," she answered with a touch of annoyance. It was the dozenth time he'd asked her that question. "Just like they're supposed to."

Good. Drake didn't begrudge the first officer's double-, triple-, and quadruple-checking, either. He was only voicing Drake's own anxieties aloud, so Drake didn't have to.

The final piece of the plan was a little surprise for the approaching cruisers. Before burning off and away from the plasma cloud, *Glory* had dropped off a dozen of her Delta Wings to sit there, systems shut down, and they waited. Drake would have preferred to drop remote charges, which they had in their fully stocked weapons stores, but the likelihood of transmission interference was too high, either from the Paragon or the radiation field itself.

Fighters, on the other hand, didn't need a QE or radio signal to do damage. Their pilots could see an incoming target on their own. As long as they maintained the element of surprise, they could light up that cloud, land some direct blows, and bug out before the Paragon knew what hit them.

It seemed like they were taking the bait.

One cruiser stayed out of the field. The other entered excruciatingly slowly, but that was to *Glory*'s advantage. With each minute that ticked by, Fredrickson got more precious time to fix their structural issues.

"Tell Engineering to be ready to move," Drake quietly

said to XO as the two men watched the cruiser crawl toward the open trap. "Soon as that lights up, we're moving on Vorkut, full-thrust."

"Aye, sir." XO nodded.

Drake hoped the fireworks would draw in the cruiser closest to them, at least initially. Maybe even give them a clear path to make a run at the moon. Even if it didn't, he liked their chances against a single cruiser caught with its pants down. "Weapons, countermeasures, tactical all at full."

XO nodded. They were ready.

"Contact!" someone at the tactical station shouted.

On the command console, the blips representing the Paragon cruisers and the plasma field were engulfed in light. "Visual," Drake requested, and on the overhead holographic display, a zoomed-in scope in the spectrum of the human eye displayed an image of fading light. The scope searched for activity, reorienting before finally settling on something that made the command deck crew cheer.

The Paragon cruiser was in flames. Around it, streaking like glow bugs, several dozen incoming missiles pounded the engulfed cruiser. There were more streaks as the fighters who'd fired those missiles departed as quickly as they'd appeared, running back into the asteroid field for safety, then eventually to *Glory*.

The other cruiser moved into the asteroid field in pursuit.

It was working.

CHAPTER FORTY-FIVE

Idri was alone.

The darkness around her was so complete that for a moment, she couldn't remember where she was, where she'd come from, or how she'd gotten there. The flashing console light brought her back.

The cube.

She'd jumped inside the AI cube, except this wasn't right. Nobody was with her. Hmm. That wasn't true, was it? There were others missing . . . but she wasn't *alone*. She could feel something or someone else. She fumbled in the dark, staggering toward the flashing light, trying to get her bearings. There *was* light in the cube, she realized. It was just dim compared to the corridor she'd jumped in from. Her eyes needed to adjust.

As they did, her attention was drawn to three things. The first was the console with the blinking light. It wrapped around the cube and had a vast array of similar lights, slowly blinking on and off. The other two items of interest were a pair of tables, each covered with a black shroud. The dim illumination from the console's blinking lights enabled her to see them. They were in the center of the room, and just setting eyes on them made Idri's stomach turn.

"Idri!" Warren's voice came over her radio's earpiece. "Idri, are you okay? Where are you?" He sounded panicked.

"I'm here," Idri responded quietly, trying to control the feeling in her gut. "I'm here, Warren."

"Inside the cube?" Over his radio, in addition to his voice, Idri could hear an alarm blaring.

"Yes."

"Jump us inside," he said. "We're all supposed to be in there together."

That was right. Her team. They were supposed to be with her; that was the plan. So why weren't they? "I tried," she said, struggling to piece together what had happened. It was fuzzy. Confusing. As Sudan would say, what in the hell was wrong with her? "I did jump us in. I . . . I don't know what happened."

As she turned around, taking in the dark room, her foot caught on something. She bent to pick it up; it was Sudan's engineering bag. Proof she had done what she remembered. She'd jumped everyone inside, so why weren't they with her? "Where are you?"

"Back in the chamber outside. I'm looking at the cube right now."

"I don't understand."

"It must be some kind of security system. We triggered an alarm that's going off out here. Maybe the AI jumped us back out."

"Then why am I still inside?"

"Yeah, I don't like that part one bit."

"I don't think I'm alone," she said, realizing what the feeling in the pit of her stomach was.

"What?" Warren sounded alarmed.

Idri moved toward the two tables, which she realized were beds. "I think . . ." she started as she reached for the closest shroud and pulled it back. What she saw made her gasp, and she recoiled from the bed with a hand to her open mouth.

"Idri! What's going on?"

A Navid male was on the table. Not a Navigator. She could tell by probing his senses. A normal, non-gifted Navid. Wires were plugged into his forehead and temples. His eyes were open but vacant and unseeing, nor did he move or respond to Idri being there. Most disturbingly, Idri couldn't feel him. When she got closer to him, she couldn't feel *anything*. A void.

Quiet wasn't the right word because you could *hear* quiet. It was nothing. She shivered. This was what she'd felt when she'd reached out to the AI during training. This was what she'd felt every time she'd looked at the AI cube in her mind's eye or even moments before standing outside it and peering through the pinhole. It wasn't neutral, the state they were in. It wasn't natural. It was malicious, with a dark intent that Idri couldn't put her finger on.

"There's a Navid in here," she said to Warren, then walked over to the other table and pulled off its shroud. A Navid woman lay in the same state as the man. "Not Navigators, but they're plugged into the computer, I think, and so *cold*. I don't even know if they're alive." What could they be doing?

"I want you to get out of there," Warren said. "Jump out. We'll figure out a way to get in together, or we'll leave. I don't want you in there alone."

Idri shook her head and took a deep breath to push away the cold dread of the void that was bearing down on her. "I have Sudan's equipment. I can complete the mission."

She picked up the bag and turned to the console.

"No, let's get you out. Do you hear me? The Paragon are on their way."

"I'm already at the console." She opened the bag. There was a mess of cables and several devices that she couldn't make heads or tails of. "Sudan, can you assist me in using your extraction unit?"

Silence on the other end except for the blaring alarm in the distance. Then . . .

"Are you looking at a data port?" Sudan asked on the radio channel. "It'll look like three vertical slits."

Idri smiled. Warren had acquiesced. "I see three vertical slits," she answered, moving to another side of the cube, where there were several such ports.

"Good. Now, you're going to need to find the yellow interface terminal in my bag and the data drive, which looks like a gray brick . . . "

"Duck!" Carrol shouted and pulled Zed down to the deck of the elevator with her.

Plasma fire peppered the corner they'd occupied an instant before, then raked the width of the elevator car, sending sparks and molten spatter over them. This was bad. They were sitting ducks, and even on the floor, out of sight, one of those plasma bolts would find them sooner or later.

Things got worse when the elevator car stopped with a heavy *clunk*. Someone below—or above—had halted their ride to the top of the cliff. With another *clunk*, the car changed directions and started creaking back down again.

"Goddammit," she wheezed. "They're bringing us back down to the facility level."

Think, Carrol screamed at herself. Think . . .

The plasma fire lessened since the car was descending. The Paragon were secure in their quarry being brought to where they wanted them, so shots only ripped through the space above them every so often to make sure they didn't get any funny ideas. Lying on her back, looking at the sporadic plasma bolts blowing chunks out of the rear wall, Carrol did have a "funny idea," thanks to Zed. She grabbed her rifle off her chest, aimed it at the roof of the elevator car, and fired.

"What are you doing?" Zed wondered from beside her.

She ignored his question and asked her own. "You still got heavy-duty multipurpose gloves in your kit?" He looked at her like she was crazy. "Fucking check!" she ordered him.

He produced a pair of thick gloves and waved them at her. Good. She had hers, too. "Make sure the mag function still works," she ordered next.

He was still frowning in confusion, but he did as he was told without protesting this time. At the base of each glove was a tiny flexible control screen. He tapped it, selected "magnetic," and turned on the function. His hands flattened on the floor with a satisfying *thunk*. They worked. Carrol hadn't time to check hers yet, but she hoped they would do the same.

"Move!" she shouted at Zed, ceasing her firing, and shoving him to the right as she rolled to the left.

From above them came a horrible creak, then a Carrol-and-Zed-sized cutout from the elevator's ceiling clanked on the floor. Beyond the hole she'd shot out, there was open air.

"I'll give you a boost," Carrol told the still-bewildered Zed, and she crouched, careful to stay below the dirty windows where her head would be a nice round target for a Paragon sniper.

Zed stepped into the cradle she'd formed and pumped his legs for a jump. Carrol timed her boost to match. He grabbed the edge of the hole and hauled himself through. He then turned and put a hand down to help Carrol.

A plasma bolt ripped through the air as he did, and he had to jerk it back. "Hold on!" he told her, and he crawled out of view. A second later, he returned plasma fire from his position on the roof. Because of the car's height, he had some cover. Carrol peeked out the window to see a couple small explosions, and several troopers fell, shot.

"Okay," Zed shouted through the hole in the roof, hand out.

Carrol jumped, caught his forearm with one hand, and pulled with all her might to get high enough to grab the roof with the other. It worked. She got purchase, and with Zed hauling her, she crawled out onto the elevator roof with him.

"Holy shit," she exclaimed as the car rocked. It wasn't because they'd been shot at. It was just that unsteady as it rumbled down along its two sets of cables, one moving down with the car attached to them, the other moving up. Weight and counterweight.

Zed caught her eyeing the ancient system. "Oh, crap," he said, realizing what she was going to do. "Seriously?"

Carrol nodded. They had to get to the top. The shuttles were up there, and those were the only things that could get them off this rock after Warren and his team blew the cube. They *had* to get to them. This was the quick way to do it.

"Grab on," she said as she donned her gloves, turned on the magnetic setting, and gripped one of the cables tightly. She hoped it would be enough for the ride.

Zed groaned but did the same, then followed suit as Carrol aimed her rifle at where the cables connected to the elevator car. She planted a big kiss on his sweaty cheek and mumbled a quick prayer to whatever god would listen. They both fired at the connection.

The plasma did its job. It took far less time than Carrol had expected, which meant that when the car broke free of the cables, she wasn't prepared. With a gut-wrenching, arm-twisting *whoooosh*, she and Zed shot toward the top of the plateau. With another terrifying *whoooosh*, the counter-weight dove past them. Now free of the weight of the elevator car, it succumbed to the forces of gravity. Carrol and Zed, on the other side of that pulley system, were far too light to balance it, and they were pulled up at great speed.

Too great a speed, Carrol realized. With nothing to stop the counterweight from free-falling, it would smash into the ground below, and they would be thrown like rag dolls into the top of the elevator assembly.

"Let go!" Carrol screamed when the cables they were holding onto started to flare out at the top of their journey. It was a split-second decision, one she'd had no time to think through, but it was the only alternative to becoming bloody smears on the top of the metal structure.

She let go.

The cable whipped them out and away from the termi-nus, then she tumbled up and up end over end, hit an apex where her stomach floated into her throat, and then started back down again, picking up speed. She couldn't see where she was going and had no sense of direction, time, elevation —nothing. She just fell as the world spun.

Smack!

She hit the ground hard enough to knock the wind out

of her, which was *much* less hard than she'd expected, and rolled. She rolled for a long time; it almost made her pass out, but not quite. When she finally came to rest, it was dark. That made her second-guess the not-passing-out part, but it didn't take her long to realize it wasn't the passage of time that had made things dark. She was covered in something. Something soft like powder. Wet powder. It was cold.

Snow.

She was face-down in it. With a grunt, she pushed up. A relief, there. Her arms were working. Mounds of powder fell off her back and shoulders, and after a stumble or two, she stood. Her legs were working as well. Several meters away, she saw Zed doing the same.

How the two had come down was no less than a miracle. Beneath the outcrop at the rear of the shuttle plateau, the one that Zed and Carrol had descended earlier that morning, large piles of snow had accumulated, most of it fresh powder from the night before. When they'd released the elevator cable, their trajectory had dumped them into those soft snowbanks, carrying them over several rows of shuttlecraft and, from the nearby shouts, several Paragon troopers as well.

Carrol tapped her chest when she realized those shouting voices were getting nearer. Her rifle wasn't there. It must have been ripped off while she was in the air or in the snow after she landed. Damn. She scrambled when it dawned on her that if it had fallen off, it was probably along the path she'd rolled down, and *that* was clearly marked through the snowbank. She spotted something black and pointy sticking up through the powder six meters away or so.

She ran for it as a group of Paragon troopers became visible, stalking through the rows of nearby shuttlecraft.

One yelled in Carrol's direction and she dove toward her rifle, letting her and it disappear into the slush. The Paragon's shot missed. Hers didn't.

She rose from the snow and fired on automatic, raking across where she'd seen the approaching Paragon. A few meters away, Zed did the same. She kept firing, pointing at anything and everything that moved until there was nothing left. Then she fired some more.

Her rifle quit before she did. It locked up from overheating. Silence descended over the plateau except for her panting and Zed's. She counted a half-dozen fallen troopers and the same number of shot-up shuttlecraft. None were alive anymore.

They'd taken the plateau.

———

The data wasn't right.

Warren looked at Sudan's remote link to the transfer Idri was running from inside the cube and felt a long-growing constriction in his chest increase rapidly. "That can't be all of it?" he asked, pointing at the system's indicator of the size of the files they were copying from the AI.

"That's all the system is reading," Sudan said. She had called him over.

"Is there more to the program that's hidden, perhaps?"

Sudan looked up at him, her mouth quivering. She shook her head. This was it. "These distance calculations are in meters, sir."

"Idri," Warren said on the radio. The chest constriction was now full-on panic. "Idri, you need to come out. Now. We're done. This is over."

"The data transfer is almost finished," she insisted, no

doubt thinking this was more of his overprotection or caution. It wasn't.

"It's a trap," he hissed into the radio. There was no doubt in his mind. Given the data Sudan had shown him, both because of the fraction of the file size it would take to construct an AI capable of jumping a ship long-distance and from the information in the data, this had all been a ruse. There was a computer program in there, and it did appear to have something to do with jumping a ship, which validated what Warren had seen with his own eyes, but the specifics of that ability were far more limited in scope than what had been sold to them. Meters instead of light-years. Inches instead of miles.

It wasn't a game-changer.

It was bait.

From deep in the research facility, Warren heard footsteps. Hundreds of them. The Paragon were coming. "Jump out *now*," he shouted to her.

Nothing happened.

"Idri!"

"I'm trying." Her voice strained with effort. "I'm . . . trying Warren, but something . . . something is stopping me. I can't jump."

"Keep trying," he ordered. He turned to Sudan. "Cut her out," he said, then addressed his radio. "We're cutting you out."

The footsteps were getting closer. Smith sidled up next to him with Cheddar in tow. "We will not have time before the troops arrive," he said and the dog growled, ears perked toward the corridors.

Warren agreed. He unslung his rifle and primed his two shoulder cannons. "Then we must repel them," he said and prepared to fire.

CHAPTER FORTY-SIX

Drake thought they might actually have their clear shot to Vorkut V until the screech came over the command deck's loudspeakers. It was loud and so skin-crawlingly high-pitched that Drake thought his brain might melt and drip out his nose. XO, blessedly, shut off the speakers, and everyone on the command deck who was assaulted through their headphones tore them off.

"The hell was that?" Drake asked, breathing heavily. A headache had bloomed, and his vision was blurred. He'd never heard anything like it.

Oh was even more disoriented than he was, so Drake stumbled over to the comm station and checked the available information. The young technician manning those controls swallowed nervously. Bidermann was her name. He gave her a reassuring pat on the shoulder and asked her what the reading on the signal was. It was still coming through loud and clear.

"I'd guess a homing signal, sir," she said. "Blanket transmission, that amplitude, all frequencies. They're looking for a response of some kind."

Drake nodded. "Astute." The signal cut off, and Bidermann's readout level fell off at once. He pointed at them. "I think they just got their response."

"Sir!" Tactical called from a few steps away. Drake knew what he was going to say. "We have incoming."

"Fire countermeasures and give me bearing on the closest Paragon cruiser." He strode over to the center console and put a hand on a fellow crew member, this one for Commander Oh, the steadying kind as opposed to reassuring.

Oh straightened. "Fine, sir," he answered Drake's unspoken question. He looked clear-eyed.

Drake nodded. "Handle the post swaps for anyone who doesn't have their bearings yet."

The first officer acknowledged and strode off. Drake turned his attention to his command console and watched it light up as *Glory's* countermeasures deflected and destroyed the attacking cruiser's barrage.

One of the other four cruisers was on top them. Of the two cruisers that had taken the bait in the asteroid field, one appeared to be disabled, given that it hadn't moved in the past several minutes. The other cruiser was alongside, presumably providing assistance. They were successfully out of the way. Three more cruisers were burning toward *Glory* at full speed, but they were still minutes away. And, as expected, Hadras' flagship hadn't moved. But the one cruiser had just pinpointed them before they'd made out of the asteroid field. It was a match that would normally make Drake salivate, but with the other ships anticipating a dive for the moon, tangling on this course would delay *Glory* just enough to be vastly outnumbered.

"Back us off," he called to Helm. Time for a change in tactic. "Bearing negative-seven mark three-five. Take us back into the asteroid field. Up alongside . . ." He searched the three-dimensional display of the space around them and the rocks that filled it until he saw what he was looking for— a giant, craggy, slowly-spinning asteroid twice the size of their ship. "There. He flicked the coordinates to Helm. "Tight pass, I'd say two or three hundred meters, then full burn like we're running."

"Tactical!" he called next. "Prep thirty plasma charges to drop during the pass at the following coordinates on my mark. Rig for remote detonation." Finally, he would get to use his RC toys.

Glory groaned under the sudden acceleration and torque on her structure as the engines fired and the ship swung away from the Paragon cruiser. She could stand toe-to-toe with the ship out there, but he doubted its captain knew that. The Paragon were used to their quarry running when spotted. Drake suspected they'd pursue, confident in their superiority, and get a nice pointy surprise for their hubris. From the deck's vibrations and the sounds they transmitted, Drake knew Fredrickson hadn't been able to finish his repairs. He also knew that *Glory* could take it. She would hold together. He could feel it in the way she moved. She'd been stitched up just enough.

"Ship is in pursuit," XO said, rejoining Drake at the center console.

Drake nodded, intently watching what lay ahead. They were approaching the large asteroid. "Tactical, are those charges loaded and ready?"

"Yes, sir!" came the response.

"Prepare an aft salvo, all ordnance. Fire on my mark."

"A little cover?" XO asked, eyebrows raised. Drake nodded. His friend was with him.

"Fire aft salvo, please."

"Aft salvo away."

Drake watched a multitude of streaks erupt from Glory's rear launchers, aimed at the oncoming cruiser, which was quickly gaining ground. An aft salvo, a coordinated firing of all the guns, missiles, torpedoes, and cannons they had pointing ass-backward, didn't have the punch a straight broadside could deliver, but that wasn't necessary for Drake's purposes. The cruiser launched its countermeasures. They formed a perfect wall between the two ships, and Glory's weapons smashed into it and exploded well short of their intended target. Except, not really.

"Drop charges!"

"Charges away."

Drake tracked the two-and-a-half dozen tiny dots that dropped out of Glory's belly and buzzed off like so many flies to various points on the asteroid, which they were currently slicing past so closely that one might lose their arm if they stuck it out a window. Behind them, the light and energy from the countermeasures curtain were fading. The Paragon cruiser burst through it, bearing down on Glory at a reckless speed.

"Veer us off at six degrees starboard," Drake called to Helm. "Hard burn. Push her as hard she'll go."

Glory groaned loud enough to make Drake doubt his previous confidence a little, but she held. Kicking and screaming like she always did, but she held. Drake watched the Paragon ship turn to match, adjusting their optimal intercept course. It, like Glory, would take them very close to the large asteroid. Drake inhaled, watching the course readouts, speed, and distance, and waited. And waited.

"Blow charges!"

The asteroid exploded in the Paragon cruiser's path. A multitude of shards blossomed from the rock, each untraceable and as deadly as a bullet from a rail gun. They pummeled the cruiser like a million cuts from a million knives.

The Paragon ship faltered. Its speed decreased.

"Helm, thirty degrees starboard, z-axis. Tactical, fire broadside salvo when you're clear. Everything!"

The ship slowed so fast the inertial compensators couldn't keep up. Drake was shoved into his center console. He didn't care. *Glory* was still nimble on her feet. She swung to put her long side flush with the staggering Paragon cruiser, then fired everything she had on that side. It sounded like thunder or a drum line. *Boom booooom booomboomboomboom.* Plasma cannons, projectiles, superpowered laser beams, missiles, and torpedoes; they all hurtled from *Glory* and crossed the void to bury themselves in the Paragon ship.

It cracked open like an egg, then disappeared in an angry flash of orange-white energy.

Fuck, yes.

The deck beneath Drake's feet lurched.

An alarm blared.

He looked at XO questioningly. The two reset their feet and hunched over the command console, looking for answers.

"Hull breach," Tactical called, flashing the information to their console in the form of a 3D model of the warship.

On Deck Seven, there was a breach in the exterior plating. Not where Drake would have expected the hull to buckle. It was fifty meters away from the mess the blowhole had caused. Had they been hit by one of the asteroid shards? But this far away? "Visual, please, on that breach." It took a second since *Glory* had a metric shit-ton of scopes looking beyond the ship, but very few pointed inward, but Drake finally got the view he was looking for.

His heart skipped a beat. "Clean that image up!" he shouted, peering at the fuzzy picture, hoping it wasn't what he thought it was. The image sharpened, and Drake knew it was exactly what it had looked like.

A Paragon hull-piercing troop transport had latched onto their hull.

Deck Seven. That was the same deck as Sickbay.

"Jesus," Drake muttered, realizing the cruiser that had pursued them hadn't really been after them. Not *all* of them, anyway. Just one person. "Have Efremova and a security squad meet me on Deck Seven," he yelled to Oh as he sprinted off the command deck.

"Sir?" XO called after him.

"They're after Markus."

CHAPTER FORTY-SEVEN

WARREN and his team were caught in a crossfire.

The spokes of the wheel they stood in the middle of were a nightmare to cover. The Paragon poured in from all sides. They were almost completely surrounded. Warren noted that the Paragon seemed to stick to the corridors with long sight lines and stayed away from those that had a quick turn; areas of possible tactical maneuverability.

Between bursts of return fire, Warren glanced at Sudan, the cannon, and the progress they were making on cutting the cube open. All three were in dire shape. Sudan was clutching her shoulder, which had a nasty plasma burn on it, the tip of the plasma cannon was starting to glow from continuous use and looked ready to auto-shutdown at any moment, and worst of all, the hole they'd made in the black wall of the cube was barely enough to stick two fingers through.

Warren refused to accept it.

Idri would *not* be taken. If that was what this was about —and deep down, he knew it was; it had *always* been about Idri—he would stop it.

He roared and grabbed the barrel of the cannon, ignoring the burning sensation that radiated through his gloved hand, and raked it around the room in all directions. Its white-bluish stream of superheated plasma worked like a laser beam powered by a supernova, melting anything and everything it touched. Warren drew a line of destruction in a neat half-circle, careful to avoid the ducking Sudan and Smith and Cheddar on the other side of the cube and making sure the Paragon didn't outflank them from behind.

Down each of the corridors, Warren heard Paragon screams, and their barrage ceased for a moment as everyone scrambled for cover. There was no cover with a plasma cannon rated this high. It cut through everything, even crash metal. Not fast enough for the cube walls, but it worked on everything else.

A dark object flew through the air.

Warren turned the cannon on it, assuming it was a grenade or explosive of some other kind. He realized too late that it wasn't. With a concussive shudder, the object imploded when the plasma beam hit it, and the oddest reverse thunderclap you could imagine followed as the room groaned and bent toward the implosion. The plasma stream did too, sucked into it. A gravity grenade. It had unleashed a tiny black hole in the room, tiny being a relative term. Some black holes were large enough to consume galaxies. This one was a trillion times smaller but still large enough to eat a person. Or a plasma stream. Try as he might, like a fishing line with a shark on the other end, Warren could not break the cannon's plasma stream away from the singularity.

Another dark object was tossed into the room. Warren dropped the plasma cannon. He'd shoot this one with his rifle. Maybe send it skittering away before it cracked open the gravity well. Again, Warren realized too late what it was.

A normal grenade. The explosive kind.

Explode it did, a meter or so from him and Sudan and Smith and Cheddar. Warren hit the side of the AI cube so hard that he almost lost consciousness, even inside the ample protection of his helmet. His ears rang, and suddenly he found himself face-down in a pile of rubble. He rolled over with a groan to see the AI cube still towering over him. It was untouched, but the room around them, particularly the floor and walls closest to the explosion, were fucked up. So was Sudan. She was lying limply a few feet away. The heads-up display on Warren's helmet told him she was still breathing, pulse detected. That was good.

He willed himself to his knees, but there was no time. The Paragon were advancing toward them. He had to find cover. The cannon was lying next to Sudan, inoperative. He grabbed the small engineer by the shoulders and dragged her toward the closest corridor with a bend. Movement out of the corner of his eye snapped his head toward the other side of the AI cube. It was Cheddar. The dog had Smith by his armor and was dragging him in the same direction as Warren.

Smart dog. If anyone had a chance to get out of this alive, it was her. She could go invisible and run off. But she hadn't. She'd stuck with Smith.

Paragon fire resumed. It filled the smoky air like lightning. They were mostly firing blind, however—the single positive thing the grenade had done for Warren. He dragged Sudan into the side corridor and around the immediate right it took. Cheddar was right behind him with Smith in tow. The Marine looked unconscious but otherwise, none the worse for wear. Warren's HUD, like Sudan, indicated he was breathing and had a pulse. He was alive. They were all alive. For now.

Warren looked down the corridor they'd just entered. It made another immediate turn, this one to the left, and a turn a few meters after that, a right. He couldn't see past that and there were no Paragon, so he figured this was good as anything for now.

He did a quick once-over on Sudan and Smith, removing the latter soldier's helmet so he could check a pulse. They were still unconscious, both of them, but alive. He scrambled back to the first elbow in the corridor, the one that led to the AI cube, and peered around the corner.

The cube was still there, now crawling with Paragon troopers. He noticed that some of them were different. They were bigger and moved more efficiently. Confidently. The other troopers deferred to them. And they wore a bright red streak over the tops of their helmets.

Warren recognized them from the last time he'd been in these halls.

Warren sighted his rifle.

Hadras was coming. Warren was going to shoot him when he arrived.

"Please," he whispered; a prayer. "Jump out of there, Idri, before I do."

In the darkness and quiet of the cube, Idri raised her rifle to her shoulder, and waited.

She'd been trying to jump outside for the past several minutes but was getting nowhere. Her abilities were suppressed inside the cube. She didn't understand how, but they didn't work. She also didn't understand why there were two non-Navigator Navid in the room or what they might have to do with the AI they were plugged into. Only one thing made sense to her: someone was coming for her.

She'd heard over the open radio channel that the Paragon had surrounded Warren and his team, and she'd heard the desperate fighting before the AI cube rocked and the radio went dead. Not being able to see what was happening had been torture, and just as horrifying had been the realization of just how blind she really was. She didn't have a term for it because she'd never realized it was there, but until this moment, Idri had always been able to sense time and space around her, including everything that occupied it. It was more than sight or smell or touch, more than any of the traditional senses. It was a connection to everything around her, a background awareness she could feel whenever she focused on folding space.

She hadn't realized it was *always* there like a warm blanket enveloping her. Not until she'd come to this place and felt the terrifying cold emptiness and solitude. She was, for the first time in her life, truly blind. *Vulnerable*. It wasn't an accident. It was intentional, directed by someone. The stillness outside meant they were close, whoever had done this to her. Idri knew all she could do, alone and blind, was be ready for them.

For a long time, it was just her and her breathing, short and shallow and shaky. Otherwise, the cube was silent. Still. Her radio earpiece was the same. No static.

Pop!

Idri couldn't feel space folding before it happened. Her senses were blanked out.

A man stood before her. A giant. He had a gold helmet on with a thin slit across his eyes. It took her a split second to register he was there, but she swung her rifle to point at his chest and fired.

Too late.

In her sense blindness, she'd failed to register that two others had folded into the cube with the large helmeted man. Two soldiers.

One grabbed her rifle the instant before she fired, and her shot went wild. The other grabbed her arm and plunged something sharp into her shoulder. With a surprised yelp, she looked over and saw a syringe being withdrawn.

She'd been injected, not stabbed. The other guard grabbed her other arm, and she wildly fought both, kicking and flailing, using the limited training Warren had provided. In the corners of her brain, Idri could feel something taking hold inside her. A drug. She had been drugged. It tore at her consciousness, and her vision began to form a tunnel. They were trying to knock her out.

Something else kicked in in her mind, ratcheting up to fight her takeover. Idri felt her mind hard and desperately feeling for something. She wasn't in control of it. What was awakening in her was primitive, instinctual, and indiscriminate. It was tearing through the space around her, searching for *anything* it could grab onto, even just jump inside the cube. It wasn't conscious thought. It was the self-defense of a primal fight-or-flight instinct. Outside the struggle in her mind, the guards had pinned her arms, gripping them so hard it felt like they would break. She was stuck inside and out.

Idri's mind found something, and she screamed.

One of the guards next to her exploded.

As Idri fell to the floor from the sudden lack of support, she was dimly aware that she'd jumped something into his head. She saw a tool like a wrench lying next to the Navid on the closer bed.

The Navid.

Something inside her told her to release them. She screamed again, and her mind found something else inside the room to jump. She latched onto Sudan's tool bag, maybe because it was familiar or just because it was close. All she knew was that she found it, and she jumped it into the hub of wires and tubes that connected the two Navid to the computer console behind them.

An explosion.

It threw her, the remaining Paragon guard, and the giant helmeted man against the walls of the cube. The wall cracked, and when Idri came to after a few seconds of dazed immobility, she realized she could see outside the thing. She could also *sense* outside the cube.

The two Navid on the beds were screaming. Their eyes were no longer glazed, no longer distant. They were there in the room with Idri, staring at her and screaming *at her*. "Run," one gasped—the woman. Her terror was not for herself but for Idri. *"RUN!"*

Idri jumped.

Exhaustion overwhelmed her as she emerged from the fold, and she stumbled. The Paragon around her were surprised and still, but only for a moment. Then they all dove toward her en masse like an avalanche. It matched the drugs coursing through her brain. They were rising like a tidal wave, pouring in. Idri fought with everything she had, instinctually, savagely, and unconsciously.

She screamed louder this time, the loudest scream she'd ever produced. Her mind randomly grabbed chunks of debris and bolts of energy, anything and everything, and flung them into body parts, weapons, and the cube. She could hear screams to match her own as her enemies exploded, but they kept coming. Someone landed a blow on her head and she fell to the floor, but she kept fighting.

She would have *kept* fighting, but there was a final *pop!* and someone new was in front of her. The person stuck something into her neck. She forced her eyes open—she hadn't even realized that she'd closed them; stars, they felt like the mass of a black hole—and saw the helmeted man from inside the cube. She staggered back from him. When had she stood up again? She couldn't remember.

Another syringe was sticking out of her, this time from her neck. She tore it out and held it in her hand. She glanced at the helmeted man, and she thought about folding the syringe inside his blank, shining helmet. Usually a thought was enough to make it happen, and when it didn't, she looked at the syringe and tried harder.

It didn't work.

The darkness gnawing at her consciousness was now a thunderstorm, its winds racing across her mind, whipped by the second dose of the drug. She knew she couldn't stop it this time. The darkness would overtake her no matter what she did.

Her sight dimmed, tunneling in from the edges. In the dead center of it stood the helmeted man. He was the last thing she saw before she passed out.

CHAPTER FORTY-EIGHT

WARREN WATCHED from the outside as the AI cube shuddered and cracked. Idri was in there fighting for her life, and it sickened him that he could not help her. It was all he could do to stick to his corridor bend and not run out there to die in a blaze of glory. He would if he went back out there: die. The Paragon outnumbered him by a hundred to one.

His sacrifice might alleviate the feelings of cowardice biting at the edges of his thoughts, but it would do nothing to help her. He stayed where he was, hiding, eye on his rifle sight, looking for a shot. Hadras would show himself. Warren knew it as certainly as he knew anything. The arch-general was here for Idri. When he appeared, Warren would be ready for him. The Paragon, it would seem, had forgotten about Warren and his team or assumed they'd run off. It only reinforced that they were here for Idri since they didn't even pursue. They encircled the cube with her inside and stayed put. Warren would make them pay for that.

Pop!

The space around the cube flashed, and Idri was

suddenly standing outside. She had managed to jump out. Warren yelled at her, but she didn't hear him. Neither did the Paragon troops, who froze in surprise for a second. The next moment, they dove at her in waves. Warren regained his focus and put his eye back on his rifle sight to search for a shot. Something clean that would help her, but it was chaos.

Idri started fighting back.

Fwoooom!

The facility shuddered and cracked when Idri let out a scream, and waves of Paragon troops were blown away from her or blow up. Warren was forced back around his corner by a shockwave of air. When he scrambled back to where he could see, Idri was screaming again.

Another concussive snap of space-time followed, and the building shook once more. The floor she was standing on exploded, taking out troopers and the facility's structure in chunks, including the AI cube, which had far more than hairline cracks in it; sections were missing. The force of the shockwaves continued to blow the Paragon troopers back. Warren ducked back behind his bend just in time to keep chunks of rock, crash metal, and Paragon flesh from pelting his face.

Out of view, there was another *snap!* A different sound from Idri's fireworks. The same sound he'd heard when she jumped out of the AI cube but different.

Warren peeked around the corner, and there was Hadras.

He was standing in front of the staggering Idri, who was bleeding from her mouth, eyes, and nose. A syringe had been stabbed into her neck, and Hadras was pressing the plunger. A gold-gloved hand still gripped it.

Idri moaned, then collapsed.

Warren yelled at her, an involuntary reaction. Hadras turned at the sound and looked at him.

Warren squeezed the trigger and hit him full in the chest with a plasma bolt.

Hadras fell. Paragon troopers swarmed to him, their first instinct to care for their superior. They recovered quickly. Before Warren could get off another shot, some of the elite troopers opened fire on his position, and Warren caught his own shot to the chest. His armor absorbed it, but the force of the blast drove him back to the opposite wall of the corridor turn, exposing him to more fire. Dozens of shots followed, and Warren rolled farther around the turn to get out of sight. He didn't know where his rifle was, his helmet was off his head, nowhere to be found, and one of his shoulder cannons was out. He scrambled, desperate to find his weapon to fend off whoever was coming for him.

But they didn't come.

Warren found his rifle on the tunnel floor, crouched to give the enemy a different eye-level, and poked his head around the corner once more.

Hadras was standing again. Alive, dammit. Idri was slung over his massive shoulder, and he was shouting at his troops, gathering them.

They were leaving. Pulling out. With Idri.

Hadras turned before following them, looking right at Warren's position. The two locked eyes. The archgeneral stared Warren down, ice-blue eyes blazing and triumphant.

Warren roared at him, wanting to fire again. He almost did, but Idri was on his shoulder. Hadras turned slightly to put her limp body in his path. He was taunting Warren. He knew he'd won. Then he turned away, adjusted his grip on Idri's limp form, and swept out of the chamber.

The special guard circled behind the archgeneral,

facing Warren. They peppered the corridor corner with a barrage of fire so fierce that Warren had no choice but to retreat.

When the fire finally died, Warren scrambled to his feet and checked the central chamber. It was empty, but he could still hear the receding footsteps of Hadras and his men.

"Smith," Warren shook the prone Marine, still where he'd been safely dragged by Cheddar. Thinking about the dog made him realize he hadn't seen her since they'd taken cover. Damn. Sudan lay just beyond the Marine, also still out. "Wake up, Marine!"

Smith sat up, eyes open. The change from unconscious to conscious was so abrupt that it startled Warren. The Marine took stock of his new surroundings, blinking. "What happened?"

"They took Idri," Warren said, opting to cut to the chase. "We have to move. They're heading out of the facility, but they're not that far ahead."

Smith nodded and cocked his head to the side. "I can hear them." He swept the area with his gaze. "Where is Cheddar?"

"I don't know," Warren said as he crawled over to Sudan to re-check her up close. She was still alive. Breathing. Pulse was strong. Gash on her forehead, and a concussion, but alive.

Smith checked a screen he had strapped to his forearm and frowned. "My tracking pad is damaged. I'm not getting a reading"

Damn. "I haven't seen her." Warren hesitated. They couldn't leave the dog behind. That wasn't going to fly with Smith, and it wouldn't fly with him. But those receding footsteps were almost out of earshot and getting farther away.

They had to move.

"Don't worry about her." Smith stood. There was certainty in his voice. "If she's concealed, it's for good reason, and it means she's uninjured. She'll stick close to us. She may even be trailing the Paragon troops."

"What if she's lost?"

Smith shook his head. "Cheddar does not get lost." He bent and scooped up Sudan. He slung her gently over his shoulder and knelt to pick up his rifle with his other hand. He primed it with a signature click and whine. "You lead the way, Lieutenant. I will keep up."

The level of activity around the facility was insane.

Hundreds of troopers poured out of the exits, hauling ass to their waiting transports. In the chaos, Carrol couldn't make heads or tails of what had been accomplished. It wasn't a retreat; that much was certain. Who would be forcing so many of them to run? Not Warren and his tiny group. Not her and Zed in a single shuttlecraft. No, this was the type of "Let's go!" that accompanied a job well done, a mission accomplished. They were meeting no resistance. With that hypothesis in mind, Carrol could make out a rear defense line setting up around a few of the facility's exits, waiting to blast anything or anyone who came out who wasn't Paragon. Read, Warren and his team.

"We need to lift off," she hissed to Zed in the front compartment. Carrol was standing in the open shuttle hatch, looking over the edge of the cliff.

"Working on it," Zed called back, trying to make sense of the Paragon controls. In the considerable history of human-Paragon conflict, very little Paragon technology or matériel had been recovered by the Fleet. Not much was known about their systems, controls, or even language. Still, a plane was a plane. He should be able to figure it out.

"Everyone is leaving."

"I SAID I'M WORKING ON IT."

KaCHUNK. The shuttlecraft's engines came to life with a cough. It jerked Carrol in the open hatch, and she caught herself just in time to avoid plunging face-first out the door as they were lifting off the ground.

Closing the hatch wasn't an option. She wanted it open so the second their teammates appeared outside the facility, they could swoop in and grab them. Falling through it because of Zed's unorthodox flying wasn't an option.

"You okay?" Zed called from the front, looking over his shoulder.

"I'm fine."

"I can set us back down."

"You focus on your flying! I'll focus on not falling out."

Carrol looked around and saw that the shuttle had modular seating. Chairs that could be installed, removed, rearranged, etc., which meant the components were likewise interchangeable. Fancy. She grabbed one of the belt harnesses, the kind that clipped one into their seat by both shoulders and across the waist. Lots of strong material for Carrol to work with.

"Why don't you strap in up here?" Zed asked as they gained altitude.

Troop transports filled the sky around them. In each were dozens of the enemy, just leaving. Getting away. It didn't sit right with Carrol, nor did just circling and waiting to see if their friends made it out alive, at the mercy of those last couple lines of defense the Paragon were leaving behind, presumably to light them up as soon as they came out. No, they needed to help. Cause some chaos. This was too easy for the Paragon.

"I have something else in mind," she yelled over the roar of loaded transports heading back to the archgeneral's ship. She found a couple handholds on the side of the hatch, looped her seat straps around them, and buckled herself to them tightly with a couple points of contact. She yanked the result and was reasonably certain it would keep her from flying out the open door if she lost her feet. Then, with a stretch to reach it, she grabbed her plasma rifle. "You have the hang of this thing yet?" she called to Zed.

"Think so." When he looked over his shoulder at Carrol in her getup, half-hanging out of the open hatch, rifle in hand, he grew a grin and a twinkle in his eye. "What are you thinking?"

Carrol cocked her weapon. "I'm thinking we get close enough to some of these transports, and a couple well-placed shots into their thruster ports could do a whole lot of damage."

"I'm thinking you're right."

"Well, then, Lieutenant, let's do some fucking flying."

"Yes, sir."

Zed punched it.

CHAPTER FORTY-NINE

THE FIREFIGHT HAD STARTED by the time Drake and Efremova arrived at the breached section of Deck Seven. A dozen of her security team were pinned by a cadre of Paragon invaders.

"Dug in," Efremova reported to Drake after a brief but concise conversation with one of her soldiers. "Not moving."

Drake peered around the shoulder of the nearest of Efremova's team and saw half a dozen white-clad Paragon troopers arranged on either side of the corridor, well-covered and not moving as advertised. "They're protecting the breaching craft," Drake shouted to Efremova. "Where is the other group?"

Efremova shook her head. "Unclear."

"About twenty of them broke off, sir, right after we arrived," the soldier in front of Drake turned to say. "Didn't see where they went."

Dammit. "We have security at Sickbay?"

Efremova shook her head again. "Comms are jammed. They were dispatched. You want to head there?"

Drake considered but shook his head. "They're coming here." He pointed down the corridor at the small group of dug-in Paragon. "They need that ship to get out of here. This is their smallest contingent. We need to throw everything we have to try to stop them *here*."

It was a good plan. Efremova had another wave of security forces coming right behind them, due in seconds. A burst of heavy fire from down the corridor, however, told Drake they would be too late.

Two dozen troopers streamed into the corridor behind the dug-in Paragon line. They fired behind them as they went and opened up on the security forces Drake was with as well, forcing them to retreat behind their cover, which was a hastily assembled pile of metal crates.

Through a crack in the crates just large enough to see through—which meant it was large enough to let a round through and get him killed if he wasn't careful—Drake caught sight of a figure in the midst of the larger group of Paragon soldiers. A tall, slight figure Drake recognized.

"Markus!" he bellowed down the hallway, standing up and out of the cover.

The Blaspheme heard him. He turned and looked at the captain. Drake could see his hands were bound, and the troopers on either side of him were holding him tightly by the arms. They were different, these troopers. Drake recognized them. He'd seen them before, though not for a very long time: Archgeneral Hadras' personal guard. 'Stripers,' in reference to their distinctive helmets. An elite unit inside the Paragon hierarchy that carried out the most sensitive of his biddings. They were the type to shoot and not miss.

Drake stared at Markus. Time slowed, and they locked eyes. Markus's were blank. Impenetrable. Drake shouted his name again, but the old man was a stone. Resigned. This had been put in motion a long time ago, and although at the very end he had perhaps wished to change the outcome, that desire had come far too late.

Damn him.

The elite guards hustled him through the punctured bulkhead where they'd breached *Glory's* hull, and Markus was gone.

Their conversation back in the airlock rang in his ears. *Even then*, Markus had asked him, *would you come for me?* Drake had said yes. Now . . . he wasn't so sure.

The Paragon fired at Drake, both those they'd been fighting all along—the standard troops—and the elites. He was tackled to the deck, or he would have acquired several new holes in his body.

"Captain!" Efremova yelled in his face. She had wrestled him to the deck, and she was furious that she'd had to.

Drake's blood boiled, but she was right. That had been foolish. "Can we stop them?"

Efremova shook her head. "Everyone back behind section bulkhead," she shouted at the top of her lungs, louder than Drake had thought possible. His next thought was to chide himself. Never underestimate a Russian.

It was the right command, and it saved lives because a split second later, the deck rocked beneath their feet, and there was the horrible sound of rending metal. Following it was the even worse hiss of escaping atmosphere. The breaching ship was tearing itself out of *Glory's* hull, leaving a gaping hole behind.

Alarms sounded, activated automatically, and the bulkhead a meter from where they were crouched slammed down. It had no safety sensors that would stop it if a person was underneath. With an atmosphere breach, you closed off the compromised section no matter the cost. Efremova's team, at her command, had moved back to the right side of the bulkhead and were free and clear. It caught some of the metal crates they'd been hiding behind and smashed them like they were balsa wood. The hiss ceased, the alarm stopped, and it was quiet in the corridor.

Drake stood and walked up to the bulkhead, which had a dirty slotted window right at head height in its center through which to look. He wiped it with his uniform sleeve and came back with decades of dust, one of the few areas of the ship XO's cleaning crews hadn't gotten to. He could see through it, albeit barely.

The breach ship was gone.

Markus was gone.

"Bridge!" Drake shouted, tapping his wristcom.

"Captain," XO's voice came back, staticky.

At least it was working. The interference was abating as the Paragon left. "Tell CAG to have her fighters intercept that breach craft."

"Yes, sir."

"Capture, not destroy."

"Understood."

Drake closed the channel and flexed his jaw, knowing the chances of accomplishing what he'd just asked were slim. Those craft were designed to be impossible to track or shoot down, fast, lightless little arrows you couldn't see until they were embedded in your hull. He looked through the slit of a window in the bulkhead again and felt sick to his stomach.

Hadras was winning.

Drake needed to find a way to change that.

CHAPTER FIFTY

AT EVERY TACTICALLY SOUND JUNCTURE, the Paragon had set up firing squads. Warren and Smith were left scrambling for cover as they tried to follow Idri but kept running into the ambushes. After an exchange of plasma bolts, it would get quiet, the two would peek their heads out, and the troopers would be gone. It was designed to slow them down, which was infuriating but a sound maneuver executed by experienced troops.

Warren would almost have preferred a kill box, an explosion, or even a surge to try to capture them. Something in his face that he could fight head-on. This . . . well, this was toying with them. Holding them at arm's length just long enough so their own arms couldn't land any blows, like the big kid on the playground holding back the head of the smaller one.

They were nothing to the Paragon now, not even worth a concerted effort to kill. Only enough to delay and sidetrack until everyone could leave. Maybe abandoning them on Vorkut V, deep in Paragon space, would be death sentence enough. That made him wonder about Glory. Was she still up there?

The footsteps were gone now. Idri got farther away with each troop encounter. Warren resolved to charge the Paragon at the next encounter. Maybe he could break through. He saw his chance when the next turn they took in the labyrinthine facility dead-ended in a closed door ten meters down a narrow hallway. There were Paragon on the other side of that door, waiting to kill him should he step into the corridor or more easily, get him to retreat to the other side to wait for them to move on.

Not this time.

Warren bellowed, rifle raised with his finger on the trigger, his remaining shoulder cannon set to fire at anything he so much as looked at, and took off down the hallway. He didn't bother to see if Smith would keep up. He knew the Marine would do so at his own pace and that he would consider Sudan's life in addition to his own. She was still unconscious over his shoulder, which kept the Marine from being reckless, a course of action Warren had committed to.

Warren burst through the door shoulder-first, his power-armor-aided speed launching him through it much faster than any normal being could go . . .

And found himself outside.

He skidded to a halt in a snowdrift up to his knees. Around him was chaos. There'd been a defensive line set up outside the door at one point. Warren could see the remnants of a large-caliber plasma cannon, entrenchments, and bodies, all burning. The Paragon had set up an ambush. Warren was almost flattered. Someone else had gotten there first, however.

Warren looked into the sky and saw who it was. A shuttle

was wreaking havoc up there, darting through the transports that were taking off from the facility, leaving everything behind. Warren squinted and his HUD zoomed in on the shuttle, using the cameras built into his helmet and visor. In the midst of the mayhem was Commander Carrol, half-hanging out of the damn shuttle, blasting away as the shuttle pulled a tight arcing maneuver to bring them alongside another troop transport. She fired into the cockpit point-blank. The transport didn't react at first, just kept on flying. When it headed toward another rising transport, Warren knew it was curtains for them. With no living pilot to adjust course and avoid the other craft and the second pilot unaware of that, the two smashed into each other, and a fireball lit the sky.

Warren cheered, then realized Idri was on one of those transports.

"Stop," he shouted into his suit radio, breaking the comms blackout. He desperately hoped the short-range would work, and that Carrol or Zed were listening. "Commander, it's Lieutenant Warren. You must stop destroying the transports."

The speakers in his helmet crackled to life. Thank god.

"Um, could you repeat that?" Zed's voice was distorted from interference but audible.

"Idri is on one of them, Lieutenant," he said, hoping the pilot could hear him. They were angling toward another transport—another target. "We can't risk shooting her down."

There was static on the radio, and Warren's heart sank. He thought none of his message had gotten through. Then Zed returned. "Well, I think you just ruined the commander's day, but message received and understood. Where are you?"

"One of the side exits," Warren said. He turned around,

realizing he wasn't sure where he was, but no further explanation was needed. Up in the sky, the shuttle had turned and was heading toward him.

"Figured," Zed said. "You like the work we did for you on that little going-away party they had planned for you guys?"

He must have meant the burning cannons and entrenchments. Zed and Carrol had neutralized those for them. "Immensely," Warren answered before quickly scanning the sky. He was grateful, but all he could think about was Idri.

Smith emerged from the same exit as Zed landed the shuttlecraft a few meters away. Warren went back to assist the Marine, taking Sudan for the last stretch between the facility and the shuttle. Carrol stepped out to help them inside.

With a deafening roar, the giant flagship above them fired its atmospheric thrusters. Even with it being three hundred and fifty meters in the air, the ground shook. The last of the transports rose into her ample hangar bays, and the ship angled toward space. Warren had almost forgotten about the archgeneral's ship, and as he considered its presence, he was surprised the Paragon hadn't just nuked them from above. They were pulling out, and that ship had the firepower to wipe them out, but it hadn't. It didn't make any sense.

Carrol was at the hatch to the shuttle to help him load Sudan into one of the chairs inside, but both paused to look up, and it wasn't because of the flagship.

The AI ship was shimmering. Its umbilical had just disconnected and was still falling toward the ground. Suddenly, Warren understood why the flagship hadn't destroyed the facility. The AI cube was in there, still controlling the ship. The shimmering built, and as he'd witnessed weeks before, it flashed a brilliant stab of rainbow-white light and was gone. While it might have been bait for Idri, it was effective. It had to be. The ship was not the long-range threat they'd been sold on, but it was still a threat, even if it could only jump kilometers. That was more than enough to turn the tide in ship-to-ship combat, which made the black thing extremely dangerous.

"Where do you think that ship is off to?" Carrol asked him.

"Glory," he said simply, then looked at the facility. The AI cube was still in there, and there was no one left to defend it. He glanced at the flagship, which was almost through the clouds. Soon it wouldn't be visible. "Goddammit, Idri, I'm sorry," he said in a barely audible whisper. She was on that ship. He knew that as surely as he knew anything. She hadn't been on any of the transports Carrol and Zed had destroyed. She was a prisoner on that ship, being taken away to do horrible things. That was why they were bugging out.

She could take care of herself; Warren knew that. At least long enough for them to figure out a way to come and get her. Glory, on the other hand, had no idea what was coming her way. That was something Warren could do something about.

Warren regarded Carrol. "Permission, Commander, to reenter the facility?" he said.

She nodded. "Hell, yes."

CHAPTER FIFTY-ONE

"ALL PARAGON FORCES ARE WITHDRAWING, SIR," XO reported the second Drake's foot touched the command deck's plating.

The sick feeling in his stomach had increased on his way back up, and this news confirmed what it was telling him. Hadras had Idri. That was the reason for the sudden flurry of activity. *Bam.* The system was alive. They'd laid in wait to spring their trap, and now that it was sprung, they were getting the hell out with their spoils.

"Pursue," Drake said, arriving at the center console panting. "The flagship," he added, pointing at the triangle-shaped dot that represented the *Scythe.* It was on the move, the most sinister sign of all. "All available speed."

Glory didn't even have time to fire her engines.

"New contact," one of the tactical officers called from his station. "Fifty kilometers off our starboard bow, sir." XO raised an eyebrow, and they both pulled up that area of their tactical display. It was empty. XO turned to question the tactical officer, but they spoke up again before he had the chance. "Amend that, sir," he said. His voice was a mixture of embarrassment and confusion. "Make that fifteen kilometers dead ahead."

Drake looked back down at his console, and this time he saw the contact. A ship. Small one, but its energy readings indicated warship-level power generation. Then it was gone.

"Contact lost again, sir," the tactical officer said and slapped the side of his console. He turned, red-faced. "I'm sorry, sir."

"Faulty scopes?" XO asked Drake.

"Countermeasures," Drake shouted, cutting him off and realizing in that same instant what it was they were looking at. Damn. "Three-hundred-sixty degrees. Now."

The ship shuddered under their feet as Tactical complied, but when the contact popped back into existence, this time a single kilometer away, Drake knew even his preemptive order would be too late.

"Brace yourselves!" he yelled.

A dozen energy signatures exploded from the new contact. Missiles and plasma, all fired toward *Glory* at point-blank range from behind the expanding cloud of countermeasures she'd just launched. They slammed into her unimpeded. Drake was thrown off his feet when the deck pitched sharply. A power relay exploded somewhere, and crew members yelled in surprise.

Drake recovered quickly and crawled back to the center console. "Return fire," he called over the crew's shouts. "Lock coordinates and return fire."

To the credit of his bridge crew, no sooner were the words out of his mouth than he saw *Glory's* front-facing batteries pump plasma into the location that had just fired upon them. The only problem was that the enemy ship winked out of existence before the shots got there.

"Heavy damage reports coming in from the front sections," XO gasped, clawing himself back to his feet next to Drake. "Reports of fires."

"Lock it down. Coordinate repair crews," Drake said, jaw flexing. He could handle his own verbal commands. Oh would handle keeping the ship together. "Tactical," he snapped, turning to that station. "Where is that ship now?"

"Bearing five-five—"

"On my console, Crewman. I don't need a verbal response. Flash it here continuously."

"Yes, sir."

The ship, and there was no doubt in Drake's mind what ship stalked them out there, was back to a distance of several kilometers, out of weapons range. Then it popped out of existence once again.

"Countermeasures," Drake shouted in response.

Again, the ship popped into existence too close for them to be effective, and again, *Glory* took the full brunt of its attack. Drake held on this time, as did most of the command deck crew. Return fire was sent on its way without Drake needing to give the order a split second after the ship reappeared, but the ship flashed out of existence before a single shot landed.

Damn.

"The AI prototype ship?" XO asked him in between calls over his personal comm to coordinate repair and medical response teams.

Drake nodded. This was very bad.

As the AI ship attacked, the *Scythe* slithered away, heading in-system with its escorting cruisers, carrying Markus and probably Idri. The bastards were getting away, and there was nothing Drake could do to stop them.

CHAPTER FIFTY-TWO

WARREN SET the last of the explosive charges on the bottom tip of the angled cube, up against the conduit that plunged hundreds, if not thousands, of meters down into the mountain range to the geothermal reactor at its base. That in turn plunged more tens of thousands of meters into the depths of the moon, drawing its energy from the tectonic heat contained there. The conduit glowed and vibrated with an accompanying *thrum-thrum*. The AI was an energy hog; that much was clear. It meant the explosion they were about to set off would be massive.

Smith came around from the back of the cube as Warren hauled himself out from the gap between it and the floor, where he'd dangled to set the charge.

The two men regarded the black structure. Damage from the battle was fresh. The hole they'd bored with their plasma cannon still gave off wisps of smoke, and every so often, chunks of the crash metal would fall from the spiderweb of cracks Idri had caused while fighting for her life. The sight made Warren feel like a failure. He could tell that Smith felt the same. The air was heavy.

"I believe the explosion resulting from our charges will set off a chain reaction in the power plant below," Smith said, breaking the silence with his quiet but gruff voice.

Warren nodded. "We'll set them for the longest delay they have."

It wasn't just the QE comms that didn't work inside the facility. Radios were down, too, at least with any sort of reliability. They'd tried to stay in contact with Commander Carrol, who was outside rounding up every prisoner or straggler she could find and herding them up the mountain to the ridge, but beyond a word or two here and there, it was mostly static. It was not a signal one could rely upon to blow multiple charges simultaneously. QE was a total blackout. That left one option: timers.

Because of the humming, thrumming power conduit pumping gigawatts of energy into the AI cube every couple milliseconds, when the cube went, it was liable to take the entire facility along with it. And the camp. And the mine. Hell, Warren figured it would take the entire cliffside and wipe it off the face of the mountain range. That meant he, Smith, and anyone within a mile of this thing needed to hustle out of there and get to higher ground.

"Six minutes."

Smith was pointing to the closest explosive charge and the small dial on its face. That was the max it would let them set the timer for, six minutes. What an odd number to specify. "I ran a six-minute mile in the Academy," he told the Marine, biting his lower lip.

"I never went to the Academy," Smith told him, raising an eyebrow. "But I ran under six two weeks ago." Warren chuckled despite the situation. How could he forget that Smith was Superman? The Marine slapped Warren on the back of his armor with a solid *thunk*. "We're in powered armor. We'll be fine."

Warren hoped so. Running on an oval track or even through the lower decks of *Glory* was very different from the winding corridors of this facility, then out in the snow and up a mountainside, even if they were in power-assisted armor. Didn't matter, though. The charges gave them six minutes. It would have to be enough.

"Commander," Warren said, trying his radio. "We're in place."

Static was all he had gotten back for so long that Warren was sure his transmission had not gone through. However, just as he was about to give up, set the charges, and high-tail it, Carrol said, "Hold . . . tenant. We've . . . isoners. About . . . of them."

"Repeat that," Warren said.

"Hold!" she repeated. "...evacuating . . . on the west side. About two hundred of them."

Prisoners. She'd found more of them. Damn. Way too many to fit on a shuttle. They'd have to be evacuated to the hills too, which would take time.

"We'll hold," Warren said. He got back a squealing wash of static that made his ears feel like they were going to melt.

"...eat that?" Carrol's voice poked through a moment later, distorted and high-pitched.

"We'll hold," he shouted, hoping she'd hear him. "Your signal."

The radio squealed again. Warren figured Carrol had heard him. When he exchanged looks with Smith, the Marine's expression mirrored his. They'd have to wait. It wasn't going to be forever. Every second they waited, *Glory* was doing battle up there and in danger of dying.

"Ten minutes," Warren told Smith.

They would give Carrol ten minutes to get those prisoners out. Then they were blowing this goddamn place.

CHAPTER FIFTY-THREE

"Continuous fire."

It was a desperate command, but Drake and *Glory* were in a desperate spot. There was no sugarcoating it. The AI ship was proving to be unstoppable. It only jumped a few kilometers at a time, but that was more than enough to make it impossible for *Glory* to find it. The patterns, the timing—it was all random, and entirely unprecedented. No Navigator had ever been able to jump so many times, so quickly. There was no book on how to defeat such an agile foe, because such a foe had never before existed. Drake was in entirely uncharted territory.

He had tried extrapolating where it might show up next, but that proved fruitless. He'd tried timing its jumps; ditto. He'd tried chasing it around with their fighter squadrons, but the area within even the few-kilometer range was far too great. It had slipped through every time without suffering a blow. Not a single shot had landed.

Glory, meanwhile, was taking a pummeling. There were fires amidship. She had a crack on the port side where the asteroid shard hadn't been fully sealed. Power was fluctuating as the grid became progressively more compromised. They were dying. The AI ship was pristine and untouched.

That needed to change.

Drake gave the only order he could think of. "All weapons," he said, following up the call for continuous fire. "In three-hundred-sixty degrees."

Oh raised an eyebrow that furrowed his sweat-slicked brow. Drake nodded to confirm he'd heard right. It was a massive expenditure of energy and weaponry. The plasma cannons would overheat after only a few seconds and take minutes to cool enough to be used again. Missile and torpedo stockpiles would diminish at an insane rate, and the same with rail ammunition.

Drake didn't care. They *had* to punch back.

Glory shuddered, and Drake held on as she poured everything she had into the void. Seconds ticked by. He watched his command display as energy levels crept toward critical across all systems. Behind him, an energy bank's surge protection failed and it exploded with a pop that reverberated through the command deck, then burst into flames. Repair crews on standby jumped into action and put out the fire before it spread. The air was heating up all over the ship, Drake knew, and other consoles started to spark and smoke. Even without his display, Drake knew the ship was about to burn out, but he held to his order. Keep firing.

"Contact," Tactical called, whirling to face the command console.

Drake saw it in the same instant. The AI ship jumped in just under a kilometer off the starboard bow. One of their cannons was firing at that spot, and the AI ship took a plasma bolt on its nose.

It staggered.

"Shut down all blind fire!" Drake shouted. "Concentrate all starboard batteries on those coordinates!"

Glory stopped quaking. Half her weapons went silent. Those on the opposite side from the AI ship could rest. Those on the other side roared in unison with a single target to focus on. The transition was almost instantaneous. It made Drake's heart swell to the size of the goddamn sun. While the other weapons could now rest and recover, the weapons that kept firing were seconds away from failure, but it didn't matter. They were no longer being fired blindly or in vain. These shots would land.

They did.

The AI ship rocked as wave after wave of energy and missiles pummeled it. It was caught broadside, and small explosions rippled along its outer hull. The command crew yelled, and Drake whooped along with them. Then, in a flash, the AI ship disappeared and reappeared again, this time several kilometers farther away than it had stalked them from before.

Damn right.

Drake ordered the rest of *Glory's* weapons to shut down. He was pleased to see the majority hadn't gone past critical. They would cool and could be used again when they were needed.

The AI ship hung back. It had a bloody nose. *Glory* had much more than that— cracked ribs, internal bleeding, hands failing, if one extended the metaphor—but the artificial intelligence running that ship wasn't used to being hit. It was in shock. Reassessing. Cautious. Uncertain.

There had to be a way to take advantage of that.

"Helm," Drake called, an idea forming. "Plot course for the asteroid field. Full burn."

"Aye, sir."

"Navigation, flash me a density map."

XO came over to Drake as an overlay of the asteroid field came up on the command display. "We're going back in?" he asked, eyebrow arched again.

Drake nodded. "We need to even the odds."

CHAPTER FIFTY-FOUR

Carrol's call came in at Minute Eleven.

It took everything Warren had to wait those extra sixty seconds, but he'd held on. "Go" was her command. "*Go go go.*"

"Commander," Smith called, jumping on the radio.

"Smith?" Carrol responded. The signal was still laden with static, her voice distorted, but it was the clearest exchange they'd had up to this point. Full sentences were coming through.

"Have you seen Cheddar?" the Marine asked. The dog still hadn't turned up anywhere the two of them had been, outside, or back in the facility. Smith had stopped checking his tracker a while back; it was dead.

"Not out here," she answered.

"Understood." Smith closed the channel with a curt nod to no one but himself. "Let's go," he said to Warren.

Warren felt for him. The dog had to be somewhere, that was certain, but where and why she hadn't revealed herself was still a mystery. He'd been confident that Cheddar was intentionally concealed during the battle, hiding as a tactical move—after all, she'd been there on second and was gone the next—but that confidence was wearing thin now that so much time had passed, and she still hadn't turned up. Maybe she'd been spooked and run off. She was trained not to. Engineered to keep her cool, but even people did that kind of thing, let alone animals.

Warren gave the Marine a pained look.

But Smith shook his head in response to the unspoken sympathy. "She will show herself," he said with absolute confidence.

He hustled to the other side of the AI cube, and from the beeping sounds that came soon after, Warren knew he was setting the charges.

Warren followed his example, shook off his worry and busied himself. He moved as quickly as he could between the charges. "Six minutes," he shouted as he flipped the last switch. Smith called back an affirmative that his charges were set.

They ran.

CHAPTER FIFTY-FIVE

DRAKE WAS ASKING THE IMPOSSIBLE.

Thousands of rocks surrounded *Glory*, each with its own trajectory, speed, and rotation. Some spun wildly, either from the inertia bestowed upon them from the millennia they'd spent in space running into and bouncing off their own kind or from *Glory's* presence, which stirred the drink as she barreled through them like a bowling ball. Even from the command deck, Drake could hear thuds on the hull.

That was the good part. Diving into the pool of small rocks had been a key facet of Drake's plan to reenter the asteroid field. The AI ship had to be a lot more careful about jumping. With all that mass floating around, one wrong move and she would jump a rock on top of her power core. *Boom.* No more AI ship.

The bad part, the impossible part, was that it was proving unfeasible to track all the rocks around them. There were still holes in the field, filled with larger asteroids, where clouds of smaller rocks had been sucked up, and the space between them was cleaner and safe to jump into.

There were enough of those holes, changing with the perpetual motion of the field, that *Glory* couldn't figure out where the AI ship would appear next. They tried to fill the gaps with weapons fire. Shoot at the parts of the field that were clear enough to jump into, and they might catch the AI ship when it popped in there. That part of the plan had been sound. It was far more efficient than trying to maintain a full three-hundred-sixty-degree barrage, but it wasn't nearly as simple. Miss a gap, and you could miss the AI ship.

And she was missing.

"Navigation," XO shouted, pointing at a portion of the three-dimensional projection of the field hovering above the command console that glowed red. "We're blind on 27-A." That indicated that the positions of the asteroids displayed there were plotted outside an acceptable degree of uncertainty and needed to be re-scoped.

In simple terms, the asteroid projections weren't accurate anymore, and Tactical was setting firing targets based on bad information. Navigation had six other portions of the asteroid field to get updated positions for. They were behind, and it kept getting worse. The pieces were too numerous to keep track of, and there was too large an area to cover.

A second later, Navigation had seven portions of the field to re-scope.

The AI ship jumped into one of those sectors, easily avoiding the covering fire because of the outdated information.

"Hard to port," XO yelled in a desperate attempt to dive out of the way of the fire that was soon to come.

It was too late. The other ship unleashed a barrage that slammed into *Glory's* starboard side, then popped back out of the field before they could return fire. XO slammed a fist on the command console hard enough for something to *crunch*. When he lifted it, there was a tiny crack in the tabletop, and Oh winced in pain. That resulted in his expression growing even angrier. He could be mad at himself in addition to everything else.

Drake caught his attention with a slow shake of his head. This wasn't working. The AI ship would prick them to death in the field at this rate, or worse, force them to become increasingly more erratic in their evasive maneuvers. Then they'd smash into one of the larger rocks and meet a fiery death.

The larger rocks . . .

Drake felt another idea forming. He scanned the asteroid field with a new interest. XO, at his side, read that his captain was looking for something and leaned in as well. "Get me a three-click scan of any rock over two million metric tons of displacement," Drake told him. "Ignore anything smaller than that."

Oh nodded and sprinted over to the bank of navigation consoles to handle it personally. Meanwhile, Tactical roared; they'd scored a lucky hit on the AI ship when it flashed into one of the gaps they'd been firing on. The ship winked out before more batteries could be brought to bear on it, however, and two dozen plasma trails were left in its place: missiles streaking toward *Glory*. They exploded topside, more than half hitting home. Even those the plasma cannon crews had been able to shoot down exploded in such close quarters that *Glory* rocked nearly as hard as she did from the ones that hit. More power conduits overloaded in showers of sparks and flame as Oh ran back over to Drake. "Sir," he said breathlessly as he flashed Drake's requested readout on the console.

Drake scanned it and found something that would work. He stabbed a finger at a dense pack of large rocks caught in each other's gravity fields. They formed a semisphere, open on one end and closed on the other like an eggshell with the tip cut off. It was better than Drake could have asked for had he designed and built it himself. "There. Get us in there."

"We won't be able to get out," Oh observed.

"Correct." He zoomed in on the opening. "But there's only one way in."

XO straightened in understanding. "Helm, take us bearing three-five mark one-seven. Full burn. Tactical, cease fire all batteries, and lay down two rounds of countermeasures, then continue at one every sixteen seconds."

The first officer had thought of the cease fire and countermeasures on his own. Brilliant. They could let their cannons recharge and the missiles and torpedoes be reloaded, and hopefully, the cover the countermeasures provided would keep them from being hit too badly as they hightailed it to their last stand.

And their last stand it would be if the AI ship took the bait. *Glory's* firepower against hers. Whoever could deliver the knockout punch would win. No more hide-and-seek. No more hit-and-run. Pure power against power.

Neither ship had shown what they could really do so far. Drake was smart enough to know that. He expected the AI ship to have some fire in it they hadn't seen yet. Even in her weakened state, *Glory* had the same. All things being equal, he'd bet on his old girl. The AI ship was designed to sneak, jump, stab, and run away at the first scratch. It wasn't a bear like *Glory*, liable to tear you apart if cornered—and he was about to put her in a corner.

Glory dove at full speed. Her beams and supports

groaned with the sudden strain, and Drake could feel the damage up and down her hull through the vibrations at his feet. She was compromised, but she wasn't broken. Not yet. Drake thought he could feel and hear that Fredrickson had finished welding the asteroid shard to the main spine. That particular shriek and shifting was gone. If they survived this, he would commend the engineer for completing the repair under the most difficult conditions one could ever be subjected to.

"Cut main engines and rotate x-axis 180," XO called to Helm as the asteroid eggshell loomed. They'd made the burn without a shot from the AI ship. Drake could see it on the edge of the asteroid field, watching them. Her circuits and computer banks were probably aglow, trying to figure out what the human ship was up to.

On the holographic display, Drake watched as *Glory* flipped around so her bow faced the opposite direction. She made the maneuver on thrusters alone, so her velocity in regard to the eggshell remained constant. When it looked as though they were about to smash into the tight group of giant rocks, XO called for the main engines to fire once more, and the ship slowed. She backed into the eggshell, nose facing outward, and came to a stop dead center between the surrounding rocks. Absolutely goddamn perfect, and not a second wasted. Drake wanted to give him a medal.

"All forward cannons, prime and prepare to fire right there," Drake called, pointing at the opening of the eggshell. That was where the AI ship would have to jump if she wanted to continue attacking *Glory*, and they would be ready for her. "All guided ordnance on standby."

"Cap," a voice called from near the navigation stations. Drake turned to see that it was CAG. "I've got two

squadrons within a two-minute burn from our current location. Should I pull them in? Set up a firing squad just on the
other side of our little funnel here?"

Drake considered, then nodded. "Do it." This was it.
Fighter fire from the other side of the opening couldn't hurt,
and if this *was Glory's* last stand, what was the point of
keeping her fighters out of the fray? They'd be orphaned
hundreds of light-years from home, left to either die in the
vacuum or be picked up by the Paragon. Better to bring
everyone together and see what blows they could land on
the mechanical ship.

Seconds ticked by, and still the AI ship hung just
beyond the edge of the field. It remained stock-still. Thinking. Assessing. Drake had observed the behavior before, but
it had never been this long. The scenario he was presenting
to the AI was probably not one it had anticipated or
prepared for. Good.

Maybe too good, however. It dawned on Drake that
the AI ship might wait *Glory* out. She didn't have a crew.
That was why she was so small, Drake realized. The ship
was solid power generation and weaponry. There were no
corridors or landing bays or sewage systems or command
decks, only a computer and its means of destruction.
What was it going to be, Computer? Stalemate or
showdown?

A flash of light on the projection gave Drake his answer.

"Fire everything!" he bellowed before he even had time
to blink. The AI ship was at the mouth of the eggshell. She
too fired everything.

Showdown it was.

The AI ship's barrage lit up the asteroid field like a
second sun, dwarfing any attack it had launched thus far. As
Drake watched it come in, his heart sank. Even in his

caution and respect, he'd underestimated the fire that small ship had in her belly.

Damn.

"Brace for impact," he yelled as he gripped the command console.

The barrage hit home.

CHAPTER FIFTY-SIX

WARREN DIDN'T HAVE a countdown running, but his HUD displayed a chronometer. They weren't going to make it. If he and Smith were on their own, they might. Their legs could churn through the snowdrifts and over the rocks a lot faster than they were now, but that was by necessity. Two dozen prisoners ran at their sides, scrambling and slipping and clawing to get away from the rigged facility.

They'd encountered them in the halls, wandering panicked and aimless, sixty seconds into their sprint. With a bellow amplified by the speakers on the outside of his armor, Warren had ordered them to haul ass since the place was about to blow.

They'd made good time getting out of the facility. The smooth, level floors hadn't been much of a challenge, even for the prisoners' emaciated legs and half-shod feet. When they'd reached the outside, their under-nourished and ill-cared-for state had caught up with them. Warren had to stop every few seconds to haul up a person who slipped or steady a stumble. One prisoner, tiny enough to be a child, though Warren didn't have time to confirm that, he'd simply slung over his shoulder and carried with one arm around her.

The chronometer in the corner of his HUD told Warren they needed to *move*. The charges were seconds away from going off, and they were still two dozen meters from the tree line, let alone climbing up the ridge that would get them off the plateau. How they were going to do that, even if they did reach it in time, Warren didn't know. It didn't matter. They just had to reach it. One step at a time.

Boooooom.

The ground beneath his feet shuddered. The group froze, Warren included, and he turned to look back at the facility, which was now several hundred meters away. A plume of fire erupted from the center of the windowless complex. The charges had gone off. Warren instinctively braced himself for the ground around him to start collapsing, the inevitable result of the destructive forces building up where the AI cube plugged into the geothermal reactor.

But the ground was quiet. The shockwaves of the charges going off around the cube subsided, and the ice and dirt beneath Warren's feet stayed solid. He wondered if he'd overestimated how large the explosion would be. Maybe everything would be fine, and that was all the destruction they would see.

Then . . .

A subtler rumbling. Harder to feel but deeper. Farther away and growing.

"*Move!*" Warren shouted to the group of prisoners as they stood frozen. "*Move, move, move!*"

He took off in an all-out sprint, grabbing people as he passed, physically hauling them into a mad scramble for the ridge. The chain reaction was coming. It would take time to get there, building from deep inside the base of the mountain, but the explosion and damage to the plateau would be as massive as he'd feared. Larger, from the way the ground beneath them was quaking. The plateau they were running on *would* come down. He saw fault lines cracking on the ridge ahead, getting ready to shear off the face of the entire fucking mountain.

"*Run!*" he shouted again. The swarm of prisoners zigzagged in front of him, doing their desperate best. Warren caught them as they fell, pulled them to their feet, and herded them forward. Smith did the same at his side. *Just keep them moving!*

As they reached the base of the ridge, a massive crack appeared in the ground ahead and started to widen. "Jump," Warren called to the group. Those who had enough strength in their legs did. Those who didn't, Warren grabbed by their clothing and flung them across with his gloved, power-assisted hands. The ground shuddered and buckled, then dropped a meter where Warren was standing. The plateau was starting to shear. He looked around wildly to see if anyone had been left behind.

A cry to his left. He turned. The small prisoner, the one he'd carried. Somehow, he'd lost track of her. She was reaching up from a crack in the ground, only her face and stretched arm visible. Warren dove toward her and snagged her outstretched hand, then braced his feet against the edge of a crumbling piece of icy dirt and launched them both onto the slope ahead.

As they landed on the mountainside, the ground they'd just left dropped another two meters, and the mountain range shuddered. Warren shouted for the prisoners to keep going, keep climbing up and away from the collapsing plateau. The ground on the slope was different. Rocky.

Warren hoped that meant it would remain stable during the explosion to come. He didn't have to wonder long.

With a chest-crushing *fwoooommmmmm* and an ear-splitting roar, the research facility exploded. A column of fire erupted from its center and blasted into the lower atmosphere. Chunks of the concrete and plastiform complex rose a kilometer into the air. Several buried themselves in the ridge, but thankfully, none landed on Warren's or Smith's heads or those of the prisoners. The mountain shook violently, then, with a great groan, the collapse began in earnest.

Warren stopped scrambling to watch. They had gone as far as they could. It was over now. The end was coming.

Like water circling a drain, the shelf upon which the Paragon complex—the facility, mine, and labor camp—sank, swirled around the lowest point in the center, and then, with a great exhale, disappeared, creating a giant cloud of dust and debris. Something roared and shook the very foundation of the mountain range, but it was impossible to see what was happening through the thick cloud.

Then it was quiet.

Warren gasped for air, hardly able to believe he was sitting—not sure how that had happened—on the mountain and not down below with whatever was happening on the plateau.

Then a chunk of snowy ice whizzed past Warren's head, and he became aware of a new rumbling under his feet. This wasn't coming from far below the base of the mountain. It was coming from above.

Warren looked toward the top of the mountain. There was a snowpack three or four hundred meters above, hanging onto the sharply pitched peak. It "sneezed," sending small bits of snow and ice tumbling down, which whizzed past Warren's head and body.

"Shit," he said, knowing what was coming next. "Everybody find cover," he shouted, his words echoing over the slope.

It wasn't clear whether Warren's shouted command, amplified by his suit, *caused* what happened next—he doubted it—but the snowpack on the peak did not stay put. With a crack that echoed over the mountain range, it cleaved from its tenuous perch and began to slide.

"Avalanche!" Warren screamed.

CHAPTER FIFTY-SEVEN

DRAKE WAITED FOR THE DEATHBLOW.

Glory had acquitted herself as well as anyone could have hoped or dreamed. She'd fought back tooth and nail for far longer than Drake expected. They'd survived the first full-on assault from the AI ship, then the second. They'd weathered the third and fourth and delivered some forceful blows of their own that had rocked the AI ship back.

The coming fifth barrage would be the last. The hull was ready to buckle in the most vulnerable places, and the defenses that protected those soft spots were down or had been destroyed. They wouldn't be able to fend off plasma bolts and the warheads, not all of them. Some would get through and hit a vital power line or breach a crucial containment, and it would be over. *Glory* would nova like the little star she was, and she would perish along with all hands.

It stung Drake's eyes to think about dying here in this godforsaken place, beaten by Hadras. The bastard wasn't even the one fighting him. The last he'd seen of the archgeneral, he was bugging out, off to cause more mayhem and destruction. Drake couldn't even launch a QE buoy to send off his logs since those controls had fried in the last onslaught. Maybe someone on the planet would survive to tell the tale and give Hadras a smack in the mouth and a taste of his own medicine.

On the command deck, the crew was silent as they waited for the end to come. Backs were straight. Chins were high. No one cowered or sobbed. They all faced the coming fate with shoulders squared, defiant to the end. Drake's heart felt like it stopped, and the moment hung there, seemingly lasting forever.

And hung there.

Drake frowned. He glanced at the tactical display, and what he saw made his heart leap into his throat.

The AI ship was drifting subtly to the side. Powerless. Its final kill shot was still in its chamber.

"All forward batteries fire," he bellowed, pointing at the AI ship. "Everything we have!"

It was probably a fluke. Or a trick. Some last-minute trap it was laying. Had to be. Drake watched breathlessly as the tactical display tracked *Glory's* weapons as they bore down on their target, and still she didn't move.

He whooped aloud when they hit home. Every one slammed into its target. The rest of the command deck joined him, and XO shouted over the din for all weapons to be fired at will. The AI ship tossed about like a rag doll. It made no attempt to maneuver, evade, or retaliate. It took whatever *Glory* threw at it like it was unconscious on the mat, and the referee refused to call the match.

"Helm," Drake shouted as he saw a distinct set of power curves emanate from their enemy. "All head full, *now*!"

The AI ship was breaking up. Her core was going critical, and seconds from now, the opening of their little eggshell would become a goddamn fireball. Drake didn't want to wait around to find out what havoc that would wreck on the million-ton asteroids that currently surrounded them.

Glory surged forward. The inertial compensators were compromised since the jolt sent Drake and everyone else who wasn't strapped into a seat crashing to the deck. He didn't mind. They had to get past the AI ship before it blew, or they'd be caught in a rocky hailstorm a hundred times worse than the one that had ravaged them when the drone self-destructed. Or worse, they'd be caught in her explosion.

The core went critical as *Glory* squeezed past. The old girl was traveling at a thousand meters per second, the capacity of her main drive, and every screen and holographic display on the ship went blindingly white when the shockwave slammed into them. It again sent anyone and anything not bolted down flying as the ship surged forward far more violently than before. More sparks, more flames, accompanied by screeching and groaning as she squeezed past. It felt like she was going to shake herself apart . . .

But that didn't happen.

Once again, *Glory* held. She should have died three times over but hadn't.

Slowly but steadily, the shaking subsided. Screens and projections flickered back on. At the front of the command deck, Helm stopped shouting and cursing and brought the ship back under control. "Take us out of the asteroid field," Drake said, his voice hoarse from the exhaustion of the battle and an unhealthy dose of acrid smoke. Air circulation was down or compromised; one thing to fix among what Drake was certain would be a list five miles long.

Glory cleared the edge of the field and slowed when she

reached open space. Being away from the tumbling rocks made Drake's lungs feel better, even if the blowers were still struggling to rid the air of the smoke.

They were alive and probably in one piece. Behind them—Drake brought up the view to be sure—was an expanding cloud of dust and microparticles. He asked Tactical to confirm, which they did. The AI ship had been destroyed. It had lost power control just in time.

Drake turned his attention to the Vorkut V moon, which was so far around the gas giant they almost couldn't get any readings from it. Someone down there had just saved their asses. Plucked them from the jaws of oblivion.

He hoped they were still alive, whoever it was.

CHAPTER FIFTY-EIGHT

THE AVALANCHE WOULD CRUSH WARREN, Smith, and the prisoners who still accompanied them. The ridge above them funneled into a V with them at the bottom, so it would send all that snow, ice, and rock at them. Other prisoners were scattered over the rest of the mountain face, and it looked as though they were out of its path; that was good for them. The avalanche wouldn't kill everyone and thus make this entire rescue operation a lost cause. That was a consolation to Warren. Small, but it consoled him nonetheless.

He looked into the sky, trying to catch a glimpse of something in orbit or the flash of a propulsion drive. Anything to indicate *Glory* was up there and still alive. That might make all this worth it. However, he didn't see anything because his face was blasted by a rush of hot air. At first he thought the avalanche had arrived ahead of schedule. Maybe it had a leading edge he hadn't seen, or a smaller flow of debris had been knocked loose and was joining the party.

But no, this was *hot* air.

"Lieutenant!" a voice shouted from above and behind him.

Warren turned to see Commander Carrol hanging out the side of a Paragon shuttle. The wind from its thrusters whipped her hair. Zed was in the cockpit, wrestling the craft into as stable and close a position as he could manage. He did quite well; the shuttle was about four feet off the ground. Carrol was beckoning to Warren. He didn't need to be invited twice.

"Over here," he yelled to the huddled prisoners, who were transfixed by the coming avalanche. "*MOVE!*" Warren reached for the closest one, a thin, frail-looking old man, and tossed him through the shuttle's hatch. He did the same with the next prisoner. He was a hefty male, so it was more shoving than tossing, but that broke the logjam. The prisoners started clambering toward the shuttlecraft.

Warren glanced at the avalanche. It was only seconds away. More shards of ice went flying past them, ejected ahead of the coming wave. Desperately, Warren grabbed at the flailing, panicked prisoners. Roaring, the avalanche came closer. Finally, Warren's hands grabbed nothing. He looked down. None of the two dozen prisoners were left.

Except one.

The tiny prisoner he'd been carrying before. She was a few paces away, half-buried in a snowdrift. She didn't have any impact marks on her head that Warren could see; she must have passed out. Warren looked at the shuttle, then at the avalanche, then at her.

"Go!" he ordered Smith, who was a step closer to the shuttle. He looked at Carrol and said the same. The avalanche was a second away, billowing, white, and deadly. "*GO!*"

He lunged for the girl as the shuttle thrusters roared.

They were taking off. It was the last thing he heard before the avalanche engulfed him.

It smacked him sideways, and for a second, Warren wasn't sure if he'd reached the girl in time. A scream into his chest told him otherwise. She was awake and holding onto him for dear life. He curled into a tight ball, hoping his bulk and armor were sufficient to protect them both as tons of snow, rock, and ice piled on top them and shoved them down the mountainside.

Except . . .

Warren got a glimpse of gray sky, then he felt the avalanche shoving them *upward*. Not down. By some miracle, they'd caught an edge, and they were riding it down toward the cliff, but they weren't buried. Warren clawed to get them farther up. The avalanche roared and bucked and rolled around them, but it worked. He pumped his legs and pushed them up higher. The girl in his arms gasped for air.

Then there was a new roar ahead.

Just above the roiling flow of the avalanche, Warren could see the shuttle with Carrol hanging from the open hatch. They were meters away, and beyond them was the cliff. Warren didn't think; he just reacted, using every bit of his suit-enhanced strength to claw them out of the snow and ice. He launched into the air, one arm gripping the girl, the other reaching toward the shuttle.

Clank.

He caught the lip of the hatch. The craft tipped toward him, then his stomach bottomed out as the shuttle engaged its thrusters to gain altitude. The avalanche surged, reclaiming his torso and threatening to suck him under. Warren kicked against it, and with the shuttle tipped toward him like a boat on the water with someone trying to crawl in, Warren shoved inside on top of a surge of white snow.

"I got her," Carrol shouted to him, taking the female prisoner from his grasp. It allowed Warren to pull the rest of his body through the hatch, which was awash with snow, and collapse to the deck after a final heave.

Roaring still filled his ears, but it was the shuttle's thrusters. The avalanche's cacophony receded as they climbed. He was safe. Everyone was safe.

Warren lay face-down on the deck for a long while before rolling over and taking an assist from Smith to get back upright. He gave the enhanced Marine a thankful nod, then looked around the cabin to see it packed asshole to bellybutton with rescued prisoners, who were variously dazed, traumatized, and grateful. All were alive. He stumbled, shaking, back to the open hatch, to which Carrol was still strapped. She was taking in the scene below them, a massive gun on her hip. Warren clutched a handhold and peered over the edge.

The dust and snow had finally settled. The extent of the damage blowing the facility had wrought could now be seen. The plateau that had contained the facility, the camp, the mine, and the forest was gone, cleaved off like a shelf fungus from the side of a tree. All that was left was an empty semicircle with a thousand-foot drop.

The last bits of the avalanche were slipping over that edge. Warren realized he'd been centimeters from doing that himself. At the bottom of that drop, Warren could see a smoldering pile of rock, all that was left of the plateau.

It was gone. Everything below had been destroyed. All over the ridge above the semicircle, Warren saw small groups of black dots. Prisoners. Dozens, maybe hundreds.

"We think that's all of them," Carrol shouted from just

outside the hatch, hair still whipping in the wind. Zed was circling, looking for a place to land that wasn't a cliff face. Carrol smiled at Warren and reached out to pat his shoulder. "You did good."

Warren nodded, then went back over and laid on the deck for a while.

Mission accomplished.

Holy shit.

It was cold on top of the ridge. Warren didn't mind. It gave him the best view of the stars, which were starting to peek out as the trademark hazy Vorkut V cloud cover cleared. Day was slipping into twilight. Close by, Carrol and Zed were wrangling the prisoners into organized groups, making sure everyone had proper cover, and handing out the pathetically small amount of rations they had left in their packs. The hope was it wouldn't need to last long. Warren had already emptied his pack. He could be helping, and he would if a ruckus kicked up, but at the moment, all he wanted to do was look at the stars.

Idri was up there somewhere. Maybe. It was foolish to look for her from where he was, given the distance between them, but he did anyway. There was nothing to do at the moment but wait. Next to him, Smith sat gazing in the opposite direction, down the mountain. At its base was a massive mound of rubble, all that was left of the Paragon facility and penal colony. His thoughts were obvious.

Cheddar might be down there. She never had turned up.

"If she is in all of that mess," Warren said, finally

breaking the long silence that had been shared between the two, "she went out like a warrior."

The large, quiet Marine considered that, then shook his head. He changed his gaze to look up to the stars, like Warren had been. "I don't think so," he said.

Warren nodded. He could accept that, because it was the only thing he was willing to accept about Idri. Wherever Cheddar and Idri were, Warren and Smith would come for them as soon as they got off this rock.

To punctuate the thought, several sonic booms clapped overhead, raising the faces of those assembled on the top of the ridge. Shuttles were diving into the moon's atmosphere. Warren recognized their shape.

Fleet shuttles.

Rescue had arrived.

CHAPTER FIFTY-NINE

IDRI'S WORLD was darkness and silence.

She came to in a state almost indistinguishable from unconsciousness. Only the feeling of breath passing between her lips confirmed she was awake. She couldn't feel the rest of her body, nor could she move it. The room around her was more than just dark and quiet. The deprivation went beyond the five senses. She couldn't *feel* it like she always felt the space around her, a sense beyond touch, sound, sight, taste, or smell. The part of her mind that could touch the stars was blind, stifled and stuffed. Nothing. Just the dark silence of the void. She was truly blind.

"It's unnerving, I'm sure," someone called from the darkness. It was so abrupt, so unexpected, Idri had to stifle a scream. Her heart pounded, and she tried to move her head to see the interloper. She couldn't even do that. Or maybe she had, but the dark was so complete that she couldn't tell. "You were quite the handful to bring in, apparently," the person continued. Given the disorientation, it seemed to be coming from all directions at once, impossible to pinpoint. It did sound familiar.

"The envelopes are effective it would seem, but only when undisturbed."

There was a mechanical click, and Idri became dimly aware that she was moving. Not through any effort of her own, but with whatever she was affixed to. Even the sensation that she was stuck on something was foreign; she felt nothing from her limbs or torso. Her face was numb, save for her eyes and mouth.

Two soft pools of light swung into view.

From the sudden point of reference, Idri could tell that they were coming toward her or, rather, she was ascending toward them. The light was almost completely absorbed by a matte black floor, which Idri realized she'd been hanging over, face-down. The table or slab or whatever she was strapped to—she was conjecturing because she couldn't turn her head to see her arms, but she imagined they were strapped down—was rotating her from a horizontal upside-down position to an upright vertical one. That orientation, which she realized was coming from her inner ear, paired with her sight to tell her which direction she was facing.

In the two dim pools of light were a pair of faces Idri recognized. They belonged to the Navid she'd seen in the AI cube. Seeing them enabled Idri to get a sense of direction for the dark void blanketing her sense ability. It was coming from them. They were suppressing her jump ability. It was smothering to look at them. Claustrophobic, like the formless black was going to choke the life from her. Seeing them made the feeling unbearable, and she had to look away.

"I can remove their illumination if it's painful," someone said. A moment later, the two pools of light vanished. Idri's panic subsided. The lights were replaced by a single, pool of light, dimmer than the others. Someone was standing in it. Idri cautiously moved her eyes to look at the person. It was at the very limit of her vision, but Idri matched the face to the voice.

"Markus," she croaked. Her throat was impossibly dry. It felt as though she hadn't spoken in years.

The tall old man didn't move. The floor was so black, it looked like he was floating. "Would you like some water?"

Idri tried to shake her head, but found the straps wouldn't allow it. She wanted water, but not like this. "What have you done?" she rasped.

"You're on the *Scythe*, flagship of the Archgeneral Hadras, Idri."

"How?"

A beat. "It was a trap. The AI ship was the bait, and you were the target."

If she exerted some effort, Idri could move her head. She managed to turn it enough to look directly at Markus. She scoffed and fixed him with as steely a glare as she could muster. The trap wasn't news. "*How?*" she repeated.

Markus swallowed and shifted his weight, but he met her stare and didn't blink or look away. "I knew if that's what you're asking me." Another beat and Markus swallowed. "I did what I had to do."

Idri made a disgusted sound and looked away from the bastard. In the dim spotlight, she could still make out the two Navid, prostrate on their tables, pierced by the tubes and machinery she'd seen in the AI cube. Idri wondered what tubes and wires had been stuck into her. A terrifying new thought. Perhaps that was why she couldn't feel the rest of her body.

"They call them 'envelopes,'" Markus said of the sleeping Navid. "They don't have your abilities, which is a rather stupid observation to make since there is literally no one in the galaxy like you. The AI ship is the closest, and it can hardly crawl compared to your light-speed. But useful in its own way, still. Very much like your two kindred here; just because they can't do what you do doesn't mean they're useless.

"They can, as I'm sure you've realized by now, *suppress* jumping ability. Control it. Make sure it doesn't run amok. I suspect it was a natural defensive evolution on your planet, Idri, however many million years ago that your species developed the ability to fold space-time. Did you know that? Yet another example of your own kind holding you back."

Idri didn't answer.

"It makes sense. Uncontrolled, such an ability could prove fatally destructive on a global level; on par with something like an atomic bomb or viral warfare. Just a single mind could cause *incredible* damage. So, those without the ability, the ones who survived those early days, were those who could dampen it. Kind of a safety blanket to drop over the special ones to make sure they didn't destroy everyone else. Fascinating, no?"

Idri remained silent, happy to let him do the talking.

"Anyway," Markus continued, looking like he'd caught himself indulging in a tangent, "you won't be able to jump out of here." He gestured at the two Navid, the "envelopes." "They'll make sure of that." He cleared his throat. "I'm am sorry."

Idri snorted. "Then get me out of here."

Markus shook his head gravely. "No. Idri, there's no getting out of here." He took a step forward, halfway out of the light. His eyes shone in the darkness, a kaleidoscope of color. They were intense and earnest, as was his voice. A warning. "One way or another, they're going to get what they want. You can either cooperate with them, Idri—do what they say, jump when and what they want you to jump

—or . . . " He swallowed again. Idri wondered what was in his throat that he was trying so hard to keep it from coming out. His cowardice, perhaps? "Or they will force you, Idri. They will keep you sedated until they need you, and even then it will be a lot like it is right now. You're pumped full of paralytics. That's why you can't feel your body, I bet. Those won't go away, and it will be worse, Idri. The Paragon have many, many ways to get people to do what they want. Horrible ways. They will use them."

"Help me," Idri said to him. "Please."

"Believe me, I am. They figured you might listen to me. *Do what they ask of you.* It's so much easier that way, and it will save you so much time and pain."

"Save me or save them?"

"Be assured . . . by the time they need you to jump this ship, you will. Whether you want to or not."

Idri closed her eyes. He was sure he was telling the truth. She'd seen Paragon methods of mind-control first-hand. The creature they'd placed inside Carrol came to mind, and she shuddered. However, even in the moment of fear as she imagined such a creature being put in her, or whatever the Paragon intended to use, she felt a rising defiance that surprised even her. Even if it delayed their plans a microsecond, the resistance would be worth it. The pain would be sweet.

"No," she said. Her voice was even as a laser beam. "I'm not a traitor."

The old man had to look away from her. Since he was still shrouded in darkness, she couldn't see his expression. When he turned back, his eyes were cold. Distant. "So be it."

His spotlight clicked off. Darkness returned, and his footsteps receded. A door opened somewhere Idri could not see. "Let me know if you change your mind," Markus called. "If you don't, you will be alone here, Idri. No one is coming for you." The door shut, and everything was black and silent once again. Idri was vaguely aware that her slab was once again rotated to place her face-down toward the floor.

Darkness ate at her consciousness. At first, Idri thought it was a result of the return of sensory deprivation, but as the sensation grew, she realized it was more than that. She was being sedated again. The dark was unconsciousness coming to consume her, to pull her back under. She fought it, but there was very little in the waking world for her to hold onto. Very little to help her stay awake.

Then the oddest, most wonderful thing happened.

Something small, wet, and sniffing pressed against her hand, and then a larger warm, wet thing flicked across her fingers. A tongue. A nose and a tongue. And then Idri smelled it. Smelled *her*, earthy, warm and nearby.

"Cheddar?" Idri whispered into the darkness.

CHAPTER SIXTY

"Disaster," Drake said, rifling his sweat-greased hair, then dropping into his cabin chair with a *thump*. There was no other way to put it. It was a disaster.

On the screen, Admiral Jack composed himself. Drake had broken radio silence. There was no point in maintaining it; the secrecy was over. It had been over since the start of the entire mission; that much was clear. "It would seem," the admiral said slowly, "that we have fallen prey to Archgeneral Hadras."

"Again," Drake added, gritting his teeth.

"Again," Jack agreed.

They'd been here before. If they survived this, Drake reckoned they would do it again. Hadras was just *that* dangerous. But Drake and Jack were dangerous, too. They'd outsmarted the damn fox before, and Drake had been certain they would here, too, perhaps in the biggest blow he'd ever deal his old foe.

That had been the irresistible lure, hadn't it? The highest stakes ever. *Glory* had the one thing that nobody else did; the ability to jump at will. Drake and Jack had known Hadras would zero in on that, obsess over it, and crave it for his own. It was why the AI ship breakthrough was so plausible. It fit. It was something Hadras would do. They'd only missed the ruse. The bait and switch. He'd never wanted to level the playing field; he'd only ever wanted Idri. "Damn him."

"Where is he headed?"

Drake shook his head. "He hasn't shown up at any of the gates we mapped coming out here, but I promise you this, Jack. He's heading for Freepoint."

"How fast will he get there?"

Drake shook his head again, thinking about where Hadras had been heading when he last saw his forces. *In-system*. Toward the star. "Unclear, but he didn't use the main gate here. It's cold. They shut it down before they left. Going to take Fredrickson two weeks to spin it back up, he says."

"They jumped out with Idri?"

"No. No, I think they used a gate tucked up against the star, Jack. Their secret little network, all far-reach gates. I'll send the information we collected on those we observed on our way out here. I'd be willing to bet there's a route through those gates that will get him to Freepoint's doorstep in a matter of days."

"A route *Glory* can follow?"

Drake blew out a frustrated breath and leaned back in his chair. "Sure, if we knew where the hell he is and which gates he's gone through to get there. We don't even know which gate he took *here*, and we think there are three of them. Go through blind, and we could end up even deeper in Paragon territory." He ran a hand over his face, thoughts swirling. "Not to mention we'd fry without a heat shield.

When I say those gates are close to the star, Jack, they are *close*."

"How much of the standard gate network have you mapped?"

"Our stolen passenger Markus made some decent progress on that front, actually. I'll send that information over too. Once the gate is back, it's enough to get us within a couple weeks of Terran space." He paused, dreading the answer the next question that occurred to him. "How close to Freepoint is your backup?"

Jack chewed on his inner cheek, thinking. "Not close enough. Probably."

"I'm sorry, sir," Drake said heavily. Guilt wracked him as exhaustion sucked away his ability to hide it. Anger kept it away, but not when he paused to feel just how tired he was.

In the midst of the exhaustion, he spared a moment to curse the bureaucratic bastards who hadn't listened to him. If they had, maybe the reinforcements Jack didn't have close enough yet would already be there, waiting to give Hadras hell when he jumped into the system. Folding space was a massive tactical advantage, no question, but it wasn't the end-all, be-all. You still had to fight after the jump was over. Enough firepower in Freepoint, and it didn't matter what Hadras did, or his fleet. He'd be squashed.

Except he wouldn't. The reinforcements weren't there yet. Nobody had listened. Nobody except Jack.

"Let me worry about Hadras for now," Jack said. He gave his friend a wan smile. "Maybe there's a miracle or two I can pull out myself. You're not the only one in the Fleet with such talents, you know?"

Drake gave him a halfhearted smile and nod in return. The admiral was trying to cheer him up. It wasn't going to work. He knew the Fleet would give Hadras hell at Freep-oint, and it might very well be enough to avoid a worst-case scenario. But nothing except being there for that battle would make Drake feel better. Nothing.

"I mean it," Jack continued, now serious. "Your duty now is to your crew and your ship, Captain. Get them home safely. That's an order."

"Yes, sir."

"I expect to see *Glory* in one piece, hauling ass into Fleet territory a few weeks from now. Sooner, if you can find a way."

"Understood."

The transmission clicked off. Drake tried to relax and rubbed his face furiously. The thought of *Glory* being side-lined while the rest of the Fleet fought to protect those ship-yards was beyond intolerable. He couldn't accept it. He refused. Goddammit, *Glory* would find a way to be there when it counted. This whole thing was on *him*. He'd taken the bait. He'd let Hadras get away with Idri, and he would do what was necessary to fix it. Drake didn't know how yet, but he would be at that battle.

They would find a way.

"Open your mouth please," Doc asked.

Carrol obliged. She sat on the edge of a med-bed in Sickbay as the tall, dark-skinned English doctor checked her. So far, so good. Bumps and bruises here and there, mostly from her fight with the Paragon trooper in the cargo bay prison, but otherwise intact. Sickbay was packed with dozens of patients. Most were prisoners from the labor camp, and there were almost two hundred more in a temporary setup in one of *Glory*'s larger hangar bays. Among the newcomers were the rest of Carrol's operations team, also getting checked out. She was pleased to see that Sudan was awake and moving fine. She would stay in Sickbay for a while, concussion protocol for the bump on the back of her head and having lost consciousness, but Doc said she looked good. Same with Smith and Warren, who looked the worst for wear of any of them. Even they were getting green checks across the board. The only absences on the team were Idri and Cheddar. They weighed heavily, but what a relief it was that the rest of the team was home safe and sound.

Doc moved away from Carrol after having taken a long look down her throat and a swab from her cheeks. Zed was next on his check, and the two of them locked eyes. Carrol felt her face flush, and she looked away. Goddammit, what was wrong with her? There were a million other things on her mind, that *should* be on her mind, first and foremost, and she couldn't even look at him without her—her . . . whatever the hell was happening to her face.

"Hey Doc," she called. "Am I free to go?"

"You're free to go," he responded without looking back.

Carrol left. Behind her, she heard Zed ask if he could go too.

"Wait up!" he called.

Carrol paused. The corridor beyond them was empty for the moment. She turned back to him, nervous. "I'm not sure we should be talking," she said to him, voice low and feeling like a coiled spring.

"No no no," he said, putting his hands up. "I'm not trying to do anything."

"I mean, with Sudan, and Cheddar, and Idri."

"Of course." He nodded, serious. No jokes. No wisecracks. Nothing of the sort. "I just wanted to know if you were okay. We can do that, right? That's okay?"

Carrol nodded. "Sure."

He swallowed. "Are you okay?"

"Yeah." There was a beat. "*You* okay?"

"Yeah." Another beat. "Things got pretty hairy down there."

"They did."

"But we were . . . good together."

Carrol nodded.

"Like, *really good.*"

Carrol flushed again and glanced away. "Yeah." When she glanced back at him, he was smiling, ear to ear. And not in any sort of juvenile, or smartass, or inappropriate way. The smile was grown up. Honest. Naked, even. His eyes shone against the dim corridor, two oceans of depth. Carrol couldn't help but smile back, feeling her entire body quake as she did.

"I don't mean to interrupt."

Snap.

Carrol jumped as if a silent world had suddenly been filled with roaring sound.

Smith was standing behind Zed, leaning out from sickbay through the open hatch. "Yes yes," Carrol heard herself stammering. She cleared her throat. Shook her head. "What is it?"

He looked between her and Zed. "I can ask someone else for assistance," he said without a trace of subtext.

"I was just leaving," Zed offered.

"Indeed he was," Carrol seizing on it.

"Thank you, Commander," he said, giving a slight bow. A bow? A fucking *bow*?!

"My pleasure. Lieutenant."

Carrol moved to step aside and let Zed pass her down the corridor, but he moved the same way, and they bumped into each other. He gave an awkward chuckle and Carrol thought it might just be better to fucking drop dead, right then and there.

But then he was gone. And Carrol was still alive.

Smith simply looked at her, patient and impassive. "I'm sorry, Smith," she said, clearing her throat once more. "What did you want?"

"Doc hasn't cleared me yet, so I'm wondering if you can go by my quarters and pick up my secondary tracking interface." He got straight to the point. No fuss. Carrol appreciated that more than she ever had.

"Your tracking for Cheddar?"

The Marine nodded and indicated the tracker on his wrist, which Carrol now saw was broken. She hadn't realized he'd been without it down there. "It might give me an indication of where she currently is."

He didn't show it obviously, but Carrol had gotten to know the Marine well enough over the past several months to tell when he was worried. This was one of those times. It pushed away everything else in an instant, and she gave him a focused, heartfelt nod. "Of course."

From Sickbay, Doc called to him. "Get back in here, Marine."

Smith acknowledged the doctor, then turned back to Carrol and handed her a security chip—the key to his quarters. She dropped it into her pocket. "You're on Deck Six, right?"

"Cabin Forty-Seven."

"I'll grab it right now."

"Thank you, sir." He went back inside Sickbay.

Carrol left, mind swirling. The feeling wasn't helped

when reached into her pocket to fish out Smith's key. There was a folded piece of paper in there. Carrol wasn't sure how it had arrived, though she suspected.

She took it out. It was a handwritten note. She unfolded it to read Zed's unmistakable scrawl.

Carrol shoved it back into her pocket afterward, body quaking all over again. Irrationally, she looked up and down the corridor to see if anyone was watching her. There was a small group of crewmen at the far end, talking about an access panel they had open. They didn't glance her way. Carrol took the note back out of her pocket and read it again. The message hadn't changed.

I love you.

Well, shit, she thought. *Shit, shit, shit.*

"It's all a mess," Fredrickson said, dumping a pile of datapads, printed reports, and data chips on the briefing room table. He gestured at the pile. "We're going to have to sort through all this data before we even begin to understand how the power matrix works or how to restart it."

The engineer's face was drawn and hollow. Drake doubted he'd slept since before they made their last jump. Stars knew he hadn't. He was exhausted, and Drake could see that the prospect of all that homework out in front of him was about to push him over the edge.

He felt the same pull. He'd ordered Fredrickson to investigate the cold Paragon gate. See what it would take to spin it back up again, so they weren't stuck in the Vorkut system. This was the result—a pile that indicated how thoroughly the Paragon had shut down their regular gate.

"How long?" Drake asked, fighting desperately not to

sound annoyed or frustrated. He doubted he was all that successful.

"A week." Fredrickson raised a preemptive hand to stop Drake from demanding less time. "I'm not kidding, sir. It'll take a week. At least."

It was unacceptable, but Drake bit his tongue. It wasn't Fredrickson's fault. None of this was. "What if Sudan helps?"

"Oh, that's assuming my entire senior staff helps, sir. Which will seriously slow down the repair crews, I might add."

"What of the far-reaches?" All power level readings of the three gates by the star indicated they were of the variety that could get you across several hundred light-years in one go. It was maddening to have them so close to the path Hadras had taken. If they could only figure out how to use them.

"No progress," Fredrickson said, his frustration seeping into his voice as he stated what Drake was thinking. "Even the probes we've tried haven't gotten within five clicks of that tight an orbit before frying. It's possible we might be able to scrounge some material from the two destroyed cruisers or the AI ship, but that would still be ignoring the obvious issue, sir."

Drake nodded. They had no idea where Hadras went, which gate he used here at Vorkut, and worse, what other gates down the line.

"Attempts to map them?"

"They're on an entirely different network. We can't get in remotely."

Drake looked at the ceiling and closed his eyes to repress a yell. Markus, it would seem, had taken that knowledge and expertise with him when he betrayed them all.

Between him and Hadras, all their routes to follow had been methodically blocked or delayed. It was maddening. After a long beat, Drake looked back down with enough composure to give his chief engineer a grateful nod. "Do as you see fit. Including balancing *Glory's* repairs with restarting the gate and working on the far-reach problem."

"I can tell you right now I think the far-reach gates are a waste of time. I've said that from the very beginning."

They weren't a waste for Hadras. Otherwise, they wouldn't be there. But Drake bit his tongue. "Like I said, do as you see fit, Chief."

Fredrickson nodded and straightened, which looked like it took a monumental effort. "Yes, sir." Behind the exhaustion and the pissy mood, Drake could see that he was grateful for the latitude and the vote of confidence. It told him he was making the right move by letting his people do what they did best. Fredrickson pointed at the pile of information on the table. "You mind if we—my team of people— use this as our research room?"

"Be my guest." It wasn't as if Drake would use the room for anything else until they were back underway. He stood as well, bones creaking. Goddammit, he felt so *old* when he was frustrated and worried.

His exit from the room was blocked when someone else entered. Smith. For a second, Drake thought something was wrong. A security issue, perhaps? But no. He was holding something in his hands, looking into the briefing room with an expression Drake didn't think he'd ever seen the Marine wear before: excitement.

"It's Cheddar," he said and hustled over to shove the device he was holding into Drake's hands. It was a datapad with a screen, the kind that attached to the forearm of powered armor. On it were data points with time stamps, dozens of them. Smith pointed at several with a giant index finger. "This is where the tracker has pinged her."

Drake frowned. He didn't understand.

Smith took the pad back and hustled over to the nearest interface built into the briefing room table. He snaked out a data cable and plugged it into the side of the pad, then projected the data up on the briefing room screen, which flickered to life. It was just the raw data, location points with time stamps, but after a moment, Smith manipulated the pad's controls to show the data as points plotted across space. Fredrickson inhaled sharply. Drake did too when he realized what he was looking at.

A trail of breadcrumbs. Cheddar was on the move, popping up in several different star systems. Unless another of her latent abilities was faster-than-light travel, she was on a starship.

"She followed Idri?"

Smith nodded.

Hadras had Idri. That meant Cheddar was with Hadras.

"I think she's revealing herself on purpose," Smith rumbled, vibrating with pride. "Taking down her concealment so we can follow her."

Drake turned to exchange looks with Fredrickson. "What were you saying about cobbling together a heat shield?"

CHAPTER SIXTY-ONE

"Probes away."

The mood on the command deck was tense. This was their third attempt, and the first two had failed in spectacular fashion. Probe Set One had failed even before making it to the gate, burning up in the Vorkut system's sun's intense radiation. Fredrickson had doubled their heat shielding, and tried again. Probe Set Two had each exploded within milliseconds of each other after emerging on the other side of their respective gates. Gravity, Fredrickson had determined after several hours of scrutiny.

Glory hung just beyond the worst of the Vorkut star's radiation field. It had been nearly a day in terms of a Terran clock. While the ship's engineering teams were performing miracles in terms of repairing and retrofitting *Glory* for the demanding journey that was ahead of her, Hadras had a full day's head start on them, and they had yet to leave the system. It took every ounce of Drake's self-control to grind his teeth and stay out of his officers' way, Fredrickson in particular. The grumpy chief engineer was watching the command console with intense, fatalistic interest. He was already shaking his head, expecting the worst—that these set of three probes, one for each of the star-powered gates, would meet the same fate as their predecessors.

"Probes approaching gates," one of the tactical deck crew called, narrating what Drake and Fredrickson were watching in three holographic dimensions on their own console. Three blinking yellow dots neared three larger steady blue discs. The yellow met the blue, then the yellow disappeared. "Contact," the tactical crewman called at the same instant.

Fredrickson drew a breath. Drake did the same.

"We're receiving telemetry!" someone called from the communications station. Raw data flashed onto the command console, strings of numbers and images. It didn't mean much to Drake, but it did to Fredrickson, who leaned in, frowning as he did. "We have position lock from the QE network."

"There," Fredrickson said, finger stabbing one of the three probes. His eyes lit up. "Right there!" He whirled to the comms station. "Concentrate all data gathering capture on Probe Two," he said, rushing over to them. "Let's see what we can on the other side."

Drake remained at the center station, waiting on edge. XO slid up next to him; he'd been monitoring repair efforts throughout the ship so Fredrickson could focus on this project. He sensed a breakthrough, as did Drake. For several excruciating minutes, Fredrickson conversed in low tones with the comms station, hopping between them, Navigation, and Tactical. Finally he turned, his normally sour expression replaced by something rarely seen on his face: a smile.

"Probe location matches our first ping," he said, hardly believing it. "They went through Gate Two."

"It's still nuts."

Drake had assembled his senior staff in the middle of the command deck, huddled around center console, since Fredrickson's team was still set up in the conference room. The discussion: their plan to exit the Vorkut system.

"Even though we've figure out how to successfully probe the gateways, we'll have to do it for *every* successive gate set before proceeding," the chief engineer said, back to his pessimistic self. "That will take time and a lot of luck that—at each—we'll find a coinciding ping from the tracker. We must hope, too, that it's an unbroken chain of pings, and we're not missing an in-between gate, because then all we'd have is a guess."

Drake cleared his throat. "The data points appear fairly regular."

Fredrickson nodded. "True. Just preparing for the worst is all. If we're missing a gate location, we'd have to do it blind and hope we can pick the trail back up on the other side."

Drake nodded. That was a risk they'd have to take. Nods around the console indicated everyone agreed.

Fredrickson inhaled, then let the breath out slowly. "That's not the only issue, however."

"Heat shield?" Carrol asked. She'd been coordinating with CAG on repairs to their fighter and shuttle complement, so she was out of the loop on the other work areas.

XO took the lead. "Heat shield will hold up to Type B supergiant, Captain. We're using a mixture of the derelict shield from the cruisers we took out and reinforcing that with some of the asteroid shards from in the gas giant's field. We're making final adjustments now."

Excellent news.

"There's one final risk to consider," Fredrickson said, re-taking the floor. He flashed up numbers on the projection screen, charts with curves on them, spreadsheets full of numbers to accompany them, and a single star chart with a blinking dot. Fredrickson started his explanation by pointing at the dot. "This is the most recent ping from Mister Smith's Cheddar-tracker." There were small smiles around the table at the term. They faded, however, when they realized what it meant. "It puts Hadras in the Perseus system."

The Perseus system was one direct gate from Freepoint's lone entrance. Hadras was a day away from his target with a day's head start. *Glory* might already be too late.

Fredrickson was looking at Drake, teeth clenched. "It's impossible to say if it will work, Captain, since we won't have the actual gravitational fields mapped out until we arrive in each system, but . . . I think it may be possible to make up much, if not all that ground."

Incredible. Except the engineer didn't look happy about it. "There's a 'but?'"

"Fuel consumption."

Drake sat back. Of course, flying in the near-bottom of a gravity well expended more fuel than out in open space. Exponentially more. And the closer they were to the bottom of that well—the tighter their course around the stars—the more fuel they'd have to expend to ensure they didn't slip in too far.

"How much would it take?"

"We'd have to hit the very top of our error margin to make it at all. We'd be completely empty when we got there."

It was nuts. Fredrickson was right. Even if they did

show up on Hadras' heels in time for the fight, they'd be dead in water when they got there.

"What do you think, Chief?" Drake asked him.

"It's your call, Captain." Fredrickson folded his arms across his chest.

"I want to know what you think."

He looked down, considering. The tight group, huddled around the console, waited with bated breath. When he looked up, Drake saw steel in his eyes. His jaw was tight. "I think we fucking go for it, sir. Pardon my language. I can put together a team to manage fuel consumption with each gate we cross through. If we don't have enough to make it, we don't have enough, and we shut it down, sit in whatever system we're in, and figure out something else. But my team, sir, can make sure we use every ounce of fuel we have to get there as fast as we can and, goddammit, get Idri back. Sir." He blinked, gathering himself. "I apologize again for the language."

Drake looked around the console. All his officers shared the same steely, determined look. They nodded one by one as he looked each of them in the eyes.

It was settled.

"We fucking go for it," Drake said with a proud smile.

CHAPTER SIXTY-TWO

"Stick to your zones," Carrol said and nodded at CAG, who was standing with a stack of datapads ready to hand out to the assembled group of pilots sitting in their high-backed, cushy ready-room chairs. Why those chairs were so comfy, Carrol would never know. No other chairs on *Glory* looked like the chairs in the pilots' Ready Room, and pilots weren't a group she felt needed to be coddled. It was tradition for the chairs to look thus; that she knew, but why? No idea.

CAG divided the stack of pads in two and handed them to the closest pilots on either end of the room to take one and pass the rest along like it was a schoolhouse. Carrol hoped they'd heed the information on those pads and the advice with which she'd concluded her presentation. *Glory* was about to fly far closer to a star—and not just one but several—than she'd ever flown before, protected only by a makeshift heat shield. If any of her escorting fighters got out of position, they'd fry instantly. Carrol would have preferred to keep everyone inside the ship, full-stop, but the risk of running into Paragon resistance was too high. They needed fighters at the ready to respond instantly. If they stayed in position, they'd be fine. The launch process would take too long for immediate deployment once the ship was clear of a star's intense heat and radiation.

CAG took several minutes to reiterate everything Carrol was thinking. To their credit, the pilots were focused and serious, taking the information with the necessary gravity. CAG had assembled a good bunch. She was far more disciplined than Carrol's efforts as the air group commander and a master at her job. Carrol could see they all loved her. Respected her.

"Dismissed," CAG called when she was satisfied the group was as filled-in and ready as they could be. They began to shuffle out, talking among themselves.

Carrol called to catch Zed's attention. "Lieutenant."

He stopped and smiled at her.

Carrol's stomach churned. "Can I have a word with you?"

Zed looked over Carrol's shoulder. Standing in the doorway was CAG. She was waiting for them with a quizzical look on her face.

Carrol took a deep breath and closed her eyes. When she opened them, she turned to look at CAG. "I'll catch up with you." They had two other flight groups to brief with the same information they'd presented here. "I only need a minute with the lieutenant." Her tone was cold and assertive. Reproachful, even, though not to CAG; to Zed.

CAG hesitated, looking at the two, then nodded and left. Carrol turned back to Zed.

He frowned. "Are you okay?"

Carrol took a deep breath. She'd been thinking about this conversation since—well since the very start. It was all starting to spin out of control. Carrol could feel it in her gut, and she needed it to stop. It was always going to be horrible, having this talk, so why not just get it over now? Before they embarked on this insanely dangerous mission. They could both have their heads clear. It would be better this way. "Our fraternization," she said, let the deep breath out. "It needs to stop."

Zed laughed. "What?"

"It's inappropriate."

He cocked his head. "Why do you sound like an HR officer right now?"

"It has to stop, Zed."

The frown returned. "Did CAG say something to you? Or Oh?"

Carrol shook her head.

A beat.

". . . You're serious."

"I am."

Zed's face fell, realization sinking in. "Is this because of the note?"

"No," she said, hurriedly. "Of course not. This is simply — . . . it's not a big deal, Zed. We both said we'd end it if things got too, you know—much. I'm just saying I think we should end it while we both still have our dignity. Before we do get caught, or it causes any negative performance. It's just better this way. It's the responsible thing to do. You know?"

Zed took a step back. He looked like he'd been slapped.

"I mean, come on, it was fun. Right? When the stakes were low. But they're not anymore. The ship's in danger, Idri's missing . . . we need to be distraction-free. You must agree with that; it's better we have our heads clear. It has nothing to do with you or me. It's really just terrible timing and circumstances. It has nothing to do with you."

But Zed wasn't buying.

"I didn't mean it," he said. His tone wasn't pleading but his eyes were, even though he tried to blink back the emotion there. His voice quavered. "I was just kidding. It was stupid."

Carrol swallowed. A lump was forming in her throat, and it was becoming impossible to look at him. She tried in vain to clear it, and she looked away. "It's no big deal," she said with a pleading shrug, but she could no longer remember who she was trying to convince, Zed or herself.

"You don't have to do this," he said.

But she did. She didn't know why. Every muscle in her body was telling her to run. To bolt. It was too much. Too dangerous. She needed her head clear. She needed space. And she needed this conversation to be over.

"I'm sorry, Zed," she choked out, and she turned and left the room without looking at him again.

Out in the hallway, she picked up pace, her speed walk growing into a jog. Her heart raced even faster, making it hard to breathe. The relief she'd been seeking was nowhere to be found.

This was right. They'd been silly. Juvenile. They could be court-martialed if they got caught, for God's sake. She'd just done both of them a favor. She'd done the responsible thing.

But if that was true, why did she feel so, *so* horrible?

———

ALARMS BLARED over the command deck. Drake slipped his feet into makeshift braces made of the material the harnesses on the command deck seats were made of. They were a new addition, courtesy of Fredrickson, who'd received word from *someone* that the captain was taking his fair share of spills during battle. The straps were just loose enough for him to wedge his boots between them and the deck plates. Handlebars had been welded to the side of the command console as well. Between those and the footholds, Drake was confident the ship could rip itself apart and he wouldn't budge a millimeter.

"Feeling steady, Cap?" XO asked, coming up next to him with a subtle look under the console.

Drake studied him, trying to figure out if it was he who'd made the engineer aware, but XO just looked ahead without flinching. It *had* been him. "The engineering team has mastered the art of making their captain feel like a dinosaur," he said archly.

"Simply anticipation of a bumpy ride, I think."

"I see." Drake's side and shoulder had some nice work done on them by Doc, but it was probably a good idea not to let himself spill too hard. Not that he'd let anyone know that, XO or otherwise.

"I will pass along your appreciation to the engineering team," XO with a curt tip of his chin. He pointed at information pouring in on the console with perfect timing. "Power levels are green, sir." All business.

Drake moment of banter last another beat with a reproachful shake of his head, then turned his full attention to the task at hand. *Glory* was ready to go. She certainly looked a mess, however. The asteroid shard still sliced through her midsection, albeit fully welded in place now with any excesses knocked away that had stuck out into space, and there were swaths of the outer decks they didn't have the time to re-hull. But Fredrickson had done extensive stress testing on each of those sections and given them the thumbs-up, which was more than good enough for

Drake. She looked a mess, but she was as structurally sound as she'd even been; she needed to be for the journey she was about to take.

As for the outer sections of the hull that couldn't be repaired on the fly, those had been evacuated and closed off from the ship. The crew was drawing into the center of the ship to get as much shielding as they could between them and the radiation they were about to be pummeled with.

Drake shook his head. It was crazy. Starships weren't made to travel this close to a star. There was no need. Gates could be powered by the most common gas giants. Energy could be easily collected from a star in much safer orbits, and everything else that a living being would find useful in any given system lay on icy, rocky planets and moons that were even farther away. Why would one want to get so close to a sun that its heat would melt your hull, its radiation would poison your crew, and its gravity would rip you apart?

Well, the Paragon had found a reason: it effectively hid a ship. Because of that, *Glory* now had to do something she wasn't meant to do. Maybe it was hubris, but Drake knew she could take it, her and her crew.

"Ready at your word, sir," XO said a few minutes later.

Fredrickson stepped out of the briefing room off the command deck. He was holed up in there with a crack team —his term—of his best engineers to actively monitor *Glory's* fuel consumption and oversee the rounds of probes they would have to launch after each gate they went through. They would use them the same way they'd used them here in the Vorkut system: to figure out where to go next. The hope was that there were no gaps in the ping trail Cheddar had laid for them and they had a location for each star system Hadras had traveled through. The chief engineer gave a thumbs-up. The alarms had quieted. Everyone was in place, strapped in, hunkered down, and ready to go.

Drake gave his feet another push into their straps, wiggling them to make sure they were secure. He *was* grateful for the addition. "Take us in," he said with a gesture to his first officer.

XO swelled his chest so his voice would fill the room. "All stations, mind your screens. We have to do this right down the line." He turned to Helm. "Take us in."

The air on the command deck was electric, and the deck thrummed under their feet. Fredrickson disappeared into the briefing room, and Drake could hear him calling out commands to his team in there as well as instructions to Main Engineering. He took the opportunity to throw the scope feed from ahead of them onto the overhead holodisplay so everyone on the command deck could see what they were diving toward.

Roiling fire dominated the view. The Vorkut star was a seething, undulating ocean of energy. It blotted out the stars, an unscalable wall of light. Minuscule in comparison was their destination, the Paragon gate. It was barely more than a dot, a black island in a sea of white, yellow, and orange fury, but it was growing. The ship's inertial systems struggled to keep up with the change in gravity and acceleration as *Glory* fell into the star's gravity well.

At a certain point, the inertial controls *wouldn't* be able to keep up with the sheer force of the pull. Fredrickson had predicted that, explaining what it would feel like: a rollercoaster. Imagining that sensation hadn't prepared Drake for the deck to pitch beneath his feet, trying to slide him and everyone else toward the star.

It *was* like going over the top of a rollercoaster in the front car: slow at first, with the feeling of dangling, and then the release as the rest of the cars went over the edge and the rush downward that pushed you into the back of your seat began. It was a relic of a comparison, but as is the wont of humankind to hold onto its past, anyone who grew up or lived in the North Americas was still familiar with the simple ancient thrill rides that dotted the continent.

The image of the sun on the screen wasn't helping the vertigo. Drake wondered if it had been a good idea to put it up there, but he left it. It was a quick and easy reference to see where they were and what they were doing.

"Gate contact in seven seconds!" Navigation called, the stress in his voice clear, reflecting the duress they were all under.

Drake didn't let his attention waver from the gate. It grew larger, increasing in size exponentially. It made clear how fast the ship was moving: faster than any other gate Drake had ever plunged through. In the last second before contact, the relative size of the gate increased so suddenly that Drake flinched. He said an internal prayer that their helmsman had that course dialed in because if they were off a hundredth of a degree, it was curtains for everyone. Around them, *Glory* creaked and groaned as the forces on her mighty beams and supports increased as exponentially as their speed.

"Contact!" Navigation shouted.

There was no need. Drake registered the sensation. His body felt as though it were being squeezed through a pinhead, then in a fraction of the time it took to blink, the sensation was over, and he was being slammed in the opposite direction from the moment before. It knocked him on his ass, though since one of his feet had stayed tucked in its strap, he didn't go far.

Beneath him, *Glory's* deck plates were rattling like a tin

roof in a hurricane, and her creaks and groans had turned into shrieks and wails.

XO lunged over to help him to his feet, but Drake waved him off. He pointed at the handholds on the side of the console as he stood. "Serves me right," he shouted sheepishly. He hadn't been holding onto them. He remedied that oversight by grabbing them and pulling himself upright. It wasn't going to happen again.

On the overhead screen, they saw a new roiling hellscape. It was similar to the last, except that the color coming through the forward scopes' filters and apertures was different. Another star. They were through the first gate.

"Contact with another gate at point-five," Navigation called.

"Helm," XO bellowed, "adjust bearing to match, off point-three degrees. Sending course correction." He glanced at Navigation. They were working furiously to come up with the precise vector they'd need to do a close enough fly-by of the gate ahead so that Fredrickson and his team could work their magic.

It was a four-step process. First, circle around the star once in an ever-tightening orbit, so they didn't lose velocity. Second, fly past the gates they encountered on that first pass. Third, drop a probe into each gate that would then, Four, give them a reading on where each gate led. Hopefully, using the process in conjunction with the coordinates they had gotten from Cheddar's tracker, they could determine which gate Hadras and his fleet had gone through. They'd dive through that gate on their second pass. No time wasted.

"Navigation," XO shouted. He hadn't gotten an answer from that busy station. "Vector now, please."

"Sending, sir," a crewman called, face slick with sweat.

"Hold!" Fredrickson called from inside the briefing room. "Hold," he repeated. On the command console, Drake could see a small window that represented the engineer's workstation; he was making fuel calculations. Something Navigation had done with their proposed vector would burn too much of it. The course ahead, marked with a bright green line and things like thruster throttling and drive percentages in blue—everything Helm would need as long as they could get it to them in time— flashed on and off, indicating it wasn't ready to implement.

"Now," Fredrickson called.

The course stopped blinking and solidified.

XO flashed it to Helm, and not a second too soon. The gate ahead was now larger than a speck, and *Glory* was going faster than she had before. The hope was that they wouldn't have to slow down. It would save fuel and maybe give them a drop or two to maneuver when they reached Freepoint. The plan to have Fredrickson make adjustments on the fly had been risky, but goddammit, it had just worked. Hopefully, that would continue.

The gate roared past in an eyeblink.

"Probe away," the engineer called.

They didn't know how far away the next would be, but because they required geosynchronous orbits for their energy supply tethers, they were almost always on the equatorial plane of their host body. Follow the star's equator, and they were bound to run into it eventually. *Glory* was at one or two percent of the speed of light at the moment, but that still meant an hour or two to circle the star, so "eventually" was the key. Drake relaxed and tried to get used to the constant shaking of his ship. Structural integrity was holding, as was the heat shield. Fuel consumption was fine. Everything was fine.

Data from the first probe started pouring in within minutes. It was a QE connection, so line of sight with the gate didn't matter. Navigation announced they had a location fix several minutes after that. It was not a star system they had a ping for. Drake took the information and gave back a sincere thank you and good job. Even though they would likely come across several more gates, one of which was probably their next ticket to chasing Hadras, it was still disappointing. Drake blew out a long breath and wondered what he would do for the next hour or two.

As it turned out, he needn't have worried.

They encountered the next gate twenty minutes or so after the first. They flew by and dropped their second probe, which, like the first, started sending back data within a few minutes of passing through the gate. This time, when Navigation got a fix, it was good news. The best.

"Location lock on our second set of location pings," the lead officer said, beaming.

Drake nodded and looked at Fredrickson, who was once again in the doorway between the command deck and the briefing room. "Is it possible to get back to that gate faster than a full revolution without running our fuel down in excess?"

Fredrickson tapped his fingers over the doorframe. "I thought you might make that request," he said, half-smiling. He called to the navigation station, "Pull up and calculate course four-beta-three, please. Send to the briefing room for confirmation."

"Helm, stand by to change course," XO called, heading to the forward-most station of the command deck to oversee things personally.

"Standing by."

Fredrickson disappeared back into the briefing room, and Drake was left at the center console to consider that it was working. It was all working. He called up a schematic of the *Scythe*, Hadras' flagship, and busied himself by studying the scant new information they'd collected on it during their time in the Vorkut system.

"Coming for you," he whispered to himself. "Sooner than you think."

THE FURSTON FUNNEL

Terran Federation Space

CHAPTER SIXTY-THREE

"CAPTAIN, WHAT ARE YOU DOING HERE?"

Idri was standing in the middle of the *Scythe's* fulcrum, and everything was quiet. No alarms. No firefights. The stars outside, filtered into the room in much the same manner as the fulcrum on *Glory*, were dark. Even the two Navid were gone, as was the black slab and the hoses and wires she'd been plugged into.

But Idri wasn't alone. Standing next to her were her friends. All of them, she realized: Sudan, the captain, Warren, and Smith. And Cheddar. She was right next to Idri, breathing softly on her hand.

"Oh, I missed you!" She flung herself at them, squeezing them to make sure they were real. They *were* real, as real as she remembered them—the way they smelled, their shapes, and the way the heavy fabric of their uniforms scratched her face when she rubbed it this way and that. They didn't speak, but she didn't need them to. She could see everything in their eyes and the way they hugged her back.

"I don't understand," she said when her thoughts had

enough time to catch up. "What are any of you doing here?"

"We're here to save you," Warren said.

Idri nodded. Of course. Why else would they be there? What a silly question. She wasn't even sure why she'd asked it. "I'm ready to go."

Her friends reached out to stop her, shaking their heads.

"I want to go," Idri said, confused.

"We're *here*," Warren repeated more earnestly than before. "To save you."

"I don't understand."

"You can't go," her friends said. "It's not safe out there."

Idri understood.

It wasn't safe out there.

She had to stay here. There was no need to question it. She was safe here. With her friends.

She embraced them all again, feeling their warmth and their strength and love. Oh, how nice it was to be with them again. She wanted to revel in it forever and . . . and she realized that she *could*. She could stay with them forever, time without end or beginning, stretching in every direction without any limits or bounds, warm, cozy, and safe. Yes, yes, how she wanted to.

Something . . . not-here . . . nuzzled her hand. It was warm. Wet. Familiar.

It made her remember . . . things. Pain. Darkness. They were in the 'not-here.' And more. Her friends where there, too. It was so confusing. not knowing what she knew, had forgotten, and was starting to learn again.

"This isn't real," she told her friends, the words sticking in her throat. She had to force them out in gasps, which brought tears to her eyes. Her friends' eyes glistened along with hers. "I can't . . . stay here."

They nodded. They understood.

She thanked them for protecting her, embraced each and kissed them, then said goodbye and faced the darkness outside the fulcrum. It was hard to let them go, but she did . . .

And there were stars, so many stars, and flashes of angry red, green, orange, and white.

The ship shook in the throes of battle.

Idri was awake and in pain, more pain than she'd ever felt or conceived was possible. Cheddar was by her hand. The pain had momentarily made her forget and driven her to protect herself by retreating into a warm, safe, dissociated place in her mind. But not anymore.

She was here. *This* was real. And horrible.

The *Scythe* was jumping. She could feel through the crack of senses that were in her control that they were some-place familiar, somewhere she'd been before. The gate to Freepoint. Hadras was about to use her to jump them into the shipyards. Drugs coursed through her body, triggering pieces of her she didn't know could be triggered, making her do things she desperately wanted to stop.

Markus had been right. When the time came, they would force her to jump whether she wanted to or not. And it was hell.

She tried to resist, but it was too late. The process had begun. The stars, smattered with the angry reds, greens, oranges, and whites of battle, were folding, zooming out as the ship, with Idri at its center, expanded to near-infinite size. She railed against it and screamed for it to stop, but some compartmentalized part of her mind had already set off the chain reaction. She couldn't stop it now. Trying to do so would only kill her, tear her apart.

So, tear me apart, then.

A dare.

A shred of self-determination, of choice.

TEAR ME APART, THEN!

The AI controlling the jump reacted to that. Something was injected into her body a split second later, and she slid back into unconsciousness. The jump was complete. The stars outside were normal again.

This time she'd woken up too late; remembered where she was too late. But even as the darkness sucked her back inside its freezing nothingness, Idri knew she'd found something.

She could fight back. If she stayed conscious and embraced the pain instead of running from it, she could resist.

It wasn't a battle she could win, not and keep her life, but that was its own sort of victory, wasn't it? It would force the machine to choose: complete its horrible task, jump the ship, and destroy Idri in the process, or back off, shut it down, and drag her back into unconsciousness.

A gruesome win-win, but a win-win, nonetheless.

She just had to remember what was real.

Another nuzzle of her hand in told her everything she needed to know. Cheddar was there, physical and real, reminding her, *you are here.*

That had been the last jump she would be forced to do. She'd die before doing another. Her last thought as unconsciousness claimed her was a dare to Hadras: test her and find out.

CHAPTER SIXTY-FOUR

"BATTLE STATIONS."

XO made the call as they passed out of the gate into the Furston Funnel. Ahead of them was carnage.

There was nothing to Furston beyond its gate hub. A single gas giant circling a cold star. No moons. No asteroids. It was just a waypoint to get travelers to their final destination: Freepoint. That's why it was called a 'Funnel.' Its only function was to serve as a doorstep to the shipyards.

And defend it as the single entry point. Those defenses were currently on fire.

Through *Glory's* long-distance scopes, Drake watched the weapons platforms surrounding the gate to Freepoint and the meager assembly of Fleet ships get pummeled by Hadras and his invading fleet. And a fleet it was. Hadras had far more than the four or five escorts that had accompanied him from Vorkut. Drake counted two dozen. Furston Funnel and everything it could throw at them paled in comparison to the firepower of the Paragon attackers.

The worst was yet to come, however. The *Scythe* was holding back, letting the rest of the fleet take the brunt of the battle. So it would be in position to make its next move. It shimmered, and the long-range scopes focused and refocused to keep it in view. Drake recognized what was happening, and his stomach turned. She was about to jump.

A flash of light and the *Scythe* was gone.

Over the blaring general quarters klaxons, Drake called for Fredrickson, seething. "Time to intercept?"

They'd made up an incredible amount of ground. A half-day minimum, maybe a full day, depending on how much resistance Furston had put up. But emerging as they were from the corona of the Furston star, they were still agonizingly distant from the action. An hour or two, Drake guessed, but he wanted to know for sure, and he wanted to push it.

"Three hours at two percent." The engineer grimaced. Two percent of light speed was damn fast, and that was their current velocity.

"Cut loose the heat shield," Drake said.

"That *is* cutting loose the shield."

Damn. "I need four percent," Drake said, knowing that was pushing it to the point of near-impossibility. Even an hour and a half was an eternity on the battlefield. All could be lost before they arrived. Already, Drake could see that Hadras' fleet was pouring through the Freepoint gate. The assault was beginning. *Glory* had to get there in time.

"We'd have nothing left when we got there," Fredrickson said, shaking his head. "Not even to brake."

Drake's head spun. Fredrickson's answer meant there was a way. They had the fuel to make a final push, but how to make it work? "We could aerobrake on the way there," he said, grasping. Even with main propulsion down, *Glory* had her thrusters to maneuver with.

Fredrickson considered, looking at the ceiling with

calculations running through his head. When he looked at the captain again, Drake could tell he hated it, but it was possible.

"Do it," Drake told him. "We'll figure out the specifics on the way."

"And the minefield, sir? On the other side?"

Drake pointed at the Paragon ships disappearing through the gate. "They're either taking it out as they pour in, or that minefield is down."

Fredrickson nodded.

"All hands," XO called over the ship-wide comm. "Prepare for sudden acceleration."

Glory surged.

FREEPOINT STATION

Terran Federation Space

CHAPTER SIXTY-FIVE

Ninety minutes had been more than enough. By the time *Glory* made its second revolution around the Furston gas giant, using its soupy-green atmosphere to slow her down enough to safely dive through the Freepoint gate, Drake had a plan. Fredrickson had wanted to return to Engineering now that his work on the command deck was done. They'd used their fuel, every last drop of it, and they no longer had to map the gates. However, Drake had asked him to stay. He had one last task for the chief engineer before he returned to the lower decks.

"Gate in twenty-two seconds," Navigation called.

Drake exchanged looks with Fredrickson, who nodded. They were ready.

"Ten seconds!"

"Thank you, Nav," XO called, his voice gently admonishing. "We don't need a countdown. Helm. Eyes up."

The rest of those seconds proceeded in silence, *Glory* quaking beneath their feet. Drake took a moment to say a silent thank you to the old ship. She'd held. Through seven —yes, *seven*—solar gates, she'd held firm. They'd had their fair share of localized failures and close calls, but she was intact and ready to fight. And she would if Drake's cobbled-together plan worked.

"Contact," Navigation called.

Drake felt the pinch of the gate as they flashed through it, still going far too fast . . .

Into chaos on the other side.

If the carnage of the attack on Furston had been disturbing, the sight of the Freepoint shipyards was unbearable. The minefield was clearly down. Hadras had figured that out, too. His fleet appeared to be intact, and they'd taken full advantage of the ninety-minutes-plus of alone time they'd had to wreak havoc on the facility.

Not that they were alone. As it all rushed past, *Glory* barreling through faster than an anti-ship missile, Drake could see that the Fleet had mustered a half-dozen ships to form a semicircle around the gate-facing portion of the facility. It was far too little. They were outnumbered four to one, even with Freepoint's built-in weapons platforms.

Paragon boarding parties stuck to the station like barnacles, and though several of the Fleet ships were still intact and firing, their line was too thin and too small to stop Hadras' fleet from outflanking them, pouring past, and swarming the station. In the middle of it all was the *Scythe*, like a pebble surrounded by stream water.

Glory dove past too fast, untouched and untouching. Not even computer-assisted targeting could help her land a shot at those speeds and distance, and the same was true for any of the Paragon. Drake had anticipated this and baked it in as part of his plan to enter the fray. They'd fly past harmlessly this time, but they'd show their teeth the second time around.

"Probe is away," Fredrickson called from the briefing

room for what felt like the thousandth time in the past two days. This, however, was the last time. Drake prayed the Paragon wouldn't notice.

"Helm," XO called, his eyes on something else: their current course toward the super-massive gas giant Freepoint Station orbited. "Adjust down-z point-oh-two."

They were aerobraking again on the largest planet yet. Plenty of atmosphere against which to buffet and slow down to get to a velocity resembling attack speed. From there, their inertia wouldn't last forever. There was no plan beyond that because they'd have to adjust to whatever was thrown at them or happened to be nearby, but they'd get a pass or two at the Paragon line. It would have to be enough.

The problem, as *Glory* angled down to the planet, was that they'd be blind. Not only would their course take them to the far side of the planet, but as they came around, they needed to brake as long as they could, which meant their scopes would be covered with friction fire. They wouldn't see a thing until they were upon the Paragon forces.

Enter the probe.

"Receiving data," Fredrickson announced, poised on the briefing room threshold. He was quivering, aching to leave the command deck and get below. See what magic he could work on their power core and fuel supply. He and Drake looked at the tactical station, waiting for them to sort through the raw information coming from the last probe.

"Identifying targets!" the lead officer barked and turned to face Drake, beaming.

The probe would be their eyes.

It was working.

Drake looked at Fredrickson. "Go." The chief engineer sprinted like he'd been shot from a cannon and was through the command deck's main hatch before Drake could blink.

"Prep all weapons, pick targets, and prepare to fire as soon as we're within range," he told XO as the ship started to rattle and shake. Inertial compensators had been unable to keep up with the punishing gravitational and acceleration forces *Glory* had endured for the past . . . Drake wasn't sure how long it had been. A day? Maybe two? No one had slept in that time. It wasn't possible with all the noise, the shaking, and the constant stress of whipping around star after star. And yet, the crew was alert, even through their exhaustion. They took breaks and swapped shifts seamlessly to let others do the intense concentrating for a while. Their stamina was much improved, and Drake still had his, thank the stars. He slipped his feet into the straps on the deck and gripped the console handlebars for what he hoped would be the last time they ever had to pull such a maneuver.

Outside was flame. Drake was sure *Glory* lit the dark planet like a torch, casting ghoulish shadows on the cloud formations as she screamed past, igniting the air as she went. XO and Helm made sure their course was erratic enough to avoid being hit by plasma, ballistic, or gravitic weaponry from the Paragon, who were growing smaller behind them as *Glory* curved around the planet. Any guided ordnance, missiles or torpedoes, would be taken care of by the intense heat surrounding the ship, which Drake hoped the battered old girl could handle. She'd just made fourteen trips around seven stars. He figured this was cake.

Several minutes later, Navigation reported they were coming around the far side of the planet. Freepoint Station was on the horizon, albeit not on their scopes. What they could see came from the probe, and the image was perfect. It was even tracking *Glory* as she came back around, giving them relative readings every couple milliseconds. Quantum entanglement was quite the special sauce when used properly. Tactical was a madhouse, pulling it all together, picking their targets, and designating *Glory's* weaponry to them, giving each the proper attention.

"Aerobraking complete in fifteen seconds," XO told Drake. No countdown this time, thankfully.

"Have Tactical fire at will, wherever we can do the most damage, and switch to normal scopes once we're clear."

XO nodded. He tensed, coiled and ready to spring.

"Free!" Navigation called.

"Firing," Tactical responded. *Glory* shuddered anew, this time differently—booming rather than creaking and quaking. A clearing of the throat.

They caught the Paragon by surprise.

Glory fired her weapons before fully exiting the atmosphere, scope-blind. She hit her targets with surgical precision, rocking several cruisers close by. They even had an extra-special punch to throw at the flagship, bombarding her with a barrage of plasma cannon fire and guided missiles. The Paragon in that section of the battle staggered. They didn't return fire right away, and *Glory* pounced.

Drake ordered as much strafing fire as they could muster. They pounded two nearby cruisers broadside, disgorging wave after wave of plasma fire and ballistic slugs. The ship on the right began to break up, and then the one on the left. Glee swept the command deck when they exploded after *Glory* left them behind. Drake ordered Helm to adjust and ride the resulting dual shockwaves into an angle that would take them clear of the station so they could glide into a turn and make another pass.

The crew's glee waned. This time, out in open space and going much slower, *Glory* was a target. "Countermeasures," XO bellowed as a portion of the Paragon fleet turned to meet them.

They had three cruisers dead ahead. The two flanking ships maneuvered broadside to unleash their firepower at the newcomer. It was formidable. *Glory* rocked from the weapons that got through their countermeasures, but still she plowed forward. The third ship came at her head-on, not changing course. Drake shifted his view of their tactical engagement with the three cruisers and zoomed out to look at what was behind them. Suddenly, the head-on tactic of the third cruiser made more sense. It was trying to get *Glory* to break off, either "up" or "down" from the head-on cruiser's position, either of which would aim them into the midst of a dense formation of Paragon ships. To hell with that.

"Concentrate all firepower on the forward vessel!" Drake shouted at Tactical, not bothering to go through XO. Time was of the essence. "Everything we have."

All XO had to do was glance at the tactical display Drake had pulled up to understand what was happening. "Helm, maintain course," he added, bless him. "Do not deviate!"

They had to either force the forward ship to break off or take it out. Drake would accept either, but he preferred Option Two. *Glory* was getting pummeled by the other two ships, but by concentrating all her efforts on the one dead ahead, she was dishing out more than it could handle.

The forward ship reached an understanding that in this deadly game of chicken, *Glory* would win. It broke off, angling above *Glory's* course, blinking first, but it was too late. They were seconds away from intercept, and *Glory* had no main drive with which to decelerate, which would give them more time to adjust course and avoid a collision. "There," he shouted, flashing the aft portion of the cruiser they were about to run into to the tactical station. "All available firepower there!"

The space ahead of them was awash with light as plasma cannons, missiles, and laser beams converged on the rear section of the Paragon cruiser at point-blank range. Something broke through, and just before the two ships collided, the Paragon cruiser exploded.

Glory bucked like she'd been slapped. Drake and the entire command deck crew tumbled, and in his wild, sporadic view, he saw bulkheads splitting open, sparks and flames belching, and masses of pipes and wires descend from the ceiling.

"Report," Drake croaked after the tumbling stopped. XO was upon him, instantly, helping him back to his feet. His shoulder was barking again, but it worked enough for the first officer to haul him up. He hadn't fallen far from the command console, though he'd lost his grip with both his hands and feet. Not even Fredrickson's floor straps could have stopped *that* fall.

Smoke hung in the air, seasoned with the tang of fire retardant. There were still flames near the rear of the deck, but the rest were out. There were several damaged control consoles, but those were being abandoned, their functions brought up on the consoles that remained.

"Approaching Freepoint Station," Helm called, communicating what Navigation normally would as they scrambled to get their bearings.

"Captain!" another voice shouted. Drake turned. It was Tactical. Behind them, the out-of-control cruiser they'd blown the backside off was careening toward one of the other two cruisers. The two made contact, ignited, and exploded. Another shockwave was coming their way.

"Hold on," XO yelled.

Drake heeded the advice before the shockwave hit. It slammed them forward this time, accelerating them for one whiplashing instant. Drake stayed on his feet, and because of it, he saw their next five-alarm fire to put out: the station was looming. It was far too close for their speed. They were going to crash into it.

"Helm, hard to starboard!" he ordered, hoping it wasn't too late.

It was.

It would buy them time as *Glory* turned to the right, giving her an angle at which she'd eventually impact against the giant metal structure, but no more than a few seconds. She would hit, and at this speed, it would destroy the ship.

"Engineering," he said into his wristcom. "Fredrickson!"

"Here, sir."

"Brake!" Drake shouted. "Anything you've got, *BRAKE!*"

He didn't get a response. Drake wasn't sure if his message had gone through, but he didn't have time to repeat it. The station was right in front of them, growing larger with every blink. Drake closed his eyes and gripped his handholds, sending out a silent prayer that this wasn't the end.

SLAM!

Drake was pitched over the command console, as was Oh, who skidded past Drake and slammed into the deck on the other side. Drake held on, however, and craned his neck to see the overhead display, still projecting their forward view from the time they'd spent spinning around stars. He expected to see nothing. He didn't even expect to have the *time* to see anything except maybe a flash of a wall of flame before it ripped through the ship from stem to stern in the blink of an eye. That was not what he saw.

He saw the outer hull of the Freepoint space station. They were so close to it, it was almost completely black.

They had, in fact, crashed into it; Drake could see from various scope angles that the nose of the ship was crumpled against it, but they were slowly moving *away* from the hull, screeching, tearing, and pulling off metal as they went until with a *snap!* they were free.

The shaking stopped. Drake hadn't been aware of it until it was gone, but it had been the main drives. They'd fired. Just in time, they'd blasted in reverse to stop *Glory* from impacting hard enough to destroy her. She'd taken a hit, and so had the space station, but they were both alive. Behind them, they registered two destroyed cruisers. The third had been close enough to the explosions to have taken disabling damage. Fredrickson had pulled off a miracle.

Drake told him so, the wristcom channel still open.

"Took almost all of our active core fuel," the engineer said, soberly having taken the thanks silently. "We're going to lose power in a few minutes, Captain. There's nothing I can do to stop it."

Drake accepted the information and repeated his thanks to the chief engineer. *Glory* was on the far-right side of Freepoint Station. Most of the battle action was toward its center. At their range, weapons wouldn't be very effective, and Fredrickson had shut that possibility down even before Drake had asked if they could continue to fire. The answer was no. They didn't have the power.

Glory was dead in the water.

CHAPTER SIXTY-SIX

DRAKE and the command deck crew were forced to watch as, toward the center of the station, the Fleet line crumbled. Hadras' ships surged forward, pummeling the administrative and living sections while his flagship held back, watching the chaos unfold.

It didn't matter. He didn't need to engage. The Fleet was losing. In minutes, Freepoint would effectively be under Paragon control. It would take them days to sweep through every nook and cranny of the thousands of Fleet troops holding out, but for all intents and purposes, the station would be lost. *Goddammit.* What could they do?

"Sir?" Tactical called. A new set of contacts appeared on Drake's console display. They were coming from . . . "Several new ships on our scopes coming in through the gate."

Drake's heart sank. *More* of Hadras' ships? It was about to be a massacre. He turned his attention to them, waiting for *Glory's* scopes to give the computer enough information for the types of craft to be identified and assessed.

Transponder codes came in first.

Drake went ramrod-straight. "Comms, open a channel to those ships!" Fleet signatures. Those were Fleet ships.

"Open, sir."

"Jack. Is that you?"

When the admiral's voice crackled over the short-range, Drake didn't hide his emotion. He whooped for joy, and slammed a fist on his command console. "We weren't expecting you for another week or two, *Glory*," Jack said, his tone belying his statement. He didn't sound the least bit surprised.

"Found a shortcut, sir."

"Well, thank you for holding down the fort."

"How many strong are you, Jack?" Drake was trying to count the Fleet ships as they flowed through the gate, but there were more coming, so an accurate count was impossible. "The situation is borderline and have us outnumbered four-to-one."

"I have most of the Fifth Fleet behind me. We should be able to chop down those odds."

Relief washed over Drake. More than a dozen ships had already come through, and the Paragon were turning away from the station. Jack was coming in hot, wedge formation, weapons blazing, diving toward the middle of the Paragon line. The invaders were slow with surprise. Jack took full advantage of it, and within a minute or two, the Paragon forces had been cloven in two.

Still more ships poured through the gate. It was a beautiful sight to behold. The tide was turning. Momentum was on the Fleet's side, and Drake itched to be part of the action, but all he could do was watch it on his console.

A Paragon ship that broke away from its fellows caught Drake's eye. It was steaming back toward the gate and firing wildly at a pair of Fleet ships that had just come through. It seemed desperate. Very un-Paragon-like, which was why it caught Drake's eye. The more he watched, the more confusing its behavior became. Even the shots it was sending the two cruisers' way were off-target and not landing.

"Tactical, I want visual on that ship," he said, a feeling gnawing at his gut that he couldn't quite place. "Overhead, please."

An image of the berserker ship flickered to life at the front of the command deck. Drake stepped toward it, squinting, looking for . . . something.

Then he saw it.

Not in the moves of the ship or how it was firing, but *where* it was firing and with what weapons. Scattershot munitions. Missiles breaking off with multiple warheads. All in the area *around* the two ships. Drake felt his stomach bottom out. "Get them out of there," he shouted to no one in particular. His comm line with the admiral had been terminated minutes earlier. It would have been too late anyway.

An explosion blossomed on the overhead. Tiny at first, but then there were two more explosions, then four, then eight, then sixteen. Faster and faster they came, and then the overhead display was awash with white as *Glory's* scopes were overwhelmed by the sudden increase in light.

The minefield had been reactivated.

Hadras hadn't taken it down; he controlled it. Likely one of his landing teams' sole missions. How he'd known where to go looking for those controls, Drake and the rest of the Fleet would have to find out if they survived this, but it didn't matter now. The mines were active, and the majority of Jack's forces were caught in the middle of it.

Drake yelled for the overhead to be shut off. There was no point in blinding everyone, and he looked in horror at his center console's tactical display. The minefield was exploding. Not all at once, though there were several large chain reactions happening like the first Paragon cruiser had caused. It was all going to come down eventually. The Fifth Fleet squadrons staggered, then ran for the edges of the field, not caring how many mines they hit along the way. It was chaos. Some of the Paragon fleet got caught in the mayhem, taking mine hits just as often as the Fleet ships.

One of those Paragon ships caught Drake's eye, and goddamn if it wasn't the same berserker ship from before. It was on fire, flying like a meteorite on the far side of the minefield, getting dangerously close to the gate. Extremely close.

Purposefully close.

There was a collective gasp as the ship slammed into the giant ring a second later and exploded. The gate, a swirling mass of blue-white energy, flickered as the ring shifted, then came back on and steadied.

A second Paragon ship hit it.

It was dragging a swarm of gravity-attracted mines. Those hit too, which doubled the size of the explosion. Someone on the command deck cried out. The gate faltered again and went dark around the section of the damage. The rest of the gate stayed on, but it flickered more seriously this time.

Rather than re-solidifying, the flickering got worse. Flames belched from the damaged portions, and Drake was horrified to see those were spreading, too. A chain reaction. The gate would fail. More than that, it would explode. A *lot* of energy went into powering a gate, particularly one with far-reach like Freepoint's. It drew that energy from the center of a super-massive gas giant. When the gate went, it was liable to take out half the star system. Certainly the planet, and whatever was in orbit around it, which currently included the Freepoint Station, both fleets, and *Glory*.

Drake staggered away from the console. His foot caught on one of his floor straps, and he fell to the deck on his ass. Still in view was the three-dimensional projection of the gate. The ring structure was starting to shake, and the explosions blooming out from the damaged portions grew.

He couldn't believe it. His mouth was open and his jaw was slack.

There was an unwritten rule in space combat; you didn't fuck with gates. It never *had* to be written. Gates were the lifeblood of space travel for everyone, no matter who your enemy was or what you were fighting over. Take one down, and you cut off space travel to that destination for decades if it was the only gate in or out. That was the same for any race—human, Paragon, or otherwise. A gateless star system was worthless. It might as well be an island in the wilderness. It was tactical suicide. Except . . .

Except Hadras had Idri, and no one else did. He could just sit back and watch it happen. Watch the rest of the two fleets scramble in panic, then jump out at his leisure, leaving Freepoint cut off and adrift in the void. Worthless to everyone. If he couldn't have Freepoint, no one could. He was a madman.

"Get me readings on that power overload," Drake said hoarsely as XO helped him back to his feet. "How much time?"

His first officer had an answer for him shortly after. "An hour tops at the current rate. Jack's scrambling repair teams to assist the onboard engineers."

Drake nodded and swallowed. He'd never seen a gate overload, but from the spreading explosions on the Freepoint gate's structural ring, it didn't look like anything that could be repaired. Drake could see Jack maneuvering ships along the structure to protect it from further attack, which was the right thing to do. Two more cruisers from Hadras' fleet attempted to ram it and were repelled just in time. They flew through the flickering gate and escaped instead.

A madman.

"Retreat!" Comm reported, cutting through the silence on the command deck. It was Bidermann. Here eyes were wide with shock. "Retreat orders have been issued, sir. All vessels."

Drake scrambled back to his command console. "The station," he said, sweeping his eyes across the chaos, trying to make sense of it. "We must evacuate."

Jack was already taking care of that. In the retreat order, a dozen ships had been assigned to facilitate an evacuation of the station. There were thousands of men and women there who couldn't be left behind. Another line of Fleet ships was forming behind them as they closed in to repel any Paragon ships that might try to pick them off as they sat docked, but that probably wouldn't be necessary.

The Paragons ships had retreat orders of their own. They were pulling back, firing as they did to destroy the station if possible. Not because rendering it useless was their task—the gate overload would take care of that and more—but because it would kill the most Fleet soldiers as they left.

Not Hadras. His flagship remained where Drake had seen it last, hanging back from the action, watching and still. Except . . . except not still, was it? It was shimmering. Flickering with the telltale signs of a jump, then re-solidifying where it was. Drake's heart leapt into his throat.

He scanned the tactical display, zooming in on the station, looking for two specific items. The first was easy to find. The second? He would be goddamned, but it was closer than he could have hoped.

"Drake to Engineering," he called on his wristcom. "How are those retreat orders looking?"

It took Fredrickson a minute to answer. His voice was rough when he did. Tired. "We're an ounce of plasma fuel away from losing all power, to say nothing of propulsion. We're dry, Captain. Bone-dry."

"What if I was able to get you a stack of plasma transport pods? How fast can you get those into the fuel lines?"

Another pause. "Go now," he answered. The connection between them cut abruptly, but not before Drake heard him shouting fresh orders to his engineering crew, preparing for what Drake was about to bring him. Plasma pods weren't designed to be injected into a starship. That was done through refueling umbilicals that had safety measures like valves that prevented backflow from an active power core, for example, but it was the still plasma, and such valves could be constructed. Drake had seen a bulky triple-shielded plasma pod transport docked one or two kilometers down the spine of the station. Hopefully it was full. Odds were high that it was.

"Carrol," Drake barked, whirling to find his second officer. She was at the flight control station. Perfect. "You stay right there, Commander. I need you to coordinate a convoy." Confusion flashed over Carrol's face and she glanced at CAG, who was standing right next to her. Surely Drake meant her?

But no. Drake shook off the un-asked question. He meant Carrol. "Grab those plasma pods and evacuate all station personnel you come across. All of them. Split teams if you have to, pods and rescue, but do it fast."

"Yes, sir," Carrol answered. She shook off her confusion,

slipped on a headset, and turned back to the communications board to work on scrambling their shuttles. Good thing *Glory* had an ass-ton of extras from extracting the penal colony prisoners.

"XO," Drake said quietly to his first officer. He stared at the command console with both hands gripping its sides to tight, knuckles white. "Take care of the ship. Hold off the Paragon until you're refueled and have the station cleared. You've still got three fighter squadrons to work with, and you'll have a hell of a lot more firepower when those plasma pods start coming in." He paused and looked up to catch Oh's eyes, then held his gaze. "Then you get the ship the hell out of here. That's an order."

Oh frowned. "And you, sir?"

Drake took a white-knuckled hand off the command console and pointed at Hadras' flagship, which was still shimmering and re-solidifying. He was trying to jump the ship and run, but someone over there wasn't letting him. "I'm getting on that goddamn ship," he said, allowing his fury to boil over. The fight for Freepoint was lost. Hadras had won what had turned out to be a Pyrrhic victory. It was over, but there was still a battle being waged on that ship. Idri was fighting back, and she needed his help.

"Cap," XO pled, grabbing Drake's arm. "You would be stranded here."

"Not if I get Idri back." XO tried to protest further, but Drake gave him a solemn shake of his head, pulled his arm away, and shut it down. This wasn't a discussion. "I have to try."

XO swallowed, then stood back with a crisp salute. "Yes, sir."

Good man.

"CAG," Drake said, whirling back to the flight control station.

"Yessir," she drawled, all five-plus-a-little-bit feet of her standing straight and at the ready.

"Haven't forgotten about you."

"Course not, sir."

Drake called her over to his console and brought up the second item he'd been searching for along their section of Freepoint Station. He pointed at one of the many "barnacles" embedded into the station's hull. "You ever flown a Paragon boarding pod?"

"Nope." She grinned. "Always wanted to, though."

CHAPTER SIXTY-SEVEN

THE POD REEKED.

Drake had been in Paragon craft a time or two, and the stench was always the same. It was hard to say if it came with the territory or if it was because they'd gunned down three of the bastards standing guard over it to enter, but it stank. The bodies had only been in the pod for a few seconds, but they were already smoldering from the inside out. Drake was inclined to believe their self-immolation had its hand in the stink.

Turned out they were lucky to get a pod. On the shuttle ride over with CAG, Smith, and Warren, Drake observed several of the nearby boarding pods releasing from the station, flaring their thrusters, and returning to their home ships. The evacuation orders apparently applied to them as well. Everyone was bugging out of the system.

Well, not everyone.

Drake eyed the *Scythe* through a half-domed forward viewing window. CAG had them heading straight for it. He would have marveled that she could fly the thing so well on her first try, but he'd long since learned to expect such things from the old pilot. She might ride a headset and chair most of the time these days, but her piloting skills were still top-notch. He was pleased to see she hadn't lost a step.

They had to be careful, at first, to hide from the other returning pods, lest they be seen through the viewing dome. But as they angled more and more toward the flagship, they had less and less companions until, finally, they were the only ones. Drake didn't know if that was a good thing, or bad thing.

"Where are we landing?" CAG asked as the large ship loomed.

Drake frowned. Good question. The *Scythe* was a ghost town. It wasn't shimmering anymore, however. Drake hoped Idri was okay. At least the ship wasn't in danger of jumping in front of their eyes. They still had time.

"Ah, never mind, Cap," CAG reported a moment later. She took her hands off the console of controls, but the pod still sailed forward, making slight course adjustments as it went. "Autopilot." The *Scythe* was bringing them in.

Drake turned to Smith and Warren. The two men towered even more than they usually did, decked out in their bulky, battle-scarred armor as they were. "Lock and load, gentlemen," he said, reaching for his assault rifle and checking its power levels. "Let's be ready for a reception."

THE LOADING DECK WAS QUIET.

Not that many pods were returning, which backed up what they'd observed outside. Drake had mentally prepared for the worst, that as one of the few pulled in by the flagship, they would stick out like a sore thumb. It had proven to be the opposite.

Two Paragon troopers were processing the intake of another pod five meters down the loading deck. It wasn't a hangar like *Glory* and other ships in the Fleet used for shuttlecraft and other transport vessels, a wide-open space with polished floors and high ceilings and a giant door on one end that harkened back to the age of aircraft in Earth's ancient history.

This was a series of docking hatches on the flagship's underbelly, rows and rows of them, that fit the noses of the hull-piercing boarding pods perfectly. The pod latched onto one of those hatches, then hung there, rear end naked to space. Outside the pod's front hatch, which had opened on its own when it clicked into place—automated like everything else in the docking process—was a long corridor that stretched for several dozen meters in each direction with a pod hatch every few meters. The flagship had capacity for hundreds of them. To their right, two hatches down, was where the two troopers were emptying another pod.

A row of armored soldiers filed out wordlessly. Their boot heels clacked on the gangplank and then on the metal deck grates. With a *hiss* and a *clank*, the two troopers resealed the now-empty pod, then turned to move on to the next. That was them. The pod between them and the one just emptied was vacant. He'd looked.

He slunk back into the darkness toward the rear of the tapered vessel and crouched next to CAG. There were no seats, unfortunately. Those ran length-wise down the hull and were of the simple flip-down variety that disappeared into the wall when not in use. Nevertheless, with the cabin lights out, it was quite dark. Drake was hoping the troopers would peer inside, not see anyone, and move on. No need to engage or raise an alarm. Quiet in, quiet out. Just in case, however, Smith and Warren were poised on either side of the hatch, weapons at the ready. Drake had his in hand as well, as did CAG.

The first trooper stopped in front of the hatch. With a small hand-held computer of some kind, he scanned something on the outside of the pod, and the computer chimed pleasantly. An identifying mark, Drake guessed. The other officer joined him and looked at the computer, then nodded. Then they waited. When no one came out, they looked into the pod. When they saw no one, the first trooper made a soft and melodic noise.

Not what he would have expected someone of its size and appearance to make. Paragon troopers were formidable-looking, and not just because they were large. Their opaque helmets were sharply tapered at the chin in a way that would be uncomfortable for a human, the armor was grotesquely tight and had striations that looked like muscle tissue, and the multitude of bright blue dots set into the white armor looked like dozens of eyes. Yet, the sound was pleasant.

Drake realized it was the first time he'd ever heard such a noise. Perhaps their language in battle or when non-Paragon were around was different from when they were by themselves and "safe." It must have been a call for anyone inside to exit. The trooper made the same sound when no one emerged.

The second trooper un-slung its plasma rifle. After the first pocketed the small hand-held computer device, it did the same.

Damn. So much for non-engagement.

Cautiously and in a crouch, the troopers shuffled into the pod's entry hatch. The second they stepped past the threshold, Warren and Smith were on them. Warren used a pair of bayonet-type blades built into his armor, while Smith used his rifle a point-blank range to muffle the energy release and noise. The two troopers dropped to the ground, lifeless. A second later, the white armor blackened in the areas where the tissue was the closest. A few moments later, the bodies were mostly ash, and the horrible Paragon stench was back.

That confirmed it for Drake. The dead bodies gave off the smell.

"I'm afraid you'll have to keep them in here," Drake said to CAG as he and she dragged them into the dark recesses of the pod. Warren and Smith took the other body. "Can't risk them being seen."

"Let's hope the Paragon don't have a keen sense of smell," she said, grimacing.

CAG was staying behind, at the ready to get them the hell out of there. So far, there had been no alarms. No pounding of boots that indicated an approaching security squad. It looked like they'd managed to sneak aboard the *Scythe* undetected. Drake hoped it would stay that way. He showed CAG his wristcom. "Wrist taps only," he said, though she didn't need reminding. She nodded. They were QE and didn't require a radio transmission. "Should be pretty safe."

He then pointed at the pod. "And figure out if these things launch from here as well, or if you need to move."

"Already on it, Cap," she assured him. "Get the hell out of here while it's quiet."

Didn't have to tell him twice. He gave her shoulder a squeeze, sent up a silent prayer for her to stay safe, and joined Warren and Smith at the hatch. They had donned their helmets and were raring to go.

"We know where we're headed?" Drake asked.

Smith nodded wordlessly and showed Drake the tracking screen attached to his armor's right forearm. There was a dot blinking steadily. Cheddar. The dog would be with Idri or close to her.

He gestured at Smith. "You're on point."

CHAPTER SIXTY-EIGHT

"Status, Third Squad," Carrol repeated into her headset, making sure she was tapping the appropriate transmit button on the comm panel in front of her. It was lit. She was transmitting.

"Little busy here," someone finally came back. Carrol recognized the voice.

"Zed, report," she said. If it had many any goddamn sense, she'd have picked someone else to make the plasma-pickup run, but Squadrons One and Two were out fending off the random Paragon fighter group that had slipped out their way and the stray missile that got loose from the heavier fighting toward the center of the giant station.

Not to mention the plasma pickup was crucial to get right. The evac airlift was equally important—Carrol had devoted three times the transports to that part of the operation—but if there was as much plasma on the station as they were hoping there was, they couldn't risk taking so much as a hard right turn with it, or *Glory* and everyone else within a cubic kilometer would be vaporized. Carrol needed pilots with skill. She had several others, but it mostly meant Zed, who was currently pissed at her. Clearly. "What. Is. Your. Status?"

"We have our hands full."

Over the comm channel, when Zed briefly had it open, Carrol could hear the noise of a large crowd. "Do we have enough transport space?"

"For the evac? Sure. Think so. But loading them with these plasma pods might get tight real quick."

Carrol's pulse quickened. "So, there are plasma pods there?" No answer. "Zed!"

"Goddammit, Commander. I'm busy."

Carrol leaned into the comm station and pressed her headset mic to her mouth, so the rest of the command deck crew couldn't hear her fury. "Cut the bullshit. I'll put fucking Oh on the line and have him ask the same goddamned questions, you hear me? *Lieutenant?* How many fucking pods?"

"There's enough." The line went dead.

Carrol ripped off her headset and threw it at the comm station. She steepled her fingers and pressed them to the bridge of her nose, wanting to scream. She inhaled slowly instead. When she looked up from her station, she expected half the command deck to be looking at her. That proved to be an overdramatic thought. Everyone was busy doing their own work.

"Commander," she called to Oh. The first officer gestured her over to the central station, busy. She got up and approached him. "Our evac squad reports they're inundated but believe they can handle the capacity."

XO nodded, not taking his eyes off the console. "And the plasma pods?"

"There. As we'd hoped."

"Do we know how many?"

Carrol swallowed, then shook her head. "'Enough' was the report, sir." She braced herself for a reprimand for delivering such unspecific information, but Oh simply nodded. "Let's hope that's true." He then eased close to her.

"Never let the troops see you frustrated, Commander. It throws them off their game."

"Yes, sir," a chastised Carrol replied softly.

He pointed at the display he was studying so intently, moving on. On it, burning a fiery red that indicated a hostile contact, was a Paragon heavy cruiser breaking off from the main group of the fleet.

It was heading for *Glory*.

XO finally looked at Carrol. "Tell you squad to hurry."

CHAPTER SIXTY-NINE

DRAKE, Warren, and Smith met their first resistance within minutes of leaving the pod loading dock. Four Paragon troopers waltzed around a corner. His team made short work of them, naturally, given the advantage of surprise, then pulled the guards into an alcove. It wasn't a closet or a storage locker because it had no door, but the small corner was out of line of sight from the rest of the corridor.

There was a problem.

"This isn't going to work," Drake said breathlessly. Holy shit, these fuckers were heavy. "We're too exposed. Stick out like a fucking lighthouse."

Warren grunted in agreement, but Smith didn't answer. He was taking out his Ka-Bar from a holster in his shin armor. He gripped it tight, then plunged it into the backside of the nearest dead trooper and ripped upwards.

Smoke and stench billowed from the cut. "What the fuck?" Warren moaned, leaning away and waving in front of his helmet. Apparently, his suit's atmospheric filtration systems didn't keep out the smell.

Smith, however, motioned for him to do the same.

"Quickly! Before they burn through." He stood, grabbed the trooper's armor by the seams he'd just cut into its back, lifted the entire thing off the deck, and shook. Oozing black pulp plus guts, bone and other tissue poured out of the fissure. That which was not already black ooze and smoking caught fire the second it touched the air, sizzling even before it hit the deck.

Drake got it. So did Warren, who went to work with his arm-bayonets. If they got the Paragon body out of the suit before it burned up, maybe it wouldn't burn the suit.

It worked.

They poured three bodies out of their suits before they self-destructed, and the men stood in their smoking, stinking, ash-filled alcove with three Paragon trooper suits. "Now what?" Warren asked. Drake couldn't see his expression behind the faceplate, but he could imagine it was skeptical.

"We try them on," Drake said, making a disgusted face. The two other men just looked at him. As the ranking officer, it was only fair for him to give it a go first.

The armor was surprisingly light in his hands despite being quite thick. It wouldn't be a perfect fit, but it didn't need to be. It just needed to be good enough from a distance or at a glance. Everyone on a starship had a job. You went to and from that job as quickly and narrowly focused as you could. As long as an intruder alert wasn't blaring, this might work.

Drake hoped.

Getting his legs in was like putting on a jumpsuit. Same with the arms and torso. The trooper whose suit he was slipping into was larger than he was, which helped in the boots and existing uniform departments. Drake didn't have to take his off since the suit fit over them. It wasn't nearly as helpful in the hands department. It was just an oversized pair of gloves. "It's fine," Drake mumbled, tugging on the suit's sleeves to get his hands and fingers into the gloves. The fabric stretched as he did so, making it worse.

The helmet was the worst part. Not all the "organic material" had sloughed off despite Drake shaking it. He put it on, and some of the black gunk splattered his cheek and burned there for one horrible second while Drake clawed the damn thing off his head. He gave it a once-over with a gloved hand, then tried again.

Pitch-darkness.

"Problem," Drake said. "I can't see a goddamn thing." Someone spoke, but the words were muffled. "Can't hear anything either."

"Point at your eyes, Captain," he heard Warren say close to the helmet.

Drake tapped on the opaque plastiform faceplate until it felt and sounded like where his eyes were. There was a whirring sound and he tried to jerk back, but someone was holding him from behind to make sure that didn't happen. A second later, with a flash of blinding light, two eye-sized holes had been burned into his helmet. A second after that, two more holes for his nostrils and another for his ears. It wasn't perfect, but it worked. "How do I look?" he asked, wishing there was a mirror somewhere.

"Like you're melting," Warren said grimly, eyes narrowed.

Drake looked down. Getting into the suit had made its dimensions even worse. It was grotesquely stretched out in places, misshapen to the extreme. He didn't understand. Why was the material so malleable? Had it been damaged when its occupant had died, even though they'd removed the body?

"Captain," rumbled Smith from behind him. He was

feeling something on the back of the suit near the base of Drake's neck. "If I may?"

"If you may what?" Drake asked him. "If it's nearly shooting me in the eye with a cutting laser, the answer is no." He shot a look at Warren, who shrugged. He still had the small pencil-shaped tool he'd used to cut the eye, nose and ear holes in his hand. A precision instrument, with preset depths it would cut to, but one slip and Drake would be blind.

"It is not a cutting laser," Smith answered.

"You may, Marine."

Drake didn't know what to brace himself for, but whatever he could have imagined was insufficient as Smith pressed down firmly on the suit's protrusion. The entire thing *crawled* like it was alive. The suit morphed, undulating and contracting like a thousand tiny boa constrictors until it was so snug around Drake's body, helmet included, that he wasn't sure he could breathe.

"Holy shit!" he exclaimed, and he staggered for a moment before realizing he could move. He could also breathe. Even the eye holes in the helmet had managed to stay in the right spot as the headpiece wrapped his noggin in an unsettlingly tight hug.

Drake looked down to see that despite the odd bulge or wrinkle here and there from the stripped-down uniform he was wearing underneath, the armor was as tight and form-fitting as that of any Paragon trooper he'd seen.

"I believe the suits are one-size-fits-all," Smith concluded, standing back to look at his work.

Warren nodded in approval. "Good shit." He turned to Smith. "Do me next."

THE SUITS WERE stretchy and one-size-fits-all, sure, but only to a point. That point did not extend to Smith's and Warren's armor. There wasn't enough material, so the two men were forced to strip to their underlayers, then each used half the remaining empty Paragon suit to make a makeshift sack into which to stuff their armor. Both men made it clear they would turn around and go home if going forward meant abandoning their suits here.

Drake couldn't argue with that. They were already going to look odd. While the suits seemed to have a built-in healing ability—they'd self-repaired the long slices down the backs of the suits when the shrinking button had been pushed, yet another feature that made them feel unsettlingly alive rather than just clothing—that ability apparently did not extend to the array of lighted blue dots. They refused to come on. Drake would wager that the helmet was looking for a neural interface his noggin did not possess. However, they only needed to pass temporarily.

Glances, not scrutiny.

They got their first test moments after stepping back into the corridor. An entire squad of soldiers turned a corner and rumbled past, their synchronized footsteps making the deck plates shake. They didn't look twice at the odd trio. Drake breathed with relief. "I think we're in business." Smith, who'd taken his portable tracker screen off his armor's forearm and strapped it to his Paragon suit, pointed. Cheddar was close by.

Security got heavier the farther into the ship they went. Patrols came every few sections here, and though the trio was able to stride past the other troops, Drake knew it would get riskier the closer they got to where Idri was being held. If there was an ID check or a security barricade, it would be curtains.

Drake's fear manifested after the next corner they rounded. A checkpoint for a restricted area. Five guards manned it, standing stock-still, ten meters down a straight section of corridor. They didn't react to the trio, neither appearing to look at or away from them. With the element of surprise, Drake was pretty sure they could blast their way through them, but there was no alcove here to hide the bodies in. It *would* raise an alarm. What other choice did they have, though? Drake adjusted the rifle in his hands and slipped a finger down to the trigger, ready to roll.

A hand from Smith stopped him and Warren, however. The trio paused.

"What?" Drake hissed to the Marine. The guards at the checkpoint still hadn't moved, but Drake knew flinching like this in their view had to look suspicious. Tarrying was even riskier. What if one of the guards asked them what they were doing? They had no way to respond.

Smith was looking at his tracker, trying to decipher something on it. Drake made an executive decision to turn on his heel and walk back from whence they'd come, around that corner and out of sight of the checkpoint. Warren followed him, but Smith, head still bent over his tracker, didn't. Drake gave him as subtle an elbow in the ribs as he could on his way past, and thankfully, the Marine responded with a grunt and followed the other two.

"She is behind us," Smith said in a low voice once they were around the corner.

"The dog?" Drake asked.

Smith nodded.

"Because I'd bet you Idri is somewhere past that checkpoint."

Warren seemed inclined to agree. Smith looked at the two. "Cheddar is extremely resourceful. She will have purposefully sought out hiding places in the vicinity of whomever she was protecting. The fact, Captain, that I'm getting her homing signal almost certainly means she's hidden somewhere right now, which is why she's not concealed. Such a hiding place could be advantageous for us as well."

Drake looked back at the corner that led to the security checkpoint, then back the way they'd come, which was quiet for the moment. Whatever they did, they couldn't just stand in the corridor with their thumbs up their asses. They needed to move. The clock was ticking.

He nodded at the Marine. "We find the dog."

"This way," Smith whispered, and they retraced their steps.

Always find the dog. That was what Drake was learning.

Smith had been spot-on. Cheddar *was* hiding. Her beacon had led them to an access panel they'd never have known existed otherwise since it was seamlessly integrated into the bulkhead. A few moments of prying, the panel came off, and stretching in front of them was an amply-sized service crawlway and one very excited dog.

Cheddar whimpered and whined while alternating between rolling onto her back to show Smith her belly and launching herself at him with full force. He let her bowl him over several times, and had to physically drag her into the crawlspace and out of the corridor lest they be seen. Inside, Smith relaxed his suit, pulled the helmet aside, and wrapped the canine into a bear hug. He buried his face into her fur.

"I worried she wouldn't be able to smell me," Smith said, and raised his head to wiped something from his eyes. Drake could have sworn it was a tear. "Paragon armor and all," he clarified. "But she still knew it was me."

He hugged the animal again, and Drake had to admit he was touched by the reunion. They'd bonded quickly, these two, in such a short time.

"We should move," the Marine said, composed again. He had his helmet back on, and his suit tightened.

Drake agreed, getting his bearings. The crawlway was massive by *Glory's* standards. Even Warren and Smith, giants though they were, could sit upright, makeshift packs on their backs and all.

"Idri," Smith said to the dog. Her ears perked at the tone of his voice and the change in his body language. In an instant, she stopped acting like a crazed puppy and stiffened to attention. She cocked her head to the side, listening intently with her large triangle-shaped ears perked. "Where is Idri?"

The dog padded deeper into the crawlspace, then paused and turned back to look at the trio of men as if to say, "Are you coming?"

"After her, I guess," Drake said, getting to his hands and knees. "Sure hope she knows where she's taking us."

CHAPTER SEVENTY

THE PLASMA POD count was alarmingly low.

As Carrol's shuttle pilots checked in, she realized that there were so many personnel to pick up from the station, her "pod squad" had been filled up with people, not pods.

"I don't know what else to do, Commander," said one of her shuttle pilots, Emmit. A vet from the invasion. "I've got two pods and I can barely squeeze everyone in here."

Carrol wasn't sure she'd ever seen a plasma transport pod in person, but she knew they were three meters by three meters by three meters and weighed several hundred kilos. They weren't small. "Between you and the other four shuttles, Emmit, we only have six. I don't know how far that will get us."

"Well," the pilot considered, "I can take maybe one more if we kick out a few passengers, but that's it. These people are desperate, sir."

Of course they were. Dammit. But if *Glory* didn't get fuel, it wouldn't make much difference if those personnel were evacuated to the ship or stranded on the station. They'd all die together when the gate blew.

"Forget it," someone said over the radio. "Shove off as is, Emmit. I'm loading the rest of the pods into my shuttle." It was Zed.

"Confirm, Lieutenant," Carrol broke in. "How many pods do you have loaded?"

"I've got thirteen. Fourteen counting this last one on the loading dock that I'm about to go grab."

Carrol shook her head. "Negative, Zed. Negative. That's way past tolerances. We need to spread those around." Plasma, like any other explosive material, got more dangerous the tighter it was packed together, and it wasn't the plan.

"Gonna have to negative your negative, Commander," Zed replied. "Everyone is already taking off, full to the brim. It would take us way too long to bring them all back, re-sort all the evacs, and divide up the pods." Zed grunted several times, accompanied by hydraulic whirring, which Carrol took to mean he was loading the last pod on his shuttle, despite her orders to the contrary. A *clang* in the background made her cringe. If that was the pod being dropped on the deck, she to fucking God . . .

"Don't worry about me," Zed continued, panting. "I'll get these back to *Glory*."

"Zed, if you take fire or even bump them the wrong way . . . "

"I believe I'm capable of a clean flight, sir," he said instead. In the background, Carrol heard the distinct chime of the shuttle's rear hatch closing. He was getting ready to take off.

"At least let's transfer your passengers over, then," she said, mind whirling.

"It's just me." The chiming stopped, and Zed sounded

like he was hustling back into the station. "And make that fifteen plasma pods. I see one more back there I missed."

Carrol inhaled. It was a short flight. A few minutes. She glanced at XO, who was communicating furiously on his headset. His tactical display was a hornets' nest of activity, swarming around the incoming Paragon cruiser. The ship looked like it was minutes away from bringing the worst of its weapons to bear on the inert, defenseless *Glory*. She knew he'd say, "Get those shuttles back here ASAP, and don't leave a single person behind." If Zed had the rest of the pods and the other shuttles had all the evacuees, that was mission accomplished. Hopefully just in time.

"Fine," she told Zed. "I'm giving all the other shuttles clearance to return. You grab that last pod and get the hell back over here."

Zed didn't answer. His line just went dead, which Carrol took as a "yes, sir, thank you, sir." She leaned back into her seat and took her headset off faster than she intended, risking a glance at the XO. They'd all be back soon. It was decided. She hoped it wasn't a mistake.

"Commander," XO called from the center console. "If your team is set, I'd appreciate another pair of eyes on Second Squadron."

As if to punctuate the request, *Glory* lurched and jerked under the impact of a weapons barrage. The Paragon cruiser was awfully close. Carrol straightened, wrapped her headset back on, and keyed the comm channels for the fighter group XO had mentioned. "Yes, sir!"

They just needed to hold out for a little longer.

CHAPTER SEVENTY-ONE

CHEDDAR LED them straight to Idri. The crawlspace the dog had been hiding in ran directly to where she was being held. Literally 'held,' it turned out. Crouched, just inside the opened access panel, Drake took in the grisly view.

The chamber was pitch-black, not only in its lack of light but also in its color scheme. There *was* light in the room, but the surfaces upon which it shone were matte and absorbent, so they did not reflect it. Unless you were looking directly at a light source, the room appeared to be formlessly dark.

As for light sources, there were three. One was close to the lone entrance to the chamber, around which stood eight Paragon troopers, all Hardas' personal guard, looking as though they were standing upon space itself.

Drake froze when he saw them, but they hadn't been detected. Cheddar's crawlspace panel was already open, and their makeshift Paragon suits' lack of lights was turning out to be a boon. They couldn't be seen, and they'd been fortunate enough not to make any noise thus far.

The second source of light was several meters from the door and the troopers. Two black slabs contained strapped-down Navid with tubes and wires running from their arms, necks, and heads. At the feet of their slabs was a bank of computers, softly flickering with indicator lights. This matched what Idri had reported in the AI cube on the Vorkut moon. Whatever had been done to her down there was being done to her here, and more.

The final and largest light source was a ring of spotlights projecting from the ceiling of the chamber. They encircled a massive cone-shaped apparatus with small lights and blinking indicators that was perhaps eight meters tall. A computer, Drake surmised, probably an AI. From that cone plunged a column of wires and tubes similar to those that pierced the two Navid, which made their way ten meters to another black slab. Idri was strapped to it, hanging face-down over the pitch-black floor. She wasn't moving. Wires and tubes were plugged into her, even more than the two Navid. Drake could see from gear-toothed metal circles on either side of her slab that it was meant to rotate at least a hundred and eighty degrees, if not more, so Idri could be oriented either vertically or horizontally. He couldn't fathom why.

The scene was horrifying. She was so small in center of it all, strapped down at every articulating part of her body, even her forehead, so tightly that Drake could see her pale skin reddening. Blood oozed from several of the tubes' entry points, and she was deathly pale, even for her. But she was alive. She was in there fighting. He'd seen it.

Warren tapped Drake on the shoulder and whispered sotto voce into his ear, "The Marine and I will enter first. Fire when we do."

Drake shook his head. Fuck that. He would not be side-lined for these Paragon bastards. He was just as capable of slipping into the chamber silently as Warren or Smith were. Probably more so, given their extra bulk. "On three," he whispered to the other two. "One . . . "

He didn't get to two.

With a snarl that echoed around the large chamber, a demon with teeth and fur lunged at the unsuspecting group of Paragon. The one unlucky enough to be chosen first screamed in surprise, then gurgled and flailed as the dog ripped out his throat. The other guards froze in shock, and Cheddar launched at the next closest trooper before he could raise his rifle.

Drake wouldn't let the dog be outnumbered. Neither would Warren or Smith. All three scrambled out of the crawlspace and opened fire as soon as they were clear of each other. The six remaining troopers fell within another second. Silence returned to the chamber.

No alarm. No shouting. Just Drake's heavy breathing, and a low growl coming from Cheddar over by the fallen troopers. Smoking fluid dripped from her half-open mouth, but it didn't seem to bother her. Perhaps it was part of her genetic enhancements and she'd been designed to with-stand immolated flesh, or perhaps she was just standing there taking the pain without a flinch. Drake would have believed either.

"Let's get her loose," Drake said, still in a low voice.

The trio rushed toward the center of the chamber. Drake nearly fell on his face two steps in. The floor was not flat. It sloped, which he hadn't expected. Looking down, he couldn't see it. Even feeling it beneath his feet and seeing that there was light in the room, it was hard to believe it was there. But it was, and it wasn't flat. As he adjusted, moving more slowly and deliberately than before, he realized it curved down like the slope of a bowl. Looking at the computer and the column of tubes and wires, he realized they were coming from a ceiling that was shaped the same way. The room was a sphere, like the fulcrum on board *Glory*. Of course it was. Drake was willing to bet that from the right angle and orientation in the center of the room, one could see an uninterrupted view of the stars, which Idri required to jump.

He saw that was true when they reached the slab, but only from a standing position. From the center of the room, he could see everything. The station. It was *crawling* with activity. Half a dozen Fleet warships with hundreds of support craft swarmed like bees in their mad dash to evacuate the facility.

He could see *Glory*. She was right where he'd left her. He hoped she was refueling, ready to get the hell out of there. He could also see the gate. It wasn't done yet, but Drake could tell it was close. Much closer than when he'd last seen it. Drake wondered why the *Scythe* was sitting so calmly amid the chaos. What escape plan Hadras had up his sleeve that no one else did? He suspected it was Idri.

"Unplug her," he said, focusing on her. They needed to *move*. "And let's get her upright." Warren found controls on the side of the black slab and rotated it upward. Idri moaned. "Jesus," Drake muttered, guilt and rage stabbing him like a hot knife. Good lord, she was pale, and every inch of exposed skin was slick with sweat. "Goddammit, let's get her out of this thing."

They scrambled to find a safe way to extract the tubes and wires that ran up and down her body, looking for twist-offs and click connections, but they found nothing. Every tube and wired looked like it had been stabbed into her, and taking them out would rip her apart. Some of the tubes were clear, and as Drake handled them, he could see various liquids pouring through them. Drugs, he was certain; they were probably keeping her sedated. Drake cursed himself for not having Doc come along. He'd know what to do.

"How about this?" Smith called from behind the head of the slab. Drake shifted to see what he was pointing at. It was a hub that all the wires and tubes ran through before integrating into the slab. Drake followed the tubes from the hub and saw that they all continued into the computer bank above them. It controlled everything, including whatever was being pumped into her.

"Can it be disconnected?" Drake asked, looking around for a release mechanism. It wouldn't free Idri's body of the wires and tubes, but it *would* sever her from the control mechanism. "I don't see anything."

Smith indicated that the captain should stand back. *Blam!* He blasted the hub with his plasma rifle. With an angry hiss, the mass of tubes and wires shot loose, sparking and spraying fluids around like a spitting snake.

Idri screamed.

Drake gasped when her eyes flew open. She was awake. Kind of. She thrashed as though she were in the throes of a horrible dream, straining with unconscious strength against her restraints. "Idri!" he shouted, jumping to her side. "Idri, it's me. Drake."

She screamed again, her eyes wild, and Drake was blown back from the black slab. Overhead, there was an ear-splitting crack, then a thunderclap echoed from the walls of the chamber as a concussive blast of air rebounded off them. When Drake managed to scramble back to his feet, Idri was on the floor, shaking and bleeding from where she'd jumped or torn the tubes from her body. The black slab had been shattered into dozens of melted shards.

The ceiling groaned. When Drake looked up, the computer and the column were on fire, with several of the slab shards buried in them. The same went for the Navid and the computer they were plugged into at the side of the room. Idri had jumped pieces of her metal slab into each of them. That explained the explosion in the room, and from her moaning and continued thrashing, she was liable to do more damage. Drake rushed to her side.

"Idri!" he said, taking a risk and grabbing her. She was bleeding from where she'd ripped out the tubes and wires, but there were more embedded in her, dripping fluids. "Idri," he repeated, turning her toward him and trying to capture her wild eyes. "I'm here. *We're* here."

Cheddar joined him at her side and licked her face. Idri stopped screaming.

The dog. She was responding to the dog. "Good," Drake told Cheddar with a rub on the head and a scritch behind her ears. Smith joined them and did the same, encouraging the canine. Warren knelt by Drake's other shoulder. In fits and starts, Idri calmed down. Her eyes focused, and she finally saw Drake, then Cheddar, then Smith and Warren.

"Are you really here?" she asked, tears welling in her eyes. She was clutching fistfuls of the dog's fur. "This isn't a dream?"

"We're really here, kid," Warren said, smiling.

Idri sobbed, and reached for them all, clutching whoever she could get hold of tightly as if she were afraid of falling off a cliff. Drake held her back, as did the other two men, and she cried into them with her entire body.

Outside in the hallway, an alarm blared.

Drake looked at Warren and Smith. Hadras finally knew they were here. They needed to move.

―――――

Deep in the bowels of the *Scythe*, CAG heard the alarm blare. She recognized it—intruder alert. Even on an alien ship, it had the same ring, the same urgency. *Someone is on board who is not supposed to be.* Footsteps thundered down the corridors, security forces swarming to find the invaders and expel them.

CAG waited for them to come.

She hunkered down, plasma rifle in hand, as two long lines of them streamed across the catwalk and headed for the pod the *Glory* crew had flown in on. She kept her finger on the trigger as they took breaching positions outside the front hatch of the pod, dropped a small flash bomb just outside it, and set it off.

Boooom!

The hangar deck shook with the explosion. The air filled with smoke, but not before CAG saw the two lines of troops pour into the pod. Bastards were smart, she would give them that. They had tracked the intruders to their point of entry, but they weren't *that* smart. She was smarter.

With a smile, she stepped away from the open hatch of the new pod she'd slipped into, two stacks up and on the other end of the row from the original one. The security forces shouted when they found it empty, and confusion reigned in the growing smoke. It was the perfect cover. She pressed the control panel on the side of the hatch to close it. It obediently thunked shut and sealed. She then hustled up to the front of the pod and tapped the controls to release it from docking. With another satisfying *thunk*, her new pod disengaged from its moorings and emitted automatic thruster bursts to push it away from the flagship.

CAG reached for her wristcom and tapped in a simple message to the rest of her crew: pickup. She could find them anywhere in the ship with her boarding pod. The thing would bore through crash metal if necessary. There was no need for them to come to her.

She trusted the message went through, guided her pod to a cloud of debris just off the large ship, shut down her power, and waited.

"We just need to get hull-side," Drake said when CAG's message come through as a series of taps on his wrist.

They were inside the crawlspace. Drake and Smith were leading the way toward the exit. Warren was assisting Idri, who had to take breaks every several meters, and Cheddar was bringing up the rear. They'd shut the access hatch behind them and taken this slower route in the hope that the Paragon would figure they'd used the front door to escape. That might buy some time and put them behind the search line.

Drake was having serious doubts about Idri's ability to travel. Though she insisted she was fine, she was not. It would be a struggle for her to maintain consciousness until the sedatives wore off. They had no idea how long that would take.

"Just a little way to go," Warren told her with a gentle nudge as she started to drift during their most recent break.

The exit hatch was in sight. Drake slipped ahead of Smith and crawled the rest of the way to it. He paused and listened carefully to the corridor beyond. The alarm still blared, but he couldn't hear anything beyond that. It seemed quiet. Gently and carefully, he grabbed the two inside handles and pushed it open. The deck was crimson, which was apparently the universal color for "Alert!" but it was empty. He motioned for Smith, Idri, Warren, and Cheddar to hurry through. Who knew how long the quiet would last?

After he'd slipped out and was standing with his rifle at the ready so the others could exit, Drake felt another tap from his wristband. At first, he thought it was CAG with a follow up message, but he realized it was different. He recognized it, though.

Tap-tap, tap-tap-tap.

Tap-tap, tap-tap-tap. It made him look down at the device hidden beneath his Paragon armor. Tap-tap, tap-tap-tap.

He shouldered his rifle and configured his wristcom to send the same signal back.

"I think it might be advisable just to carry her," Smith said, breaking Drake's concentration.

He looked up. Idri was out of the crawlspace and leaning against Warren with her full weight, head lolling on his shoulder. "We could give her the stimulants," Warren said with a gesture at the armor that was still bundled and strapped to his back. Doc had sent them each with a little packet of injectables, anticipating that Idri would likely be drugged.

"Just carry her for now," Drake said, shaking his head. "It's probably best to let her body work out whatever's still in her system. Save the stims for if we really need them."

Warren nodded, hoisted the small Navid without so much as a grunt and slung her over his shoulder.

Goddammit, Drake was worried about her, but the mission stayed the same: get her off this ship and to Doc ASAP. If anyone were to give her more drugs, it was best that it was him. Drake pointed down the corridor to their left. "The outer hull is that way, I believe. CAG is waiting to pick you up wherever you are, so when you get to the edge of the ship, call her in."

"Sir?" Smith asked with an arched eyebrow. "Where will you be?"

Drake looked down at the small bump his wristcom made in his suit, then back at the Marine. "I'm going after Markus."

"What?!" Warren bellowed too loudly. He lowered his voice before Drake could give him a dirty look. The soldier's eyes burned with fury. "Captain, he's not worth the energy of the plasma bolt he deserves through his face."

Drake shook his head even though half of him agreed with the lieutenant. "I can't just leave him," he said, voicing the other half, and wishing it wasn't the side winning.

"Why, sir?" Warren was at a loss.

Drake ground his teeth, already hating the decision. "No man left behind," he said, simply.

Warren fell silent. "We'll wait for you at the pod," he said after a long, anguished beat.

"You will do no such thing," Drake told him. "You will get Idri off this ship. That is an order."

"Captain, I will come with you," Smith said.

Again, Drake shook his head. "Warren already has his hands full, Marine. He needs you more than I do. You will both take Idri off this ship."

The two men were torn. Pausing in the red corridor, exposed, was excruciating. "Move," Drake insisted, unslinging his rifle. "That's another fucking order."

He headed down the corridor to the right, letting the taps on his wrist guide him.

THE OLD MAN was apparently close.

Drake felt the frequency of the wrist taps quicken not far from where they'd entered the crawlspace. It was around the corner, where the secured checkpoint had been . . . which was now empty and abandoned. Idri *had* been the prize they were protecting. With her on the lam, those guards were scouring the ship, looking for her. A stroke of good fortune. It seemed Idri hadn't been the only prize they'd been protecting.

Drake slipped past, looking carefully for cameras or motion detectors he would trigger, but he saw none. Didn't mean there *were* none, just that he couldn't see them. *Move fast and careful.* That was the strategy.

He rounded another bend in the corridor and came within spitting distance of two Paragon guards. He already had his finger on his trigger. *Blam, blam.* The two guards dropped to the deck without firing a shot. They weren't stripers. These were regular troopers. Another stroke of luck, Drake figured. The stripers would not have been caught flat-footed.

Drake regarded the door they'd been guarding. It was locked from the outside, and Drake's wristcom was tapping furiously now, screaming "In there! in there!" He looked at the door's controls but quickly abandoned them since he couldn't read Paragon. He stepped back, raised his rifle, and shot the damn thing in what he figured was the power supply. Obediently, the doors hissed open. Good. Apparently, they worked the same as Fleet doors and were designed to open using gravity when power was cut.

It was dark inside.

"Markus," Drake hissed as he stepped inside, rifle raised and finger next to the trigger. His wristcom was tapping near-continuously now. At the very least, Markus' wristcom was inside. Markus had to be too, since it had been activated. "Markus!"

"Captain?" the old man called from the rear of the room.

It was pitch-black back there, but as Drake stepped cautiously forward, he caught sight of two glowing kaleidoscope eyes. Relief washed over him. "Markus," he called. "It's me."

Markus and his distinct eyes stepped forward, catching the glow of a light strip in the wall nearby.

Except it wasn't Markus.

It was a towering figure dressed in Paragon military finery, pristine white with ornate gold and red threads woven in complex and ornate patterns. It had an ostentatious gold helmet on its head, red plume erupting from the top, and a thin severe line across the eyes. It was a uniform Drake knew from decades of battle.

Hadras.

Drake yelled and fired on pure instinct. The shot struck the archgeneral in the face. He bellowed and his helmet flew off, clanging off the wall behind him. Drake stepped forward to fire again, seizing a moment he'd waited so long for: to burn this monster so full of holes he could never cause anyone harm again.

He was slammed to the floor from behind.

Two bodies piled on top of him. Guards. Had to be. Drake fought for his life. He fired wildly around the small room before a giant fist crunched down on his trigger finger, and the rifle was kicked away. Drake grabbed the fist and the arm it was connected to and wrenched them with his entire body weight. He felt a snap and heard a grunt above him. The weight pinning him down rose, and he surged to his feet.

Slam!

He was tackled onto his chest, and this time two iron arms wrapped him in a full nelson. He heard the unmistakable click and whine of a rifle being charged to fire.

"Wait!" came Markus' voice. He said something in Paragon before returning to Standard. "Wait. Don't shoot him. Not yet, anyway."

Drake was hauled to his feet in one swift motion without the hold abating in the slightest. The pressure on his neck and shoulders was excruciating. In front of him was one of the two guards who'd tackled him, the one whose arm he'd broken, holding a charged rifle in his good hand and looking like he *really* wanted to waste Drake then and there. He was huge. Bigger than even Hadras' personal guard, un-helmeted, and with two piercingly blue eyes. He wore the Paragon insignia for a Second. Behind him . . .

Hadras stepped into view.

"Remove his mask," he told the Second, still speaking Standard. "I want him to see me."

A giant hand gripped the tight material and ripped it open. It tore like flesh, and Drake's helmet was gone. The guard behind Drake released him and poked his rifle butt sharply into his back in the same movement to make sure he couldn't react. It was all Drake could do to stand up straight.

The archgeneral was standing before him. He uniform and insignia were unmistakable. His face, like his Second's, was naked too. His helmet still on the deck somewhere from when Drake's shot had sent it flying.

But it was Markus. Markus was standing there in the uniform of an archgenenral.

Markus was Hadras.

His smile was cold and heartless. "It's so nice to finally, truly meet you, Captain."

CHAPTER SEVENTY-TWO

GLORY ROCKED under the incoming cruiser's attack. Half the stations on the command deck were charred ruins, and although repair crews were busily trying to swap them out, Carrol knew it wouldn't mean much if there was no power to run them. On her console, she could see that her fleet of transports and shuttles was docking. There were plasma pods on the vessels, but it had long been a question of whether *Glory* could last long enough for them to be unloaded and injected into her power systems so they could maneuver or fight back.

The answer to that question, it would seem, was no. If they were going to make a last stand, it would have to be now. Not later. They couldn't wait.

XO was on the horn, saying exactly that to Fredrickson in Engineering. "Everything you have," the commander told him, his tone grave and desperate. "It's come down to that."

"One barrage," Fredrickson told him. "And that eats most of our emergency battery power, which gives us about ten minutes of life support afterward."

XO nodded. It would have to do. If they didn't stop the

cruiser's attack, they were space dust anyway. "Thank you," XO told the engineer, then whirled toward the tactical station. "All weapons, on my mark," he called to them. "Helm! Bring us broadside."

Glory groaned under the stress of the maneuver, slight as it was. She didn't have much left, but "not much" wasn't nothing. Carrol sent out the call to her fighter squadrons to let them know *Glory* was about to fire and to coordinate an attack run in the aftermath. The response was disheartening. They'd do what they could, but they had their hands full with the cruiser's fighters and keeping them away from hitting *Glory* with their own bombing runs.

Carrol could feel the ship spinning up. Power levels surged, and the core, the heartbeat of the ship, roared. The lights on the command deck flared, previously dim or dead consoles flashed to life, and the deck trembled.

"Fire," Oh said.

The ship erupted. Every remaining weapon belched into the void and screamed toward the Paragon cruiser. Half the missile tubes were empty, but more importantly, half weren't. Carrol watched it all unfold on the overhead holoprojection: a thousand streams of smoke and light tracing an ever-tightening trail toward their target. The resulting explosion when they hit was enough to blind the scopes, as was the secondary explosion, which made Carrol's heart swell.

It had been enough!

Maybe it had been enough.

Glory whirred down. All lights went off, the floor was still, and deep within the ship, the core was silent. Empty. Spent. A moment later, dim emergency lights clicked on, bathing the smoky bridge in ominous energy-saving red light. They were down to expending the last of their battery power.

A few consoles flickered back to life, including Carrol's and the center station. On it, Oh had the forward scope view of the Paragon cruiser. It was still glowing white and overloaded, but the interference of the massive energy release was starting to abate. The image flickered, went awash with static, and then crystallized.

Carrol couldn't believe what she saw.

The cruiser, although on fire and clearly in critical condition, was still coming toward them. It wasn't firing anymore. It looked as though *Glory's* magnificent final barrage had deprived them of that ability, at least. But she was barreling at them. Ramming speed.

Someone on the command deck sobbed. Someone else joined them. XO, standing stock-still, eyes fixed on the image as if he couldn't believe it, just shook his head.

There were no options left. None.

"*Glory* flight control." The voice was coming from one of the loudspeakers on Carrol's console. Carrol realized her headset had come unplugged during the battle. "Requesting permission to land."

It was Zed. All eyes turned to him, or rather, the speaker his voice was coming out of. Carrol laughed and shook her head. She was about to press the transmit key and tell him to veer off and get far away from them when he transmitted again.

"Just want to remind you, Control, that I'm carrying no less than fifteen fully loaded plasma pods. Would be quite the fireball if something were to happen to it, so you let me know if I need to adjust course."

Carrol staggered as if she'd been slapped.

No . . .

"Don't talk nonsense," she said, diving toward the transmit button and slamming it down. "We have no ability to provide cover fire and clear a path, so an auto-course and bail isn't possible."

"I'm not talking about bailing."

Silence fell over the command deck.

"Navigation," XO said hoarsely from behind Carrol. "What would time to intercept for that shuttle and the Paragon cruiser be?" Carrol looked at the first officer, her panic rising. His expression was pained.

"The margin is only a second or two, Commander," was the answer. "But he might reach them in time."

"And is that a sufficient payload to head off the cruiser."

Tactical nodded.

Carrol stumbled. Her knees gave out, and she had to hold onto her chair to keep from crashing to the deck. Her head was swimming. XO stared at her. It was her pilot. Her call. On the console projection between them, the Paragon cruiser was bearing down.

"Control?" Zed asked over the loudspeaker, then softened his voice. "Eunice, are you there?" Her finger was still on the transmit button. He'd heard the reports. "Let me do this."

Carrol couldn't allow it to happen. No. *Absolutely fucking not* no Zed no it wasn't supposed to happen this way there was another way he was NOTGOINGTODOTHIS.

"Incoming shuttle," someone said, not Carrol. "You may adjust heading point-three-oh-seven, full throttle."

XO's mouth hadn't moved. No one's had, which meant it had to be her. She didn't understand. She would never give an order like that, not to the person she . . . Who she . . . didn't even get to say 'sorry.'

No.

"Acknowledged, Control. Adjusting course."

Zed's shuttle beelined for the oncoming cruiser on the command display. Carrol tried to watch it, but her vision was fuzzy. She had to sit down, but she wanted to stand. Wanted to watch what she'd done.

Zed was still transmitting. Static cut through as sporadic unaimed weapons fire ripped past the shuttle. The Paragon had seen him and surmised the truth; he was a threat. He had enough of a payload to destroy the ship if he hit it in the right place, like in the stern, back near the power core. They had to shoot him down before he did, but it was too late. Breathing heavily and cursing as he banked his shuttlecraft in one astonishing maneuver after another, Zed flew like the fucking wind. He dodged every bullet, every blast, everything they threw his way.

"Woohoo!" he shouted, sounding gleeful as he shot past the nose of the cruiser and strafed its underside. "I can see —" His transmission cut off.

Time slowed as the shuttle made a tight loop and aimed at the cruiser's soft underbelly. Carrol watched in horror, wanting to scream. No. This wasn't right. But the shuttle finished its graceful loop, flared its engines in one final burst, and slammed into the cruiser going several hundred meters per second.

Boooooooommmmmmmm!

Screens went white. *Glory* bucked backward, slapped by the shockwave.

Carrol fell to the deck, backed up against her console, and stayed there. When the command deck settled, everyone was deathly quiet.

"Tactical," XO said, piercing the silence.

"Target destroyed."

A roar erupted from the crew, then people hugged, shouted prayers of thanks to that pilot and the sacrifice he'd made, clapped other crew members on the back, and wept— a cacophony of gratitude, relief, and joy. She was vaguely aware that XO was giving orders.

Carrol watched it all like she was an alien. Distantly, she knew she should be sharing in the celebration or weeping on the floor or screaming at the image of the destroyed Paragon cruiser, which was a slowly expanding cloud of debris, and Zed along with it.

She could do none of those things. She'd left her body.

XO stood in front of her sometime later, asking if she could scramble more shuttles.

Shouldn't they be evacuating?

No. They were staying. Something about a boarding party, a rescue.

It was all so far away, like he was talking to somebody else, and she could hardly hear. Shuttles and troops. Could she help him get it organized? They had just enough time.

Her body rose. She heard herself speak, but it wasn't her. Carrol was still floating away. Becoming nothing. Whatever was still on *Glory* saying yes, sir and this and that and sending shuttles to rescue people was someone else.

That was fine with her.

She felt like nothing.

Carrol didn't exist anymore.

Carrol was dead, just like Zed.

CHAPTER SEVENTY-THREE

"It was you."

Drake stood motionless, his mind reeling as all the pieces fell into place. Markus hadn't been used by Hadras. He hadn't been coerced or victimized. His hand hadn't been forced. He *was* the abuser. He was the coercer, and he was the force. This had been his plan. He was the conductor and the orchestra.

"But you were a prisoner. They beat you. You . . . helped me save my ship."

"A gambit. One which had to be followed through until we had her."

He meant Idri, of course. It was dizzying, everything he'd done to get her; everything he'd risked *personally*. "You almost died."

Hadras gave a small, self-hating smile. "I was uniquely qualified to play the part."

Yes. Because he looked human.

Looked human.

He was not. And Drake was fool for ever thinking so.

More guards poured in from the back of the room, and

Drake's hands were bound. It roused him, and he used his free fingers to tap a quick message on his wristcom. *GO*. They were already supposed to have done that, but Drake knew those two bastards would wait if he gave them any reason to.

GO! Hadras saw the movement and reached around to rip the wristcom off his hand. Drake took the opportunity to head-butt him in an attempt to break his face.

The archgeneral shouted in pain and surprise and staggered back. The striper behind Drake jammed the barrel of his rifle into Drake's back so hard, he doubled over in pain.

He waited to die.

He heard rifles being raised and more voices shouting. The end was coming. Drake straightened, refusing to be cut down hunched over.

Much to his surprise, Hadras' voice stopped them. *"Do not shoot him,"* he said, enunciating each word carefully. The archgeneral spoke through a hand pressed to his bleeding nose. Not profusely, which was a big disappointment, but Drake had hurt him more than enough to warrant being shot dead, if simply *being* in this place wasn't enough. But it wasn't, not for Hadras.

The archgeneral accepted a piece of fabric from his Second and used it to replace his hand. "You can't kill me," Drake said when he realized. "Because I saved your life."

A flash of cold fire appeared in the archgeneral's eyes. That was it, and he wasn't happy about it. It made his displeasure with being saved take on a much more chilling tone in retrospect. "Believe me, Captain," he said, voice tight and dark. "That was not part of the plan."

Drake mustered a significant amount of satisfaction from that. Even caught so unawares, he'd managed to fuck it up for the bastard in some small way. Maybe not so small. "Neither was losing the shipyards, I bet."

Hadras was impassive. The cold fire was gone. "Unfortunate," he conceded. "But not unforeseen. Its destruction was still calculated to be sufficient to tip the balance of the war."

He dabbed at his nose. It had finally stopped bleeding. He held the cloth out to and handed it back to his Second, disgusted at the sight of his blood. Drake noted it; the self-loathing hadn't been an act. "Boastfulness is offensive to the Light," he continued, "but . . . " and he leaned forward again as close as he dared. "I think you will find that there is *nothing* that we have not foreseen."

In the closeness, Drake could see past the mask of impassive superiority. He could see the cold fire still burned behind it. He saw what stoked it, and he understood. If only he'd seen it sooner.

"It still won't make you one of them," Drake said, almost a whisper. "You'll never be Paragon, Markus."

It wasn't a taunt. It was the truth. One he knew the archgeneral would never accept.

In a move so lightning-fast Drake wouldn't have believed it possible from his old body, Hadras tore his Second's plasma rifle from his hands, cocked it, and pointed it at Drake's insolent face. His finger quivered on the trigger. It was clear that he wanted very much to pull it. Drake briefly considered if he was wrong to have given the old man such truth. Hadras *would* do it. He would kill him right there, heaven be damned.

Instead, in another lightning-fast move, Hadras whipped the butt of the rifle around and smacked Drake in the side with it, right in the spot where the asteroid shard had stabbed him, freshly stitched up by Doc. Drake gasped in pain and doubled over. When he was able to look back up, he saw Hadras was cold again, like a stone.

The Second approached the archgeneral. He whispered something into his ear; Drake caught only tones, like song. When he finished his message, he acknowledged and dismissed him, then stooped to pick up his helmet. He looked at Drake when he straightened.

"I was hoping you'd bring the girl with you when you came for me," he said, running a finger over the blackened streak where Drake had shot the helmet. "It would have been so neat and orderly that way. But you are messy. Humans are messy. Which is why all the planning and scheming is so necessary to make sure it goes right."

He blinked. "Which it has." He donned his helmet. "She has been intercepted, along with your friends. Would you like to see them before they die?"

Drake's heart sank.

Hadras registered it. "I wouldn't be too hard on yourself," he said with feigned sympathy. "The best traps are laid in broad daylight, and we walk into them anyway."

"Fuck. You."

Hadras once again took one of his Second's rifle, and this time shot Drake in the foot with it. The captain bellowed in pain. "My ledger may not allow me to kill you," Hadras said. "But for every curse you issue in my presence, I will shoot a new hole in your body. Do you understand?"

All Drake could do was moan.

"Good." Hadras handed back the rifle. "Now. Let's go kill your friends."

CHAPTER SEVENTY-FOUR

WARREN, Smith, Idri, and Cheddar had been caught within sight of the exterior bulkheads. As Drake, still bound and limping from the shot to his foot, was half-walked, half-dragged toward the foursome. He could see portholes to the stars and the chaos outside. The two men, meanwhile, were being held—kneeling on the deck, Paragon disguises ripped off at the helmet like Drake's—by no fewer than twenty troopers with rifles drawn. Idri was still unconscious, head against Warren and body limp. Cheddar was hunkered down next to Smith, teeth bared but still. They'd been so close. It made Drake furious all over again.

"The girl is unharmed?" Hadras asked when he reached the prisoners. It wasn't clear if he was asking them or his guards. The archgeneral clarified by slapping Warren across the face. He jumped to his feet, ready to return the assault, but two red-striped troopers intercepted him and twisted his arms behind his back while he half-stood, half-crouched.

Warren gestured at Idri, who had slumped against the bulkhead when he stood. "She doesn't look unharmed to me." The soldier's eyes widened as he caught Hadras' eyes and locked gazes with him. Recognition. He looked at Drake aghast, searching for confirmation. Drake nodded. Yes, it *was* who he thought it was. "You *bastard*," he finished.

If Drake thought his rage and betrayal were deep, it was nothing compared to Warren's. The giant man's face went purple, and from the quiver in his body, Drake knew he was going to do something that would end his life then and there. He was about to shout at him to stand down and save it for a better time, but in a remarkable display of self-control, Warren restrained himself. Drake didn't know how, but he was impressed. "I saved your life," he said, horrified and trembling.

"Our ledger is clean," Hadras told him, face stoic and impassive. "It is true, you saved me in the snow. I saved you on the shuttle dock. I owe you nothing."

"You saved me from a situation you yourself created. It's not quite the same."

Anger flashed over Hadras' face, and Drake realized it was a cover for something else. Guilt was a reach, but maybe not. Did the archgeneral, deep inside, feel remorse? It was impossible to tell because on the surface, there was only anger bubbling beneath his skin, waiting to explode. He stepped back, and indicated to his guards that they should do the same. They formed a firing line.

"As much as I would love to discuss our time together more in-depth," he said, "my engineers keeping an eye on the gate that's about to explode tell me that we don't have the time." He addressed his guards. "Take the girl."

A pair of guards surged forward and snatched her from the deck. Warren caught Drake's eyes as they did. He was staring at him intently, trying to communicate something. Drake frowned. What was it? Warren glanced down at the deck, then back up at Drake. Drake followed the look. As he did, Warren moved a boot aside, and beneath it was crushed ... plastic or glass. And a tiny needle.

A syringe.

Realization slammed into Drake. The stimulants. Warren had injected Idri. She was probably awake already. Good man. They just needed an opportunity to catch Hadras and his twenty guards off-balance ...

As if the prayer had been mainlined to God himself, such an opportunity came a second later.

From down the hallway, just a stone's throw away, something small and round rolled into view. Drake recognized it—a Fleet-issued combination flash and smoke bomb on a five-second fuse. Its pin had been pulled. Drake counted. Four ... five ... He pinched his eyes closed.

It exploded with white light, and smoke billowed from the corridor.

The deck beneath them rocked from the concussion, and the firing line of guards staggered, confused, and turned to face the intrusion. There were shouts from the hull-side corridor, and from the slowly-clearing smoke came plasma fire. Fleet troops. From *Glory*. Drake caught his ships' insignia on a flash of armor.

"Now, Idri!" He shouted as he slammed into the arch-general, bound hands, bum foot, shoulder, side and all, using his body weight to trip the old man and knock him to the deck. Hadras bellowed for his men to fire, but they had their hands full with the invading forces.

Drake hit the deck with Hadras squirming under him, and saw Idri's eyes flash open. She cried out in unbridled fury, and Drake felt the space around them ripple and flex, then tear.

Crack!

There was a sound like a thunderclap. Drake was tossed into the air. Screams. Splatter as bodies exploded around him. Drake was slammed down, but he didn't hit the deck again. He continued to fall. His ears were barraged by the sound of tearing metal, and he fell into the screeching and rending darkness, sliding, tumbling, and clawing in free fall.

Slam!

He hit something face-first hard and tasted blood again. Then . . .

Darkness.

CHAPTER SEVENTY-FIVE

"Boarding parties are in."

XO acknowledged the report.

He'd disobeyed Drake's orders. They hadn't hightailed it for the gate the second they'd refueled. He couldn't do it. He couldn't just leave Drake over there, nor could he fail to stay and gather the stragglers still trying to flee. The fighters, shuttles, and carriers not currently engaged with the Paragon flagship were sweeping every last nook and cranny. No one would be left behind, not while there was still time.

Speaking of which . . .

"Time?"

Expert minds elsewhere in the fleet had been keeping an eye on that. The gate, apparently, was building a feedback loop with an eminently predictable progression. Everyone fleeing or preparing to flee had a countdown clock.

"Twenty minutes, sir," the crewman answered.

Well. There it was. A hard out. Go time.

"Comms, send out system-wide message. Twenty minutes. That's the last ship out." The rest of the Fleet had withdrawn or was doing so. The Paragon fleet, too. Only *Glory* and the *Scythe were* left. Somehow, that seemed right.

"Come on, Cap," he whispered, imagining Drake on the other side of the void, fighting for his life. "We'll wait as long as we can."

CHAPTER SEVENTY-SIX

DRAKE WAS STILL.

It was dark. Gone were the screaming, the tearing metal, and the weapons fire. Slowly, painfully, he became aware of activity above him. Shouts. Words. *Far* above him.

"Captain?" called someone Drake could finally understand. They had been calling for a while. "Are you down there, sir?"

Drake groaned. Or maybe he stopped groaning. He wasn't sure. He put his still-bound hands on the hard thing that had stopped his fall and felt the sharp texture of catwalk grating. It hurt to do so, but he pushed against it to roll over and face the person above him.

Light. Blinding, but only at first. His eyes adjusted. It was still dark. He couldn't see who was calling to him. There was stuff in the way. Wires, bent and torn metal, girders and beams. And an overhead corridor light inches from his face that had collapsed along with the ceiling.

He'd fallen two or three decks. The twisted, mangled mess of a hole stretched a dozen meters above him.

"Can you hear me, Captain?" It was Warren. He was up where Drake had fallen from, calling down.

"I'm here" he responded as loud as he could. "What happened?"

"The deck collapsed when Idri jumped the guards into each other. All of them. At once."

Well, shit. That would create quite the explosion. "Is she okay?"

"She's all right, sir. Worried about you."

"Was that a boarding party from *Glory* I saw, Lieutenant? Right before the jump?"

"Yes, sir. I have the rescue team right here with me, and there are several more at various points of the ship."

"You take her and you go right with them," Drake called, putting a lot of effort into getting to his feet. That didn't work, so he let himself sink to his back on the floor. "Get her off the ship, Warren. Smith, Cheddar, all of you."

"We're going to figure out a way to come down and get you, Captain. You seem to be somewhere no one else is going to be able to get to."

"Goddammit, Lieutenant! How many fucking times do I have to order you to get the hell out of here? Do it. I'll find my own way out."

"With all due respect, sir," said someone else. Their voice was higher, not Warren's baseline rumble, but it was steely, nonetheless. "We can't do that. I *won't* do that."

"Idri," Drake said, dropping the bluster, the rank, and orders. He didn't need them. All he needed was the truth. "We're out of time, and you're more important than me. You have to go to safety, Idri, away from here. I need you do to that for me."

A long pause. Then, "Yes, sir."

Good soldier.

"And, sir?" It was Warren again.

"What?"

"We don't have eyes on Hadras, sir. I think he may have fallen down there with you."

That brought things into focus for Drake. He rolled onto his chest and used both hands to push up into a plank, brought his knees forward, and finally got to all fours. "Understood," he shouted. "Go."

"I'll wait for you as long as I can," Idri called. She sounded emotional. So had Warren, for that matter. That was their prerogative.

"Fine," he said, willing himself to his feet. "Now, go!"

He had to get to the edge of the ship. Maybe be lucky enough to run into a group of his troops. The problem was he had no idea where the hell he was. Pipes. Catwalks. Even steam. He was in the bowels of the *Scythe*. It looked like heat processing and possibly water treatment or storage. It was humid, hot, and empty.

Drake found a jagged, twisted piece of metal from the collapse, cut through his bindings, and shed the rest of his stolen Paragon armor. He was pleased to discover his limbs all worked. His foot still hurt like a mother, and that shoulder was iffy, but he was able to use both. A few moments later, he was walking. Hobbling, more like, but moving. He wasn't immobile.

"Hadras!" he shouted. With the congestion of pipes and tanks around him, his voice didn't carry far. There was no answer. Drake looked for a weapon, perhaps a misplaced tool. Nothing appeared in his immediate vicinity, even with the cave-in above.

Which way to go? The catwalk he'd smacked into went off in four directions, their paths only visible a few meters into the maze of pipes. Drake was still disoriented from the fall. He had no idea which way was which and which direction led to the outer hull. He picked the way he was facing. Why not? There was no way to know.

A few paces in, Drake found an arm-length piece of busted pipe on the catwalk. He picked it up and found it had a decent heft. He figured it was a good omen and continued on.

As the stars would have it, it was apparent Drake had picked the right direction.

After two minutes of walking and running into dead-ends, Drake saw a porthole at the end of a straight catwalk. The edge of the ship. He rushed forward, gritting his teeth at the pain of his foot. When he reached the porthole, he pressed against it and looked out. He could feel vibrations in the hull of the ship. Movement. Clanging. He looked up and saw he was directly beneath a docking port, and there was a ship attached. A Fleet ship. He was below one of the troop carriers. He saw flashes of flurried activity through the one-size-fits-all airlock and its tiny windows.

"Hey!" he shouted, pounding. "*HEY!*"

There was nothing to carry his voice to the deck above. They couldn't hear him, and they wouldn't. He had to get up there. He pushed off from the porthole and looked around wildly.

Stairs. There were stairs five or six meters to his right, and they led up. Drake had taken one step toward them when he was struck from behind. The vicious blow was meant for his head, but his movement had made it only clip it. The brunt of the blow landed on his shoulder instead. The bad one.

He moaned and crashed to the catwalk. Everything went fuzzy, the deck felt like it had tilted and was swinging, and he struggled to breathe. His fall had knocked the wind out of him. A foot slammed into his ribs, throwing him against a rail. He looked up, and his vision cleared.

Hadras was standing over him. He had a pipe in his hands.

CHAPTER SEVENTY-SEVEN

"Ten minutes, sir."

Oh nodded. It would take the boarding party's shuttles five minutes to return and land. *Glory* had another three minutes to bum-rush the gate. Two minutes to run on the other side. He'd never seen a gate explode, but he had to imagine it would send a hell of a lot of energy through the other side in addition to destroying its own side. *Glory* didn't want to be caught in that.

"Idri, Lieutenant Warren, Smith, and the canine are on a transport," the reporting crew member added.

"The captain?"

The young man shook his head. "The carriers must return if we are to leave in time, Commander."

The command deck was silent.

It hollowed Oh out, but he had to say it. "Then they must return." He nodded at the comms crewman. "Give the order."

Oh hung his head. He glanced at Carrol and the void in her from Zed's loss. He knew about them. He was the XO and supposed to know that stuff, but they worked well together. If it ain't broke... But how would *Glory* work without her captain? Oh stared at the deck but found no solace and no answers.

CHAPTER SEVENTY-EIGHT

Drake reacted by instinct. He used every ounce of his strength and swung at the attacking Hadras, hardly remembering that he too was holding a pipe. It connected with a wicked crack, and Hadras fell, then toppled backward.

Drake tried to jump back to his feet, but the movement was far too fast. His head screamed, and a lack of balance threatened to spill him onto the catwalk. He grabbed a nearby pipe and arrested his fall. The pipe was burning hot, and Drake yelped in surprise.

Hadras laughed. It was an utterly foreign sound that took a second to register as laughter. Drake couldn't recall seeing the old man do such a thing. It was maniacal and sadistic. He hobbled a few feet away, gingerly touching his shin where Drake had smacked him. He was between Drake and stairs. He wasn't laughing at Drake's mishap with the hot pipe. He was looking through the porthole. He pointed for Drake to see.

The troop transport had disengaged from the airlock.

It was returning to *Glory*.

Without him.

Hadras dangled something. A bracelet. *Drake's wristcom.* He dropped it to the deck and stomped on it with his boot, destroying it with a definitive *crunch.* "So much for 'no man left behind,'" Hadras said, grinding it into the grating with a turn of his heel.

It was Drake's turn to laugh. He gestured to the leaving transport. "She's getting away," he said. "Idri's on that shuttle."

But Hadras only grinned. "Also not unforeseen. Similar to the shipyards, Captain, possession of the girl was not the only option for turning the tide."

Drake felt his heart stop. Realization drenched him like cold water. "You . . . did something to her."

Hadras' kaleidoscope eyes twinkled. "Maybe."

"Maybe?"

He shook his head, still grinning like a maniac. "You'll have to wait and see, won't you?" He laughed again. "I'm not going to tell you anything you don't already know, Drake. No." He moved back and forth in the space between them, crouched, readying to strike again. "Not until everything is all played out."

He swung.

Drake dove past him, underneath the blow, and swiped again at the archgeneral's legs. He connected again. Exactly where, he wasn't sure. He hit the deck in a roll and cried out in pain as his bad shoulder took the brunt of the impact. Groaning, he rolled over, flailing the pipe with his good arm to fend off any follow up attack from Hadras. But the archgeneral hung back, hobbling now on both legs. Drake's diving blow had struck home.

Drake hauled himself to his feet. The shoulder wasn't dislocated again. It only hurt like a mother.

Hadras ground his teeth and tried to shake off his own pain. "You can't beat me, captain," he said, chest heaving.

Drake was gasping as well. "And you can't kill me."

"There are so many things worse than death."

Hadras slowly began to circle. Drake gripped his weapon and mirrored opposite of him.

"The things I'm going to make you see, Drake," Hadras continued, consumed with the point he was making. "You have no idea. Freepoint is just the beginning. And you'll be there to witness it all. So, annoying as it is, perhaps its better this way. You will be there for the end, to know, truly, that you were *beaten*."

"None of that has happened yet."

The archgeneral's insane eyes flashed maniacally. "It will. I have foreseen everything."

Drake swung. It surprised Hadras, and Drake's swing connected half on his neck, half on his chin. He staggered. So did Drake, from the effort. Bellowing with naked rage, Hadras lowered his head and shoulder and launched into Drake's midriff.

As he made contact, Drake twisted so he would land on top of the old man when they crashed to the deck. Hadras took the brunt of it, smacking the back of his head against the metal grate. Drake's wrist smacked the grating as well, and his pipe clattered away. Before he could roll off to get it, Hadras raised his weapon and swung.

Drake caught it before it hit his temple.

Hadras snarled and seized the pipe with his other hand, attempting to wrench it away from Drake. Drake mirrored the move, grabbing it with both hands as well. The two grappled for position, but Drake had the upper hand. He was on top. And Hadras, perhaps, wasn't as strong as he would be otherwise; he'd sacrificed much of his body in his charade as Markus. With a snarl, Drake pivoted at the waist and leveraged his body weight to twist the pipe lengthwise in line with the old man's shoulders, perpendicular to his neck.

Drake threw everything he had left into the pipe, driving it down toward Hadras' neck. The old man took the opportunity to slam his forehead into Drake's face. Pain bloomed from his nose. Fucker got him right in the same spot he'd headbutted him. Favor returned. But Drake didn't relent.

He pushed harder. Hadras resisted, but the pipe continued to descend. Hadras screamed, thrashed, and pushed back against Drake, but the pipe inexorably moved lower. The screams became gurgles and Drake looked into the archgeneral's face. His eyes were wide to the point of bulging, and his skin was starting to turn purple.

He was dying.

"Did you . . ." Drake gasped and pushed down as hard as he could, "foresee— . . . *THIS*?"

As Hadras squirmed and choked, Drake could see that he had not. This unplanned for. Perhaps even shocking. That made Drake as happy as anything ever had. He pressed harder, finding reserves he didn't know he had.

The bulkhead behind them exploded.

Drake tumbled head over heels, slamming into boiling-hot pipes. He finally came to rest against the stairs he'd been trying so hard to get to. Blearily, he looked back at where the explosion had come from. Something was poking through the side of the ship with big, spiky metal claws. Smoke and debris billowed from the breach. A squat and sturdy figure stepped onto the catwalk.

"You need a ride, Cap?" CAG called.

Drake could have kissed her. He stumbled to greet her,

but his injuries were now far more numerous than the foot. She caught him. "Am I glad to see you!" he gasped. "How did you find me?"

"Your wristcom, sir. Didn't get a ping on it for a while, then a flash saying it had been damaged."

When Hadras had smashed it under his boot, he'd unknowingly made it ping. A built-in feature if it was damaged or destroyed.

"I was looking for you when I heard everyone else had been found. Lucky you were right out on the edge of the ship."

Drake nodded, then looked around. "Where is he? Hadras?"

CAG shrugged. "Didn't see no one, sir."

"He's still here, then."

"Don't mean to rush you with whatever you were doing here, Cap, but we need to *go*. Everyone's heading out. Now!" Drake let the sturdy officer drag him back into the Paragon breaching pod while he peered down the catwalk's corridors, looking for the bastard. "You okay for me to let you go?" she asked him once they were inside the pod. Drake nodded, and she slipped out from under him. He braced himself against the inside seal of the breaching hatch as she motored up to the front of the craft, readying to seal them back up, retract those breaching claws, and wrench the ship out of the *Scythe's* hull.

Then he saw the archgeneral.

He was standing in the middle of the long, straight corridor. He had a plasma rifle in his hands. Where he'd found it, Drake couldn't fathom. The old man's face was bare, helmetless, and contorted with rage. "This is only the beginning!" he screamed down the corridor, then raised the rifle.

He fired before Drake could dive out of the way. The bolt struck him in the shoulder and sent him stumbling back. Before Drake hit the deck, the airlock doors on the pod slammed shut, and the craft broke away from the Paragon ship's hull.

For a moment, Drake wondered how he could be alive, but when he realized he was, with great difficulty he clambered back to his feet and hauled himself to the rear hatch's window to peer behind them.

Like blood from a bullet hole, atmosphere and debris poured from the breach the pod had made. Smoke, steam, and sections of the catwalk were all sucked into space. Everything in the vicinity of the jagged hole. Drake even saw the pipe he'd nearly killed the archgeneral with spinning into the void.

But he didn't see Hadras.

The cloud of debris had been thick. Maybe his body had been sucked out before Drake had gotten to the window. It was possible, but there was no way to know.

"You all right back there, Cap?" CAG called from the front.

Drake, with colossal effort, pushed off from the hatch window and picked his way slowly, carefully, and achingly to the front of the pod. There was a second seat next to the pilot's, and Drake collapsed into it. "I'm fine," he said, feeling as though he just might sit there forever. He looked at his friend. "Thanks to you."

CAG shrugged off the sentiment. "No one left behind, right?"

Drake smiled. "Right."

"How're those?" she asked him with an eye to his nose and shoulder.

Drake looked at the latter. The bad one. It was smoking,

now, from Hadras' shot, though the Paragon suit seemed to have taken the brunt of it. The former felt broken. "Fucked up," Drake said, and put his head back on his seat. "But I'll live."

"Well, buckle up, because we have to do some real fancy flying here, Cap."

In the end, it was a combination of CAG's fancy flying and *Glory's* turning to meet them halfway that saved the day. That cut the intercept time in half, and while CAG still had to haul ass into the hangar bay and crash land, there was time afterward to crawl out of the smoking wreck of the Paragon breach pod and gather by the open cargo door to behold the end of the Freepoint gate.

The deckhands and flight crew were gathered there when Drake joined them. The yawning opening crackled with its nearly invisible atmospheric barrier, offering an expansive view of the disintegrating gate. The *Scythe* was running for her life. She dove through right as it went. The entire circle was in flames when the flagship hit the membrane, then *flash*. A blinding light more powerful than anything Drake had ever seen. It lit up the system like a second sun, casting shadows over the structures in the ship-yards, the minefield, and the fallen vessels, both Fleet and Paragon. An expanding sphere of energy bellowed forth from it, vaporizing everything that stood in its path.

As Drake watched Armageddon arrive, he felt the awe-inspiring sensation of he and his ship and everyone on it expanding with the universe like a cosmic breath, reaching out and touching everything, even the stars, to the edge of infinity and back again as Idri jumped them to safety.

THE FURSTON FUNNEL

Terran Federation Space

CHAPTER SEVENTY-NINE

"You really do need to return to your bed," Doc told Drake, annoyed with the captain's insistence on looking over his shoulder. Drake ignored the advice.

He was supposed to be getting regenerative treatments for the plasma bolts he'd taken in his shoulder and his foot, the stitches he'd knocked loose in his side, and a broken nose. It wasn't going to set perfectly, Doc suspected of the nose, even with the treatments, about where Drake had busted Hadras with blow of his own. Drake didn't mind. There was a symmetry to it. It made him wonder if the bastard had planned it that way.

But Drake was not getting his regenerative treatment. He was hovering over the good doctor's shoulder as their latest round of scans on Idri came in. She was alert and clear-eyed and looked annoyed on one of the more advanced bio-beds in *Glory's* Sickbay. They were with Jack's fleet—the ships that had survived and escaped, anyway, licking their wounds and regrouping in Furston's Funnel. More support was on the way, but the Paragon fleet seemed to have retreated under the cover of the explosion fallout that had poured through this side of the gate from Freepoint. This system was quiet for now.

Drake's first priority had been to get Idri checked.

"Normal," Doc said, letting out a relieved breath as the scan results came through. "All normal."

"I feel normal," Idri said, hands crossed impatiently over her midriff. Doc nodded and told her she could sit up. He unplugged suction cups from her forehead and temples as she did.

"No trace of the drugs in her system anymore, and I'm not seeing any long-term effects to her tissues." In places, the skin was being restored after the removal of the Paragon medical devices.

"What about anything else?" Drake asked. Hadras' insinuation that he'd done something to her rang in his memory. "Anything out of the ordinary."

Doc shook his head. "Nothing, Cap. She looks tip-top."

Drake nodded. She looked okay. Maybe the bastard had just been bluffing. That was possible. Anything was possible . . . "That's good. Good."

"It's excellent." Doc smiled at the young woman. "We were all very worried about you."

"I was worried about you, too," she said.

"I want to do more detailed scans when we get to the next Fleet facility," Drake said, wondering where that might be. Here and now, he would let it go. Idri was healthy. That was wonderful news. Drake glanced at the doctor. "If you would give us a moment," he asked.

"If you promise that afterward, you're heading right back to your own bed and finishing your treatment."

"Orders understood."

Doc bowed and retreated from the biobed, leaving Drake alone with the Navigator. "Idri . . ."

The young Navid braced herself. "Back to restricted duty?" she asked. She wasn't defiant. Resigned was more apt. And disappointed.

It caught Drake off-guard. "N-no," he stammered. "No, Idri, no."

She blinked. "I— . . . are you not about to tell me how foolish it was for me to have gone on the mission? You were right? And it was an unacceptable risk?"

Drake looked down and shook his head. "No. I am not going to say that." He lifted his head back up so he could look her in eyes. "Because it's not true. I was *wrong*, Idri. Not you. You saved my life over there. You saved all our lives."

"But you wouldn't have even been there if it weren't for me."

"You, Ship's Navigator, *are* probably the most coveted, most desired person in the galaxy at the moment, and that is not going to change. But that is also exactly why I was wrong. They fear you. Hadras is afraid of you, Idri, that's why he tried so hard to get you. And he should be afraid of you. Every one of our enemies, in fact, should be terrified."

Idri blinked again, this time with tears in her eyes. "Really?"

"Idri, you don't need protection. You protect *us*."

He straightened. "I could not see that, and it was my failing. Not yours. I offer you my sincerest, deepest apology. You are a full member of this crew . . . and I will not fail you again."

Idri let a single tear fall down the side of her face, then she wiped it away and straightened to match him. She aged years before Drake's eyes. "Thank you, sir," she said with a crisp salute that would have made a drill sergeant proud. "Apology accepted, sir."

Drake returned the salute.

"Captain," the doctor called from behind him. "If you are just about done bothering my other patients, one of my nurses is waiting for you over on Bed Fourteen."

Drake hid a smile. He wondered how much the doctor had heard. All of it, probably. He nodded at Idri, then turned.

"Coming."

THE MAIN HANGAR bay was in chaos.

Carrol walked through the mess of shuttles, fighters, transports, work bubbles, escape pods, and the multitude of other craft *Glory* had collected during its final sweep of the Freepoint facility as the last ship out. The crew was drowning under the task of sorting the shocked, frightened, and grateful personnel, to say nothing of cataloging the equipment. Queues at a hastily set-up series of check-in stations were hundreds deep, with people yelling into the cavernous space, trying to find their friends and loved ones.

She didn't need to be down there. It wasn't her duty shift. She'd floated through that until they were on the other side of the explosion and had been dismissed by XO to get some rest. She hadn't fought him on it. She hardly even remembered what she'd done during those hours. A hollow blur. Rather than rest, this is where she'd come, hoping against hope. She walked up and down the lines, scanning faces. Strangers, all of them.

He wasn't in there. He wasn't going to be among them because he was gone. He was dead.

She couldn't do it. The thought was overwhelming. Numbing. She felt nothing, which was far more terrifying than feeling because she didn't know if she would ever feel anything again. She didn't even want to. How was she going to live like that?

This had been a mistake. A horrible, horrible mistake.

She turned to leave and . . . there he was.

Zed.

In the middle of the chaos, covered in soot and grease, uniform tattered and burned, he was standing there, looking at her.

No.

She stared, sure it was a mirage or a ghost. A trick her mind was playing on her. She was going crazy. She couldn't handle it, and reality was breaking. Then he smiled at her, closed the distance between them, and reached out to hug her.

Instead, her legs collapsed, and he caught her as she fell to the deck.

Carrol gripped his arms with every ounce of her strength.

He was there.

He was real.

She emitted the kind of wail that only someone with a broken heart could. Her keening echoed through the hangar bay, and it made everyone in the chaos stop and think about the loved ones they'd lost.

Or nearly had.

And found again.

CHAPTER EIGHTY

Idri caught Warren in his quarters, putting the last of his sparse belongings into a duffel.

"You're leaving?" she asked, leaning against the half-open hatch.

He paused, looked down at his packing. "Yeah."

"Where to?"

"Um . . ."

She smiled and shook her head. "You can't tell me."

"Afraid I can't."

"So, you're not retiring?"

Warren straightened and cleared his throat. "No."

"How come?"

He shrugged but told her the truth. "I don't know, really. Another mission came up. I said yes. Like I always do."

She nodded and rocked back and forth on the shoulder she had pressed against the frame. "You know, you could stay here."

"No." Warren shook his head. He resumed packing his things.

"I see."

He looked at Idri and saw hurt in her eyes. Disappointment. "Kid," he said, then took a breath and let it out slowly, "if I ever did settle down with one crew, make roots in one place . . . " He looked around at the old walls and listened to the chatter of the crew members in the hall. "This would be the ship."

Idri nodded. He could tell she knew he meant it, but the sadness remained. She rocked her shoulder again on the frame. "I'm not a kid anymore," she said, looking at him.

He smiled. "No. You've turned into quite the soldier," he told her. "I seem to remember being somewhat skeptical about that once. I shouldn't have been."

Warren grabbed his bag and cinched the top. Idri stepped away from the threshold to let him through the hatch. He stepped through, paused, and then turned around to embraced her. She squeezed him back tightly.

"I'm going to miss you," she told him.

"Me too," he said.

He let her go. She stared at him with her big, big eyes until he cleared his throat, gave her one final 'goodbye' nod, and then left before she could change his mind.

———

ZED WAS ALL STITCHED UP. His burns were healing, as were the broken bones. Everything he'd suffered after bailing out of the shuttle at the last second and riding an EV booster pack at seven gees to run from the resulting explosion. A miracle he'd made it in one piece and another that he'd been found by an evacuation transport, one of the last to land before *Glory* jumped.

Carrol waited until the doctors and nurses and technicians were finished, then longer for Sickbay to clear as the casualties were taken care of or moved one by one. Eventually, with Doc tucked away in his office and the only other medics in the room over helping someone with some physical therapy, Carrol and Zed were alone.

"I can't do this," she told him, tears welling in her eyes.

"I know," he said.

It was too much, and not because of the sneaking, or the games, or the threat of a reprimand and her record or any of those things. None of that mattered. That was child's play that paled in comparison to the true reason. "I wanted to die," she said, thinking of the order she had to give.

"I understand."

"You do?"

"I do."

"You're not mad at me?"

He gave a sad shrug and a smile. "What can we do? It's too much for me too. For anyone." He looked down. "I put in a transfer request." He looked back up, afraid of what her reaction would be. "It's already been accepted, actually. I ship out as soon as I'm cleared by Doc. The *Intrepid*."

Carrol just nodded. "Good. That's . . . that's good."

"Yeah. Good."

He stood as if he was going to leave. Carrol stopped him with a hug and pulled him in for a kiss. It was passionate. "I love you," she said as she held onto him, trembling. "*I love you*. I'm so sorry, Zed. I was such a coward for not being able to say that to you. I have *always loved you*."

"Come on," he said as he kissed her back gently. "I know that." He took her by the shoulders so he could look at her. "I love you, too," he said.

Carrol felt tears falling down her face. "Then you have really terrible taste in women, because I'm an idiot."

"Why are you an idiot?"

"Because this feels so much better now that I *know* that I love you."

He wiped her tears away. "Okay, but you're a really *pretty* idiot."

She laughed and buried he face into his uniform. "That's so shallow," she said.

"You're the one in love with a fighter pilot, Commander. So."

She laughed again. And cried.

They held each other for a good long while. "What are we going to do?" she asked, eventually.

"I don't know," he answered, honestly.

Then they parted, eyes dry. She held his hand. He had to go. "We'll figure it out," he said.

"Okay," she said, not wanting to let go. "We'll figure it out."

———

"Come in, please, Commander."

Carrol didn't even have to knock. Drake knew she was standing awkwardly and fearfully outside his quarters. He'd summoned her and left his hatch open a crack. Through the sliver, she could see him sitting at his desk, going through paperwork, reports, transfers, etc. He didn't glance up at her, just motioned her inside. "And shut the hatch, please, on your way in."

She stepped through and closed the heavy metal door with a *clunk*.

Drake finally looked at her. "There was a lieutenant once," he started, folding his hands on the desktop. "I was an ensign at the time, and she hated me. We were assigned on a mission together, a consultant to the resupply team I was on, if I remember correctly, and I hated her right back. So, naturally, it wasn't long before the two of us were making out and then seeing each other whenever we could throughout that run. Then, of course, my CO caught wind and I nearly lost my commission."

Carrol wanted to shrink down small enough to crawl into the ventilation cover on the floor and disappear.

"People don't like being lied to," he said.

"Who else knows?"

"Everyone knows." He was furious.

Carrol swallowed, body at rigid attention. "It's over, sir."

"I know it's over. I signed the transfer papers myself."

"Of course, sir." Goddammit, of course he had.

"It's your men and women on this ship, Commander, that you're going to have to square yourself with."

"Yes, sir." Carrol swallowed again, not daring to look at him. A beat. "How, uh, did you square yourself, sir, back in the day?"

Another long beat. "I picked up KP for my squad for the next ninety days, which went a decent way toward my penance."

"I'm happy to do the same."

"I'd suggest you make it six months."

"Yes, sir. And, sir . . . " Carrol had to clear her throat to finish. "It won't happen again. I swear to you."

Drake sighed, which released the tension in the room. His expression softened, and he nodded. "I know," he said. He was still looking at her, now with understanding sympathy. "You really found out why the regulation exists, didn't you? It's not just an arbitrary bullshit rule written up by a desk jockey, is it?"

"No, sir."

"Are you okay?" The question was soft, and heartfelt.

Carrol had to clear her throat to answer. "I'm better now."

Drake swallowed. "I'm glad he's okay."

"Me too." There was another silence, then, "Sir, if I may?" Drake gestured for her to continue. "You and the lieutenant. Did . . . you love her?"

Drake sighed. "As a matter of fact, yes. I did."

"And what happened with you two?"

Drake smiled. "Oh, I married her."

Carrol's mouth opened in shock. Drake nodded to confirm what he'd said was true.

She sputtered. "I . . . I didn't know you were married, sir."

"I'm not married. Well, not to her anymore." He leaned back in his chair, an amused smug look creeping over his face. "And there's a whole lot you don't know about me, Commander."

He let the moment linger, then waved.

"Dismissed."

CHAPTER EIGHTY-ONE

THE HOLORECORDING WAS GRAINY, even with all the post-production and effects *Glory's* top communications specialists and Fredrickson's data retrieval experts could throw at. It was still nearly impossible to make out.

It was an image of the Freepoint gate on the Funnel side just as it was exploding. In the center of the image was a speck, a black dot that looked like the nose of a ship, and there had only been one ship heading through the gate when it blew.

"There's no way," Doc said, shaking his head at the image.

Admiral Jack stood next to him, similarly skeptical. "Even if it was, he's right at the membrane when the gate is blowing. It probably snapped him in half."

Drake, the final member of the trio, wasn't having it. He wasn't convinced, and he never would be. Not until there was incontrovertible proof.

"The radiation fallout from the explosion," Jack continued, "even the fraction of it that came through before the Funnel-side gate was severed, unfortunately, was the perfect cover for the Paragon ships to escape. It's unclear how many were able to get away, though I think it's safe to assume that most of them did. It's also probably safest to assume that the *Scythe* was one of them and that Hadras is still alive."

"He's alive." Drake reached over and shut off the recording. They weren't going to get anything else from it, and he didn't need to. He knew, deep in his gut, that the archgeneral was still out there. "He told me himself; he'd prepared for every contingency. I'm absolutely certain that included destroying the gate, and how much time he needed to get out of there if we managed to get Idri back."

"How is she?"

"Doc says she's in perfect health."

Jack nodded. "Lucky, then, I suppose."

Drake didn't think so. The loss of the shipyards was . . . well, devastating, as he'd predicted from the very start. Their ability to replenish the Fleet for the war ahead was now critically endangered, putting Earth and all her colonies at great risk. They had survived, yes, but Hadras had just handed them a *massive* defeat.

"You were right," Jack told him, seeing the torment Drake was putting himself through. "From the very beginning."

Drake shook his head. "No, I wasn't. I was wrong about what really mattered. That bastard set a trap for me that I fell right into."

Jack put a hand on his old friend. "A perfect trap." The admiral's echo of Hadras' words haunted Drake. "That we *all* fell into."

"But it all hinged on him," Drake said, still shaking his head. "The AI ship? Sure, that was a masterstroke. The type of bait it would be foolish to ignore. But none of it works, Jack, unless I believed *him*. Markus. And I did. He fooled me. *Me*. Not anyone else. If I'd seen through his bullshit, none of this would have happened."

"Drake," Jack said, putting some bass in his voice. "Now, I want you to listen to me, and listen to me good." He put his thumb and index a millimeter apart from each other and held them right up to Drake's face. "We were this close from absolute disaster. We could have lost *everything*; you, Idri, *Glory*, the entire damned fifth fleet, and the Paragon bastards could be setting up shop at Freepoint right now." He dropped his fingers. "But we didn't, did we? We survived. You destroyed that bastard's AI ship. You got back your Navigator. And the Paragon have scurried back to their hole to think very, very carefully about what their next move is going to be because they pissed us off and they'd *better* think carefully about their next move. And you know who made all of that possible?" He slapped the briefing room table. "You, you son of bitch. You, your ship, and your crew. So instead of sulking or thinking this was some kind of defeat, Captain, I need you pissed off and thinking about next time."

Drake swallowed and tried to accept it. "Next time, we'll be ready for him."

"You're goddamn right we will."

Drake looked up at the admiral. He was right. Next time was coming, of that Drake was sure. Hadras had said it himself: this was only the beginning.

And they all needed to be ready.

They would be ready.

"Next time," Drake said, "its payback."

Glory, Drake, and his crew will return in *Glory: Humanity's Warriors*
PRE-ORDER NOW ON AMAZON

IF YOU LIKED THIS BOOK, please leave a review. We love reviews since they tell other readers this book is worth their time and money. I hope you feel that way now that you've finished this first volume in what could be a six-book series. Please drop us a line and let us know you like *Glory*'s adventures and want them to continue. This is my new favorite series. I hope you agree.

Keep reading since we have a few extra tidbits just for you...

MORE FROM THE AUTHORS

If you liked this story, you might like a couple other military science fiction series that we recommend...

Battleship: Leviathan – One ship against many in a war that has lasted a thousand years...

AVAILABLE NOW ON AMAZON

Metal Legion - **Victory or death!** _Fight to survive_
by CH Gideon (Craig Martelle's pen name)

The complete set in one package – as much military science fiction adventure as your heart can handle. Aliens. Galactic conquest. Grunts. And firepower. Humanity learns that it's not the biggest or the baddest in the universe, but that doesn't stop them.

AVAILABLE NOW ON AMAZON

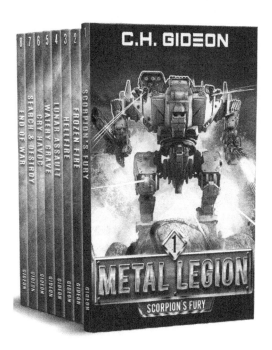

Starstuff – by Ira Heinichen

The galaxy is dying...

Starstuff is an epic space opera perfect for readers of any age.

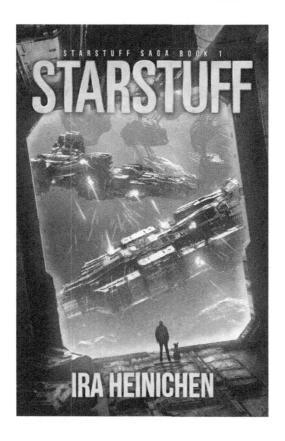

AUTHORS' NOTES

Ira Heinichen
Written November 5, 2022

First, the thank yous.

Thank *you* for reading this book.

Thank you, Craig Martelle, for shipping out with me yet again. You're the best collaborator a writer could ask for.

Thank you to Liz for your love, support, and feedback. I'd never get anything done without you.

Thank you to Cooper and Coco for being the perfect pups.

This one was quite the ride. A little longer than we'd expected, but we listened to where the story decided to take us. Our thought after the first book was that Glory needed a *villain*. Not just the faceless troopers, or the monolithic superiority of intolerance . . . but someone flesh and blood that we could fear. And respect. And maybe hate a little bit. Someone *devious*. Hopefully, we got close with Hadras. If we did, you'll probably see a lot more of him. And if we didn't . . . well, there are a lot more baddies among the ranks of the Paragon. Drake and his crew certainly have his work cut out for them.

There are more tales to come. I'd love to get them to you faster, and I'll tell you what's incredibly, deeply motivating in that regard: your reviews. My god, I am overwhelmed by the things you had to say for the first book. I can't speak for

Craig, but it certainly took me by pleasant surprise. I sincerely hope you enjoyed this book as well. If you did, please let us know. Write a review. It's the words so much more than the stars that mean the world.

It also means the world that you read this story.

Thank you.

———

Please join my Newsletter (iraheinichen.com), or you can follow me on Facebook, Twitter, and Instagram.

You can also email me anytime authorira [at] gmail.com – I would LOVE to hear from you. I try to answer every email I receive.

If you enjoyed this story, please consider leaving a review! I cannot adequately express how much seeing an encouraging review helps motivate me to write the next book.

Amazon—www.amazon.com/author/iraheinichen
Facebook—facebook.com/iraheinichen
Website—www.iraheinichen.com
Twitter—twitter.com/iraheinichen
Instagram—instagram.com/iraheinichen

———

Craig Martelle
Written November 5, 2022

Thank you all for joining us on this great ride conceived and executed by Ira (with a little dash of me).

It's been a long and fruitful year, considering this book came it at over 152,000 words to begin with and trimmed up to 143k. It's a massive beast, but every page is pulse pounding. Every page matters. Ira is a great storyteller. I'm glad he included me on this ride.

I lost a few people over the last year. As I get older, each makes a greater impact on my life. Learning to do without isn't an easy task, but we power forward because there's so much left to do for now and the future.

In a few days, I'll be traveling to Las Vegas for an annual convention that I run for authors of all shapes and sizes, in all genres. Most of the beta reading team comes and that's important to me. They do so much for my stories. Like other authors, too, who share news of *Glory* and all that she brings.

The series will continue! There's more to the universe that the Paragon, maybe there's another enslaved race that needs to be freed. We shall see over the next year what trials the crew is put through.

In the interim, if you liked *Glory*, then definitely give the completed series *Battleship Leviathan* a read. And if you've read both of those series, then try *Metal Legion*, another completed military science fiction series of mine. Coming in 2023 is *Starship Lost*, another military science fiction adventure with some post-apocalyptic elements thrown in. It should be a great ride.

And there we are. Another book finished, and I hope, a great way for you to enjoy a break from your everyday trials.

Peace, fellow humans.

***

Please join my Newsletter (craigmartelle.com—please, please, please sign up!), or you can follow me on Facebook.

If you liked this story, you might like some of my other

books. You can join my mailing list by dropping by my website craigmartelle.com, or if you have any comments, shoot me a note at craig@craigmartelle.com. I am always happy to hear from people who've read my work. I try to answer every email I receive.

If you liked the story, please write a short review for me on Amazon. I greatly appreciate any kind words; even one or two sentences go a long way. The number of reviews an eBook receives greatly improves how well an eBook does on Amazon.

Amazon—https://www.amazon.com/author/craigmartelle

BookBub—https://www.bookbub.com/authors/craig-martelle

Facebook—https://www.facebook.com/authorcraigmartelle

In case you missed it before, my web page—https://craigmartelle.com

Krimson Empire (co-written with Julia Huni)—a galactic race for justice

Zenophobia (#) (co-written with Brad R. Torgersen)—a space archaeological adventure

Battleship Leviathan (#)– a military sci-fi spectacle published by Aethon Books

Glory (co-written with Ira Heinichen) – hard-hitting military sci-fi

Black Heart of the Dragon God (co-written with Jean Rabe) – a sword & sorcery novel

End Times Alaska (#)—a post-apocalyptic survivalist adventure published by Permuted Press

Nightwalker (a Frank Roderus series)—A post-apocalyptic western adventure

End Days (#) (co-written with E.E. Isherwood)—a post-apocalyptic adventure

Successful Indie Author (#)—a non-fiction series to help self-published authors

Monster Case Files (co-written with Kathryn Hearst)—A Warner twins mystery adventure

Rick Banik (#)—Spy & terrorism action-adventure

Ian Bragg Thrillers (#)—a hitman with a conscience

Not Enough (co-written with Eden Wolfe) – A coming-of-age contemporary fantasy

Published exclusively by Craig Martelle, Inc

The Dragon's Call by Angelique Anderson & Craig A. Price, Jr.—an epic fantasy quest

A Couples Travels—a non-fiction travel series

Love-Haight Case Files by Jean Rabe & Donald J. Bingle – the dead/undead have rights, too, a supernatural legal thriller

Mischief Maker by Bruce Nesmith – the creator of Elder Scrolls V: Skyrim brings you Loki in the modern day, staying true to Norse Mythology (not a superhero version)

Mark of the Assassins by Landri Johnson – a coming-of-age fantasy.

For a complete list of Craig's books, stop by his website—https://craigmartelle.com